AN EVIL
GUEST

BY GENE WOLFE

FROM TOM DOHERTY ASSOCIATES

THE WIZARD KNIGHT
The Knight
The Wizard

THE BOOK OF THE SHORT SUN
On Blue's Waters
In Green's Jungles
Return to the Whorl

THE BOOK OF THE NEW SUN
Shadow and Claw
(comprising *The Shadow of the Torturer* and
The Claw of the Conciliator)
Sword and Citadel
(comprising *The Sword of the Lictor* and
The Citadel of the Autarch)

THE BOOK OF THE LONG SUN
Litany of the Long Sun
(comprising *Nightside of the Long Sun* and
Lake of the Long Sun)
Epiphany of the Long Sun
(comprising *Caldé of the Long Sun* and
Exodus from the Long Sun)

AN EVIL GUEST

GUEST

GENE WOLFE

A TOM DOHERTY ASSOCIATES BOOK   NEW YORK

AN EVIL GUEST

Copyright © 2008 by Gene Wolfe

"Walk in the Reign" is quoted by permission of the composer, Rory Cooney, and GIA Publications, Inc.
"Oh Why Have I" is quoted by permission of the composer, Rebecca Spizzirri.

A Tor Book
Published by Tom Doherty Associates, LLC
175 Fifth Avenue
New York, NY 10010

www.tor-forge.com

Tor® is a registered trademark of Tom Doherty Associates, LLC.

Library of Congress Cataloging-in-Publication Data

Wolfe, Gene.
An evil guest / Gene Wolfe.—1st ed.
    p. cm.
"A Tom Doherty Associates Book."
    ISBN-13: 978-0-7653-2133-6
    ISBN-10: 0-7653-2133-5
    1. Actresses—Fiction. I. Title.
PS3573.O52 E95 2008
813'.54—dc22

                                                                2008028716

First Edition: September 2008

Printed in the United States of America

0   9   8   7   6   5   4   3   2   1

This book is dedicated to
Joe and Rebecca Bushong-Taylor.

Gold is the kindest of all hosts when it shines in the sky, but comes as an evil guest to those who receive it in the hand.

—SIMONIDES OF CEOS

AN EVIL
GUEST

WASHINGTON

They sat at ease in the Oval Office. Had the president looked at his guest, he would have seen a handsome, ageless man, dark-haired, with a smooth oval face and a flawless olive complexion. Had he looked into this man's eyes, he would have seen the night looking out through a mask; it was because he had looked there once—and had not liked what he had seen—that he did not look again.

Had the president's guest looked at him, he would have seen a lean and hard-faced man of sixty-three who might have been a farmer or a county agent.

In point of fact, the president had been a rodeo rider whole decades ago. He still looked the part. Like all the best politicians, he looked like anything but a politician.

"They git you his picture?" the president asked.

His guest shook his head; on Earth, this guest was known as Gideon Chase.

"Well, I'm glad." For a moment, the president's hard blue eyes glinted. "I got a bunch, an' I want to git 'em out of my desk. Give 'em to the FBI when you're through."

Gideon picked up the first and glanced at it.

"Perfec'ly ordinary, ain't he, Dr. Chase?"

"There are no ordinary men, although so many believe themselves so."

"You're right, he ain't. He's ordinary lookin' is what I mean."

Gideon shook his head and tapped the figure in the photograph with a fingernail, at which the figure said, "Woldercan's a beautiful place, one I'm sure I'll miss often. But right now retirement looks awfully good to me and I'm heading for the South Seas."

"A perfec'ly ordinary-lookin' man, but if I was asked to name one evil man in our entire nation, an' if the fate of the whole damned U.S.A. was ridin' on my answer—well, sir, I'd name him."

The president waited for Gideon to speak, but Gideon did not.

"Brought up in the buildin' trade. His pa was a contractor. Become a contractor hisself, an' was smart enough to see the big money went to them that had friends in high places. You want to bellyache about it? I have, more'n once. Don't do any good."

"There is no good," Gideon murmured. His voice was level, expressionless.

The president raised an eyebrow. "I know you made a reputation writin' that shit. You really believe it?"

"My belief or disbelief will not change the truth," Gideon murmured.

The president grinned. " 'What's truth?' said jestin' Pilate."

"That there is no good."

"Well, sir . . . what about evil?"

"It does not exist."

"Well now, I'd call that hombre whose picture you're lookin' at evil. If there's a evil man in the world, he's the one."

Gideon, who was not in fact looking at any of the pictures, said, "There are none."

The president smiled again. "I wish I could believe it. It'd be comfortin'. Only I s'pose I'd have to give up good, too."

"No. May I explain? You can't have a great deal of time."

"For this? I'll take as much time as I think will do any good, an' let the bastards go hang. Explain."

"Briefly, then. Today, most people think evil the mere absence of good.

Darkness—which many confuse with evil—is the mere absence of visible light, after all, just as silence is the absence of audible sound. If these people were correct, there would be no evil, only a lack of good. They are wrong, and when they discover they are wrong, they leap to the opposite error."

"Mine," the president said.

"Yes. Would you say that evil is synonymous with cruelty? With greed?"

The president nodded. "I sure would."

"Then you cannot be correct. Cruelty and greed are very different things. Cruelty is delight in the pain of others. Greed is an insatiable desire to possess. You do not like the result of either one—unless the greed and cruelty are your own. You avenge yourself upon them by calling them evil. There is no difference in kind between your position and that of a woman who shouts "bad dog" when the puppy soils the carpet. The difference is in degree. Only."

The president pressed a button on his desk. "I think we'd best git down to business."

Gideon nodded. "So do I."

"I talked to you the way I did, 'cause I wasn't sure you was the right man for this job. You are. A wizard's what people call you, an' if anybody's qualified for this, you're the one."

Gideon rarely smiled and did not smile now, though there may have been a gleam of humor in his disturbingly dark eyes. "The only evil man meets the only qualified man," he whispered.

"Not really—come in, John! I said if there was only one evil man in the whole world, it'd have to be Bill Reis. There's a hell of a lot of evil men in the world."

"Three in particular," the man the president called John added.

"We haven't gotten to that yet, John, an' I don't think we will." The president motioned toward a chair. "Sit down."

"My error, Mr. President. I didn't know you were excluding the Senate." John was forty plus, and starting to get fat. The thick, round lenses of his glasses gave the impression of blindness.

"Explain our problem," the president told him. "Our problem with Bill Reis."

"Sure. Do you know who he is, Dr. Chase? That will save some time."

Gideon shook his head.

"He was a major contributor to President Ingstrup's first campaign. Also to his second, though that doesn't really come into it. Major contributors are often given ambassadorships. Perhaps you're aware of that."

"My father was an ambassador," Gideon remarked. "He was the U.S. ambassador to the only intelligent nonhumans known to science. . . ." He paused.

"To the Wolders," John said.

"There were older sciences," Gideon murmured, "to which other intelligent races were known. So I've heard. But, yes. He was ambassador to Woldercan, as you say. I was born there. No doubt you know."

"We do. That was one of the reasons I suggested the president consult you. It wasn't the chief reason but it figured in our thinking."

"Perhaps you might like to tell me the chief reason." Gideon swept the remaining pictures toward him as he spoke.

"Your reputation. You specialize in solving problems every other expert declares are impossible or outside his area. You're expensive, we realize—"

"Not as expensive as government." Gideon was looking at the pictures as he spoke, glancing at each in turn, then laying it facedown on the president's desk, his hands sure and swift.

John laughed. "You've got us there. Of course not. But expensive. You'd have the entire cooperation of the Federal Bureau of Investigation."

"You can commit them?"

"Yes. You would be an adjunct to our investigation."

"How flattering." Gideon's gleam returned. "If I were to—"

The president interrupted. "Your dad was a patriot. I didn't know him personally, but I've talked to some that did. He served this country ably as a private citizen an' a diplomat. None of the people I talked to said you were much like him, but I've found out that every man in the world gits certain traits from his folks. As I told John, your not resemblin' your father on the surface tells me you'll be like him down deeper."

Nodding, Gideon swept the photographs into a neat stack and pushed the stack away.

"We can't give you a lot of money," John said, "but we have other ways of rewarding people who help us. You would be recommended to friends of the president's who might make use of you. If you'd enjoy a professorship at one of our leading universities . . ."

"I'd like to know what this man Reis has done," Gideon murmured.

"Well, think it over, Dr. Chase. You have a Ph.D., don't you? Some private college in Massachusetts?"

Gideon nodded.

"There you are. It would be easy. A professorship at Harvard or Princeton could be readily arranged. It would involve very little actual work and would convey a great deal of prestige."

"What has Reis done?" Gideon spoke to the president, not to John.

"He's a spy," the president said, "an' that's just for starters. We can't nab him 'cause we got no evidence. But he travels around. He stops at sensitive spots. He don't stay long, but soon afterward our sources in—well, never you mind. In a certain foreign country, okay? They tell us certain people there have got holt of somethin' we were tryin' to hold close to our vests."

Gideon shrugged. "Have him killed."

"Not 'til we find out how he does it."

John said, "He's found a flaw in a security system we thought just about flawless—not something he can exploit now and then, but something he can exploit whenever he chooses. We've got to know what it is."

"That he can exploit," Gideon murmured, "only when he is in close proximity to the facility in which your secret operations are being carried out."

"He's a blackmailer, too," the president said. "We know that."

"For money?" Gideon's gaze roved the room.

"Sometimes." John cleared his throat. "More often for other things. Sexual favors, at times. Introductions and information."

Gideon said, "You will have considered that he may be blackmailing someone at each of the industrial plants and laboratories he visits. They are plants or laboratories? Most of them? May I assume that?"

"He would have to meet with them, or telephone them at least," John said.

Gideon looked amused. "E-mail them? Write letters? What about carrier pigeons?"

The president's hand came down on his desk with a resounding smack. "This ain't fit for humor."

"Then you shouldn't tempt me to it. Neither of you should, and both of you have." Gideon leaned back in his chair. "You'll be listening in on telephone calls. Data mining? Isn't that what you call it? You'd pick it up. You're certainly tapping the lines of those laboratories or whatever, as well as the telephones of everyone privy to sensitive information. If you prattle about cell phones now, I shall go home. I'm beginning to miss my little apartments already."

John murmured, "Just assume that we're already doing everything every ordinary person would think of. Because we are. Assume, too, that it's not working. If it were, we wouldn't have called you. We don't want you to guess what he's doing. Any such guesses would be pure fantasy. Wild guesses are of no use. We've made plenty ourselves, and they haven't helped."

The president grinned. "John's guesses, mostly. Wild as blue quail, every one of 'em. Thought readin'. Talkin' to ghosts."

"Neither are impossible." Gideon sounded pensive. "I have done both in the past, and will doubtless do both in the future. One or both may well explain Ambassador Reis's success, although I doubt it."

John began to say something; the president silenced him with a gesture. "Didn't either one of us call him that."

Gideon made a small, disgusted sound. "So now you're wondering whether I've been reading your mind. I haven't been, but you'll have to take my word for that; I can't prove it. John wanted to know whether I knew that major contributors are often rewarded with ambassadorships. He also told me that this man Reis had contributed liberally to an earlier president. The inference was obvious. My father was succeeded by a man named Klauser, but Klauser will have been replaced years ago. I surmise that Reis was ambassador to Woldercan during the Ingstrup administration. Is that correct?"

"It is," John said.

"Good. Is he spying for Woldercan? To the best of your knowledge?"

Speaking simultaneously, the president said, "Yes," and John, "No."

Gideon suppressed a smile. "Not proven, I take it."

There was a pregnant silence while John waited for the president to speak. At last John said, "There are only two ways to communicate with Woldercan."

The president muttered, "That we know of."

"Ethermail can be monitored," John continued. "It's odd stuff—you probably know. Sometimes a second message gets there before the first one. Sometimes, well . . ."

"One picks up messages that have not yet been sent," Gideon said.

"The whole question of time . . . of—which things are simultaneous and which are not—is . . . I mean, when you've got worlds light-years apart . . ."

Gideon rescued him. "One the best astrophysicists suggest is insoluble."

John nodded gratefully. "That's right, and ethermail won't solve it. It only introduces more complications. I read once that congratulations from

Earth on the birth of his son reached an ambassador on Woldercan before the baby was born. Back here, the State Department had received an ethermail from him saying his son had been born and even giving the son's name. I don't recall what it was—"

"Gideon." He turned to the president. "Your advisor doesn't think this man Reis is spying for Woldercan. You do. Do you have evidence?"

"Evidence that will stand up in court? No, sir. No, I don't. Only I look at what a man does." The president aimed an imaginary rifle, squinting at its sights. "Where does he go for chow, huh? When does he do it? Where does he drink, an' where does he bed down? Know them things an' you can bag the wiliest old buck that ever corralled him a harem."

Gideon nodded. "I've been known to hunt men the same way. So have you, I'm sure. What does Reis do?"

"It ain't what he does, it's what he did. He started in the minute he got home from Woldercan, an' he's got tricks I know damned well he didn't have before he went. They turned him. Think that don't happen? Think again." The president's *again* was almost *agin*. "They turned him an' they taught him, knowin' I'd want to pull him out an' replace him with my own man."

Gideon pursed his lips. "The news I've heard and read—I confess I hear and read very little—has given me the impression that Woldercan is behind us."

"Technologically?" John's shoulders rose and fell. "We like to think so, but it's hard to say."

"Your opinion? I was still a child, you understand, when my family left."

"Behind us in some areas and ahead in others. Ahead in biology, for example, but behind in physics. Behind us in military science—if it may be so called—but ahead in sociology. There are a number of areas I wouldn't want to guess about."

"Optics?" Gideon did not smile, but his voice and eyes hinted at amusement.

"That's one of them."

"Then tell me this, please. Where is Reis now?"

John shook his head. "I don't know."

"In Washington? Off in the desert at one of your secret sites?"

"I don't know, Dr. Chase, and I know of no one in government who does."

"Can you at least guess at the state? Nevada? Utah? Could he be aboard a hopper going back to Woldercan?"

"I told you. I don't know."

The president said, "We want you to find out how he does it an' make him stop doin' it. That's what it comes down to. You've heard what we're offerin'. What do you say?"

"That there is a great deal you're not telling me. You talked about hunting a wily buck, knowing his habits. Surely you've had men, able agents, studying Reis."

"Will you do it?" The president looked grim. "Do what we want?"

"More the point," John added, "*can* you do it? In your own opinion."

Gideon looked down at his own hands—long, dexterous hands, whose slender, ringless fingers might have belonged to a musician. "I'll answer you first. What's your last name, by the way?"

"It doesn't matter."

"In that case, John, I won't answer you at all. I'll answer our president, however. His name, at least, I know. Mr. President, I still don't know enough to say whether I can do what you wish. You've told me nothing about this man Reis's crimes other than espionage and blackmail, for example, although other crimes have been hinted at, at least twice. As it happens, I know something of those already, assuming alchemy to be criminal. I feel sure you know much more. Empty the bag for me, and we can talk rationally. Otherwise, I'll go."

"I have a file," John said. "It's long and detailed, and we didn't have time to get into all that. Agree, and I'll give it to you."

Gideon did not look at him. "As you have outlined my little assignment thus far, it's senseless. You know that—you're far too shrewd not to. Pick up Reis. Take him to a safe house. You wouldn't have to employ torture. There are drugs. There is even hypnosis, with which a skillful operator can do much more than the public has been led to believe."

No one spoke.

"You have no comment?" Gideon rose. "Very well. I'll try with the trifling information you've given me. For my service, I want that professorship and fifty million dollars. I want both in advance."

The president snorted.

"A billion is nothing to you, but a billion is one thousand millions. I'm asking one-twentieth of a billion, and you'll have three-quarters of it back within a year through taxation."

"When the job's done, Dr. Chase. Not before."

"You don't trust me. Why in the world should I trust you? I can't and I don't." Gideon turned and went out.

The question, or so he thought as he was escorted out of the White House, was whether he would be followed.

No, there were two questions. The first was whether he would be followed. The second was whether he was being followed already. Since he knew the answer to neither, he would have to act as though the answers were yes, and yes.

He had been followed before, and in some cases had succeeded in evading his followers. It would be important to begin as though he suspected nothing.

And to tire his unseen companion—or companions—if he could. The Secret Service agent who had accompanied him out of the White House offered to flag a cab for him on the far side of the concrete barriers that had long closed Pennsylvania Avenue. Gideon declined the suggestion, said something inane about the beauty of the stifling day, and declared that he would walk.

THE airport would certainly be watched, if the president had in fact ordered the FBI to monitor his movements. The same was true of his hotel room, which would have been searched by now.

Had a bug been planted on his person? It seemed unlikely, but it was certainly possible. It was even possible that the president had anticipated that he would filch one or more photos of Reis. Bugs could be planted in thick paper, such as photographic paper, and often were. When he felt (or at least hoped) that anyone shadowing him had been both discouraged and lost, he stopped at a camera store. It cost him eight dollars to make copies of the pictures he had stolen, image only; when he had them, he ripped up the originals—wires, chips, and all—and threw them away.

IN THE BLACK CAR

Cassie Casey had read about Gideon Chase more than once, and had seen him interviewed on vid more than once as well; if she found the folded note tossed through her bedroom door something of a shock, she can hardly be blamed for it.

Even so, it was not the identity of the sender that surprised her at first; having left the theater alone, she had supposed herself alone in her apartment. The contents of the note itself supplied the second surprise. And the third.

You do not know me, though you may know of me. My name is Gideon Chase, and I need your help. I am prepared to reward you liberally for it. Help me and you will be rich—and a star.

Wait in the Baskin-Robbins on the corner of 15th and Madison. You may see a man in there who resembles your second husband. Look well, and not hurriedly. When he comes, he will show you where you may find me. When you do, I may confide the means by which you can become mistress of a small fortune within a year. I may also make you a star.

    Tonight. Tell no one.

                                                   —G.C.

As she read, she heard the outer door of her apartment close. Hurrying out of her bedroom, she bolted and chained that door for the second time that night; her alarm system, a costly one that was supposed to be the last word in such things, had been switched off—though not by her.

The note had been printed on a computer using the same program hers did, and the paper was, or at least might have been, her own Miracle Magnawhite. He had printed it out on her personal computer, almost certainly. Had he done more?

Ten minutes later, she shrugged and put her computer on SLEEP. If Dr. Chase had left a souvenir of his passing on her hard drive, it was too subtle for her antivirus software. Unfolding his note, she read it again. A small fortune. Stardom. It was not signed and so not provably his, although his fingerprints might well be on it.

She had a friend on the *Sun-Tribunal*; it was entirely possible that her friend was not yet asleep. Speed dialing made the call easy.

"Hello, Sharon? This is Cassie. I'm terribly sorry about bothering you so late, but this is pretty important. Or it might be."

"It's okay." Sharon sounded drowsy. "I was just lying here thinking about lipstick."

"Lipstick?"

"I try to name shades from A to Z. You know, Apricot Passion, Bathsheeba Pink, Coral Number Ten. It puts me to sleep."

Cassie took a deep breath. "This isn't going to help. It'll wake you up, more likely. It isn't for the paper, either. Or at least, not yet. I need a little friendship, and there may be something by and by. What do you know about Dr. Gideon Chase?"

Eighteen blocks away, Sharon made a small sound.

"I'm not just curious. It may be—no, it definitely is important. I don't know a lot, and I'm not sure about some of the things I think I know."

"Man of mystery . . ." Sharon paused. "Good-looking, too, if you like the type."

"Tell me something I don't know, okay?"

"How should I know what you don't know? Mid-thirties at a guess. They say he's some kind of wizard. Not like in kidvid, but somebody who can do stuff other people can't even begin to do."

Thinking of her alarm system, Cassie said, "I'm one of them. I say that, too. I had a little experience with him tonight. What else?"

"Tell me!"

"Later maybe, but not now." Cassie shook her head. "Does that sound like I'm shaking my head?"

"Definitely. I can hear the rattle."

"Great. Because I am. I need info. I'll give you some if I ever understand this." Cassie paused, whitened white teeth gnawing at her lower lip. "Listen up, Sharon. This is strictly confidential."

"Got it."

"He wants me to go in on something with him. Big, big money, or that's what it sounds like. I don't know which way to jump."

"Illegal?"

"Maybe. I don't know. He says he needs me. Needs my help. He'll pay big for it, and . . ."

"Cassie?"

"I was just thinking. I may do it, Sharon. I just might. I'd have to know a lot more before I'd tell him to get lost. If I do, I mean. I guess I'd rather not have to. You said he was a wizard."

"Yeah. What I meant was he's somebody that people and companies with lots and lots of money go to when they've got something bad they absolutely can't handle themselves. I've talked to a couple of them. They both said he costs the world, but he delivers the goods."

Cassie took a deep breath. "Tell me. As much as you can, all right?"

"Promise you won't try to find out who these people are?" Sharon was wide awake now, and sounded nervous.

"Okay."

"You won't even try to find out. And if you do—if he tells you, for example—you won't brace them with it."

"You've got my word."

"Swell. I trust you. How was the show tonight?"

"It was all right. House about half full. Everybody a little teary. You know. We close tomorrow. Final performance and see you around. Break a leg, you were great. All that stuff. Are you stalling, Sharon?"

"Maybe I am. Maybe I need time to think. Or maybe not. You got a new gig lined up?"

"Huh uh. I may vegetate awhile. My agent's been talking to Hollywood, but there's nothing definite yet. Now tell me."

"Before I do, has it hit you that he might have picked you because of how things are right now? Because you'll be loose and he knows it?"

"No. . . . Well, by gosh! I hadn't thought of that. Thanks. You're sharp, Sharon."

"And a good friend?"

"Yes. A very good friend."

"Swell. I'm going to be a good friend some more. One was this very rich woman. She wasn't married anymore, but she had a little kid. A leftover kid that hardly anybody knew about."

"And?"

"She loved him—she still does as far as I know. The kid is her whole life. He was a little piece of a man she loved and lost."

"A boy." Cassie nodded to herself.

"Did I say that? Yeah, I guess I did. Okay, it's a boy, only he was—wasn't right. Birth defect like. You know?"

"Deformed or mental?"

"It doesn't matter. He wasn't right, and it broke her heart. Nobody could cure him. She went to Chase, and her son's just fine. Smart, good-looking. Maybe a little too brave, but normal for sure."

Cassie made a mental note. "How about the other one?"

"This was a company—a big corporation. They owned oil fields in a country where the government didn't like them much. It was going to nationalize. Take everything and tell them to take a hike."

"He fixed it?" Cassie shook out the folded note. "Gideon Chase fixed it?"

"They're big buddies now. That government loves the company, and the company loves that government. Hey, you ought to be interested in this. There's a national theater there, funded by the company. They're going to—well, never mind. They've done a lot of things for the country, and they're planning a lot more. Why not? They've still got the oil."

"I understand. Is he gay?"

"I don't know, but three women I know don't think so."

Cassie took a minute to digest that. "When he comes on vid, being interviewed on a cable news show or whatever, they always say he's a philosopher."

"Right. He is. Sort of quasi-irreligious. God's quit on us because we quit on Him. He's written books."

"I ought to have a look at them," Cassie said.

She could almost hear Sharon's shrug. "I don't think they'll tell you much about him."

"Talking to him might tell me a lot." Cassie glanced at her clock radio.

"I doubt it. Not beyond what I've told you. He's smart, and he's smart in funny ways. Maybe he's smart in ways that just about everybody else is as dumb as a box of rocks about. If it tells you more than that, you let me know. Okay?"

BASKIN-ROBBINS was deserted except for the teenager behind the counter. There were a few high stools in front of it, and Cassie sat down. "How late are you open?"

"Midnight." The girl sounded sleepy and bored.

"It's almost that now."

The girl nodded. "I know, ma'am. Just seven more minutes."

"What would it take to get you to stay open later?"

The girl said nothing.

"Twenty bucks?"

The girl shook her head. "I got to go. My mom'll be all upset. I'm closin' in seven minutes."

"Call your mom. I'll talk to her."

The girl shook her head.

"I'm a customer," Cassie declared, "and you've got to wait on me."

"I guess. . . ."

Cassie scanned the menu posted behind the counter. "I want a double sherbet papaya delight, and I'm staying until you make it and I eat it."

The girl said nothing.

"Wait a second." Cassie rummaged through her purse. "Here's the twenty. See it? I'll give it to you if you'll just tell me what *would* make you stay open later."

"I wouldn't tell you," the girl said deliberately, "even if I liked you. Ma'am."

"You can't close while I'm in here. What would you do? Lock me in?"

"You'll see." The girl had found a rather fanciful plastic dish and was scooping sherbet into it.

"One's yellow," Cassie commented, "and that other one looks like raspberry. I thought papaya would be pink."

The girl said nothing.

"Has a man been in here? Maybe a man who said he was looking for somebody?"

The girl laid down her scoop and went to the door. A switch beside it darkened the outside lights.

"You're two minutes fast," Cassie told her.

"So sue me." The girl locked the door and pulled down a shade.

Cassie sighed. "I wish we could be friends."

"I've got three friends." The girl drizzled cloudy syrup on the sherbet. "Rita, Amber, and Christabelle. I don't like any of them very much, but I like every one of them fifty times more than I like you. Even Christabelle."

"Puts me in my place. You got a spoon?"

A pink plastic spoon stabbed the raspberry sherbet. "I even like Rita's little brother better than you."

There was a knock at the door. The girl looked toward it, but did not move.

"I'll get it," Cassie said, and stood up.

"No you don't!" The girl beat her to the door, pushing her back.

The knocking became pounding. Something as hard and heavy as a carpenter's hammer was striking the door.

The girl pulled the green shade an inch and a half to one side and peeped out. After a moment she unlocked the door and stood aside.

The man who entered was both tall and wide, nearing middle age. Cassie gasped, "Scott . . . ?"

"Who's that?" His voice was deep and a trifle raspy.

"A—a certain man I used to know. A gentleman. Or I thought he was."

"Not my name, Miss Casey. You ready?"

The girl said, "She's gotta pay for this."

The man who looked so much like Scott leveled his left forefinger at her. It was an unusually large forefinger. "You shut the fuck up," he told her.

His car was roomy, cheap, and new. A good portion of the dash taken up by what looked like a computer screen. A remote keyboard occupied the passenger seat until Cassie moved it.

"Fasten your belt, Miss Casey."

She did. "You know my name. That's the second time you've used it."

He started the car.

"Since you know my name, I think I ought to know yours."

"Scott." There was little traffic this time of night, and "Scott" jammed down the accelerator.

"You're not Scott. You look kind of like him, but you're not him. It's not really that close." Cassie craned her neck for a look at the numbers flaming before him: *40, 50, 60* . . . She tightened her seat belt. "You're a cop, Scott."

He glanced at her.

"This car and the way you drive it. The whole bit. That girl wouldn't have unlocked the door for Jacob, Jack Pot, and Joan of Arc; but she unlocked it for you because you showed her a badge."

"You new in town?"

"Does it matter?"

"You're not a cop." The car swerved right to pass a speeding cab. "I'd know you. If you're a grifter, you'd have to be new. I know the local gals. High class. Red hair. Forty?"

"Not quite." It was hard to smile, although she did.

"You'd be a bunco gal if you were a grifter. But I don't think so."

"You could check the police files, couldn't you?"

He seemed not to have heard her.

"Where are you taking me, Scott?"

"Show you in a minute. Got a cigarette?"

"Heck no." Cassie looked as if she wanted to spit. "How long have they had a cure for cancer? Eighteen months? Something like that. Just eighteen months, and everybody smokes."

"Never mind. I'll buy some soon as I drop you off up here."

"Where's up here?"

To her surprise, he pointed. "Right there. In the parking lot."

"You're going to leave me there and drive away? It'll take me twenty minutes just to hike someplace where I can catch a cab."

The car slowed.

"In heels!" She hoped that it sounded as bitter as she felt.

"You see that black car over there? The dead black one. It doesn't shine." She nodded.

"Sweet. You get out of this car and get in that one, and that's *all* you do. It's unlocked on the passenger's side. Get in. Right side, front. Wait."

"Suppose I don't?"

"I kick your ass out of my car and after that you're on your own. Twenty minutes? That what you said? Get in the black car and you probably won't have to wait that long. So which is it?" He grinned. "I'm a good kicker, Miss Casey. Try me."

"I've got a gun in my purse."

He held out his hand. "Right here. Fork it over."

"You want me to take it out and give it to you?" She was incredulous. "I could shoot you."

"But you won't. Fork it over."

She opened her door and slid off the seat. "I was lying. Fibbing, all right? I haven't really got one."

She had thought her purse out of reach. It was not. He snatched it from her and straightened up.

"Hey!"

"Shut up," he muttered. He was fumbling with the catch.

"I could call the police. I could have you arrested."

That brought a smile. "Well, for one thing, Miss Casey, I've got your cell phone."

"And for another, you're a cop yourself. What do they call you, a plain-clothesman?"

"Stupid, usually." He looked at her. "There's no gun in here."

"I was lying. I told you."

"Sure. Cell phone, compact, nail file, lipstick." He pulled the cap off. "Hard to tell in this light. What do they call it?"

"Ultra-natural ash rose."

"Got to watch that one. It'll put you to sleep." He dropped lipstick and cap back into her purse. "Billfold. Looks like about three hundred bucks. Driver's license. Union card. Another union card—I guess the second one's for vid. Visa, MasterCard, and Discover." He closed her billfold, dropped it into her purse, and shut it. "Plus Kleenex and chewing gum."

"Is that still in there?"

"Most women carry a lot more."

"So do I. There should be a pen in there."

"You left it someplace. Catch." He tossed the purse to her. "Shut the door, and there'll be no hard feelings."

She shut it.

The black car was low and oddly angled, of a make she failed to recognize.

The front door on the passenger's side opened easily; she slid in and found the upholstery delightfully soft and luxurious.

WHEN she woke, the car was speeding along a highway. She coughed, swore, and blinked half a dozen times before she remembered how she had come to be there.

"I let you sleep," the driver told her. "You're not going to get a great deal of sleep tonight, and I thought it wise to let you sleep as long as you could. If you'd like coffee, we can ask for some."

She was staring. "You're him. You're Gideon Chase."

"I am."

"You were in my apartment tonight."

"I was."

"You broke in."

He nodded. "I did. And did some damage, by the way, in the process. I would think that building management would pay for the repairs, if the matter were put to them in the right way."

"Besides, you're going to make me rich."

He glanced at her, his teeth flashing in the dim light. "I suppose I said that in my note. It was hastily written. I'm going to show you how you can become rich, yes. Not easily. And not safely. But quite quickly, if you have the fortitude for it."

To her surprise, she found that she was warming to him. "Does this involve murder, Dr. Chase?"

"That," he said, "depends on how you mean it. I do not plan to kill anyone. Is that what you're asking?"

"I suppose."

"Then you have your answer. Nor do I intend that you should kill anyone. If you did, however, it wouldn't be murder. You'd be acting in defense of your country, and would thus avoid blood-guilt. Morally."

"You're telling me that America's in danger."

"Every country is always in danger. All the time."

She sensed that he was smiling.

"Let's get back to murder. The man we're after has committed several. Thus he might murder you or me. In that sense, murder is certainly involved."

"How risky is it?"

"Very risky. Mathematically? Let me think." Gideon paused. "I'd say there's about one chance in fifty that you'll be killed if you do what I ask. I should tell you however that your present risk is at least equally grave. As things are right now, there's about one chance in fifty that this man will kill you."

"That is going to take some digesting. And coffee."

He nodded. "Com Pu Ter, please fill the thermos under the instrument panel with coffee."

Gurgling and hissing followed a brief silence. When they stopped, Gideon said, "It's ready now."

Cassie groped under the instrument panel, found the thermos, and brought it out. "Only one cup. Want to drink from the other side?"

Gideon nodded. "I do. Thank you."

She poured. "Cream. I usually take it black, but tonight I'll make an exception."

"And sugar."

"Here you go. It's only half full."

"Wise, I'm sure." He accepted the cup and sipped.

"I—Dr. Chase, I just saw how fast we're going."

He sipped again, seeming not to have heard her.

"A hundred and forty? Is that right?"

He took the cup from his lips. "About that. We have to reach Canada and travel another hundred miles or more before sunrise. Or so I think. You see, I believe that you'll agree to what I'm proposing. At this point you have nothing to lose, after all. And much to gain."

Cassie drew breath, let it out, and filled her lungs again. "I've been looking out the window. Everything's whizzing past. I feel like I'm in a low-flying plane."

Gideon nodded, smiling. "I wish I had one. But if I did, there'd be no place to land it where we're going. A hopper would be better, but the Mounties are on the lookout for smugglers. Are you up to some hiking?"

"In these heels? Absolutely not!"

"No. You'll have to take them off. You know, I ought to have thought of that."

"Brought shoes for me?"

He shook his head. "Told you to take off whatever shoes you might be wearing and put on walking shoes."

"You know, I like you. But if I weren't crazy, I'd be demanding that you turn this—this hot rod of yours around immediately."

"And yet you are not."

"No. And you haven't told me anything. Not anything beyond the less than charming fact that I may have to hike for miles barefoot."

"I will try to tell you whatever you want to learn," Gideon said, "provided I know the answers myself. Ask a question."

"How will you make me a star?"

"Ah!" He turned his head and looked at her so long that she felt a thrill of terror.

"Drive! Please drive! If we hit something at this speed . . ."

"We won't." Gideon looked ahead again. "There's some slight danger, though, that we might buzz right through the checkpoint. It must be close."

"We'll have to stop? Thank God!"

"It's to be hoped that God won't keep us long. We've very little time. You were slow coming to that ice cream shop, which made me think I might have misjudged you."

"I'm glad you said that. Now I know what my next question will be, if you ever answer my first one."

"How I'll make you a star? It's almost easier to do than it is to explain. Every human being contains a whole grab bag of qualities. Some are inactive, others active. You have the quality that makes stars, but it is latent. The old mesmerists called it personal magnetism. We who think ourselves so much wiser have no better term for it."

He sipped more coffee and handed her the cup. "One of my own qualities is the ability to manipulate qualities in others. With difficulty, and only to a limited degree, but I can do it. Tonight I'll try to awaken your star quality. To change it from a latent quality to an active one. As active as I can make it. My mind will reach into yours, find that quality there, and drag it into the light."

After that Cassie was quiet for a good three minutes. At last she said, "Why do I believe you?"

"Because you sense my honesty. Honesty is a powerful force."

"You mean that."

Gideon nodded. "With all my heart."

"All right. I'd walk barefoot all night and all day if it would make me a star. If there's a ghost of a chance that it will."

"There's an excellent chance," he told her, "and it's not a terribly high mountain. A couple of hours should be more than sufficient."

"We'll drive up as far as we can?"

"Correct." He braked, seeing the lights of the checkpoint ahead.

THREE

THE MAGIC MOUNTAIN
AND BEYOND

Gideon Chase got out of the car. Cassie Casey watched him talking to some-body who might have been a Mounty and to somebody else who might have been a customs officer. After speaking with Gideon for a minute or two, the Mounty came to her window and tapped on the glass. She lowered it, admit-ting night air that held a spring chill.

"Are you a U.S. citizen, ma'am?"

She nodded.

"Talk out loud, ma'am. I need to hear your voice."

"I'm not," she told him. "My position is a great deal higher. I'll have you know I'm an undocumented national of indefinite residential status. Our government cherishes me, so if you mess with me you'd better look out."

"Mexican?"

"Russian."

"You don't sound Russian." The Mounty himself sounded impatient.

"I 'aff lied." Cassie's eyes were cast down demurely. "I am uf Byeloruss. Een my own country vimen such as I are calt belles. Here you tsay ding-dongs."

The Mounty heaved a sigh. "Let's see some ID."

"I haf a tattoo." Looking up at him, she licked her lips. "Ees var' preety. Tzum private place, da?"

The Mounty reached into the car and grabbed her purse.

"That's twice tonight I've had my purse snatched," she told him. "It was an American cop the first time."

The Mounty nodded. "He has my sympathy." After glancing at her driver's license, he returned her purse.

Smiling, Gideon slid back into his seat and shut the door. As their car glided silently away from the checkpoint he said, "Any questions I haven't answered?"

"Five or six hundred. Will bringing out my star quality make me a star?"

"Yes."

Cassie felt a sudden pang of sympathy for the Mounty. "Enlarge on that a bit, will you?"

"If you were . . ." Gideon waved his hand vaguely. "A factory worker. In that case it wouldn't, and I'd have to bring you to the attention of the right people. I could do it, but it might take a week. As it is, I don't have to. You're an actress already. That will be sufficient."

"My show is closing—what time is it?"

"Two fifteen."

"Ummm . . . You didn't look at your wrist. Or at the clock in front of me, either. I see it now."

Gideon said nothing.

"All right, I'll let that alone. Our show is closing tonight. Just a tiny bit under twenty-four hours from now I'll be unemployed."

"You will be my partner in a difficult and dangerous enterprise that will make us rich."

"I haven't said yes yet."

He shrugged.

"I see. It doesn't matter. Are we going to Toronto?"

He shook his head.

"Well, that's what the sign said."

"We'll turn off. Another five miles or so."

"There was a question I was going to ask you before we stopped. Only I know the answer now. I'm going to ask it anyway, to see how honest you really are. Why did the cop who brought me to this car say ultra-natural ash rose would put me to sleep?"

"I can't say. When you were talking to your friend Sharon you mentioned lipstick, then you said your news would wake her up. I suppose the implication was that lipstick was dull and so induced sleep."

"You heard us, too. You must have planted a bug in my apartment."

He shook his head.

"I heard you leave, Dr. Chase."

"You did not. You heard your door open and close, and assumed I had gone."

"You were in there all the time."

"If you mean all the time that you yourself were, yes. I was. I came in before you did and left after you had gone."

"Taking nothing. Right?"

"Wrong. I took away knowledge I didn't have when I arrived. I know you're wearing a gun on your right thigh, for example."

Cassie stared. "You—you watched me dress. . . ."

"I did not. I can explain later."

"You can explain now!"

"As you like. Before you came home, I had found your gun in the nightstand. Under it was what's called an ankle holster. The straps on those things have to be long enough to circle the calf of a powerfully built man, so they would presumably circle your thigh. When you left, your gun and holster left with you."

"I could have had it in my purse."

"You could have, but it didn't seem likely since you had taken the ankle holster, too. It was much more likely that your gun was strapped to your leg. To your calf if you were wearing slacks. When I joined you in this car, I saw that you were wearing a skirt. Besides, that Canadian officer poked through your purse. If your gun had been in there he would have found it."

"The cop you had pick me up looked in my purse, too."

"Did he?" Gideon's shoulders rose and fell. "I don't suppose he found anything."

"No, but he'd tapped my phone. He knew about Sharon naming lipsticks to get to sleep."

"Or he had tapped Sharon's." Gideon sounded bored. "Or your talk was broadcast at some point. If the number you called was that of a cell phone, it had to be. Or he spoke to Sharon afterward. I could go on."

"You want me to go partners with you. If I do, you'll have to trust me."

"Exactly." Gideon nodded. "And this sort of thing is the only way I can do it. Suppose you'd called Bill Reis instead of Sharon. Reis is the man we're going after."

"I don't even know him."

"You will."

"I . . . see." Cassie looked thoughtful.

"So I hope."

"We'll become friends. Reis and I. Is that your idea? But all the time I'll be feeding information to you, maybe even setting him up for a neat little murder."

Gideon touched the brake pedal. "No. I don't do murders."

"Comforting."

"Bill Reis does, however. Haven't you noticed that I haven't objected to your gun?"

"Yeah. Did you mess with it? Take out the bullets or the firing pin?"

"No. Why should I?"

"Darned if I know."

The black car slowed again and swung off onto a side road.

"Where are we going, Dr. Chase?"

"To a certain mountain. There's a road for most of the way up. Beyond that, we'll have to hike to the summit. When we reach the summit, you'll become a star. That will take another hour or two, I'm afraid. After that, we'll return. It's important that you make the final performance of that play."

"I'm going to name a price."

"Are you?" His teeth shone in the dark.

"I am. A firm, hard price, the amount I want for going along with this from this point on."

"If you want cash now, it had better not exceed five hundred dollars. I don't have much more than that with me."

"I want your word that I'll get this much if I play ball. Your word of honor."

"You'd trust me to that extent? I—well, Miss Casey, it's flattering."

"Yes, I would. Besides, I have to." For a second or more, Cassie wrestled with her thoughts. "I would anyway. I don't know why, but I would. You're a wizard. Sharon said that, and she was right. But you're a good wizard."

"Famous," Gideon remarked dryly, "for saying there is no good."

Cassie nodded. "I think I understand that now. You mean it's extinct. I never did before. When I saw you on vid, I mean. Now I've got it. Or I think I do. Is this supposed to bring my price down?"

"I suppose not."

"You suppose right." Cassie drew breath. "Have I said this is firm? It is. One hundred thousand. I'll keep on with this—be your Rose O'Neal—for one hundred thousand dollars. Payable on demand, in cash."

Gideon chuckled. "I asked the president for fifty million. I haven't told you about that."

"The president?"

Gideon braked, swinging his strange black car around a sharp curve. "Yes."

"You saw him? Face-to-face?"

"Right."

"I don't like him. Did you?"

"More than I expected to, yes." The black car slowed again. "I don't believe he can have many friends, but he's probably loyal to those he has. In general, I think he's as honest as he can afford to be."

"Which isn't very," Cassie said.

"Is it ever?"

"And you?"

Gideon grinned. "A man of shining integrity wherever there's a dollar to be made. Or an honor to be gained, for that matter. They offered a full professorship at Harvard. Or Yale. Princeton. Wherever I wanted to go."

"To hell with that. Did you get the fifty million?"

"No. I didn't expect to, either. Though I'd have taken it if they had surprised me. I wanted to see how they reacted."

"Who's 'they'?"

"The president and an advisor of his. He's a federal agent named John Ferguson. I'm not supposed to know that, but I've researched him since."

"How much did you get? Will you tell me, honestly?"

"Yes. I got nothing. My shining honesty is very much in evidence in that statement. No professorship, no money. Nothing."

"If you can't afford a hundred thou—but you can. I know you can."

"You're right. I can."

The road angled up sharply. Cassie could sense no downshift of the transmission.

"Since I'm being honest," Gideon said, "I should tell you that John's called me twice since. Seventeen million the first time. Fifty the second time, but with strings. I refused both offers."

"No wonder you researched him."

Gideon nodded. "There's a great deal of money to be had. I don't know how much, and it may be that no one does. Still, it's very large indeed. Billions, almost certainly."

"This Bill Reis will be my assignment?"

Gideon nodded again.

"Tell me about him."

Gideon handed her two photographs. "Put these in your purse, and have a good look at them when you've a better light."

"This is him?" Cassie was peering at the photographs.

"Supposedly, yes. My guess is that they're good. We don't have much time, so I'll just cover the most important points. The first is that he's terribly dangerous. You'd have asked for more than a hundred thousand dollars if you'd known how dangerous. The second is that I suggested the obvious course—that they pick up Reis and sweat the information they wanted out of him. My suggestion was ignored. It wasn't rejected. It wasn't even discussed. What does that tell you?"

Cassie thought. "That they don't think they could make him talk? Like maybe he'd kill himself instead?"

"I don't believe so. I have the advantage, obviously, of having been there—of having sensed the atmosphere. It means that it's been tried and failed. That they can't pick him up, although they seemed to know something about his past movements."

"Huh!"

"Indeed." Gideon's hand touched hers. "It's just possible that they have picked him up, only to have him escape before they could learn anything. Possible, but unlikely. I believe my first supposition is correct. He's as slippery as an eel, either way."

"They can't hold on to him?"

"Exactly."

A yellow sign loomed in their headlights. Gideon stopped the car. "Leave those shoes behind."

"All right, but you may have to carry me."

"I will if I must." He opened his door and stepped out into the moonlight. "Come along. We've got to walk from here, and walk fast." He opened a rear door and pulled out a small canvas carryall.

"This is where you're going to magnify my star quality?"

"I can't. It's innate. Most people have little or none. You have a lot, but it's not active. This is where I energize it."

"If you can do that, I don't understand why you didn't do it back in the city. Why bring me here?"

"Do you ask why your surgeon wants to operate in a hospital? If he can do it, he could do it in your flat, couldn't he?"

"So this is better."

"It is. There are mountains, and then there are mountains. Have you been to Africa?"

"No." She was hurrying after him.

"I have. To Egypt and the Sahara, and to the semidesert edges of the Sahara. Once I looked across a wide, dry landscape and saw bushes."

"And?"

"Some of those bushes were bushes and some were ostriches. All mountains are stone. Most have no life. This one is alive. You won't believe that, and I'm not going to prove it to you. But it is."

"Wait up! Just a minute. Please!"

He did. "It is alive and sentient. It can speak, though it rarely does. It has a wife who lives in one of its many caves. She is—a laundress. Let's leave it at that. She isn't important, but he is. Important to us, here, tonight."

"I'm starting to think you're crazy, Dr. Chase. I—"

"What is it?"

"I'm barefoot, and you're not."

"Yes. What are you getting at?" He had set down his canvas bag; as he spoke, he picked it up again.

"I felt the ground tremble. Not a lot, just a tiny tremor. They, do they have earthquakes up here?"

"You were born on this planet." Gideon sounded angry. "You live on it, yet you know nothing about it. Antarctica is the only continent wholly free of earthquakes."

"The mountain . . ."

"Didn't like what you said. Correct. Have I told you that his wife is not the only thing that makes its home in his caves? She is not. Not by any means."

Cassie gulped, still shaken. "Got it. I'll shut up for now."

"There's an inn sign, the Silent Woman. Maybe I'll take you there sometime." Gideon looked back at her, smiling, and began to walk again.

Ten minutes later (or it may have been fifteen) she asked, "Does this get steeper?"

"Yes. Quite a bit steeper just before the summit. If you like, we'll turn around and go back to the car."

She shook her head. "I'm game if you are."

"Barefoot."

"Barefoot and bleeding. You can walk faster than I am, but you won't walk farther." She pointed. "Up there. Is that the top?"

"It is."

"I—" She gasped for breath. "Tell me about that flat rock."

A dozen more steps carried Gideon to it. "It's an altar. Are you afraid I'm about to sacrifice you on it? I'm not."

Cassie caught up to him. "I can see where something's been burned on it." She sounded as if she were choking.

"Exactly." Gideon zipped open his canvas bag and took out what appeared to be a bundle of pale sticks. He turned his back to her as he laid it on the altar. When he faced her again, a small fire blazed there.

"I don't—I don't even pray to God, Dr. Chase."

"That is none of my affair." Taking a jar from his bag he poured the thick liquid it contained on one side of the fire, letting the last drops fall into the fire itself.

Cassie sniffed and sniffed again. "I know that smell. Is it—"

"It's wild honey. You think I'm about to worship pagan deities. I am not, but there are certain persons with whom I wish to communicate. I'm preparing to do it. Now sit down—that high stone over there. I'll sit on the low one facing you." He sprinkled a powder on the flames, and the odor of honey was replaced by a new one, an odor pungent and sweet.

"Perfume?" Cassie had not yet taken her seat.

"Or incense. As you like."

"I . . ." She coughed. "I wouldn't want to wear that. It's, well . . ."

"Sit down." Gideon sat on a smaller stone facing hers.

"Dark." She found that she was seated, although she had not intended to sit. "There's a bitter undercurrent."

"Correct. Be silent now and look at the moon, which is very beautiful indeed. I have a great deal to explain, and very little time in which to explain it."

For a few seconds that might have been much longer, there was only the sighing of the night wind.

"The first thing I must explain is how badly you need sleep. Tonight you'll have to take your part in the final performance of *The Red Spot*, and yours must be the greatest performance of your life. You've had very little sleep, and I'm sure you must be exhausted. I want you to sleep in the car as we drive home. You should sleep all morning, if you can. I know you must be very, very tired. . . ." Behind him: great, dark wings.

The moonlight, Cassie reflected, streamed down upon this barren mountaintop as upon no place else on Earth.

CASSIE woke in her own bed, in her apartment. For a time that seemed terribly short, that fact did not trouble her in the least. She had returned from the theater, gone to bed, and had a strange dream.

Sometimes she had strange dreams. Didn't everybody?

Dreams, in her experience, faded quickly. They became less real, less and less compelling, as she thought about them. This one seemed to solidify, like a jinni coalescing from lamp smoke. Before she finished brushing her teeth, her hands were trembling.

Her door was closed and locked, bolted and chained. Her windows were locked as well. The alarm was on. The dress she had worn home from the theater hung neatly in her closet. The warmer dress she had put on for the short walk to Baskin-Robbins hung neatly beside it. Its loden wool held a sweet and smoky aroma, with a bitter undercurrent.

Her white bra was in the clothes hamper. So, somewhat oddly, was a pair of taupe panty hose she recognized as her own; oddly because the feet hung in shreds.

The pictures! Suddenly, vividly, she remembered that the dark slender figure in her dream had handed her two photographs. She had peered at them in a bad light for a second or two, and put them in her purse.

They were there. She lay them on her coffee table: image-onlys of a middle-aged, clean-shaven man who wore glasses only in the full-length shot. "Soft face," Cassie murmured. "Hard eyes. Big shoulders? Thick neck."

She turned one over; someone had written on the back.

6' 2" About 240. Jogs. Often wears sports clothes, sunglasses. Watch is a cell phone. Former builder, diplomat. Blackmail, espionage, murder, alchemy???

Walks unseen.

On the back of the other:

Up to something big. Find out what it is, Miss Casey. Be very careful.

She tapped Reis's image, but heard only silence.

Sharon might be anywhere now, and was most likely out of the office on some assignment. Cassie dialed her cell phone.

"You have Sharon Bench."

"It's Cassie, Sharon. Can you talk?"

"Absolutely! How was Dr. Chase?"

Cassie paused, wrestling her uncertainty. "Weird. Much weirder than I expected. Sexy, and I hadn't expected that either."

"Did you . . . ?"

"I don't know."

"Come on, Cassie. Come clean. I won't print it."

"I don't know. There's a—a vacancy, I mean. A blank spot. Things must have happened last night that I don't remember. I thought it was all a dream at first."

"Is this really Cassie? You don't quite sound like her. Your voice is . . . I don't know. Maybe you're getting a cold."

"Maybe I talked a lot last night and don't remember it."

"Like that, huh? Booze?"

"No. I had nothing to drink. Nothing to eat, either. I—I stuck a little pink plastic spoon in some sherbet once. I remember that. But it never made it to my mouth. Right now I'm hungry enough to bite off my own fingers."

"Well, fix yourself something."

"I'm going to Walker's as soon as we hang up. I'm going to order every-thing."

"Not the apple thing. It would feed an army."

"Dessert," Cassie said firmly. She licked her lips. "Listen, Sharon. Can you meet me there? I'll buy your lunch."

"Maybe. When?"

"I'll need forty minutes to get dressed and get there. Get a table if you get there first?"

"Maybe. Listen, Cassie. Do you remember my mother? You met her when she flew up from Florida."

"Sure."

"What's her name?"

"First name? Martha. Martha Grossman."

There was a long pause before Sharon said, "See you at Walker's."

WALKER'S served the world's best omelets but made Cassie think of a cuckoo clock. Its windows were stained glass, and its roof was spiky with turrets. Its walls were, to be charitable, busy.

None of which were actually bad. That was left to the people waiting on chairs and benches. There were twenty at least, and some appeared to have been waiting there for quite a while.

Cassie approached the frazzled girl at the reception desk. "My friend may have gotten here first and gotten a table for us. Okay if I look?"

The girl's mouth opened, then shut again.

"My age? Small, brown hair, big purse? Her name's Sharon."

"I—I know you," the frazzled girl whispered. She sounded as if she had lost a lot of blood. "Only I c-can't think of your name."

Cassie gave it, although the frazzled girl did not seem to hear her.

"I'd better tell Ben." She seemed to have come to some sort of decision. "I'll go get him. May I have your autograph? While I'm gone, I mean." She fumbled below the counter, at last producing a paper napkin. "It's not for me! It's for—for my sister." She whirled and was gone.

Cassie borrowed a pen from a disconsolate man on a folding chair and wrote *Cassie Casey, with all good wishes.*

She had just returned the pen when the frazzled girl reappeared with a youngish man who wore a blue tie with a purple shirt.

"A pleasure, madam," the youngish man said. "Your friend's expecting you. Drinking coffee, you know. Said he wouldn't order until you arrived. Please follow me."

He? Cassie followed anyway, through one noisy room crowded with tables and redolent of good food and into another, this one equally redolent though smaller and not quite so crowded and noisy.

A slender, olive-skinned man sitting alone at a table set for three looked up from his menu as they approached. It was Gideon Chase.

FOUR

THE UNSEEN AUDIENCE

"I've got just one question." Cassie lowered her voice. "Who the hell gave you permission to tap my phone?"

Gideon almost smiled. "No one."

"You—you slick little bastard! I thought we were friends."

He nodded. "As did I. May I add that I haven't tapped it?"

"You didn't know I was coming here? This is pure coincidence? I don't believe it."

"I knew. I came here to meet you and Sharon Bench. May I explain?"

"It had better be good!"

"It will at least be truthful. This morning it struck me that you had called someone named Sharon as soon as you had read my note. Thus it was reasonable to suppose that you might call her again on awakening. When you two talked last night, you implied that she worked on a newspaper."

Gideon paused, glancing back at his menu, until Cassie had nodded. It was a reluctant nod, but a nod nonetheless.

"Since you clearly knew her, it was also reasonable to assume that Sharon's paper was local. Three newspapers are published here. You look surprised."

"I am," Cassie said.

"Two are quite small, and one of those is given away. As it happens I know—or at least I believe that I know—everyone who works on the other small one. Thus it seemed likely that Sharon was on the large one, the *Sun-Tribunal*. I called their offices and asked to speak with Sharon. The operator asked whether I wanted Sharon Wilks or Sharon Bench. Forced to guess, I said Sharon Wilks."

Cassie grinned.

"When I had Sharon Wilks on the line, I explained that I was a friend of yours and that you had mentioned your friend Sharon in my hearing. Sharon Wilks told me she had never met you—though she knew who you were—and gave me a number for Sharon Bench. I called her, and she asked for an interview."

Slowly, Cassie nodded. "Begged for one, I imagine."

Pad in hand, a waitress cleared her throat.

"We're waiting for the third member of our party," Gideon explained.

"Go on," Cassie said.

"I will." He watched the waitress's departing back. "Now then. I told Sharon I'd be happy to give her an interview on one condition. It was that she call me if you called her, and report what you'd said. To her credit she told me that she would not do so if she had agreed to keep your call confidential."

"She didn't. I never asked her to."

"I'm glad to hear it. What do you think of the blueberry pancakes?"

"They're dotty. She called you and told you I was meeting her here for lunch. Except it's breakfast for me."

"As for me," Gideon said. "You're correct of course. She told me you'd called and that you seemed different. Her word was *spacey*. She said you'd described me as weird and sexy."

"That's better than spacey."

"I suppose, although I'd guess that I am both. She said you'd slept long, and that you had difficulty deciding which of your experiences had been mere dreams."

"I didn't say that. Or not exactly."

"Newspapers are not notorious for their painstaking accuracy."

Sharon came in, and after a moment Gideon waved. In a whisper he added, "Follow my leads and I'll follow yours. For your life, don't mention those pictures or the man in them."

Cassie nodded almost imperceptibly as Sharon perched on the edge of a chair.

When they had put down their menus, Sharon looked from one to the other. "It seems like you two are an item."

Gideon nodded. "We are."

Cassie said, "Get real, Sharon. Just because I meet a man for breakfast . . ."

"Gee, it seems like only yesterday you were calling me to get a line on him. You're a fast worker."

Cassie smiled.

"That is *beautiful*! Wow! Can you smile like that for a picture?"

"I'll try." Cassie smiled again.

"Great! Put your hands under the table, both of you, like you're holding hands." Sharon's purse had yielded a small camcorder. "Move your chair closer, Dr. Chase. That's it!"

The camcorder lit.

"Let me move over just a trifle. Keep the smile."

Sharon dropped to one knee.

Gideon raised his free hand in protest. "That's enough, surely."

"One more shot . . ."

After more footage taken from a new angle, Sharon sat again. "This is s-o-o-o great! I've got the lead already. Now where did you two go?"

The waitress reappeared. "Anybody want to order?"

When she had gone, Gideon said, "We went on a drive. I kept Miss Casey up most of the night, I'm afraid."

"A drive where?"

Cassie said, "You wouldn't know the place, Sharon, and it's quite a ways from here anyway. It's a sort of—of a scenic overlook."

"I won't pry." Sharon grinned.

"But you'll speculate."

"Sure I will, I can't help it." The grin intensified. "This is going to be so big—"

The waitress who had just left returned. "She's a star, isn't she?"

Gideon said, "Correct."

"I knew it! I told the other girls, and they're taking peeks. Nobody can think of her name."

"Neither can I," Gideon told the waitress firmly, "but I believe I can recall the name of the manager here. Isn't it Ben Janas? I seem to remember that."

The waitress backed away.

Cassie whispered, "I thought you didn't lie."

"Of course I do." Gideon's tone was normal. "I've been mistaken for various things at various times, but never for a saint. Though I suppose they must lie, too, now and then. What I meant to say, and should have said, was that I could not think of you without feeling a trifle dizzy. You are, after all, the most desirable woman in the world. And I was, after all, holding hands with you just a moment ago."

"Aren't you going to turn on that tape recorder gadget you wear?" Cassie asked Sharon.

"She did," Gideon said. "She turned it on as she came into the room. That's how I knew she was Sharon. Did you drive here, by the way?"

Cassie shook her head. "I took a cab. I don't have a car."

"I do," Gideon told her. "I have one here, I mean. Not the one we used last night. I'll be happy to give you a lift when we've finished eating."

LATER, in a small brown convertible with the top up, Cassie asked, "Is my phone tapped, by the way?"

"I don't know. It isn't tapped by me, if that's what you mean. It's possible that the man in those pictures has tapped it already, although it is not probable. What is, is that he'll tap it soon."

"I was thinking of your pet cop," Cassie said.

"He may have, though I doubt it. I think it's much more likely that he talked to Sharon Bench—or that Sharon talked to him."

"I hadn't thought of that." Small white teeth nibbled at Cassie's lower lip. "I didn't know she knew him."

"He's a detective lieutenant and she's a reporter. It would be surprising if they did not know each other. You called Sharon and asked about me. Didn't it occur to you that when you had hung up Sharon might call others to try to get more information for you?"

"No. It should have. How did you get him to pick me up for you?"

"By telling him the truth. I told him that I thought I knew who had committed a crime he's investigating. I named the man, and said that I was trying to locate him. As I am. I asked him to help me, promising to help him in return, as I have in the past. Do you want his name? I'm afraid I haven't memorized his badge number."

"No. I want—are you going to tell me the truth?"

Gideon nodded. "If I can, yes."

"Good. Where are you taking me?"

"Back to your apartment."

Cassie glanced at her watch. "I'll need to get a cab to the theater before long."

"I may be able to drive you. There's something in your apartment I need to show you. After I do, you and I will have to talk a little more."

"We won't have much time. I hope you realize that our romance is going to be all over town after five o'clock."

For a moment, Gideon's eyes left the traffic ahead. "As fast as that? In a newspaper?"

"Not in the *Sun-Trib*. That won't hit the streets till tomorrow, but Sharon does a gossip spot on Channel Three. It's the same company that owns her paper. Want to watch in my apartment?"

"I do indeed." Gideon was smiling.

"You want everybody talking about us?"

"Correct." He nodded emphatically. "Fundamentally, there are two ways to find a man, Miss Casey. One is to go looking for him. The other is to have him come looking for you."

"Okay . . ."

"I've tried the first, and failed. Now you and I are trying the second."

"This is the man that cop wants, isn't it? And it's the man in those pictures."

Gideon nodded.

In the elevator he said, "I want you to go into your apartment. Shut the door, but don't lock it. When I knock in a minute or two, let me in."

"What are you up to, Dr. Chase?"

"I want to see whether your neighbors have come home, that's all."

"They're on vacation."

The elevator stopped, its doors sliding open. He motioned urgently, and

Cassie stepped out and unlocked the door of her apartment, entered, and shut it behind her. A moment later, she heard his loud knock at the door of 3B.

JIMMY'S smile fairly glowed as he opened the stage door for her. Jimmy was at least sixty, probably nearer seventy; he always smiled, but Cassie had never seen him smile quite so warmly.

She smiled back. "Everything all right, Jimmy?"

His smile widened. "Everything's fine now that you're here, Miss Casey."

Her tiny dressing room seemed to be exactly as it had been the night before. Was the phone tapped? Was the room bugged? Cassie decided that the answers were no and yes. No, because there was no phone. Yes, because there were roaches.

Quite a lot of them, really; but everybody knew that it was the fly on the wall that spied on you. The roaches hid till you went to sleep, so they could raid your peanut butter.

By the middle of the first act, she had been in the wings for ten minutes at least, peering out at the audience (the lack thereof, really) through the spy hole and more than prepared to make her entrance as Veronica's dearest friend, Mildred. The usual lines spoken in response to the usual cues from the usual people.

Except that when she stepped out onstage something was very different. . . .

A lot of things, really. The theater was the same and the play was the same, but . . .

For one thing, Alexis Cabana was looking daggers at her. The eyes above that mocking smile wanted to kill, and that was utterly and completely new.

For another, Bruce Sandoz's eyes were devouring her alive. He was (his eyes declared) a famished lion. She was a strawberry ice cream cone. When he licked his lips, Cassie wrote and underlined a mental sticky to lock her dressing-room door.

For a third, the play had become far more serious and real, a real life—*hers*—watched not at all strangely by several hundred people sitting in the dark. A real life (still hers) in which she herself was the center of every silent watcher's attention.

Brad Kingsley was determined that he and Jane Simmons would tour the moons of Jupiter in his new hopper on their honeymoon; while she, knowing all they risked, was equally determined to stop them. Sorrow, fear, and determination poured from her lips unbidden, a triple stream that filled the theater with wailing ghosts and the echoing threats of drums.

She stole a glance at the audience while Brad was arguing and stamping around. A second-row seat that had been empty a minute before was occupied now—occupied by a big soft-faced man who wore glasses.

A man she knew at once.

When she had exited, she used the peephole again. Reis was no longer in the audience. Had she imagined him?

SEURAT strangled her—Act Two, Scene Two—and she lay gasping and trembling on the darkened stage until he helped her rise and supported her as he led her into the wings. In real life, Donny Duke was small and swishy and reeked of Nuit de Marseilles; but Cassie clung to him until he had to leave to take his bow.

There was a scattering of polite applause.

Hers came after his. *"And now, "* India Dempster's voice echoed from the walls, *"Mildred Norcott, Kingsport's own Cassie Casey!"* The applause rose as surf rises when a storm races toward the coast. In less than half a minute it was thunder. A man stood up, and another, and another. Women were rising as well, smiling and clapping. Someone was slamming something hard against the back of a seat. Somewhere a woman with a fine, strong contralto called, "Brava! Oh, brava!"

Cassie bowed and bowed again, and fled to the wings, only to be grappled by Mickey, the stage manager, and thrust out onstage once more.

At last it was over. Bruce Sandoz came out, the roar subsided, and the audience resumed its seats. By the time Alexis took her bow, the theater seemed almost silent.

The tiny, dirty dressing room that Cassie had always detested had become a place of refuge. She shut and bolted the door and sat down before the smeared mirror, ignoring both burned-out bulbs.

The woman who stared back at her was herself—was her true self, and not the foreign and slightly shoddy knockoff who had looked at her from a thousand other mirrors. "I am *me*," she said, and only afterward realized she had spoken aloud. Before the mirror, she removed her stage makeup and combed and brushed her hair. That done, she stripped and practically bathed in her favorite cologne, a baptism of the new self by the new self: a ritual cleansing in Lily Delight performed while someone tapped very softly at her door.

When it was complete she called, "Just a minute! I have to put on a robe."

With the robe in place and securely tied, she opened the door.

"Miss Casey." A small, gray woman smiled hesitantly, bobbing her head. "You don't know me, but I'm—"

"You're Margaret, Alexis's dresser."

"I was, Miss Casey." The smile faded and returned. "For the length of the engagement, you know. Well, I'm at liberty now, so I thought I might give you my card. You'll find me loyal and efficient. Hardworking, Miss Casey, and clean. An expert seamstress and laundress, and a discreet companion." She was offering a somewhat battered business card.

Cassie accepted it.

"When I was with Miss Sinclair . . . You must know of her work? Miss Easter Sinclair, Miss Casey—"

Margaret had been interrupted by India's rapping the door frame with hard, directorial knuckles. "Can I see you for a minute, Cassie?"

Cassie nodded and pointed to Margaret. "How much?"

"Only nine-fifty a week, Miss Casey, and—"

"That's too much." Cassie looked around for her purse, found it, and opened it. Neither cop, it appeared, had taken her money. "Here's twenty. I want a sandwich with lots of meat in it. Hot pastrami, understand? On rye with thousand island. A big coffee to go, sweetener but no creamer. Go get them, and we'll talk about your pay when you get back."

India shut the door behind Margaret. "I see you know," she said.

Cassie, who had not the least idea what she was talking about, nodded.

"If you'd played Mildred like that from the beginning, we'd still be running. Hell's belles! By this time you'd be Jane Simmons."

"Something was different tonight," Cassie said; mostly to herself she added, "I don't know . . ."

"It sure as shit was."

"And now I'm about to hire a dresser who'll cost me—do you happen to know what Alexis was paying her?"

"Eight twenty-five? I think I heard that." India dropped into the dressing room's one tattered chair, leaving Cassie the stool.

"A man owes me a hundred thousand." Cassie sighed. "I guess I've started spending it already. I'd better collect."

"Good luck. Can I tell you what I wanted to talk to you about?"

"The cast party? If you'd rather I didn't go, I won't."

"Screw the cast party. No, I take that back. You've got to go. It'll look bad if you don't."

"Bad for you?"

"Hell, yes." For a moment, India seemed worried and a trifle angry. "Bad for me and bad for you, too. Bad for everybody in the show."

"Alexis has decided she hates my guts."

"So what? She won't be there."

"How do you know that?" Cassie wondered whether she looked as surprised as she felt.

"It stands to reason. All the bees will be buzzing around you. She can join the buzz or stand in the corner and pout. Or not go. Which one would you pick?"

For a moment, Cassie could only stare.

"You think I'm kidding? I'm not."

"All right, I'll go. Now tell me why you want me to."

"See here, Cassie . . ." India's voice dropped to a stage whisper. "I've got this angel. Heavy, heavy guy. Wants to back a big musical. You sing, right?"

She nodded. "Not so you'd notice. I try."

"And dance?"

"Last time I looked."

"Well, you'll wow him. Give him the smile, give him the voice, and we're in."

"I've got a question, India. Don't string me on this. I want an honest answer, and I want it now."

"How much? We're not talking hard numbers yet, but it'll be big."

"How long have you known this guy?"

Someone knocked. It was neither Margaret's soft tap nor Mickey's rapid pounding. Cassie motioned India to silence and opened the door.

Jimmy stood there holding his watchman's cap, looking resolute and a trifle embarrassed. "I'm sorry to bother you, Miss Casey, but I have to deliver a message. There's a man in the alley, and he's got a nice present for you. That's what he said. I . . . Well, I promised I'd tell you right away."

India said, "Okay, you've told her. Disappear."

It seemed to Cassie that Jimmy's normally ruddy face paled somewhat. "Don't go yet." Jumping up, she caught his arm. "I need to talk to you."

India rose, too. "Well, I don't. You're coming to the party, right? We can talk more there."

Cassie nodded. "I'll be along."

"I won't be," Jimmy muttered.

"Got it." Cassie motioned for him to come in, and closed the door. "I like you, Jimmy. I consider you a friend, and I stick by my friends. If somebody's out to get you fired or something, I'm on your side. I mean it. Is that clear?"

"Thanks, Miss Casey."

"You're scared about something. If it's India I can fix it, but I don't think it is. What is it?"

"Nothing, Miss Casey. Honest. Everything's fine. It's just . . ."

"Just what?"

"Just that he gave me a hundred to come up and tell you he was waiting. Waiting, and he's got this present for you. Something really nice, he says."

Cassie slapped her dressing table, jarring four jars. "Let's get this straight. I don't accept gifts from men I don't know. There are a thousand guys out there who give you something and feel like they've bought you. If I know the man, maybe I'll take his gift and maybe I won't. If I don't know him, forget it."

Jimmy nodded. "I'll tell him."

"Great. Next point. If he wants his hundred back, tell him you earned it. You found me and told me about him and his gift, and that's what you promised to do. You can't deliver me like a package. Nobody can. Call the cops if he gets ugly."

Jimmy did not nod.

"Last point. What did he look like? Did he give you any kind of name? First name? Nickname? Anything?"

Jimmy shook his head. "He just gave me a hundred—it's a hundred-dollar bill, I could show you—and said to tell you he was waiting for you with a nice present."

"What did he look like?"

"I couldn't see him very well, Miss Casey." Jimmy was backing toward the door. "It was real dark."

"Big? Small?"

"Big. He sounded big." Jimmy turned, almost bumping into Margaret.

Then he was gone, walking away so quickly that Cassie suspected he would have run, had he still been capable of running.

"Here's your change, Miss Casey. Is everything all right?" Margaret was carrying a white paper bag.

"No." Cassie dropped into a chair. "Things are not all right. Far from it. You got the coffee and sandwich?"

"Yes, Miss Casey. Sweetener, no cream. Hot pastrami on rye."

"Good. Let me have 'em. There'll be food at the party, but I'll be talking to people and it's . . . an hour and twenty minutes. Besides, we don't want to be there when it starts. Half an hour late should do it. You're coming?" Cassie had opened the white bag and was looking over her sandwich.

"Thousand island," Margaret told her. "It's what you said, Miss Casey."

"Right. They should've used more. Tell them next time, if you're working for me. What about the party?"

"I don't think I'm invited, Miss Casey."

"Phooey. They didn't give you a straw?"

Margaret shook her head.

"You should have asked for one. Preserves the makeup. I don't have lots of money, Margaret. If I hire you, we may hit a place where I can't keep paying you. You'll be free to split, of course. But that may not be long. I don't know."

Margaret smiled. It was a very small smile but a smile just the same, a tiny candle lit in her colorless face. "I know how it is in show business, Miss Casey. I've been doing this quite a time."

"Good. I'll pay you eight hundred a week. That's firm. Do a good job, and you'll get raises. But eight hundred to start. Want it?"

Margaret hesitated. "I wasn't . . . Miss Cabana owes me back pay, Miss Casey. It's over three thousand dollars."

"I don't know how I could put the arm on her." Cassie gave it a few seconds' thought. "But I'll do it if I can figure a way."

"If you could just let me have the first week in advance . . . ?"

"Like that, huh?"

Margaret nodded.

"Are you going to cry on me?"

"No, Miss Casey."

"Good. Don't. I hate criers. I do it way too much myself. If I had the money on me, I'd give it to you. I don't, and you probably can't take a card."

"No, Miss Casey. I can't."

"I didn't think so. I'll give you the eight hundred tomorrow. It'll mean you'll have to wait two weeks for another payday. That's firm. No more advances."

"I understand, Miss Casey."

"And I'll get you into that party, if I can. It'll be a good test, and I think we're going to pass. Now go find Mickey for me. Tell him I need to get out of the building without being seen. Not the stage door and not the front. Something else. Scoot."

FIVE

DATING THE VOLCANO GOD

The Red Spot party was at Rusterman's, upstairs. "Cast only!" announced a Teutonically uniformed attendant at the door. "Cast *and* guests," Cassie snapped, and sailed into the room with head high and Margaret bobbing in her wake.

India was nowhere in sight. Ebony, her assistant, was loading a plate with beautiful brown fritters and terrine de lièvre. "Don't get fat," Cassie warned her. "What are you going to wear when you can't fit into a size four?"

Ebony grinned. "I never get fat. You tasted these?"

"Not often enough. How's life in India?"

"Ha, ha. Listen, Cassie, you got a new gig?"

"Right now?" Cassie shrugged. "Yes and no. Let's just say I don't want one."

"India's got an angel." Ebony's voice fell. "This's humongous stuff—try it out here and maybe Springfield and open on Broadway."

"So I heard." Cassie selected an oyster wrapped in something that might have been prosciutto but probably was not. She twirled it on its toothpick, studied it with a dietician's eye, and set it back down.

"Okay if I ask what Alexis's dresser's doing here?"

Almost inaudibly, Margaret said, "I'm Miss Casey's dresser now, Miss White."

Brian Kean appeared at Cassie's elbow. "Can I get you something? Champagne? Highball?"

Cassie smiled. "Just a glass of Chablis, please. Would you like anything, Margaret?"

Margaret shook her head.

"I'll fetch my own," Ebony announced. Brian appeared not to have heard her.

At Cassie's other elbow, Tabbi Merce whispered, "You were devastating tonight, Cassie. Absolutely devastating! They were throwing flowers at the stage."

"They weren't!"

"Oh, yes, they were! Boutonnieres and corsages. Orchids and carnations. You were seeing—I don't know what. Counting the empty seats or something while the audience went bananas."

Cassie smiled. "If you're trying to make me feel good, you're succeeding."

Brian pressed a glass of white wine into her hand, and someone else handed her a midget's plate heaped with food. She smiled again. "What are these fritters, anyway?" It was a general question, directed to the group around her. Norma Peiper, perhaps the heaper of the plate, said, "Wild mushroom. Delicious!"

"I'd like an anchovy fritter. This place is famous for them, and I've never had one."

"I'll tell them," Brian said, and hurried away.

Ebony asked, "Want to sit down?"

Cassie nodded. "See if you can't find us a table, Margaret."

Norma touched her arm. "Come on. I've got one already."

"So do I," Tabbi protested. "Cassie can sit with us."

"She certainly can." It was Bruce Sandoz. In a tone only slightly lower he added, "We featured players should cleave together, Cassie."

"I'd better sit with Ebony," Cassie decided. "India will be coming, and I promised we'd talk here." She called Margaret back.

Porter Penniman was seated there already, apparently holding the table. With a smile as broad as a piano's, he raised his exceedingly impressive four hundred pounds and indicated the chair on his right. Like all of Rusterman's chairs, it was massive and looked medieval.

Cassie managed to drag it back while Margaret squirmed into the chair on Cassie's right.

"De-lighted. Ah'm mos' surely de-lighted, Miz Casey." Porter Penniman's voice belonged in Walker's, blackstrap molasses drowning a cinnamon waffle.

Cassie smiled. "You know, Mr. Penniman, you've always seemed a little sinister to me, onstage and off. You've changed now, and I like the new you."

He raised a hand that looked as large as a dinner plate. "Ah mos' solemnly swears, Miz Casey, that Ah shall never agin enlist no smelly li'l foreigners to wring your pretty li'l neck."

"Friends forever." Cassie offered her hand. "And call me Cassie, please."

He took it, grasping it rather as an ogre of unusual size might have held a dove. "An' you mus' call me Tiny, which all mah other fren's already does."

A waiter leaned between them, proffering a platter of smoking fritters. At Cassie's other elbow Brian Kean said, "Anchovy fritters, made fresh for you. I haven't sampled them. They're very hot."

The waiter added, "Rusterman's best," and set his platter in the center of the table.

" 'Til I come heah," Tiny intoned, "Ah had believed this place heah to be solely in Noo Yahk."

Margaret whispered, "It's a chain now."

Brian had taken the chair to her right. "Speaking of chains, I understand that India wants to enlist people for a new show."

"It seems to me like it's way too early for anybody to commit to anything," Cassie said. She turned to Ebony, who was sitting to Porter Penniman's left. "How long has India had this angel? Do you know?"

"No," Ebony told her. "I don't. But not long. Or I don't think so."

"I can always make a good living doing commercials," Brian declared. "Still, there's nothing like the stage, is there? Live audiences and reviews next morning."

Ebony grinned. "The roar of the greasepaint and the smell of the crowd."

Porter Penniman had picked up a fritter. He popped it into his mouth as he might have eaten a peanut.

Cassie sipped Chablis.

Ebony rose, waving. "Over here, India!"

From behind Ebony, Tabbi murmured, "I thought she was bringing the angel."

India pulled out a chair and dropped triumphantly into it. "Wallace Rosenquist will be along shortly, kids. I've made firm arrangements for them to let him in, and Bruce is waiting there to raise holy hell if they don't. He saw our show tonight, and he's eager to meet all of you."

She turned to Cassie. "How were the utility tunnels?"

"You heard, huh?"

India nodded. "Mickey told me. Unwelcome company?"

"If you want to call it that." Cassie picked up a red something on a toothpick, conveyed it to her mouth, chewed—and swallowed before she realized she did not know what she had eaten. "I saw a man I knew in the audience. After the show, Jimmy came around to tell me somebody was waiting for me in the alley. Waiting to give me something, okay?"

Ebony said, "Careful time."

"Right. I'm not saying I don't want to see this guy. I'd like to talk to him as a matter of fact. But there are very few people I want to meet in dark alleys, and he's not one of them."

Margaret whispered in Cassie's ear, and she added, "He'd scared the heck out of Jimmy, and I didn't like that. He'd also given Jimmy a hundred, but Jimmy was scared just the same."

India said, "So?"

"So the utility tunnels. They run from building to building and there are electric wires in them. Pipes and all kinds of stuff. Mickey showed me how to get down in there. Then he took me on through when he saw how scared I was. We came out in the basement of the Marcus Building."

Cassie stood. "I don't mean to be impolite or anything, but where's the Jane?"

Ebony said, "I'll show you," and Cassie followed her, hoping that Margaret was following as well.

She was. When they were alone, Cassie opened her purse. "I said I'd give you a raise if you did a good job, remember? You can earn that raise right now. Here's ten bucks."

Margaret accepted it, pushing it into her sleeve.

"Maybe you've heard of Gideon Chase. He's a friend of mine, and he's got an apartment someplace in the city—I don't know where. He teaches close to Providence, so he's probably got another one around there. Got it?"

Margaret nodded.

"Get on the phone—directory assistance, the Babybell Search Engine, all that stuff. Find him. Tell him who you are, and tell him I'm here and I'm scared. Tell him to get himself over here quick."

When Margaret had gone, Cassie held the door open to watch her hurry away. The party at Ebony's table seemed unchanged. Ebony had resumed her seat, and India was holding forth. It occurred to Cassie that she need not rejoin it. Other tables dotted the tapestried room; there was even a crowd around the bar. After washing her hands twice, she slipped out of the restroom.

She was halfway to the bar when Palma pounced. "You were marvelous tonight, Cassiopeia Fiona Casey. Truly and absolutely marvelous! It was a privilege and an honor to tread the boards in your distinguished company. You made my poor scheming detective look very poor indeed, and that was all to the good. I know that the audience, God bless 'em!, made bold to let you know how *merveilleux* you were; but none of these hams will, so I intuit that I should do it myself. One strives, one endeavors, you know, to leave our poor old Earth a better place, eh? You have, and I do my own threadbare trifle by telling you how greatly you dazzled us. Come sit by me, and I'll tell you much, much more."

Palma had been steering her as a tall and unusually cruel tomcat might steer a captive mouse. They had nearly reached a table at which Donny Duke sat sipping something green, and at which Norma was in the act of sitting. "I was going to the bar," Cassie protested weakly.

"Donny will fetch it for you, Cassiopeia. Be seated, tell him your desires, and it shall be done."

Tempted to ask for a beach cottage, Cassie refrained. "I don't care what you get me, Donny, as long as it knocks my panty hose off. If you and Vince have to carry me out of here and pour me into a cab, you'll have done your job."

Borne up by half a smile, Donny floated from his chair and drifted toward the bar.

"I take it you're celebrating," Norma said.

"Try taking it that I'm scared."

"Cassie shall prophesy evil," Palma intoned, "but she shall not be believed. Save by me. Alone."

"Tell us," Norma said.

"There's nothing to tell." Cassie looked around for the Chablis she had left on Ebony's table, and failing to find it took a healthy swallow from Donny's glass. It was like drinking toothpaste.

"The Irish," Norma remarked, "are rarely afraid of nothing."

Palma smiled, and brushed an invisible yellow feather from his lips with a manicured and be-ringed paw. "She has heard the banshee."

"Seen it," Cassie said, "and I think I'm going to be going out with it in a day or two."

"Why Cassie!" Norma was grinning. "You always seemed so hetro."

"English speakers," Palma lectured her smoothly, "are invariably deceived by the second syllable. It merely conveys that banshees are to be numbered amongst the Grey Neighbors."

"I'll be damned if I've the foggiest idea what that's supposed to mean," Norma said, "but doesn't Cassie have a gray neighbor right now?"

"She's talking about me," Margaret whispered.

Turning, Cassie caught her arm. "Did you get him?"

Margaret shook her head. "I tried all those things. I talked to answering machines at both his apartments. I left a voice mail—"

Cassie raised at hand. "That's plenty for now. You can tell me the rest later. Find a chair, sit down, and talk about something else if you want to talk."

Donny returned bearing a tall and narrow glass thick with frost. Solemnly he passed it to Cassie, who sipped, shuddered, and sipped again.

"Would anyone care for ugly news?" Donny inquired. "Perhaps everyone has already heard? Am I to know shame because *I* had not?"

Cassie wet her lips from the glass and licked them. "It depends on what bad news you have in mind. My God! I don't think I'll ever get used to this stuff."

"You weren't planning on two?"

"Lord no!"

"Are you going to be displeased because I bribed the man to mix it to my own specifications?"

Palma touched Cassie's elbow. "I had supposed you celebrating, Cassiopeia darling. I see how mistaken I was. Rest assured, I beg you, that your friends—and everyone at this table is your friend—will stand by you through thick and thin."

Norma had taken out her compact and was studying herself in its mirror. "The cavalry's not coming, Vince. You've made westerns. I know you have. The Apaches are closing in, and back at the fort nobody knows. You've got to learn to listen."

Donny raised an eyebrow. "Listen to . . . ?"

"You weren't here." Norma snapped her compact shut. "To Alexis's dresser. Cassie sent her to the colonel, but she couldn't find him."

"This is my personal thing." Firmly, Cassie set the frosted glass down. "Whatever you've heard, Donny, wasn't. Or I don't think it was. So tell us."

Margaret returned with a glass, sat, and sipped primly.

"Well, I um . . . ?" The scarlet dots of Donny's pimples stood out like bloodstains on a sheet. "Was the security guard back at the theater a, er, special friend of anyone here? I believe his name was Jeremy? I, ah, perhaps you thought I knew him?"

"I consider him a friend," Cassie said. "I did and still do. Has he been fired? He always seemed like such an honest, cheerful sort of man."

Margaret spoke more loudly than usual. "He was, Miss Casey. I knew him about as well as I know anybody. James K. Warshawsky was his name, and he's passed away."

In the silence that followed, she added, "Or that's what they say. I think that's probably what Mr. Duke heard at the bar."

Donny nodded.

"Let me guess." Cassie closed her eyes. "They found him in the alley outside the stage door, and he'd been shot. Maybe stabbed. Is that right?"

"Oh, shit!" Norma spoke under her breath, adding, "I'm back in the show."

"I didn't hear about shooting or stabbing," Donny said, "did you, Margaret?"

She shook her head.

"Quiet, everybody! Quiet!" The voice was India's; she was standing in the middle of the room, speaking into a mike.

It had the desired effect.

"Thanks! We call this the cast party, but it's not all cast. Some of us were never onstage, but we're all in showbiz and that's what this's really about. Now I'd like to introduce you to a gentleman you really ought to know. He's in showbiz, too, or he soon will be."

There was a subdued buzz of talk. Cassie gulped her drink.

"It always seems like big stage musicals are few and far between," India continued, "but the legitimate stage is coming back. Maybe it's just a cyclic thing. That's what some people say. Maybe it's all these hoppers, and people vacationing on barren worlds. Honeymoons on the moon, when grandpa was happy just to do it on his honey. All that shit. I don't pretend to know, but I do know that lots and lots of the old movie theaters are reopening as legitimate playhouses, where people can sit and watch talented people like you onstage doing a show." She fell silent, looking toward the door.

"Some of you may have heard rumors about a big new musical called *Dating the Volcano God*. Okay, if you want to know more we've got the man right here." She motioned urgently to a big man in a pin-striped teal suit. "Let's have a real standing 'O' for a real angel—Mr. Wallace Rosenquist!"

The applause was loud and prolonged. Cassie took advantage of the cover it afforded her to open her purse and glance at two photographs she took from it. Nodding to herself, she crumpled them and let them fall to the floor.

The man Gideon Chase had called Bill Reis took the mike from India, coughed once, and smiled. "First of all, I want to say that our show's still in the planning stages, very much so. India and I hardly know each other at this point. We haven't even started looking for a set designer and a choreographer."

From his left, India put in, "Tomorrow, Wally."

"I have the book, however, and some ideas about the music. Plans already made and plans I'm still shaping. What's more, I have the money and the determination. This afternoon I found my director."

Raising her arms, India shook her own hands like a prizefighter.

"I talked to her over lunch, and she was good enough to give me a ticket so I could watch a fine example of her work. I did, and want to say how much I enjoyed it. You are artists, and I mean that sincerely. There won't be parts for everybody here in our new show, and I realize that some of you will already have commitments elsewhere. That will be our loss. We'll be talking about commitments and contracts, roles and all the rest of it in the days to come. Right now, tonight, I just want to say that I wish I could have all of you."

There was a burst of spontaneous applause and some scattered cheering.

"Having said that, there's one member of your cast I'd like to pay particular tribute to. You're well ahead of me now, I feel sure. I'm told Miss Cassie Casey is at this party."

Palma hissed, "Stand up, Cassie!"

She did not.

"I have a gift for her," Rosenquist continued. "I want to give her this little keepsake, whether she will consent to be our leading lady or not."

India said, "Come on, Cassie! Who the hell ever heard of a shy actress?"

Rising, Cassie handed her purse to Margaret, pushed back her chair, and came forward smiling. "You want a Dumb Dora, don't you, Mr. Rosenquist? If that's what it is, I'll be perfect."

"Has anyone told you, Miss Casey, that you're even more stunning in person than onstage?"

She dropped him a mock curtsy. "Make that stunned."

Rosenquist was reaching into his coat pocket. "I had this designed and fabricated months ago. At that time, I didn't know to whom I would give it. When I saw *The Red Spot* tonight, I knew I had found her."

The leather-covered box he handed Cassie was eight inches long, two and a half inches wide, and remarkably heavy.

"I should have had it wrapped," he told her, "but I'm afraid the ribbon will have to do."

"Open it," India directed.

Ebony seconded her from the audience: *"Show us, Cassie!"*

She slipped the gold ribbon off, and found that her hands were trembling. "I don't think I can. I feel like I've just won something I don't deserve."

"You deserve much more," the man who had given it to her said.

Bill Reis, Cassie told herself. *Bill Reis said that.* India had given him another name, but she had forgotten it.

Her fingers found and released the catch. Reis took a step backward and urged India forward.

"Show me!" India sounded eager. "I want to see it."

From the table Cassie had left, Donny called, "What is it?"

"It's . . . a bracelet. A great big gold bracelet." She pulled it from the box and dangled it above her head. "It's—well—massive."

"Solid gold," Reis told her. "Eighteen karat, which means it's pretty soft. Be careful with the clasp."

"Put it on," India said. "Here, hold out your arm. I'll do it."

She did, adjusting the catch and wrapping the heavy bracelet around Cassie's wrist. Cassie, who already hated it, said, "It's very pretty."

"Lovely," India muttered. "Simply lovely."

A large hand took the box from Cassie. *"I need to speak to you privately. I'll meet you at the front desk downstairs in twenty minutes."* Reis's whisper was a trifle hoarse, deep yet sibilant.

India was using the mike to field questions about *Dating the Volcano God*. No, she had not seen the songs yet, but she knew they would be good. As the show now stood, there would be seven major parts, a dozen minor ones, and perhaps forty parts for dancers and singers who would play male and female natives, missionaries, and seamen. There was no hard casting date yet, but it would begin soon.

That question had been from Palma; as Cassie returned to his table, India asked him to stand. "I want Wally to see you. I know he's seen you already onstage, Vince; but I'd like him to see you again without makeup. Think you might be loose?"

Palma licked his lips. "You'll direct, India?"

Reis rumbled, "Absolutely. Tomorrow I'll have her under contract."

"In which case," Palma declared, "I shall cancel my commitments."

"Reading the synopsis," India told him, "I kept seeing you as the Volcano God." She turned to Reis. "How about it, Wally? What do you think?"

"I'd certainly like to see you try out for it. How tall are you, sir?"

"Six feet four, and . . ."

Cassie did not hear the rest. She had the bracelet off and was handing it to Margaret. "Keep this for me. I'm leaving now, but I want you to stay right here. Stay here for at least another hour. Understand?"

Margaret nodded. She was looking at the bracelet.

"You can go to the restroom or change tables, but that's it. Have you got a pen?"

Margaret did, taking the pen from her purse and putting the bracelet into it.

"Here." Cassie scribbled her cell phone number on a napkin. "Call me tomorrow afternoon."

She was gone before Margaret could reply.

Ebony stopped her on the way out. "You look like death warmed over."

"I had a scare, that's all. Well, no, it isn't. Not really. Have you heard about Jimmy?"

"Sure. Heart attack or something. It's a damned shame."

Cassie nodded. "I liked him, and two people sprung it on me fast. I was shaky already, and now—well, I'm going home."

"You're going down to the bar with me," Ebony said firmly. "You need a drink and some quiet talk."

"I've had two drinks, and the second one would peel paint. I think I drank about half, and my head's swimming. So no."

"So yes." Ebony followed her. "You can have a Coke or something. I need to talk to you."

Cassie stopped abruptly. "God knows I need to talk to somebody. Listen, Ebony. I promised someone—a man I like a lot—that I'd do him a little favor. It—well, it was easy to promise then. Now I'm . . ."

"Afraid."

Mutely, Cassie nodded.

"You need to talk it out, that's all. You need—"

A deep, hoarse voice interrupted. "What she needs," Bill Reis said firmly, "is a strong friend, an intelligent and resourceful friend. She has one. Come with me, Miss Casey. I've a limousine outside."

The night had turned cool. Rusterman's white and gold canopy sheltered them from the light rain, but not from the wind. "Fall soon," Cassie muttered.

"Our show won't be ready for this season," Reis told her. "We'll need scenery."

A uniformed chauffeur opened the limousine's wide rear door.

"And rehearsals." Thinking of things she had heard the night before, Cassie shuddered.

"You're cold. Have you a fur coat? Mink? Ermine, perhaps?"

"Wool. But it's real wool and looks nice on me. I like it."

"Get in, please. I'll go around."

She did, and the chauffeur closed the door with the merest whisper of sound.

At once, or so it seemed, Reis was sitting beside her. "Blue mink, I would say. I hopped here today to meet you. You cannot have known that, Cassie, but I did. One hour from Berlin in a friend's hopper. Have you been into space yet?"

She shuddered again and shook her head.

"I should be getting you a drink." Reis gestured. "This little cabinet opens into a bar. You must've seen that from the glasses. Brandy?"

"Nothing, please."

"This will be a very ordinary cognac, I'm afraid. Our Earth's a small place, Cassie. You see that clearly from out in space. I could have hopped from Berlin to Beijing just as easily. We weren't ready for space travel when science gave it to us." He poured three fingers of amber fluid into a pony glass and handed it to her.

"I've heard people say that."

"It's true. A hundred years ago, men dreamed of it. They thought there'd be a world government long before it came, that ignorance and poverty would've been eliminated."

"It'll never happen," Cassie whispered. She pretended to sip.

"No world government?"

She shook her head. "I was thinking of poverty and ignorance."

Reis poured for himself. "When I show you Earth from space, when you see how beautiful it is, you'll realize how easily it might be put right." Reis appeared to hesitate. "Poverty and ignorance . . . they're relative terms. Let's see that everybody has enough to eat and a place to sleep. That everyone can read well enough to enjoy reading."

"That would satisfy me. May I ask why you wanted to meet me? Wanted to so much that you hopped from Berlin?"

"Isn't it obvious?" Reis seemed oddly embarrassed.

"Not to me."

"I want you for Mariah. You haven't read the script, I realize. Mariah Brownlea's our star, the woman who dates the Volcano God. A year from now, Cassie, you'll be ready to open on Broadway. There'll be a film, a year or two after that. You'll star in the film, too. I won't have to insist on you because everybody will insist on you."

Cassie's purse played the first three bars of "Pigs in Paradise." She opened it, found her cell phone, and said, "Hello?"

"Cassie?" The voice (a pleasant voice that she found she remembered very well) sounded concerned. "It's me. I just learned that Reis is in town. Are you someplace where you can use my name?"

She glanced at her watch. "No," she said, "and you're about six hours late."

As she spoke, she felt the limousine glide away from the curb.

SIX

TOO DEARE

They met for breakfast at the International House of Toast, a plastic-cum-Formica palace less crowded and noisy than Walker's. Gideon ordered the Renaissance French Toast, and Cassie the Fontina Toast aux des Raisins Secs.

"If there's something you don't want to talk about," Gideon said, "give me an idea of what I ought to stay away from. I'm going to have a lot of questions."

Cassie nodded. "So am I."

"But you don't want to talk about . . . ?"

"How scared I was. What a coward I am."

He shook his head. "I doubt it. But fine, we won't talk about that. Or at least, I won't."

"I had my gun on my leg in that holster thing you saw. Left leg, inside, just high enough that a long skirt still covered it when I sat down. I kept thinking I ought to get it out and stick it in his face. *Stay away or I'll shoot!* Only I never had the guts."

"You didn't want to talk about this."

"I didn't want *you* to talk about it. I still don't. I felt like my insides were going to run out and soak the backseat. I was afraid I was going to fall when I got out. My knees were that weak."

"Our friend would have picked you up."

"Right. And helped me to my apartment and wanted to come inside for a drink, and Cassie, I've done you some big favors already and I'm going to do you a lot more. I'd like just one little one from you. Take off that dress."

Gideon, who had been toying with his fork, put it down. "I doubt it. He's not that crude."

"He wanted to know about the bracelet. He'd given me a bracelet—this was in public, when I couldn't turn it down without losing every friend I had."

"Including me," Gideon said.

"Right. Because you want me to play footsie with a tiger and find out exactly how he bites their necks. Well, I didn't turn it down. Happy?"

"Very. What was it he wanted to know about it?"

"Where it was, and why I wasn't wearing it. I told him half the truth, that I didn't want him to think he owned me. The other half is that I hate the damned thing. He has lousy taste."

As a waitress in a frilly lace cap brought coffee, Gideon said, "I've never thought so, but perhaps I have poor taste myself. You said he wanted to know where it was. Where was it?"

"I gave it to Margaret and told her to keep it for me. Margaret's my dresser. A dresser is someone who helps you with your costumes." Cassie paused. "I'm talking like I've had her for years, but I only hired her yesterday."

Gideon sipped. "Could she be working for Reis?"

"I doubt it. She was working for Alexis Cabana when *The Red Spot* opened. Alexis let her go when it closed, I assume because she doesn't have anything lined up. You said you had lots of questions for me. Can I ask you one?"

"Certainly. Go ahead."

"You and I had breakfast yesterday. Sharon came in and took pictures. That afternoon one was on vid, and she talked about us. You know she did, because we caught her part of the show. That evening—I'd be shouting here, if I were onstage—you-know-who was in the audience."

Gideon nodded.

"Last night he said he'd had lunch with India, so he got onto us awfully, awfully fast. How did he do that?"

"I don't know, and I wish I did. I can offer two speculations. No, three. Do you want to hear them?"

"You bet I do."

"All right. He's attracted to glamorous women. I've looked into his background, and it shows very clearly. I'm certain you recall what Sharon told her audience on trivid, and while we were at Walker's there was a good deal said about your beauty and desirability. About your being a star, and so forth. An online edition of her paper could have had her story as soon as she wrote it. Suppose Reis had software searching for news items in which those words were used."

"I don't believe it. I know any good programmer could do the computer stuff, but he wouldn't hop halfway 'round the world because of something Sharon wrote."

"He'd have seen you. Perhaps even heard you speak."

"Thanks, but I still don't buy it. What are the other two?"

"That first one, the one you're dismissing so easily, is my favorite. I don't like this one as much. It's that he's done at least one search using my rather distinctive name, having realized at some point that I was looking into his operations. I've tried to be careful, of course; but it's entirely possible that I haven't been careful enough. He wants you as a way of getting to me."

"I like that one better," Cassie said.

"In which case you should like the last, too. He has people watching me."

"Ouch!"

"Indeed. I've been acutely aware of the possibility ever since I talked with the president. Did I tell you about John's call, by the way?"

Their food arrived.

"If they're watching you, would they have followed us up north?"

"I doubt it." Gideon was spreading whipped butter on his French toast. "Why do you ask?"

"If you had said yes, I'd have asked how they could do it."

"Because of the car, you mean?"

"Because you drove so fast. You burned up the roads and we never got stopped. I've been wondering how you got away with that."

"Nothing complicated. We went late at night in a black car that's invisible to radar."

"You're kidding!"

"Certainly not, and your toast is getting cold."

Obediently, Cassie cut a small triangle from the uppermost slice and conveyed it to her mouth.

"When one feels one may be watched," Gideon murmured, "one is constantly eyeing strangers."

"How in the world did you get hold of a thing like that?"

"As a bonus, that's all. I did a little work for a company that builds military hoppers. They wanted to give me some sort of gift, so I asked for the car."

"As easy as that."

"Yes. We've gotten far off the track with all this. I'd like to get back on it. Margaret has that bracelet. Positioning devices and listening devices can be made smaller than you would believe."

"Then it would be easy to put them in there. It's a great big clunky thing. Did I say so?"

"I don't believe you did." Gideon took another bite of French toast.

"Well, it is. You know who'd wear something like that? The Volcano God, that's who. It's—it's barbaric. He's got volcano gods on the brain, and where did he get that show anyway?"

"What show?"

"Didn't I tell you about it?"

"No. You've actually told me very little. Tell me about the show."

"It's a musical laid in the Pacific in sailing-ship times. I'm Mariah, a missionary's daughter. I date the Volcano God, and that's all I know about it. Reis says he's got the book—that's the spoken lines—but not the songs. There'll be singing and dancing, costumes and big sets, all the stuff they'll need for New York and London."

Cassie paused, looking thoughtful. "You know, that bracelet really does look like something the Volcano God might give a girl. Primitive."

"A diamond bracelet? I doubt it."

"It isn't. There aren't any stones at all. Just a lot of gold." Cassie's fork halted halfway to her mouth. "I said something, didn't I? What was it?"

"You may have. I don't know. You don't have the bracelet now? You gave it to Alexis's dresser?"

"I didn't give it to her." The morsel of toast on her fork attained its fated destination, and Cassie chewed and swallowed. "All right, I gave it to her to keep for me, but she's not Alexis's dresser anymore. She's mine."

"She still has it?"

"As far as I know."

"Do you have a number for her? When will you see her again?"

"Her business card should be in my purse." Cassie opened it and began to search. "I said for her to call me . . . When was it?"

"I have no idea."

"I don't think I was very specific about it. Just call me this afternoon. What time is it?"

"Twelve thirty."

"Why do you wear a watch? You never look at it."

When Gideon said nothing, Cassie added, "How's the French toast?"

"Delicious. First, I wear this particular watch because it once belonged to someone I admire. Second, I wear a watch—a watch in the abstract—to keep people like you from asking why I don't. Third, I wear a watch because there are times when I wouldn't know the time if I didn't have a watch. Satisfied?"

"Yep. Can I see it?"

"You may." Gideon took off his watch and handed it to her.

"You don't wear it when you sunbathe. Or climb into a tanning cabinet. Or whatever it is you do."

"I don't do those things. This is the way I was born; I would have thought my eye color and hair would make that clear. Aren't you interested in my watch?"

"Yes, but I'm a lot more interested in you." Cassie turned the watch over. Its back read: *RC from his friend HPL.* "This is a man's watch," she said. "Its face is twice as big as the one on my watch, and it has a big heavy gold-plated band. Are you following me?"

Gideon said, "I don't think so."

"Well, this watch is a lot smaller, and a whole lot lighter than the bracelet our angel Wally Rosenquist gave me."

"Wally Rosenquist?" Gideon raised an eyebrow.

"It's what I have to call him. Mr. Rosenquist. Same initials, assuming Bill's short for William. He's probably got monogrammed stuff."

"I imagine. Cassie, I want that bracelet. You let Margaret keep it for you. Would you be willing to let me borrow it for a few days? I won't damage it."

"Too bad. I was hoping you would. Yes, I will—with bells on. I'll have Margaret meet us wherever, and hand it over to you as soon as I get it back."

"Fine. You were talking about dating the Volcano God, and you seem to have shared a cab with—"

"A limousine. Huge. Built-in vid. Built-in bar. All that stuff."

"I stand corrected. What I want to know is whether you dated our friend W.R."

"Not yet."

"What did you do, in that case?"

"Went home. I had said I wanted to go home. Ebony wanted to talk to me in the bar instead. This was at the cast party—have I said that?"

Gideon shook his head.

"Well, it was. Wally got me away from her and into his limo. We talked a little, and drank some stuff that tasted like lighter fluid. Then he took me back to my apartment. I told him he didn't have to come upstairs with me, but he said he wanted to see me safely to my door. So he did. I kept telling myself that if he tried to force his way in I was going to pull my gun and shoot him. I was tight by then, and I might have done it."

"But he didn't?"

"No. He's not like you. How did you get into my apartment, anyway?"

"I meant to show you," Gideon said, "and I'd rather show you than tell you, so I'll try to make this brief. The apartment next to yours is the mirror image of yours. That arrangement simplifies plumbing and wiring, including the trivid connection; so it's very common. Specifically, the living room mirrors yours. Thus there's a couch with its back to your own, on the other side of the wall."

Cassie nodded.

"I entered that apartment without difficulty after having learned that the family wasn't home. There's a hole in your wall now, behind your couch. I made it, pushed your couch aside, crawled through, cleaned up a little wall-board dust, and put your couch back before you returned from the theater." He looked apologetic. "Now tell me more about last night."

"Just like that? You broke into my place."

"You're right, I did. I apologize, but I strongly suspected I was being watched and the matter was urgent. Our friend frightened you. If I'd simply arranged to meet you they might have gotten to you first. Do I have to say these things, Cassie?"

"I guess not." She sipped coffee. "Last night I was still scared, even after I'd shut the door and bolted and chained it, and turned on the alarm. I went to the balcony windows and looked down at his limo. It was white and as big as they come. The driver was standing by the open door in back waiting for Wally to come out, and I wanted to see him leave my building and get into his limo and go away. I never did, but he must have because the driver closed the door and got in front."

"He drove away then?"

Cassie nodded.

"But you didn't see our friend come out . . . ?"

"No. But I don't think he got into my apartment. He didn't toss me notes or mess with my computer or anything."

"Unlike some others."

Cassie smiled. "Hey, you got it."

"I did indeed. Did you do anything in back of the limousine besides talking and drinking?"

Cassie cut a slice of fontina toast in two and ate the smaller half before she answered. "We held hands. Are you jealous?"

"Is that all?"

"All I'm going to tell you about, yes."

"I see. May I ask what you talked about?"

Cassie held out her right hand and scratched the palm with her left index finger. "I promised to spy for you for a hundred thousand dollars. Remember? Payable on demand. It was before you made me a star."

"I do."

"You promised, and I went through with your ceremony on the mountain. Now I'm mixed up with somebody you tell me is terribly dangerous." Cassie paused. "That's what you tell me, and I think you're right. He is. He scares the holy bejabbers out of me, Dr. Chase. He talks very kindly and reasonably, and it's like hooking up with a friendly tiger. He wants you to hang out with him—until he gets hungry."

She took a deep breath. "So I want to see some money. Now. A whole bunch of money. Enough to prove once and for all that you haven't been stringing me."

"I see. And that would be . . . ?"

"Twenty thousand. At least that much. Twenty thousand dollars."

Gideon nodded. "If you want it in cash, we can go to my bank and get it. If you're willing to take a check, I can write you one right now. You can deposit it today; if it bounces, you ought to hear about that from your own bank within twenty-four hours."

"You think I'll be scared, carrying that much money."

Gideon raised well-tailored shoulders and let them fall. "I don't think anything, though anyone might be a bit apprehensive."

"Yeah. I've got a better idea. You can write me a check now? There's that much in your account?"

"In this account. Yes."

"Good. Write me the check. When we leave here we'll go straight to your bank, and I'll use your check to open an account there."

"All right." Gideon pursed his lips. "You know, that's clever. I hadn't thought of it."

"Need a pen?"

He shook his head and got out a checkbook.

"While you're writing my check, I've got a question."

"So do I. Cassie or Cassandra?"

"Cassie. My name's not Cassandra, and I always go by Cassie."

Gideon wrote.

"Here's my question. Is it all right if I hock the bracelet? I don't like it and I don't want it around. If I hock it, I can go back and get it if Wally makes too big a stink."

Gideon nodded to himself as he signed. " 'One may buy gold at a price too deare.' Who said that? Spencer?"

"I haven't the faintest idea." Cassie accepted the check. "Are you about ready?"

"No. I want more coffee, and I have more questions."

"So do I. Is it all right if I get my wall fixed?"

He nodded as he handed her the check. "Go right ahead."

"Thanks." Cassie was studying the check. "Barclays Bank? Isn't that English?"

"Correct. It's the U.S. branch of a British bank."

"You get around. What about the bracelet?"

"I want it, and I've said so. The more I hear about it, the more suspicious it sounds. I want to examine it thoroughly, and I want to have some people I know look it over. When they've checked it out, you and I can decide what—"

Cassie's purse played "Pigs in Paradise."

"My cell phone," she muttered, and answered it. After what might have been fifteen seconds she said, "Naturally you were afraid. I understand. . . . Don't worry about it."

She fell silent for a few seconds longer, then said, "Listen, I want you to come to my apartment at three." She gave the address. "I'll be there, we'll talk this over, and I'll give you that eight hundred." Soon she repeated, "I understand," pushed a button, and dropped the telephone back into her purse.

"Something's happened," Gideon said. "What is it?"

"Our friend—Mr. Rosenquist is what Margaret said—came to see her. She must rent a room somewhere. That's what it sounded like. He wanted his bracelet, and he must have known, somehow, that it was still in her purse."

"She probably looked toward it when he asked about the bracelet. People do that unless they train themselves very carefully not to."

"Fine. She looked, and he opened her purse and got it. He had a long black jewelry box, she said. It sounded like the same box he had the bracelet in when he gave it to me. Anyway, he got out this box and put my bracelet in it and left. Then she called me. All this was just a minute ago."

"She didn't call the police?"

Cassie shook her head. "She'd have told me about it if she had, I'm certain. Do you want her to?"

"No. That's the last thing I want. He must have given her some excuse when he asked for it back. Do you know what it was?"

"She didn't mention any. Just said that he asked for it back."

"A long black box . . . No further description?"

Cassie signaled to the waitress, who brought them more coffee. When she had gone, Cassie said, "I told you it sounded like the box it was in when he gave it to me. If that's right, it's about this long and covered with black leather. It was lined with white silk, or something like that."

"You handled it?"

"No," Cassie said. "I mean yes. Yes, I did. He gave it to me and I took the ribbon off and opened it. Then I took the bracelet out and handed the box back to him. He must have put it in his pocket."

"Was it heavy?"

"The bracelet or the box? The bracelet was as heavy as lead. I don't know about the box."

"You handled it," Gideon said, "even if it was only for a moment. Please try to remember. This is important."

"I'm trying. I remember how heavy it felt when he handed it to me. I couldn't imagine what it was. Then the bracelet . . . You know, I think it was. I think the box was heavy, too. You shouldn't smirk."

"Was I smirking? I apologize." Gideon sipped his coffee. "He may give that bracelet back to you. I doubt it, but he may. If he does, don't wear it more than you have to, and get in touch with me right away."

"Do you carry a cell phone? You must."

Gideon nodded.

"I want the number. I was trying to get in touch with you last night, before you called me. I couldn't reach you."

"You tend to be indiscreet on the telephone. That's why I haven't given you the number."

"I won't be. Never again." Cassie raised a hand. "Honest Injun. And I won't pester you for dates."

Gideon grinned. "Pity."

"Oh, you want to be pestered? Then you will be. But I've got to have the number."

He took out a business card and wrote it on the back; his numerals, while somewhat stylized, were as neat and disciplined as print.

"Thanks. You said you had more questions. All right, Dr. Chase, let fly."

"If you're going to ask me for a date," Gideon said, "you really should use my first name."

"Fine. I will. In a day or two, I'll be calling you Giddy. What are the questions?"

"I suppose I invited that. Very well. I don't think you can possibly know the answer to the first one; but it's by far the most important, and if you have speculations I'd like to hear them. Why did Reis give you a bracelet and take it back?"

Cassie stared. "I have no idea. I was so happy to get rid of it that I didn't even think about that."

"Do so now."

In the momentary silence that followed, the waitress laid a small blank book and a pen on the table in front of Cassie. "It's not for me," the waitress explained, "it's for Ida. She collects them, only she's not your waitress and she's shy. Could you sign it for her? Best of luck, Ida? Something like that?"

SEVEN

STAY TUNED

Much impeded by traffic, they drove from the House of Toast to Barclays Bank. When they had at last completed their business, Gideon took Cassie to her building on West Arbor, and at her insistence let her out at the curb. Parking places were hard to find at that hour; but he found one, walked four long blocks back to her building, and stationed himself across the street for a time.

There he thought about a great many things, including (but far from limited to) a sculptor of ancient Greece and the beautiful woman George Bernard Shaw had called Galatea. "I could reverse it," he told himself, "but time and chance will do that soon enough." As soon as he spoke, he knew that for him no reversal would have the least effect.

Returning to the brown convertible, he drove to his own Pine Crest Towers several miles away, where he parked in the space assigned to him. A doorman smiled, nodded, and touched his cap. "Professor Chase."

There seemed to be nothing wrong. Why then, he asked himself, did he feel so utterly certain that something was? The impression was so strong that he would not have boarded the elevator if there had been anyone else in it.

He was walking down the long second-floor corridor when the sound of a pistol slide being racked made him turn. For an instant he saw the muzzle of the gun and threw himself against the door of the nearest apartment with all his strength.

It gave way, and he staggered into someone's living room as the gun spoke in the corridor behind him. He had nearly reached the kitchen before he felt the stab of pain in his right calf.

He had known there would be no way out of the kitchen save one window. There was no time to break that window or climb through it, but kitchen gadgets hung above the sink. He threw a cleaver and saw the gunman stagger backward, his bleeding face in both hands.

With a meat tenderizer in one hand and a carving knife in the other Gideon tried to pursue him, but found that it was all that he could do to walk without falling. Before he limped away, he picked up his assailant's gun and left three hundred dollars under a book on the coffee table.

MARGARET was fifteen minutes late. "There was a phone call, Miss Casey. Miss Dempster called wanting the number of your cell phone."

Cassie nodded. "You must not have given it to her."

"I didn't. You had given it to me, but I didn't think you would want me to give it out. So I told her I didn't have it."

"What's this!" Cassie's smile would have broken the heart of every man in sight, had there been any. "You lied to India, Margaret? Tsk, tsk!"

"I didn't, Miss Casey. Things like that really bother me, so I don't do it unless I've got to. You had written your number on that napkin. Remember?"

"Right, I do."

"Well, before I told Miss Dempster I didn't have it, I got the napkin and threw it away. I've got a pretty little round wastebasket next to my phone."

"Handy," Cassie remarked.

"It truly is, Miss Casey, and while we were still talking back and forth I took your napkin out of my purse and dropped it into there. Of course after we'd hung up I looked down real careful and read the number. I copied it into my book, only there was a good deal said between Miss Dempster and me before. Before she'd let me off the phone, you know."

"Wait a bit," Cassie said. "What would you have done if you hadn't been able to read the number?"

"Why I'd shake the wastebasket, Miss Casey, just like anybody would. Made that napkin jump around in there, you know, until I could read it."

"Golly, I should have thought of that. What did India have to say?"

"Ever so many things." Margaret looked vague. "A read-through was one. She'd got the Tiara, she said, by telling them her new show might open there. One tomorrow afternoon, it will be."

"I'm not signed," Cassie remarked.

"I don't think anybody is, Miss Casey. Or nobody but Miss Dempster and Mr. Palma. She said he was, come to think."

"I see."

"Only she said she's been talking to Ms. Youmans and it's all settled except for signing. She said to tell you she absolutely had to have you and you'd be letting them all down if you wouldn't take it, so she was ever so very glad you were going to do it. Because of Mr. Rosenquist is what she said."

"I've got it. Before I sign, I want to talk to Zelda. She's sold me down the volcano much too cheaply, unless I'm badly mistaken."

Margaret tittered. "Then, too, she wants to know how many solo songs you'll do."

"None," Cassie said firmly.

"That Mr. Rosenquist wanted five, she said. Only Miss Dempster doesn't want you to strain your voice. She is trying to get him down to the three, she said. There is a voice coach, too, now. I don't recall the name."

"Doesn't matter. Dammit! I can sing along with two or three other people, but I'm no singer."

"You sing beautifully, Miss Casey."

When Cassie objected, Margaret raised her voice. "I know you do, Miss Casey. I've heard you talking. I'm hearing you right now. There's nobody in the world who can talk like you who can't sing."

"You're a very nice person, Margaret, but no. I've . . . The other night . . ."

"What is it, Miss Casey?"

"Have you ever heard of a mountain that was alive, Margaret? Honestly, now. A mountain whose wife washed clothes?"

Doubtfully, Margaret shook her head. "A dream, Miss Casey? I was going to say I sing in the choir. In church, you know, when I'm not on the road, because there's hardly ever a show on Sunday morning. I'm not much of a singer, but I know some good singers and I know how they sound."

"Do you really, Margaret? Give me a sample. What do you sing?"

"I'll try to get the tune right, Miss Casey. It's such a lovely song, but I'm not good with tunes unless I have the music." She sang, her voice quavering a bit on the high notes. When she had finished, Cassie applauded.

Smiling gratefully, Margaret said, "Now let's hear you sing it, Miss Casey. You can't help but be better than I was."

Cassie stood and coughed to clear her throat: a soft, apologetic sound.

"As close as tomorrow the sun shall appear,
Freedom is coming, and healing is near."

"Louder, Miss Casey!"

"And I shall be with you in laughter and pain
To stand in the wind and walk in the reign,
To walk in the reign."

The song seemed to fill her, a host of angels caroling through the corridors of her mind.

"The sower is planting in acres unseen
The seeds of the future, the field of God's dream.
Those meadows are humming, though none sees them rise.
The name of the sower is God of Surprise.
God of Surprise . . ."

When she had finished singing as much as she could recall, Margaret clapped enthusiastically. "Wonderful! You have a wonderful, wonderful voice, Miss Casey. I knew it. Why, I declare, it was like—like I don't know what. If you could come to church just once—"

The telephone rang. Cassie excused herself with a gesture and picked it up.

"Was that you singing?"

"I'm afraid so." Cassie managed a rueful smile. "I'm sorry I disturbed you."

"I—Pickens is my name. Brian Pickens. I have the place above yours, and I work at—it doesn't matter. I got your name from your mailbox. I wanted . . . I was out earlier today, and I saw you come in. I hope you don't mind."

"Of course not. And it won't happen again, Mr. Pickens, I promise."

"I'd like you to break that promise. Holy tornado! I'd *love* for you to break it. I just wanted to say that you're—well, I've seen you now. And I've heard you. And there's nobody like you. Nobody at all."

For a moment it seemed to Cassie that Brian Pickens was being strangled.

"For the rest of my life I'll be telling people about somebody I talked to on the phone once. Thanks for that—thank you a million. I mean it." He hung up.

Very slowly, Cassie hung up, too.

"Miss Casey?"

Feeling dazed, Cassie turned toward Margaret. "Yes?"

"Trouble, Miss Casey?"

"No. Maybe. I don't know. I promised you eight hundred dollars."

Margaret nodded. "I'd really appreciate it, Miss Casey. I need it pretty badly."

"I'm going to give you a raise. Nine hundred a week. I'll advance you the first nine hundred now." Cassie got out the envelope of checks given her by Barclays Bank. "I opened this account today, and they printed these up for me. The ink's barely dry and you get check—" She glanced at it. "Number triple-zero one. It will be good, though."

Breath sighed in Margaret's nostrils. "I don't know what to say, Miss Casey. This is such a relief."

The telephone rang, and Cassie said, "It's probably the man upstairs again. Get it, will you?"

Margaret did.

As Cassie signed the check, she heard Margaret say, "I'll tell her, ma'am."

Cassie looked up. "A woman? Was it India?"

"She gave me her name, Miss Casey, but I'm not sure I heard it right. She said do you know where he is? I asked who she meant, and it was the man you asked me to find last night. I said I didn't think so, and she said turn on the vid. She said call her if you knew."

"This sounds interesting. Here's the money. Put it away before I lose it."

Margaret put the check in her purse. "She talked fast, and I could hear people talking behind her. Shirley—Shirley . . ." A faint tinge of pink crept into Margaret's cheeks. "Shirley Ladydog? It was something like that."

Cassie had the remote. "Sharon Bench."

Pressing a button expanded her living room to include a long desk, a framed map of the forty-seven states, and a wall of books. A young woman at the desk said, ". . . recap all of our top stories, including the shooting of a famous scholar, right after this."

The remote fell to the floor.

After a moment, Margaret picked it up. "Should I mute these, Miss Casey?" Cassie did not seem to have heard her, so Margaret did.

Silent bottles of ketchup invaded the living room. One opened its own top and emitted a crimson fountain.

"Margaret . . ."

"Yes, Miss Casey?"

"She wanted to know if I knew where he was. Is that right?"

"Yes, Miss Casey."

"Then he's still alive. Still moving around."

"I think so, Miss Casey."

"So do I." Suddenly, Cassie smiled. "If the guy who shot him was the guy I think it might be, I may be out of a job."

"I hope not, Miss Casey."

"Well, I do. And that doesn't mean you'd be out of a job, Margaret. I'd get a new gig."

"I know, Miss Casey."

The desk was back. So was the woman behind it; but the map had become a map of the city. "A train has struck a school bus near the intersection of Fifty-eighth and Moore. We're getting conflicting reports regarding the presence of children on the bus at the time it was struck. Regardless of the presence or absence of children, traffic on Moore is backed up for miles. Use alternate routes.

"In an unrelated story, the Supreme Court has extended the period for post-parturition terminations to one year. Civil rights organizations continue to press for five for defectives.

"Mayor Houlihan has declared the city's streets safer than ever as a result of the previously announced decline in police violence. Most citizens seem to agree."

Cassie muttered, "Why can't they get to it?"

The end of her living room that had been occupied by the map and the books had become a park. In it, a large perspiring man in gym shorts told an interviewer, "I would say the danger's seriously overrated. Late at night there may be a certain risk, but from dawn to midnight no one's got anything to worry about." He mopped his dripping face with a towel that seemed sodden already; his hands and arms were noticeably muscular.

Margaret said, "Maybe you could call that lady who called, Miss Casey."

A young man with acne and a nascent beard shrugged. "I go out whenever. Everything's chief." His shirt, open to the waist, revealed an obscene symbol worked in gold and suspended from his neck by a heavy gold chain.

There was a knock at the door. Cassie opened it far enough to see a middle-aged man in coveralls.

"Come to do your wall, miss," he said. "Want to let me do now or come back later?"

"It goes clear through," Cassie told him. "Can't you fix the other side first?"

"Already done, miss. You hear me in there?"

She shook her head. "We've had the vid on."

"See there, miss? Only takes a moment and doesn't make much noise."

On the other side of her living room, the ketchup bottles had been replaced by equally silent beer bottles. Cassie told Margaret to get off the couch, and unchained the door.

"Hear 'bout the bloke got shot in Pine Crest Towers?" the man in coveralls asked as he moved the couch.

Cassie shook her head. The rectangular hole behind her couch was surprisingly small, less than a foot square.

"Gore everywhere, poor devil." The man in coveralls disappeared into the hall outside and returned pulling a small tool cart. "Board's cut a'ready, miss. You'll be shocked how quick it goes in."

BREAKING NEWS flashed on the erstwhile map.

Margaret pressed a button.

The young woman behind the desk said, "We told you earlier that the internationally famous scholar Gideon Chase had called police to report that he had been shot, that he was told to wait at the scene, and that he was not present when the police ambulance arrived. Now I want to welcome Sharon Bench of the *Sun-Tribunal*. Sharon's been looking into the story for us."

Sharon's apparition strode into Cassie's living room and took the chair next to the young woman's.

The young woman said, "What have you got for us, Sharon?"

Sharon smiled. "A lot, Dorothy. First, Dr. Chase hasn't been located. He's not in his apartment and his car's gone."

"That suggests that he hasn't been abducted."

Sharon nodded. "It does, although abductors might have gotten his keys and taken the car. There's an all-points bulletin out for it. It's a café-latte Morris convertible. A bumper sticker reads "Honk If You Love Woldercan." Anyone who spots it should call the police."

The erstwhile map flashed a license number.

"Second, my sources in the police department tell me there's no question now that a shooting occurred. An empty cartridge case has been found at the scene, and a bullet was lodged in the wall."

"We'd heard that there was a great deal of blood," the young woman said.

"There was. My sources confirm that. Do you know about the cleaver?"

The young woman shook her head. "Perhaps you should tell our audience exactly what a cleaver is."

"It's an instrument heavier than a butcher knife used for chopping meat," Sharon explained. "They're also called meat axes. As you can imagine, a cleaver makes a fearsome weapon."

"You say one was found there?"

Sharon nodded. "Not only was one found there, but it was covered with blood. What appears to have happened—this is what my police sources tell me—is that Dr. Gideon Chase, whose apartment is on that floor, observed that the door of a neighboring apartment had been forced. He seems to have gone inside to investigate and surprised the burglar, who shot him. Apparently Dr. Chase ran into the kitchen, where he found a cleaver and used it to defend himself, cutting the burglar deeply at least once."

"He must be a brave man."

"He certainly has that reputation," Sharon said, "and my guess is that he deserves it. He's a world traveler who often inserts himself into dangerous situations."

"You've met him? I know Tommy Pergram's had him on several times."

Sharon nodded. "I've interviewed him, and a friend of mine's dating him. We showed this clip on my five fifteen spot yesterday."

Suddenly Sharon and the young woman she called Dorothy were displaced by Cassie herself and Gideon Chase, smiling and holding hands at a table in Walker's.

"That brings us to my third point," Sharon's voice continued. "I've been in touch with her—she's the famous actress Cassie Casey, and the *Tommy Pergram Show* ought to have *her* on sometime."

Dorothy and Sharon returned, and Dorothy said, "The deeper we get into this, the more interesting it gets."

"That's my feeling exactly," Sharon agreed. "Cassie's terribly distraught. She doesn't know where Dr. Chase is and wanted to know whether he was in the hospital. The police are watching the emergency rooms, of course. So far he hasn't been to any of them."

"Doctors are required to report gunshot wounds, aren't they?"

"They are. This isn't one of the points I came to make, but maybe it's more important than any of them." Sharon paused to look straight into the camera. "You know me, Gideon, and you know I'm on your side and Cassie's, no matter what happens. You're not wanted by the police. You haven't been charged with anything, and nobody I've talked to thinks you will be. You won't be arrested if you seek medical attention."

Sharon turned back to the young woman. "I have one more point, Dorothy, and it may be the most interesting of all. May I give it?"

"Of course! We want to hear it."

"It's that the FBI is looking into this case. Nobody seems to know why, but an agent's flown up from Washington. He's questioning the people who live in that apartment as we speak."

"We'll have more on this," the young woman announced, "as soon as we learn something new. Stay tuned."

Cassie took the remote from Margaret and switched off the vid. A moment later, she became aware of the man in coveralls and said, "Yes?"

"Wanted to tell you I'm finished, miss. Your wall's patched and caulked. Caulk's still wet, so I wouldn't push on the patch. Be dry tomorrow, and I'll come back to paint soon as I can."

"Thank you," Cassie said. "Do I owe you anything?"

"No, miss."

Margaret said, "The building takes care of it, I'm sure."

Cassie nodded absently as the man in coveralls let himself out. "Do we have anything else to discuss?"

"Will you need me tomorrow at one, Miss Casey?"

"I don't see why I should. It's just a read-through. I'm going to phone Zelda—wait. There is something. Two somethings. Sit down, please."

Margaret did.

"Here's the first thing. Mr. Rosenquist took that bracelet from you, so there's a chance he may give it back to you. If he does, tell me right away." Cassie paused. "Nobody knows where Dr. Chase is now, but that could change. If he's around, give it to him. Either one of us, but as fast as you can. Is that clear?"

"Yes, Miss Casey. Absolutely."

"Good. Here's the second one. Have you heard what happened to Jimmy? You seem to have known him better than any of us."

Margaret shook her head. "I'll try to find out, Miss Casey."

"Do that, please. And tell me what you find."

When Margaret had gone, Cassie dialed a familiar number.

"Youmans Agency, stage, vid, and modeling."

"Zelda? This is Cassie."

"Great! I was getting ready to call you. We've got a contract. *Dating the Volcano God?* India Dempster said you knew all about it."

"I don't, Zelda. I don't know how good my part is or what they're going to want me to do. I don't know how good the show's likely to be. Or—"

"I've taken care of that, Cassie. You'll see when you vet the contract. There's extra money for you if they cancel before the first performance. There's more money if it runs more than three months. They gave me everything I asked for. You'll see."

"Yes, I will, and I'm not signing till I do. My guess is that I won't sign at all, but don't tell India that."

"She'll be pressuring you."

"I know it, but I think I've got a way to pressure back if I need to. How much money's behind this, Zelda? Have you any idea?"

"Uh-huh . . ."

"That was a smirk, Zelda. I couldn't see it, but I could hear it. What do you know that I don't?"

"Oh, lots and lots of things. I couldn't tell you all of them. It would take all day, and I'd be selling out my sources. But there's *a lot* of money."

Cassie went looking for something to pry with. "It's not all this guy Wallace Rosenquist, is it? I figure he has backers."

"You figure wrong." Zelda's voice had become deadly serious. "Backers have him. He operates under a dozen names, and one of my sources thinks he may be the richest man in the world. He's not somebody you want to cross, Cassie."

"I'd heard he was dangerous."

"You heard right," Zelda said. "Can you meet me for lunch tomorrow? One o'clock at the Greek place?"

"I'll try."

"We need to talk face-to-face," Zelda told her, and hung up.

There was a knock at the door, and Cassie hung up, too.

It opened before she got there. Gideon Chase stepped in, shut it behind him, and threw the bolt.

EIGHT

BLOW THE MAN DOWN

"You're limping," was the first thing Cassie said.

Gideon nodded. "I took a bullet through my right leg." There was no grin.

"Sit down! For God's sake, sit down."

Gideon dropped into the only armchair, leaving Cassie her well-worn blue couch. "I might argue with that from a philosophical standpoint, but I need to sit too badly."

"They're looking for you."

He nodded. "Whom do you intend by 'they,' Miss Casey?"

"Call me 'Cassie.'" It was said as firmly as a trained actress could manage. "You sound like Margaret for Pete's sake. I'm going to call you 'Gid.' You're going to call me 'Cassie.' That's settled!"

He nodded again. "I've got it, Cassie."

"Now—where the hell have you been? They're looking for you."

"I'll try to tell you, Cassie, but not until you tell me who's looking for me." He laid a polished brown walking stick across the arms of his chair.

"The police and the news media. Sharon, just to start with."

His smile was small and pained, but unmistakably a smile. "That's good. That's very good. I'm putting you in danger, Cassie, just by being here. Listen carefully, please. Are you a good liar?"

"I'm an actress, Gid. Use your head. Yes, I'm a terrific liar."

He nodded. "As a good liar, you will know that there are times to lie and times to tell the truth. I want to give you a little guidance regarding those times. Before I do—don't volunteer any information to anyone."

"I've got it."

"Fine. Remember it. If anyone asks, tell them the absolute truth about my coming here today and my leaving here. What time I came, how I looked, and when I left. Tell that to anyone who asks."

"You're sure that's smart, Gid?"

"Yes. Certain of it. Regarding what I say while I'm here, you'll have to pick and choose. Use your judgment."

"I will."

"Elaborate stories get liars found out. If you really are a good one, you know that. What you say should be the truth, though not the whole truth."

Cassie nodded.

"To whom have you talked recently?"

"Recently being since you dropped me off here? The building super. You'd told me about that hole you cut in my wall. I told you I was going to get it fixed, and you said fine. The super said he'd send a man up right away, and he did."

"Who else?"

"Margaret. I'd promised her an advance, and she came to collect it. I gave it to her out of my new account at Barclays."

"What did she have to say, and what did you say to her?"

"All of it? Wow! We talked quite a bit, but I'll try to make it short. She talked about needing the money, and I gave it to her. She taught me a church song, 'Walk in the Reign.' I sang it and got kind of carried away. The man upstairs called about the noise, and I talked to him.

"After that, I think it was, Margaret apologized for handing my bracelet over to you-know-who. He seems to have scared the heck out of her, and I told her I knew just how she felt. I said he might give it back to her, and if he did she should give it to you or me right away."

"You said she should give it to me?"

"Or to me. Either of us. What's bugging you, Gid?"

His right hand rubbed his forehead. "I've overlooked something, and I hate myself when I do that. I overlooked the possibility that Reis might return the bracelet to Margaret. You thought of it, and I should have. If he were to return it to you, you might think he was demanding you wear it. If he returned it to Margaret—"

"I might think he was a good guy after all. You're right."

"I believe I understand the secret of that bracelet, Cassie. Before I say more, I ought to confess that I don't really know. That's why I wanted the bracelet; there are tests, and I know people I can trust to make them. They haven't been made, so I can't be sure."

Cassie leaned forward. "How's your leg?"

Gideon shrugged. "Not good. I should stay off it, and I haven't been able to. Or not much."

"Would a drink help?"

"Yes, but I can't afford it. I have to keep a clear head, and the pain makes that hard enough. I think I've guessed the secret of the bracelet, as I said, and I had better tell you what I've guessed. There were two clues. The first was that there were no stones in it. The second—the thing that makes me feel certain I'm right—is that the box felt heavy. Not just the bracelet, but the empty box. That's correct?"

Cassie nodded.

"I was born on Woldercan. I've been interested in it all my life as a result, although I was still quite young when we returned to Earth. Bill Reis was our ambassador there for eight years. Perhaps I've told you."

"I don't believe you did."

"He was. When I talked to the president, his advisor made two statements which, although they were true as he intended them, were more than a little misleading. He said the Wolders were ahead of us in biology but behind us in physics." Gideon paused, reflecting. "Statements of that kind depend on what we consider important. A girl who was hoping to marry soon might say that Jones was a better man than Smith, while a fashion consultant would say that Smith was better than Jones."

"One's a better catch but the other one's a better dresser. You see that all the time."

"Exactly. The president's advisor said the Wolders were ahead of us in biology but behind in physics. The biology thing is interesting and I need to talk about that, but it's physics that's central right now."

"Central how?"

"Remember Smith and Jones. To John, the president's advisor, the warp drive that lets us probe the universe in hoppers is what's important. He could make an excellent case for that, and so could I. We have the warp drive, and Woldercan doesn't."

Cassie nodded.

"Still, physicists on Woldercan know things we don't, and as a result can do things we can't do. One of the things they can do is transform other materials into gold by altering their atomic structure."

"Wow!"

Gideon shrugged. "Actually we can do that, too; but the cost is very high and the amounts minute. Woldercan has brought the cost way down and the yield up. Endless riches?"

"You don't sound like it is."

"Correct. There's a flaw. The flaw is that while you're making large quantities of gold, which is what you want, you also make small quantities of other elements, and some are quite radioactive. The result is that the gold you make is radioactive for practical purposes. You can't purify it enough to weed out everything. I don't mean that one day's exposure to that gold will kill you. It won't even make you sick, unless there's a lot of it. But months or years—protracted exposure . . ."

"You're saying that's what my bracelet was. I believe you."

"I believe it, too." Gideon looked glummer than ever. "As of now I can't prove it, but I believe it. The first clue was that it was a massive gold bracelet without gems. You called it barbaric, but that's not Reis's style. The weight of the long box he kept it in made my conclusion almost certain. He wouldn't have wanted to carry it around without some shielding. There are millions of craftsmen who could make him a long box of thin lead and cover it with leather. Ian Mersey might manage it. I wouldn't be surprised."

"Who's Ian Mersey?"

"Oh. The man who repaired your wall."

"You know him?"

"Slightly, yes. He seems a good all-around handyman; but I'd like to talk about biology, and we don't have much time."

"I'm not ready yet. Where do you think our friend got the radioactive gold?"

"I believe he made it. I suppose you're right—it isn't really clear that he did, but it's what I think. I think it because it explains other things."

"Like why the president wants him," Cassie said.

"Exactly." Gideon gave her a sad nod. "They want him, and they want him alive. Alive because they want him to tell them where his equipment is and how to operate it. Why they've found him so hard to catch is another question, one I can't answer yet. May I talk about biology?"

"No. Where were you, Gid? What happened? I want to know about those things."

He nodded. "You should know them, too. I was walking down the second-floor hall of my building, on my way to my flat. I heard a noise and saw a man behind me with a gun. I broke down the nearest door, hoping to hide in there. He shot me as I was going through the doorway."

"You can't be sure? I want to see your leg."

"You won't, because I'm not going to take the bandage off. Not yet. Anyway, he followed me in and I threw a cleaver at him. It hit him in the face and must have cut him pretty badly. He dropped his gun and ran."

"And?"

"I tied dish towels around my leg and drove over to see a man I know. He's not a doctor, but he knows a lot about treating bullet wounds. He told me I was lucky; the bullet hadn't hit anything important and had gone through, so he didn't have to worry about getting it out. He took out some scraps of cloth—tiny scraps, you understand—sewed me up, dressed the wounds, and gave me a couple of injections. After that, I came here."

"To see me."

"Correct. I wanted to tell you what the situation was, and see whether they had gone after you."

"Is that all?"

"I wanted to see you and hear your voice. One more time, knowing it might be the last time." Gideon, who did not often meet her eyes, was meeting them now. "I don't think Reis is going to hurt you. Not soon at least, and perhaps not ever. But he's decided to kill me, and he may succeed."

She took his hand. "I said I didn't want to talk about biology, Gid, but we're talking about biology."

He nodded.

"Is he watching this place?"

"I don't know. He may well be. If it was watched when I came in, I may have been seen. If it's watched now, they may get me when I go out. I have no way of knowing."

"You're certain this wasn't just some criminal?"

"I am. They don't do that. Fire at a man walking down a hall? Fire without warning, without any demand for money?" Gideon took a deep breath and let it out. "He wanted to kill me. That was his objective. I know of no one other than Reis who might want me dead, so it seems safe to assume Reis sent him. From what I've learned, he must have hundreds of millions. Perhaps a billion or more. He could pay for any number of assassinations and never feel the pinch."

"From poisoned gold."

"Poisoned gold and other things. I can't prove it, but I'm confident the gold's his principal business. He'd prefer that it weren't poisoned, presumably; but he can't decontaminate it, so he sells it as is. I'd be very much surprised to learn that he handled big shipments himself."

"So would I. Want a drink? Last chance—we close in five minutes."

"No, thanks."

"Well, I do." Cassie disappeared in the direction of the kitchen and returned with a glass of wine. "Can I ask a question?"

"About biology? Certainly."

"Nope. About Dr. Gideon Chased."

He tried to smile.

"Margaret was in here. So was the man who fixed my wall. You showed up as soon as the coast was clear. Was that coincidence?"

He shook his head. "You're very perceptive. I was listening."

"Where the people have gone to Europe?"

"Correct. You're going to say that the repairman was in there. You're right; he was. I tried to stay out of his way until he left."

"The man you know just slightly." Cassie sat down and sipped. "Sure you don't want one of these, Gid? It's just Chablis."

She made a living portrait, Gideon thought: *Lady in a Spring-Green Gown.* Aloud he said, "Very unsure. I do want one. In fact, I want half the bottle. It's simply that I can't afford to drink half a glass."

"They're looking for your car, the brown one. Did you know?"

"No, but I'm not surprised."

"If they find it, will they find you?"

He shook his head.

"I didn't think so. Aren't you afraid they'll come here? You think our friend's had you watched. Anybody who's been watching you would guess you might come here."

"You're right. I'm testing. I don't think Reis will want you to see me die. If I'm right, I'm safer here than almost anywhere else; if I'm wrong, I'll find out when they break down your door."

"What if they're watching the building?"

Gideon shrugged. "I think they are. Certainly I have to behave as though they are. As I will.'

He picked up his walking stick. "Biology, and then I'll go. I'm not sure where I ought to begin, so let's try this. Are you aware of shape-changers? Werewolves and their ilk?"

"I suppose everybody's heard of them. Are you going to say there really are such things?"

"There are. I know a few. Some human beings can transform themselves, Cassie. The cells of their bodies rearrange themselves. It's actually a lot more complex than that, but that's the basic idea. The weight has to stay the same, you understand. If a hundred-pound woman becomes a she-wolf, it's a hundred-pound she-wolf. Wolves, dogs, and leopards are the most common forms."

Cassie set down her glass. "Either you're kidding me, or you're crazy. Which is it?"

"Neither." He shook his head. "The most common forms, I said. The most common forms but not the only forms. Keep that in mind, please. It's important."

"I'll try. Wait a minute! You were talking about that advisor—I forget his name."

"John."

"Right. He said they knew more biology on Woldercan. Are you going to tell me they can change themselves into dragons or something?"

"They cannot transform as we do. Not at all. What they can do—this is a side issue—is the thing that made John think they knew more biology. You see, he knows what they can do, but not what his own kind can do."

"My life was so simple before I met you." Cassie sighed. "I ought to dump you and go back. Why don't I do that?"

Gideon's hands flexed the walking stick as though he wanted to break it. "Because you know I love you. With all my faults . . . I have a great many, believe me."

"I don't." Some unfamiliar emotion had Cassie by the throat. "I don't know anything about any faults of yours, and I wish you'd come over here."

"You'll encounter more as we go along." A painful smile flickered and died. "Indifference to you will never be one of them, however. Hasn't it ever seemed strange to you that though some humans can become animals, we never hear of animals becoming human?"

"Weremen, Gid?" She wondered whether she sounded as puzzled as she felt.

"That would be man-men. But yes, that's the idea."

"I'd never even thought of it."

"It almost never happens because it is much, much easier to go down than to go up. It's so easy to go down that werewolves have trouble maintaining their human forms at times."

"I still don't believe you." Cassie looked stubborn.

"You're beautiful like that. Of course all your other expressions are beautiful, too. You must believe me, but that doesn't worry me. You will."

"John didn't."

"We didn't even discuss this. He knows that male Wolders can hybridize with lower animals, the males having the ability to alter the DNA in their semen enough to make it acceptable to the female's reproductive system. Like you, he doesn't believe that any human has the ability to transform."

"I should be talking to him. Are you going to tell me you're a werewolf?"

"Let's get that out of the way. No, I'm no werewolf. I don't have the ability to transform at all. Not down, and certainly not up. Those human beings who can transform up find it almost impossibly difficult. In almost every case, they require expert assistance."

Bewildered, Cassie shook her head. "I don't get it. Do they become angels? Or—or . . ." She froze, one hand clutching her glass, the other clenched.

"Yes." With the help of the walking stick, Gideon rose. "I may die today. It's entirely possible and almost probable. It is easy, terribly easy, for someone who has transformed up to slip back down; and it wouldn't be right for me to die without having warned you. Without having warned you and without having told you I love you. I have, and now I'll go."

NOT long afterward, the maintenance man who had repaired Cassie's wall loaded a large cardboard box into the back of his pickup. Lettering on the box indicated that it contained a toilet particularly adapted to the needs of invalids and the handicapped. It was clearly heavy; but he was just as clearly strong, lifting it from his cart and sliding it onto the back of his truck with only a small grunt of effort.

When the truck had covered about three and a half miles, Gideon (who was finding the interior of that box almost unbearably stuffy) opened the top and risked a look around. After another quarter mile he had established to his own satisfaction that the truck was bound for the remote suburb of Sweden Hill. For the moment, he had escaped Reis; and he was seized by a presentiment that he would eventually triumph. A song he had heard years ago—a chantey he would have sworn that he had forgotten—slipped back into his consciousness.

"We're a Liverpool ship with a Liverpool crew.
Yo, ho, blow the man down!"

His clear tenor rose above the hum of the tires.

"A Liverpool mate and a scouse skipper, too.
Give me some time to blow the man down!"

NINE

THE DOTTED LINE

"Please understand, Cassie. Please!"

She felt sure India was striving to sound sympathetic.

"If you don't sign, the deal will collapse. Everybody will be out of work. All your friends. The whole cast."

The read-through had wound up a quarter of an hour ago, and they stood upon the darkened stage of the Tiara and conversed in stage whispers. Ghostly echoes of lines spoken long years ago had muted India's voice and now muted Cassie's as she said, "Everybody being you and Vince. I've got it."

"A lot more, Cassie. Norma's already on board, and I'm planning to sign half a dozen other people."

"Norma's signed?" Cassie raised a carefully darkened eyebrow.

"Today. Before you came."

"Before you heard her read the sister. Before you even knew she'd be right for it."

"No! I know what she can do, and she could play Jane Brownlea with her eyes shut. She's like Vince. Like you. A natural for her part."

"Who's going to play the sailor?"

India shrugged. "Up for grabs. I've got feelers out to various agencies."

"Bruce?" Cassie smiled.

India shook her head. "He's great for spoiled rich guys. Not for the mate of a whaling ship. I want somebody not too tall, tough-looking, and muscular. Sexy. Bruce is sexy, I admit, but not sexy in the right way."

"As I am." The smile had gone inside.

"Exactly. You can get out there and be the reverend's twenty-year-old daughter, brought up in exciting prayer meetings and hotter 'n hell's horoscope. It came through in every line you read. I'm pretty damned sure you can be sexy in a dozen other ways, too. Bruce has only got one."

Cassie considered that, her head tilted to one side. "Tell me something, India. Make it as honest as you can. Woman to woman."

"At your service. Sisterhood forever."

"Would you get in bed with him to save the show?"

"With Bruce?" India shook her head.

"Of course not. You know who I mean. Would you?"

"I'm not into men, Cassie, and they're not into me."

"That's a no. You're expecting me to do something you wouldn't do."

"Holy snot, Wanton Woman!" India pushed back a stray wisp of coarse, dark hair. "Cassie, darling, everything you just said was wrong. That wasn't a no, I was saying it would be harder—I mean tougher for me, and a whole lot less likely. Yes, I would. I wouldn't enjoy it, but I'd yell and cry on his shoulder and put on the best damned act he ever saw. We're soul sisters—women together. Right? You said that."

Cassie's nod was guarded. "Sometimes we are."

"Good. This's one of the times, and I wouldn't ask my sister to do something I wouldn't do myself. Only I never asked you to, Cassie darling. I want you to sign on the dotted line, that's all. I want you to be Mariah Brownlea and give Wally a sporting chance to talk you into the sack. If he does, fine. He won't be any happier than I will. If he doesn't, just string him along for a year or so. He's not the type to give up easily."

He's not the type to give up at all, Cassie thought. Aloud she said, "Somebody's listening to us. Do you know that?"

"Ghosts." India shrugged.

"Maybe. But somebody's listening, somebody who hears every word."

"We can go somewhere else."

After a moment, Cassie shook her head.

"All right, keep your voice down and try to forget it. There's nobody here except us. How many men have you made it with?"

"That's my business, India. Mind your own."

India grinned. "You can't remember."

"The hell I can't. I've been married twice. How's that?"

"I'm going to guess. I'm going to say a dozen."

"Nuts!" Cassie turned away.

"You won't tell, so I have to guess and that's mine. What are the odds that Wally will be worse than anybody in the first twelve was? Pretty long, huh? And Cassie dear—" Ponderously, India circled to face her again. "Here's a sure thing, a lead-pipe cinch. He'll be richer than the first twelve put together. One hell of a lot richer."

"Good point." Cassie's smile would have etched steel. "When you work, you ask what you're worth, don't you? I always do."

Reluctantly, India nodded.

"Well, I'm worth a whole lot to you. And to—what did you just call him? Our friend?"

"I called him Wally. I call him Wally and he calls me India."

"I know another name," Cassie said.

"Really? What is it?"

"Indie." Cassie smiled again. "Don't you think Indie would be nicer? Rhymes with undies."

As India turned and stalked away, Cassie bowed to six hundred twenty-one empty seats. "I hope you liked our little show."

Applause reached her out of the darkness, the sound of a single pair of hands clapping.

VERY few people can maintain their concentration while reading legal prose, and Cassie was not one of them. On page seven, she discovered that she had just read the same paragraph three times, and still had only the foggiest notion of what it meant.

A knock rescued her. She dropped the sheaf of papers and jumped up to admit Margaret.

"I'm awfully sorry to bother you like this, Miss Casey," Margaret said as she trotted through Cassie's doorway, "but Miss Dempster won't leave me alone."

"I know how you feel."

"So I said I'd measure you. You said it would be all right. On the phone?"

Cassie nodded. "I remember."

"I've got my tape measure and my notebook. That's all I need now, and my little camera. Pictures help sometimes. Take off your slip, Miss Casey? That would be the best."

"I'm not wearing one." Cassie demonstrated, dropping her skirt and stepping out of it.

"You can keep on your briefs and bra," Margaret told her, "but I'll need you to take off your blouse and those shoes."

Cassie did.

"Hold your arms out to the sides, please, Miss Casey. Do you know, I never did believe that tiny little waist. But it's real. How do you do it?"

"I don't," Cassie said. For a moment she was tempted to say that Gideon had done it.

"I always measure twice to be sure." Margaret whipped her yellow tape around Cassie's waist for the second time. "That's the best way, and that way I don't—"

There was a knock and Cassie said, "Get that, will you please?"

Margaret put on the security chain and opened Cassie's door two and a half inches. "Whom may I—"

"Cassie! It's me! Have you read the contract yet?"

Cassie picked it up, laid it on the coffee table next to her cell phone, and told Margaret to let Zelda in.

"You're getting measured for your costumes. That's great! This show will make you famous."

"This show sucks." Cassie held her arms out to let Margaret measure her chest.

"Cassie, Cassie, Cassie!"

"Zelda, Zelda, Zelda. It still sucks."

"There'll be beautiful costumes . . ."

Cassie raised a hand. "Stop right there. I play a missionary's daughter. Gingham. High neck, long sleeves, and a long skirt. What's anybody going to do with that?"

Margaret muttered, "A lot."

"Right." Zelda nodded. "Plus there are two dream sequences. India told me."

"In other words, you haven't read it. I heard the readings, Zelda. And it sucks. I told you that."

"And I told you over and over why you ought to sign." Zelda dropped heavily onto the sofa. "Let's have this out here and now. Tell me why it sucks."

"People make speeches. *Everybody* makes speeches. Brian makes speeches about God. Norma makes speeches about whatever pops into her head. I make speeches about Kansas, and I don't even get to holler for Auntie Em. Vince makes speeches about coconuts for Pete's sake! My sailor makes speeches about love. You want more?"

"She needs to measure your hips." Zelda's tone was dry. "Stand up straight, hold out your arms, and put your feet together."

"I know how to do it!" Cassie took a deep breath. "And I don't think she's got a tape measure long enough." She stood up straight, held out her arms, and put her feet together.

"Only thirty-seven and three-eighths, Miss Casey," Margaret muttered.

"This is a new show, Cassie." Zelda was firm. "It's not Shaw, it's not Ibsen, it's not *Oklahoma*. It'll try out here, try out in Chicago and half a dozen other places, and it'll be fixed. New shows have to grow up. They do, and this one will."

"I won't—"

"I'm not through! Shows fold. I've seen a few of them fold. They fold here or in Rubesburg—in little towns you've never heard of. There are two reasons for folding—just two. Lack of money and lack of talent."

Margaret muttered, "Stand up straight, please, Miss Casey."

There was a knock at the door, and Cassie sighed. "Get that, would you, Zelda?"

"All finished, Miss Casey." Margaret was smiling. "You're going to get some lovely low-neck costumes. Lovely spring-green outfits that show skin in the middle. You'll see. All right if I take a few pictures?"

Zelda grinned as she opened the door. "She'll sell 'em to a tabloid, Cassie. Do you mind?"

"I wouldn't, Miss Casey." Margaret sounded shocked. "I'd never do a thing like that."

"She's kidding," Cassie told her. "How do you want me to pose?"

"With your arms above your head, please. I'll take front, back, and one side."

From the chained door, Zelda said, "It's a man from the building. He won't talk to me. Only you."

Margaret's little camera flashed.

"Tell him I'm not dressed. I'll call him."

"Want to see how you look, Miss Casey? I can show it to you."

"Fat. No, spare me the trauma."

"In back now. Hold still."

"Fatter," Cassie said under her breath.

The camera flashed again.

"Sell it to the tabloid, Margaret. It'll make a great headline—CASSIE'S CONTROL TOPS. Then everybody will want to know who Cassie is."

"Side now, Miss Casey. You wait 'til they see your profile!" The camera flashed a third time.

"Right here," Zelda murmured; she had taken a gold pen and a little leather-bound notebook from her purse.

"Can I relax?"

"One more, Miss Casey. I let it wiggle a little."

"Tell him I'll call him later," Cassie told Zelda.

Sharon Bench's voice came from the other side of the door. "Cassie! Tell this woman to let me in!"

The little camera flashed for the final time as Cassie said, "I thought you said it was a man."

"It's Sharon!" Sharon called.

"There's a woman, too," Zelda reported.

"Wait 'til I get my clothes on."

The telephone rang.

"Should I get it, Miss Casey?"

Cassie shook her head. "It'll be one of the neighbors complaining. Let it ring."

Margaret did, buttoning Cassie's blouse instead.

Zelda shut the door and took off the chain. "Should I let the woman in, Cassie? She says she's a friend."

"Wait 'til I get my skirt on. Then you can let them both in."

"It's too big," Margaret told her when the telephone had fallen silent. "I can fix it for you if you want me to, Miss Casey."

"Not now."

"He's gone," Zelda said. "He wrote you a note, but I don't understand it. What about the woman?"

Reluctantly, Cassie nodded.

The security chain rattled, and Sharon burst into the room. "Any news?"

"You're supposed to tell me." Cassie pointed toward her worn blue couch. "Sit down. You're going to referee."

"Between us?" Zelda asked. "If that's what you mean, you'd better introduce us."

"Sharon's the star of the *Sun-Trib*." Skirt in place, Cassie dropped into her reading chair.

"Straight news," Sharon announced. "Gossip, and human interest. Sports. You name it. Seen me on vid?"

Zelda said, "You know, I think I have."

"Monday through Friday," Cassie told her. "Channel twenty-three. Afternoons only."

"Unless I've got something really big," Sharon added.

"Unless she's got something really big. Sharon, this is Zelda Youmans. Zelda's my agent."

Sharon said, "Hi," and waved.

"Your job," Cassie told her, "is to decide between us. Zelda wants me to sign for *Dating the Volcano God*. She'll tell you why she thinks I ought to. But not about her ten percent. I'll have to tell you about that."

Sharon nodded.

"I'll tell you why I think it's a bad show and a bad contract."

"Then I decide?"

"Then you decide. Here I go. The show stinks. It's a turkey from the git-go. It will maybe, if they're lucky, play on two or three stages. Could be eight weeks in all. After that, flopsville."

Sharon nodded.

"That was my first point. Second point. The money's not anywhere near what I'm worth to—to the people who are organizing things. To the director and the angel. I'd be ashamed to tell you what they're offering in this contract. I've known secretaries who made more than that."

"She hasn't," Zelda said firmly.

"Third point. The angel expects me to sleep with him. He's—"

Sharon leaped to her feet. "Wallace Rosenquist? He's romancing you, Cassie? Oh, wow!"

"You know who he is?"

Sharon's hand had strayed to a pocket of her jacket. "I—oh, my God! This is so big . . . Cassie, Wallace Rosenquist controls half the banks in this city, and from what I hear he could control the other half tomorrow if he wanted to. All the financial people knew he was here the minute his hopper landed. It's the size of a super tanker, so how could they miss it? They've been as jumpy as stray cats ever since. Can you get me an interview?"

"No," Cassie said firmly, "I can't. And if I could, I wouldn't. Should I sign or not?"

"She should." Margaret's voice was just above a whisper.

"Hold on!" Zelda snapped. "Wait up, everybody. I get equal time. Can I call you Sharon?"

Sharon nodded.

"Good. Sharon, Cassie's been talking as if this were straight salary. It isn't. She had points and I've got more. The money's okay, to start with. It's more than she was making in *The Red Spot*. That's Zelda's point number one."

Sharon nodded again.

"Number two. For each quarter after the first, her salary goes up ten percent. Say that it runs a year, and a good show will play New York, then London, then Melbourne, then back to Broadway. You probably know that, and by the time it hits Broadway again it may have been running for five or six years. If not more."

Zelda paused for breath, and Cassie said, "A *good* show, which this isn't."

"But say a year. Just one year. For the final three months of that year Cassie will be making thirty percent more than she'll make on opening night."

Sharon said, "I've got it."

"Next point . . ."

The telephone rang. More quickly than a woman without experience might be expected to, Cassie unplugged it.

"My next point," Zelda continued, "is that she's down for two percent of the gross. Not two percent of the profit, two percent of the gross. Let's say the theater seats two thousand. That's small but let's say it. Let's say that tickets average twenty bucks, which is dirt cheap for a hit show. The gross is forty thou a night. That's eight hundred over and above salary per night. If there are six performances a week, which is low, one month is about twenty thousand. Should I give you the figure for a year?"

Sharon shook her head. "I can to the math."

"Meanwhile, her salary keeps going up and up and up."

"If," Cassie muttered.

"Not if. Here are my next to last and last, and I'll make 'em fast. There are months of rehearsal ahead. A bad book can be fixed. Bad songs can be fixed, and dance numbers the same. Shows fold because they don't have backing. I don't have to tell you who's backing this one."

"Rosenquist?"

"Exactly. Last point, shows fail because the talent's not there. The redhead in the big brown chair's going to star in this one. You may think she's ordinary now—"

"I'm not blind," Sharon said.

"When we did lunch, everybody looked. Men, women, even kids, and they kept looking. By the time we'd gotten a table and ordered, I knew I was sitting across from a fortune. Something happened before *Red Spot* closed. I don't know—"

Cassie rose and Margaret said, "What is it, Miss Casey?"

"There's too much noise in here, too many people talking. I need to be alone, and I'm going out on the balcony for—for as long as it takes me to sort things out. You can go home if you want to, or stay."

She scooped her cell phone off the coffee table "I know this isn't polite, but I've got to think or scream. Screaming wouldn't help, so I'm going to step outside."

Zelda asked, "Is this about signing?"

"You can make coffee or tea, or have a glass of wine. Or leave. Whatever you want. Watch vid." Cassie opened the French doors through which she had, not long ago, seen a chauffeur shut the rear door of a white limousine.

The air on her balcony seemed purer and sweeter than the atmosphere in her apartment, delightfully cool rather than cold. Autumn was on its way, but today it dallied by the roadside.

She shut the French doors behind her, turned her back to them, and scrolled up a number she had by now memorized.

"This is Gideon Chase, but my telephone is temporarily out of service. I have to sleep sometime . . ."

It was the familiar message. Cassie pressed OFF.

Five floors below, pedestrians hurried past the narrow strip of lush green lawn in front of the building. Parked cars littered the street, although cars were not supposed to park there. Trucks and buses made far too much noise, and cabs dawdled, hoping to be flagged down by a doorman. Across the street, a man in a dark doorway lit a cigarette, his face visible for a second in the flare of his lighter.

Above it all, an aching blue sky assured her that it cradled Mariah's island even as it stretched over her dirty northern city. "I hope you're nicer there," she told it. "I wish I could be there instead of just playing at it."

"ARE you ready?" Zelda asked when Cassie stepped back into her living room.

"I think so. I'm sorry to have kept you waiting."

Margaret clearly wanted to hug her but did not. "It was only about ten minutes, Miss Casey."

Sharon said, "I'm going to report what I hear here, unless you ask me not to."

"About sleeping with Wallace Rosenquist?"

"I won't say it like that. I'll hint. You know."

Zelda said, "Good publicity, Cassie."

Sharon nodded. "It will be. They'll want to come to see you, and maybe see him."

"I don't think so," Cassie said, "but I don't know. Maybe they will."

Sharon asked, "Do you want to know what I've decided?"

"I ought to feel terribly tired," Cassie mused. "I know I should, but I don't. I'm getting my second wind or something. Have you ever wanted to help out somebody you loved, and known that the only thing you could do for him was some tiny stupid thing that was a lot of trouble? And done it anyway? Any of you?"

Margaret nodded.

Sharon said, "Not me."

Zelda said, "Yes, for Joe-Boy. I don't think you ever saw him."

Cassie shook her head.

"He was my son and he was in the hospital, getting ready to go. He wanted one particular toy. I ditched work and went looking for it. It took all day to find it, but I did and brought it to him. He couldn't talk by then, but he smiled. It was the last time I ever saw him smile. He passed away that night."

Cassie nodded, finding she could not speak.

"The boss called me in the next day and fired me. And—listen, Cassie. Listen really, really carefully."

She nodded again. "I am."

"That was when I opened my own agency. Inside a year I was taking in more than I ever had in my life. Getting fired was the best thing that ever happened to me."

"I didn't know any of this," Cassie said. "Thank you. I owed you a lot already."

Sharon said, "Enough to sign?"

"Yes. And if I weren't such a bitch I'd have done it straight off."

Zelda cleared her throat. "I thought I was done, and I ought to be. Now I may queer a deal that would make me rich—but I feel like I've got to do this. Remember the note the building guy wrote?"

Cassie nodded, seized by a sudden dread.

"I've read it and I've got no idea what the heck he's talking about, but it sounds like it might be personal. I was going to hang on to it until you signed. Or didn't. Now . . ." Zelda shrugged. "I guess I'm chicken."

Margaret took the note and passed it to Cassie.

Five words, written in a hasty scrawl: *Infected. He is getting treatment.*

"That settles it," Cassie said. "Have you got a pen?"

SHE waited until they were gone before playing the message the first call had left on her answering machine. The voice was male, deep, and somewhat harsh.

"This is Wallace Rosenquist. I'll pick you up for dinner at seven. I realize you may not want to join me, and may have other plans. But I assure you that if you will consent to dinner you will learn something to your advantage."

DATING WALLACE
ROSENQUIST

Usually, Cassie reflected, the question was one of dressing to make the best possible impression. This was more like the blind dates she had suffered through in high school and college. Did she even want to make a good impression?

Perhaps not.

After much thought, she wore her second-best black dress, black pumps, and a little necklace her mother had given her long ago. Those, and her watch.

She had expected him to be prompt, but his white limousine pulled up to the curb at seven fifteen. The chauffeur got out and went into her building without opening the rear door. She was about to turn away when the rear door opened. She waited and watched until her telephone rang.

She picked it up and said hello.

"Miz Casey? This is Preston, the doorman. There's a driver here who says he has a message for you. I think you can probably see his car out front if you look out your window. The big white one?"

"I'll take your word for it," Cassie said.

"Should I let him up?"

"I don't think so. Is it a note?"

"I'll see, Miz Casey. Wait a minute."

There was a lengthy pause during which Cassie sat down; she could hear the voices of two men arguing.

"Miz Casey?"

"Still here, Preston."

"He says he has to speak to you. He won't tell me what it is."

"All right. Put him on."

Another pause and more argument.

"He won't, Miz Casey. He wants to come up."

Cassie grinned. "Please tell him I'm not about to let anyone who won't talk to me on the telephone come up."

"I will, Miz Casey." Preston sounded pleased.

After a brief pause, an accented voice said, "I am Carlos."

"Señora Casey. What can I do for you, Carlos?"

"You must let me in."

"I won't," Cassie said, and hung up.

There was no local news on vid at this hour. She watched the state news channel instead, waiting for the telephone to ring.

As it did, ten minutes later.

"Hello." She tried not to sound smug.

"This is Wallace Rosenquist, Cassie. I had planned to escort you from your apartment to my car. An urgent matter intervened. I'd like to apologize."

"I understand." She made it sympathetic.

"My driver takes my instructions a bit too seriously at times, I'm afraid. Would you be willing to meet me at Rusterman's? Carlos will drive you."

"I'd love to. Meet you when?"

"I'll be there as soon as I can. It shouldn't be long."

"Wonderful. I'll go right away."

After hanging up, she switched on the alarm system.

Carlos held the door of the white limousine for her. He looked taller and darker than the uniformed man she remembered seeing when she had looked down at the white limousine. A sheet of glass—thick glass that looked as if it might stop bullets—separated them. There was a speaker below it through which he could presumably have spoken to her, and a microphone through which she could presumably have spoken to him.

She was tempted to say, "I wasn't going to shoot you anyway, Carlos," but did not.

Rusterman's seemed calmer and richer than it had on the night of the cast party. Its unsmiling hostess might have posed for *Vogue*. "I'm to meet Wallace Rosenquist here," Cassie told her. "I assume the reservation is in his name."

"Of course. Of course!" Had some passing spirit kindled a candle within the hostess, she could have glowed no brighter; her smile looked a little forced, Cassie thought, but it was big and bright beyond all questioning.

An imperious gesture summoned the head waiter, who bowed deeply and escorted Cassie to a private room of medium size that, tonight at least, held only a single table and two chairs. "Would Madame care for wine? We have excellent wines. I shall summon our sommelier."

"Just water, please. Water and a little ice."

Her cell phone played "Pigs in Paradise" as the head waiter left; feeling the music far too appropriate, Cassie answered.

"Your alarm's gone off, Miz Casey." It was Preston. "I've called the cops. They say they're on their way, only no sirens. I thought you might like to come on back."

"It was good of you to call," Cassie said, "but I can't. Would you ask one of the policemen to call me at this number when they've investigated?"

"Sure will, Miz Casey. Okay if I open the door for 'em?"

"Yes. Of course. Preston . . ."

"What, Miz Casey?"

"There's a very nice man who works in our building. He fixed my wall."

"That's Ian, Miz Casey."

"Is he there now?"

"No, he's not, Miz Casey. Ian works days."

"Please leave a message on his computer for me. Give him my number and ask him to call me in the morning. Will you do that for me, Preston?"

"Sure will, Miz Casey, only I got to go. The cops are here."

She hung up.

After a time that might have been five minutes or fifteen, a beautifully uniformed waitress brought a tall blue bottle of Swiss spring water that had probably cost more than most wines. With it came a crystal goblet almost as tall as the bottle, a small silver bucket, and a pair of tongs.

Cassie halted the waitress with a gesture. "Do you know Alexis Cabana? Know who she is?"

The waitress smiled and shook her head. "I'm afraid I don't, ma'am."

"She an actress. I asked because you remind me of her, although you're better-looking."

"Thank you, ma'am." The smile widened. "I'm not half as beautiful as you are, I know. People do say, though, that I'm—well, some people do, that I'm not bad at all." The waitress bent closer. "Are you really meeting Mr. Rosenquist?"

"Supposedly." Cassie glanced at her watch. "I'll give him another ten minutes."

The waitress's voice fell to a whisper. "Everybody's got to treat him like he was the governor. He's a friend of Mr. Rusterman's."

"Is there really a Mr. Rusterman?"

"He's the company president. There was another Mr. Rusterman years and years ago, and he opened the first one. But now this Mr. Rusterman is the president of our whole chain. He's a cousin or something. I don't know."

"I see. Wait a moment, please. Do you happen to know Mr. Rusterman's first name?"

"It's Wade, I think, ma'am."

Reis came well after the ten minutes were up. "I'm sorry I'm late, Cassie. I was unexpectedly delayed."

He pulled out a chair and sat. "Do you mind if I call you Cassie? India says that's what everybody calls you. And now that you've signed, well, I hope you're not angry with me."

Cassie smiled. "Not at all, Bill. Did you find anything?"

His expression changed, and he said nothing.

It was in the eyes, Cassie decided. His eyes had been lying before, and lying skillfully; now they had stopped.

The waitress returned, this time with menus. Cassie studied hers for a few seconds and laid it down.

"Yes, ma'am? What would you like?"

"The half capon Souvaroff, I think, with a tossed salad."

"We have just about every dressing there is, ma'am. Would you like me to list them for you?"

Cassie shook her head. "Ranch will be fine."

Reis looked up. "I felt sure you'd order the green goddess."

"I like ranch."

"You'd like this better. Waitress, I want you to bring both dressings. A cup of each, not on the salad."

The waitress said, "Yes, sir," and wrote. "Would you care for some soup, ma'am? It comes with your dinner."

Cassie shook her head, and Reis ordered.

When the waitress had gone, he said, "You've saved me a great deal of time. Weeks, perhaps."

"I'm glad. Want to tell me what's in green goddess dressing? I'm curious."

He smiled. "A great many things, and I couldn't name half of them."

"What makes it green?"

"Money. If I may go back to an easier question, yes. I found several things of interest in your apartment."

"Before the police got there. I thought you looked like a fast worker."

"Sometimes. One was a note. The first word was *infected*. Do you know the note I mean?"

Cassie shook her head. "I had a lot of company this afternoon. One of them must have left it."

"No doubt. I don't think I've told you why I want you to try the green goddess. It's because I think of you like that. A green goddess. You were wearing green the first time I saw you."

"In the play? I wasn't. That was brown."

"So it was. I was thinking of the party. I took you home, remember?"

Cassie nodded. "Thank you. You saw *The Red Spot*, though. The final performance."

"I didn't. I know I said I did, but that was . . ."

"Diplomacy?"

"Yes, exactly. India had given me tickets, and I didn't want to admit I hadn't used them."

"I see. What else did you find?"

"One other thing that interested me even more. You have a brand-new checking account. Only one check's been written on it."

She smiled. "So I do! I'd almost forgotten about that."

"It's a great deal of money."

"For you? I know better."

The sommelier arrived, and Reis ordered wine. When they were alone again, he said, "Would you tell me where you got it, if I asked?"

"Are you saying you don't know? I don't believe you, Wade."

"Call me Wally, please. I prefer it. Here."

"As you wish, Wally."

"Thank you." He actually looked grateful. "No, I'm not saying I don't know. I simply wanted to see if you'd tell me the truth."

Cassie grinned. "I won the lottery. That's the total, absolute, brassbound truth. Good enough?"

"You're saying you lie."

"So do you, Wally. You've lied to me already tonight. Once for sure and probably more than once. Let's turn off the lights on this one. You'll lie to me anytime you think it's to your advantage. Whether I'll lie to you depends on the question you ask, how you ask it, and how I'm feeling just then."

"You're frank, Cassie. I admire frankness."

"In that case, I'll stop."

"So will I. I'm going to tell you things tonight. You'll doubt everything I say, but you'll have no reason to. I'm going to tell you a lot, and it will all be true. Every word of it."

Their wine arrived. Reis tasted it and nodded. The sommelier poured each of them half a glass.

"I've said I was going to tell you the unvarnished truth. I will, and I'll begin by saying that you are the most attractive woman I've ever met. I want to win you. Most of all, I want to win your love. I may not be able to do that, but I'll deserve it. You'll see."

Cassie nodded and sipped. "Pure truth so far."

"I'm a businessman. I've been one all my adult life, even when I was supposed to be a diplomat. It's the only thing I know how to do, but I'm good at it. I'm so good that I often need to pretend to be somebody else. There are antitrust laws, for one thing. There are other reasons as well. Almost every day I deal with sums greater than the annual budgets of many nations, so you can imagine."

"I can *only* imagine," Cassie said, "but I can do that."

"Good. Two years ago I hired a consultant. He is an academic, and like so many something of a charlatan, but he gets results. His name is Gideon Chase. It will save time if you don't pretend you don't know him."

"I won't," Cassie promised. "It would upset Sharon."

"Yes, I'm sure it would. He did what I wanted, and I paid him liberally.

He realized I commanded very large sums and decided to despoil me. He's been trying to ever since."

As their food arrived Cassie said, "I wish him luck."

"I know you do. Twenty thousand dollars is a large sum, as I said. You've gotten that much from him, and hope to get much more."

"This smells luscious. Thank you."

"I won't bother telling you that you might get fifty times as much from me. You understand that already. The things you don't know are what you might have to do to get it, and whether I can be trusted to keep my promises."

Cassie's eyebrows went up. "Can you?"

"Yes. You won't take my word for that—although it's good—but as you come to know me better you'll realize that in business matters I can be trusted absolutely. I do not cheat. Most particularly, I do not cheat my partners."

"Good for you!" She sampled her capon.

Reis's smile was principally in his sharp brown eyes. "Exactly. It is good for me, Cassie. It's good business. The criminal impulse—something your friend Chase has in abundance—is self-defeating in the long run. Would you like to try this ragout?"

"No thanks. I'm trying not to eat too much. I won't sleep if I do."

"I always sleep well. My days are long and strenuous. A good night's sleep is my reward, and I collect it every night."

"May I ask a question?"

"I invite it."

"Why did you take my bracelet from Margaret?"

"Because I was afraid of Margaret. Of her honesty. Can I explain?"

Cassie nodded. "I wish you would."

"You hated my bracelet and did not want to wear it. I saw it the moment it was on your wrist. It hurt. It hurt a great deal. I had designed that bracelet myself. It was special order, and I had paid a German craftsman extra to get it as soon as I did. He had worked nonstop, and sent it to me here by International Express. I deal in gold, as well as certain other commodities. That was why there were no diamonds."

Cassie nodded again.

"I had hoped that you would love it, that you would think fondly of me each time you wore it. I'd failed. I don't fail often, but I don't lie to myself—or to those I value—when I do. If I'd thought your Margaret would steal it, I'd have written it off and tried to forget it. After looking into her background, I decided she wouldn't. She would return it to you, and you'd wear it as a duty, detesting it the whole time. Objection?"

"No," Cassie said.

"When the show closed, as it would eventually, you would sell my bracelet. That would be the end of it." Rosenquist's well-tailored shoulders rose one-eighth of an inch, and fell. "I got it back and had it melted down."

"It's gone?"

"It is. Destroyed utterly. I suppose another like it might be made, but it will not be made to my order. Does that make you happy?"

"I don't know." Cassie felt thoughtful, and felt, too, that she must look foolish. "I'll have to mull it over. You scared Margaret."

"I had to. She wouldn't have handed over my bracelet otherwise. I won't try to make amends to her. It would only frighten her more, if I've read her right. I'll make amends to you, however. Let's do that now. I promised you'd learn something to your advantage if you'd join me for dinner."

"I'd forgotten."

"I hadn't. Here it is. The price of gold is almost two hundred dollars an ounce today."

"If that's supposed to help me, it's coming a bit late."

"I have more." Reis took a tall wallet from the pocket of his jacket. "I don't suppose you ever weighed your bracelet?"

Cassie shook her head.

"It weighed ten ounces. I gave my German craftsman ten ounces of gold and told him to use it all, and that's what he did."

Reis pulled out a green check half again larger than those Cassie had received from Barclays Bank. "This isn't twenty thousand, but it will have to do for tonight—two thousand dollars, the value of the gold in that bracelet."

Nodding, Cassie picked it up. "If I were a lady, I wouldn't take this. Fortunately I'm not."

"I understand. Gentility is the luxury of those who can afford it. I can't. Honor has to be enough for me, and it is. No doubt you're the same."

"I'm afraid not." Unable to smile, Cassie sipped her wine. "The first time I got divorced, Herbie and I split up the stuff in our apartment. No fault, you know? Fifty-fifty. He got the honor. Probably I got something, too, but I forget what it was."

Reis smiled. "In that case you're for sale. I'm delighted to hear it."

"Maybe and maybe not." She picked at her capon. "It depends."

"On the price."

"On the price, the conditions of sale, and . . . Oh, lots of other stuff. Herbie and I—Herbie was my first husband. Do you know about him?"

"No, but I will."

"You certainly will." Cassie grinned. "One more glass of this and I'll tell you everything, most of it true. Well, anyway, Herbie decided we needed a border terrier. He found a breeder and was all enthusiastic about it. It was going to cost a lot, but we'd get a good one. I wasn't as crazy about it as Herbie was—we were on the road a lot back then—but I went along."

Reis said, "I'd much rather talk about you."

"We are. Herbie and I went to see the breeder, and he wanted to know if we had a fenced yard. We said no, we lived in an apartment, but we'd walk the dog twice a day. He wouldn't sell to us. Herbie offered him more than he'd been asking but he still wouldn't sell. So this is about me after all. Do you get it now?"

"I believe I do. Chase has a fenced yard."

"Wrong!" Cassie shook her head. "He hasn't bought me. He hasn't even tried to."

"He gave you twenty thousand."

"Not to buy me. To hire me. Want a truffle, Wally? They're really delicious."

"Thank you, but no. Have you tried the green goddess dressing yet?"

"You know, I haven't. I've been too busy with the chicken. And his truffles. I will."

She did.

"You're right, Wally. I like it. I like it a lot. I guess it's the taste of money."

"I thought you would. You say Chase has hired you. Would it be possible for me to hire you as well?"

While chewing salad, Cassie nodded.

"In that case, we ought to talk about salary and terms of employment."

"Huh uh." She swallowed. "You already have. I've signed to play Mariah, remember?"

"Are you saying you'll keep an eye on Chase for me without asking more money?"

"Within limits. What would you like me to do?"

"You might begin by telling me what you're doing for Chase."

"Come on, Wally! You're smarter than that." Cassie held out her glass. He poured. "I'm not as sharp as you may think. What is it?"

"I'm having dinner with you."

"On Chase's instructions?"

"Kind of."

"He wishes you to cultivate me."

"Exactly. See there? I knew you'd get it. And why shouldn't I? You're an attractive man, rich and maybe ten years older than I am, which I like. Herbie was younger than I was, and a little bit of that goes one heck of a long way. The man should be older than the woman is what Mom used to say, and I always thought buckshot." Cassie belched. "It took the first third of my life and another bad marriage for me to find out Mom was dead-on. Excuse me. I've been eating too fast."

"So have I." Reis laid down his fork. "Where is Chase now?"

"You'd have to sweeten the pot quite a bit for that if I knew. I don't, though, so you can have it for free."

"He was the subject of the note I found in your apartment, wasn't he?"

"How would I know?"

"You'll agree that it seems likely?"

Slowly, Cassie nodded. "Sharon's been covering the story, so it was probably something somebody'd passed to her. He's been shot? That's what I heard. Shot wounded, I mean. Not shot dead."

Rosenquist nodded.

"He hasn't been in contact . . ." Cassie's fork conveyed a sliver of meat to her mouth; she chewed it reflectively.

"What is it?"

"I told you I had a lot of people at my place today. Which I did. Margaret, Sharon, and a couple others. The phone rang and I didn't answer it. A lot was going on."

"I understand."

"That was you, and you left a message on my machine. What do they feed these chickens that makes them so good?"

"I'll find out and let you know. Go on with what you were saying."

"Right after that, the phone rang again. Was that you, too?"

"No. More wine?"

Cassie accepted another glass. "I didn't answer that one, either. I unplugged the phone instead. That could have been . . . *Up!* Excuse me. Gid.

Dr. Gideon Chase. I've been trying to phone him, Wally, and that could have been him. I never thought."

SHE had clung to his arm while they left Rusterman's, having found that she was none too steady. Now, as the white limousine glided along Arbor Boulevard, Rosenquist whispered, "I'm going to win you, Cassie. I doubt that you believe me, but you'll see. When I first heard of you, I wanted to find and destroy you. It was to be an exhibition of my power, something to frighten Chase—to frighten him into my camp if possible. Almost at once I realized you were worth a hundred Chases."

She smiled, not unkindly. "This is very flattering, Wally."

"I no longer want to destroy you. I want to win you—I, alone, out of all the world. I want to feel the envy of every man who sees us together, as I did tonight. I want to dress you in diamonds. When I was younger, I wanted to own an island. An island with beaches and palm trees where I would reign as king."

Something almost mystical had crept into Reis's voice. "I have that island now, but I've seen a better one. A blue isle in a sea of black. I fight for it every day, and I'll win. With a green goddess at my side."

He saw her to her door; she kissed him there, pressing herself against him, and her kiss was long and deep. When they parted she whispered, "I'll win *you*, Billyboy. I know you don't think so, but I will. Just watch."

ELEVEN

THREE MONTHS LATER

VOLCANO GLOWS WITH PROMISE

Dating the Volcano God kicked off the fall season at the Majestic. Rev. Brownlea and his long-suffering sister were visibly nervous as they discussed what effect the family's move from Enterprise, Kansas, to the South Pacific might have on the reverend's daughter. The audience was nervous, too, and your intrepid reporter made a mental note: "This volcano has DISASTER stamped all over it."

After three minutes that seemed more like ten, the daughter appeared in the form of Cassie Casey, an auburn-haired actress about whom I have had good reports. As she floated onstage, the audience fell deathly quiet. All of us were looking at her—"staring" might be a better word—and I doubt that there was even one among us who could have said why.

She spoke, and the plywood tree outside the Brownleas' window had become a real palm; an intangible breeze carried the scent of tropical blossoms. There is such a thing as magic, no matter what the materialists may say.

Most especially there can be magic in the theater.

THEY had opened in Springfield. As Cassie stood in the wings waiting for her first entrance, Mickey the stage manager whispered, "You're the only one who's not nervous, Cassie. How do you do it?"

She grinned. "I'm jumpy as a cat. It's just that I'm good at hiding it."

The curtain rose, the Reverend Brownlea and his sister exchanged worries, and very soon after that it was time for her first song:

"It's all been put behind me, left in Kansas far away.
Life started fresh and new when the sun came up today.
Out on the beach Sun's trumpets rang the anthem of God's torch,
While at my feet the waves came up like chickens on our porch . . ."

Behind Mariah, the grass house on a nameless tropical island was wholly real. Before Cassie, the men in pink and mauve dinner jackets and the women with hair-fantasies and pearls were equally real, her people, her audience to be loved and cherished. The song filled her and poured forth of its own volition. It filled the theater, too, although she did not know it—filled it, and a thousand hearts.

Brian Kean and Norma Peiper joined their voices to hers in the chorus. As the last note faded, Brian said, "We've been talking about you, Mariah, and your aunt Jane is—"

At which point the applause began.

MARGARET recognized India's knock and let her in.

"Congrats, Cassie. You were simply wonder-fuel. You set the damned place on fire." An old wooden chair groaned beneath India's weight.

Cassie handed Mariah's long green gown to Margaret. "Congratulations to us all. Standing ovation? It doesn't get much better than that."

"Standing ovation for you when you came out to take your bow."

"For us all, when we bowed at the end."

"What did you think of our dear sailor?"

"Dean? He was all right."

Margaret shook her head ever so slightly.

"His tenor isn't what I was hoping for. His dancing isn't what Pfeiffer was hoping for, either."

"He'll come around. Pfeiffer's good, and . . ."

The telephone rang. Margaret answered it, and after a momentary silence handed it to Cassie. "I believe you had better talk to him, Miss Casey."

Cassie said, "Hello?"

"This is Agent Martin, Ms. Casey. I'm with the Federal Bureau of Investigation."

"Really?"

"Yes, Ms. Casey. Really. We've been trying to catch up to you."

"I'm afraid I can be difficult to reach. I'm sorry about that."

"No offense, ma'am. We have an office at Third and Grand. I wonder if you could be there at ten tomorrow?"

Cassie took a deep breath. "No, Agent Martin. I couldn't be. Not unless you tell me what it's about."

"Is there anyone there with you, Ms. Casey?"

"Our director and my dresser."

"If they can overhear you, it might be better if you didn't call me 'agent.' Better if you didn't use my name, too."

"All right, I won't. But I'm not going to lie in bed tonight wondering what I've been accused of and who has accused me." Another deep breath. "And I'm not coming to your office. Not voluntarily. If you want me down there, you'll have to arrest me."

"We will if we have to. I was hoping to have your cooperation as a good citizen."

"I doubt that I am one, and I'm darned sure nobody's going to think I am by the time you're through with me."

"Can I explain why I wanted you to come to our office?"

Cassie said, "Do it," then covered the speaker with her free hand. "Will you wait, India? This could be important, but I'll wind it up as fast as I can."

India nodded.

Agent Martin was saying, "People don't always believe us when we present our credentials. That happens often. I want you to come downtown so you can see for yourself that I'm who I say I am. I'll still show you my badge and ID when we meet, even if you don't."

"Are you there now? In that office?"

"I am. Three of us are working late."

"Something hot. I've got it." Cassie hung up, and immediately dialed Directory Assistance, giving city and state. "I'd like the office of the FBI."

Behind her, India stirred in her chair.

On her line, the phone rang once. "Agent Martin."

"This is Cassie again. I believe you now."

"Good. When can you meet with me?"

"I can't." Cassie's grin was inward only. "You'll have to catch me. I hear you're good at that."

She hung up. "Unplug it, will you, Margaret? He's calling back. See if you can find the thing."

"Yes, Miss Casey." Margaret threw an anguished glance toward India and hurried to comply.

"The FBI wants you?" India asked.

"They want me to cooperate in an investigation. I didn't ask what it was about because I wanted to talk to you. He probably wouldn't have told me anyway."

"I'd like to know."

"You will, as soon as I do." The chair in front of the dressing table was wire-backed, and rather too large for a doll's house. Cassie sat, taking care not to miss the seat.

"Are you going to go along?" India sounded as worried as she looked.

"Depends. Maybe, if I like what he's doing. Maybe even if I don't like it, if he's got some kind of an arm lock."

"Tell me when you know. What I want to talk about . . . Cassie, my job's to bring the rest of the cast up to your level."

"You want the false humility?"

"Hell no. Here's the straight shit. I can't. Nobody could, not even if you helped. You dance like—I don't know. Like you'd been starring with the Ballet Russe for the past three years. Dean stumbles around after you and looks ridiculous. I've had words with Pfeiffer already. He goes . . ." India shrugged and sighed like a vacuum cleaner. "So if you can do anything, please do."

"I'll try," Cassie promised.

"That's all I ask. Vince wants to ham it up. In his part that's okay up to a point, but we've got to keep him on a short leash. You're onstage and I'm not, so snarl at him anytime he gets out of control."

"I'll be your bitch, but I thought he was fine."

"He was, tonight. He was maybe one-tenth as good as you were, and if I could get the rest up to that I'd be a happy broad. Only he'll be worse to-morrow night if we let him."

"Norma was fine, too."

"Norma was lousy. She was nervous until you came on, and after that she couldn't stop smiling. Aunt Jane smiles once during the whole stinkin' show. Once!"

When India had gone, Margaret said softly, "It didn't really stink, Miss Casey. It was good. Everybody loved it. You had to do all those encores."

"Oh, did I? Tell me about it." Cassie kicked off her dancing shoes. "I'm so tired I may pass out."

"THERE are three critics here from New York tonight, Miss Casey. That's what everybody says. The *Times,* *The New Yorker,* and Channel Some-thing." The gingham gown had been hung away as Margaret spoke. Cassie's bra followed; it would be replaced by one that vanished at a distance of eight feet, save for plastic blossoms over her nipples.

Cassie said, "Full house. Did you notice?"

"I did, Miss Casey. Everybody did."

"I keep looking for an empty seat down front. I haven't seen one."

"No, Miss Casey."

"Body powder, Margaret. More body powder." The skirt of faux grass hung low on Cassie's hips, and as she studied it in the long mirror she found herself recalling something Margaret had told her while taking measure-ments. It left—how much? Ten inches of bare waist, Cassie decided. She turned to get a side view.

Onstage once more, she pulled Donny Duke out of the line of prancing sailors; they danced a wholly unrehearsed hornpipe to the deafening ap-proval of the audience.

TWO days later, Margaret asked, "Were you expecting company, Miss Casey?"

"No, but company might be welcome." Cassie was still radiant from her final bows. "Who is it?"

"He wouldn't give his name, Miss Casey. He wouldn't get out of your dressing room, either."

Smiling, Cassie threw open the door; the man inside was a stranger, much taller than Gideon Chase.

He rose and took what appeared to be a black leather wallet from a pocket of his ash-striped gray suit coat. Flipped open, it revealed a gilt badge and a photo ID.

Striving to hide her disappointment, Cassie sat down. "Good evening, Agent Martin. Did you enjoy the show?"

"What I saw of it, yes."

"That's good. Well, you've caught me. What is it you want?"

"To speak to you in private." The tall man glanced at Margaret.

"I have no secrets from my dresser, Agent Martin."

"Maybe not, but I do. Let me make my position clear, Cassie." He sat again. "I haven't caught you in the sense of wanting to arrest you. I don't. Just the same, I'll arrest you if you make me. We need to speak privately. I can do that by putting the cuffs on you and taking you down to my car. After that we'll drive to some nice quiet spot, and after that we'll see."

Something savage had crept into the tall man's face. He reached behind him; and his hand emerged with a pair of handcuffs, still shiny but not quite new. "Here—or the quiet spot. Which is it?"

Cassie motioned for Margaret to leave, and Margaret did.

"Thanks." The tall man was replacing his handcuffs.

"I could sue you for false arrest," she told him, "and if you arrest me, I'll do it."

"You could sue the federal government, Cassie." His grin was almost a snarl. "Not me. It's your right as a citizen—if they let you—and I wouldn't deprive you of it."

"But it doesn't worry you, Marty?"

"Hardly. The Department of Justice has billions of dollars and a thousand lawyers, including me. Let me get to the point."

"I wish you would."

"You're on good terms with a college professor from Rhode Island, a Ph.D. named Gideon Chase. That's public knowledge. Do you know where he is now?"

Cassie shook her head. "I wish I did."

"I hope you're telling the truth, Cassie. There's a law against obstructing an investigation. Did you know that? Most people don't, but you can be sent to prison. Want to try again?"

"If I knew where he was, I don't think I'd tell you," Cassie said, "but I don't." The telephone rang, and she added, "All right if I get that?"

The tall man nodded, and she picked up the handset and said hello.

"This is Gid. Can you talk?"

Cassie looked annoyed. "Not now, Norma. I'm busy. I'll meet you for a drink later if I can, but I may not make it. Don't wait for me."

"Our friend is back in the U.S. I think you'll be seeing him soon." There was a click as Gideon hung up.

"Don't worry about that—it'll be all right. See you later." Cassie hung up, too.

"I won't keep you," the tall man said. "We can get through this in two or three minutes. What do you know about William Reis?"

"I've heard of him." Cassie looked thoughtful, and felt the same way. "Very, very rich. He used to be our ambassador to that planet. The one that's got people on it."

"Woldercan."

"Right. Wasn't he the ambassador there for a while? Other than that . . ." She shrugged. "He's a big financier and knows politicians."

"He's a master criminal," the tall man told her. "His legitimate businesses—and you're right, he's got a lot of businesses, construction, shipping, and God only knows what else. He has those businesses to launder his money. We want to get him, and now we think we've finally got enough evidence to put him away for life. It's taken us years to collect it."

"I wish I could help you."

"I wish you could, too, Cassie. Did you know he's trying to kill your friend Professor Chase?"

Cassie's mouth opened, and closed again without a sound. At last she said, "I knew somebody tried. They shot him and he called the police and reported it. He wasn't there when they came, though. Sharon Bench told me, and I saw it on the news later. Most people seem to think he's dead."

"But you don't."

She shook her head. "No. I don't."

"Why not?"

Suddenly she smiled. "Because they tried to kill him and screwed it up, Marty. He got away, and he was still alive and safe enough to make that phone call. Have you ever met him? Met Gideon Chase?"

"Not yet. I'd like to."

"He pulls rabbits out of hats. Sometimes I like him and sometimes I want to strangle him, but he wouldn't be easy to kill."

"He's not easy to find, either, Cassie. I know it because I've been trying to find him. Either the man who tried to kill him was working for William Reis, or it was William Reis himself. If it wasn't Reis, we think it was one of his top aides. Dr. Chase's testimony could be helpful in both cases."

"You said you had enough on this William Reis to get a conviction, Marty. Why don't you arrest him?"

"Two reasons." The tall man cleared his throat. "I'm going to open up for you and give them both. The first is that there's no such thing as too much evidence in a case like this. Reis is as slick as they come and rich enough to hire the top legal talent in the country." The tall man hesitated. "Maybe I shouldn't have started talking about this, Cassie. I don't want to scare you."

"I'm not scared." She grinned to prove it. "What's the second reason?"

"We can't find him. He's seen here and he's spotted there, but when we get there he's gone. We'd love to pick him up and sweat him, but thus far we haven't been able to do it."

"You can't find Gid either." Cassie switched on a small black fan, wishing she could take off her costume instead. "Maybe they're together."

"Chase and Reis? I doubt it. Reis is seen all over, as I said. Chase isn't seen at all."

"You want me to tell you if I see him."

"Exactly. Where you saw him and where you think he might be going. I'll be out of the office pretty steadily this week and next, so I'll give you my cell phone number." The tall man scribbled on the back of a business card and handed it to her.

By the time she had found her purse, Margaret had returned. "Miss Dempster's auditioning understudies for Mr. Heeny."

"At this hour?" Cassie cocked an eyebrow.

"Yes, Miss Casey. She and Mr. Pfeiffer. I thought you might want to watch."

"I do. I'll be there as soon as I get into my street clothes. What about you?" Margaret nodded.

The last set was still in place on the darkened stage. Before it a young man bobbed and spun to the music of Jules Pfeiffer's Hyper-Deeper iPod.

Cassie took the seat next to India's. "Understudies?"

India nodded and said firmly, "Understudies."

"In case something happens to Dean?"

India nodded again. "Right."

"Like he might get fired? Something like that?"

"Holy snot, Wanton Woman!" Cramped in the narrow theater seat, India turned enough to face Cassie. "I hadn't thought of that. But yeah, he might. Like, the first time Wally sees him onstage. Even sooner than that. Could be. You never know."

"Would it help to see them dancing with me?"

"It might." India turned to Ebony. "Go ask Pfeiffer. Tell him Cassie'll dance with them so he can see it."

When it was over, India said, "You must be ready for a teddy, but if you'd like a drink, I'm buying."

"No drink, I'm swearing off. What I'd really like is some hot tea."

"Yeah." India licked her lips. "You know, I could go for coffee and a cheeseburger."

Ebony said, "There's a little place down the street that's open all night."

It was all white save for polychrome plastic stools, and self-consciously old-fashioned. "Pfeiffer didn't like any of them," Ebony said as they found places around a small white table.

"We know." India sounded gloomy.

"Well, what about you? What about Cassie?"

The counterman said, "What about four Doubleburgers?"

Cassie and Margaret asked for hot tea, India a Giant Doubleburger and coffee, and Ebony a grilled cheese on whole wheat with bacon and a glass of milk.

"I'm swearing off grilled cheese sandwiches, too," Cassie announced. "I just decided. No more grilled cheese. Nothing but cooked veggies, raw veggies, bottled water, and maybe a little fruit."

"You look great," India told her. "Tired, sure. But great otherwise."

"No more ice cream." Cassie sounded pensive. "Hit me over the head, Margaret, anytime I look like I might order ice cream."

"You're not fat, Miss Casey."

"If I get any fatter that grass skirt's going to slide down to my knees. Live and onstage."

India muttered, "We should all be that fat. You can't go much over a hundred pounds."

"I don't know. I'm afraid to get on a scale. I kind of liked the blond one."

India shook her head.

Ebony said, "The thing is, Cassie—India explained it to me. We need somebody who will make you look as good as possible. That doesn't mean somebody who's as good as you are, which we couldn't get anyway. It means somebody who's pretty good, but in a mix-and-match way. You're female. Very, very female, but in an energetic sort of hoydenish tomboy style. He ought to be a supercharged bad boy, and very male. Isn't that right, India?"

"Exactly. That kind of a tenor, who can act a little and dance a little, too. The blond guy you liked was a scarecrow. A good scarecrow but a scarecrow, and that's not what we need. Dean's just bad. Male, but a second-rate tenor and a third-rate dancer. Donny Duke can dance the paper off the wall, but he's not male and he can't sing for shit."

"So what are you going to do?" Cassie asked.

"Keep looking. That's all I can do. I've buzzed all the agencies." India heaved a sigh that bid fair to blow the chrome napkin-holder off the table. "If it gets any worse, I'll put an ad in the paper."

As he set her coffee in front of her, the counterman said, "There was a guy in here earlier. I bet he could do it."

"Send him over," India told him. "It couldn't hurt."

Ebony tittered, and pretended she had not when India glared at her.

A stocky man in a Delft sack suit was chatting with the desk clerk when Cassie got to her hotel. He followed her to the elevator and flipped open a badge case as soon as the doors had closed. "I talked to you on the phone, ma'am. Remember? I'm Agent Martin of the Federal Bureau of Investigation."

TWELVE

ROYALTY IN REALITY

"The show won't start for another hour, Miss Casey."

"You're here." Cassie was staring out the dressing room's small and dirty window.

"I always come to the theater early, Miss Casey, to make sure everything's all right before you put it on."

"That's good."

"What's troubling you, Miss Casey?"

Cassie pointed. "See that phone? I'm waiting for it to ring."

"Really, Miss Casey?"

"Yes, Margaret. Really." Cassie took a deep breath. "Margaret, I'm going to tell you something that I'm not going to tell India. I left a note for her, and I left a note for what's his name? The stage manager?"

"Mickey, Miss Casey. Mickey Urbani."

"I left a note for him to send India in here as soon as she came in.

Remember the man in the gray suit? He was waiting in my dressing room last night."

"Yes, I do, Miss Casey."

"This phone rang while he was in here. I didn't want to spill the beans, so I pretended it was Norma Peiper. It was really Gideon Chase. This is confidential, Margaret. Don't repeat it to anybody."

Margaret was opening her sewing kit. "I understand, Miss Casey. I won't."

"So he's still alive, and I want—I want to see him again."

"Yes, Miss Casey."

"I want to help him if I can, even though I don't know what I can do. I've been waiting for him to call." Cassie paused. "I just thought of something, Margaret."

Margaret nodded while biting a thread.

"How did he get the number? They have directories for these old-fashioned land lines, but I doubt that this one's in there. The only number for this theater is probably the box office."

"I can look, Miss Casey."

"Do that, whenever you have time. Well, anyway, I'm going to tell India about the tall man in the gray suit and another man. You'll probably hear all that, but I'm not going to tell her about Dr. Chase."

Later, onstage, Aunt Jane sang.

"And how I love his boiling lava
Steaming like a cup of java.
His passionate voice, his skin like guava . . ."

Cassie, standing in the wings beside Vincent Palma, whispered, "Where the heck is India?"

Palma only shrugged.

A few minutes after that, when they were deep in the second dream scene, Cassie glimpsed India in the wings—and a familiar face next to hers. They were gone by the time the scene was over, and Margaret was there instead.

A small folding screen shielded Cassie from prurient eyes while she exchanged her faux-grass skirt and flowered bra for Mariah's ankle-length white cotton nightgown. "I saw Zelda, Margaret. She was standing here with India, so something's up. Do you know what's going on?"

Margaret shook her head. "I don't, Miss Casey. They went into your dressing room. Miss Dempster has a key. I told them they shouldn't, but they said they'd leave if you didn't want them in there. Shall I tell them to go?"

"If necessary—how's my hair?"

"Beautiful, Miss Casey. Only I really ought to braid it."

"Over my dead body."

At which point Cassie had to sneak onto the darkened stage and into bed.

IN her dressing room after the show, she leveled fingers like pistols at her visitors. "I told Margaret that I'd drive you two out with a stick if I had to. I might do it, too, but not before Zelda tells me what made her take a hundred-mile drive."

"I hopped."

"Well lah-de-dah!"

"You're down for two percent of the gross, Cassie, and I'm down for ten percent of you. I get two-tenths of one percent of everything this show brings in. I've got a cute little pink hopper now with three years to pay, and I don't think they're going to be repossessing it."

India announced, "We've been negotiating a recording contract for you, Cassie. I represented Wally—he owns the songs. Zelda represented you."

"It doesn't mean a darned thing . . ." Cassie's voice was muffled as she struggled out of her green gingham gown. "Unless I sign it."

"*Until* you sign it," Zelda said firmly. "You will. Wait 'til you see it. For one or two mornings' work."

"I sleep in the morning." Cassie switched on her fan.

"Ten to one, maybe. We can work that out with the studio."

"I get up at eleven, don't I, Margaret?"

When the contract had been signed and Zelda had left for her hotel, Cassie said, "I meant to talk to you about the FBI. I said I would, and I want to. But darn it, I need tea. I want to sit down and breathe and drink tea. Cookies, too. Gingersnaps or something. Only we can't talk about this in a restaurant."

"That stuff," India said firmly, "is what assistant directors are for." She got out her cell phone and gave orders.

"There was a man in here who said he was from the FBI," Cassie began. "I'd gotten a call from the FBI, from an Agent Martin." She recounted both conversations.

"This guy wasn't for real?"

"No. He said he was from the FBI. He showed me his badge and every-thing, and he was carrying handcuffs."

"He had a gun, too," Margaret added softly.

"I didn't see it, but he probably did. He said he was Agent Martin and he was looking for Gideon Chase. He gave me his card. Wait a minute."

Margaret handed Cassie her purse.

"Are you sweet on this Chase?" India asked. "There was something in the paper about you two."

"No! He's just a friend."

"Right." India sighed. "Got it. Come to think of it, you're supposed to be sweet on Wally."

"I'm not!"

"One word, Cassie. Diamonds."

Cassie looked up. "What's that supposed to mean?"

"Just keep it in mind. Diamonds."

Margaret said, "Get a box at the bank, Miss Casey. Miss Sinclair's jewelry was stolen while I was with her. One of those bank boxes is a lot safer."

"You two are so out of it!" Cassie held up the tall man's card. " 'Bernard B. Martin, Special Agent, Federal Bureau of Investigation.' Read it for your-self."

"Buy some card stock," India said, "and you can print up all the cards you want on your computer. You ought to know that."

"Well, I believed him, and I was supposed to call him and tell him any-time I saw Gid. Then I went back to the hotel, and the real Agent Martin was waiting for me."

India nodded thoughtfully. "You made sure the second guy was the real deal?"

"You bet I did. I looked at his ID and read every word and wrote down the number on his badge. Then I called the FBI office here and got the woman to describe the real Bernie Martin. After that I badgered her into looking up his badge number. She was even meaner than most cops, by the way . . ."

"What is it, Cassie?"

"I just remembered something, that's all. Back home, I saw a guy. It was only for a second, and I couldn't think who he was. It just hit me."

"None of my business?"

"Right. It isn't important anyway. He's a friend of a friend, and he gave me a ride one time. That's all. I was going to say I called Sharon Bench, too. I got her to describe the FBI guy who'd been talking to the people who lived in that apartment. The one Gid was in when he was shot. I had to promise I'd tell her the next time I dated Wally. I'll do it, too, if there is a next time."

India sighed. "You're our star, Cassie, and you're knee deep in something I don't understand. Knee deep, and sinking."

"I don't understand it either. But I don't think I'm getting in any deeper."

Margaret said, "I do, Miss Casey."

They were arguing about it when Ebony appeared with a pot of steaming water, half a dozen tea bags, four thick china mugs, six cookies, and four sandwiches.

"Reuben on rye. That's yours, India."

India nodded. "You bet it is. Only I'm not sure you're invited to this tea party. Cassie?"

"Oh, let her stay." Cassie was dousing Earl Grey with hot water. "Margaret's here, and I know you trust Ebony."

Ebony smiled her thanks. "Ham and Swiss. That's on rye, too."

Margaret took it.

"BLT on white. That's mine. So this one's yours, Cassie."

India winked. "No calories, right?"

"Right," Cassie said firmly. "How about filling Ebony in while I eat?"

"If you want." Grunting, India shifted her position to face her assistant. "Cassie's been getting visits from the FBI. The first one was a fake. Is that right, Cassie?"

Chewing, Cassie nodded.

"The second one was for real. She told him about the fake, right?"

Cassie nodded again and swallowed.

"What I want to know," India continued, "is what the second one wanted. Cassie will have to tell us."

"That's not what I want to know," Cassie said between bites. "What I want to know—what I'd love to know—is why the first one was so hot to find Gid."

"That's Dr. Gideon Chase," Margaret whispered.

Ebony nodded gratefully.

"Was he?" India asked. "Really anxious?"

"He didn't seem like it, but he had to be. Posing as an FBI man is serious. You can go to prison. He went to the trouble of faking a photo ID and a badge. He even had handcuffs. But why?"

Ebony said, "Why's India been looking so hard for somebody new to play the sailor?"

India said, "That's different."

"I don't think so. India's looking for somebody with a better voice. For a better dancer."

"I think I've found somebody, too." Briefly, India looked pleased. "It's freaky and Cassie will have to okay it, but I like this a lot. He's my Hitler."

Cassie sipped tea. "I don't see what it has to do with Gid."

"Well, it's always the same." Ebony was smiling, but sounded serious. "I don't know your Gid, but either he's got something this fake guy wants or he can do something this guy wants done."

"Okay." India sighed. "Sure. Gee, Ebony, I'm glad I let you sit in on this. Now that we know—"

"You don't have to be sarcastic."

"About the fake, what was it the real one wanted him for, Cassie?"

"It wasn't that he wanted something. He said that the president knew him, and now that he'd dropped out of sight the president was worried about him. He's asked the FBI to find him, and it'll protect him if he needs protecting."

India grunted. "Smooth."

"You don't believe him."

She shook her head.

"He was the real thing. I told you."

"Yeah. I believe that. What I don't believe is that business about the president being worried. Nuts."

Margaret put down the sandwich she had been nibbling. "If someone wanted to get Cassie to cooperate . . . ?"

Frowning, India nodded emphatically. "If somebody wants Cassie's cooperation, they couldn't have dreamed up anything better. Only it's too damned good to be true."

Ebony said, "Are you going to, Cassie? Cooperate?"

Cassie swallowed the final bite of her sandwich and reached for a cookie. "I haven't decided."

"She'll ask him." India stood. "That might be smart. I don't know."

"Wait!" Cassie waved her cookie. "Aren't you going to tell me about this new dancer you found?"

Ebony said, "If she won't, I will."

India grinned. "Have you ever seen anybody dance on one leg, Cassie?"

She shook her head.

"Neither had I, but he can do it. He had a peg leg made up, like a pirate. He can dance on it, and he's got one hell of a voice."

Ebony murmured, "Good tenors are terribly hard to find, Cassie."

"I know. Can he act?"

"That," India told her, "is what we're going to find out. Can you come in early tomorrow night? I'll have him here then. His name's Corby."

"He's kind of short, too." Ebony bobbed like a cork in India's wake. "We want somebody who'll make Vince and Tiny look bigger."

THE white limousine was waiting for Cassie when she left the theater. She stopped abruptly, staring at it and at its driver.

"For you, señora." The driver opened the rear door with a flourish.

"You're wearing a gun, Carlos."

"Sí, señora."

Reis's voice floated through the open door. "I got him a license." There was something slightly spectral about that voice. "Under the circumstances, it seemed advisable."

"Hello, Wally. I was hoping you weren't here." Cassie had not taken another step.

"Am I as bad as that?"

"No. I am. I've been eating . . . well, sardines and onions. A sardine and onion sandwich. I love them, but my breath would gag you. Let me get a cab, please."

Reis chuckled. "Get in. I have a gift for you, and news. I only regret I can't kiss you—I'm eager to test your theory."

"Really, Wally—"

"Unreally, Cassie. I'm not here. I'll see you and hear you, but I cannot touch you, however much I wish it. Nor can I smell your breath."

She shook her head.

"You're frightened."

She smiled. "Not frightened enough to admit it if I am, Wally."

"Then why won't you get into my car?"

"Because I'm knee deep in a terrible mess already. And sinking. That's what your friend India says, and I'm afraid she's right. On top of that, I'm as tired as five-cent roses. I want to go back to the hotel and go to bed. Nothing else. No side trips." Cassie turned away.

And discovered that Reis's driver was standing in front of her. Very softly he said, "No, Señora Casey."

"Allow me to offer a compromise, Cassie. Will you listen? Carlos could fold you like a paper doll. I won't have him do that, you understand. I wouldn't even think of it."

Less loudly than she had intended, Cassie said, "No indeed. Of course not."

"Right." If Reis had been struck by her sarcasm, his ghostly voice conveyed no sign of it. "First, let me say that I'm a man of my word. I may break the law at times, and in fact there are so many that nobody can live without breaking them. Now and then I may cheat a man who would've cheated me if he could. My word is good, however. Good always. Good to everyone, but particularly to you."

Cassie's nod felt forced.

"Here's my compromise. If you'll get into my car, where I can see you and you can see me, Carlos will return to his place behind the wheel, leaving the door open. I'll tell you my news then. I may or may not give you the gift I mentioned. It was expensive, even for me, so if the moment doesn't seem appropriate I'll withhold it."

Her courage had returned. "Please do, Wally. I don't like to take gifts from men. If you're a friend, you don't have to prove it by giving me presents. If you're not, I don't want anything from you."

"I'm financing the show you're in as a vehicle for you, Cassie."

She nodded. "I suspected that, and I'm grateful. But I didn't ask for it, and if you'd asked me whether I wanted it, I'd have said no."

"Please sit down." Reis's voice was spectral as ever. "You're tired, as you said. Your face says it for you, and more forcefully. I never enjoy cruelty, and I detest the idea of being cruel to you. Sit down. You have my word."

As she slid onto the white leather seat, Reis's face floated above a seat facing her own. "That's better. Much better. Is the door still open?"

Her eyes darted toward it. "Yes. Thanks, Wally."

"You're very welcome. If you'll look to your left, you should be able to see into the front seat. Is Carlos there?"

She nodded. "He's just getting in."

"Good. Look at this."

Reis's face vanished. The stage replaced it, and she herself stood singing on that stage.

"It's only when I'm quite alone
that I can see my soul,"

Her vidimage stood beside her, and seemed about to speak.

"It's then that I am Woman
the one thing God made whole."

She clasped hands with her soul, and the two began to dance.

Her images vanished. After a half second of darkness, Reis's face filled the screen once more. "I wanted you to see yourself as others see you. I wanted you to see what the audience sees—what I've seen so often, playing and replaying the Cassie Casey captured for me by a friend's digital camcorder. Now that you have, do you understand why every man who sees you wants you so badly?"

"No." Cassie shook her head. "No, I don't, Wally. There are a lot of good-looking women out there."

"Could they play Mariah Brownlea? Would they draw the crowds you do in the part?"

Cassie said nothing.

"I came back to America to entrap you, Cassie. To entrap and destroy you. When you came up to the microphone to take my gold bracelet, I realized I had made a horrible mistake. For a time—a brief time—I continued on the path I'd laid out for myself. I'm stubborn, and I can be stupidly stubborn."

"Wally . . ."

"While we sat together in this car, I scrapped all those plans. Every man who sees you desires you, Cassie." Reis smiled. "I will win you. I alone, out of all the millions. Would you like to be a queen?"

She could only stare.

"I'm talking about real royalty. You'll be a queen who rules, as well as a queen who reigns. You'll sit on a throne, a throne of black basalt carved immemorial ages ago, and wear your crown when you choose to. If you choose to elevate a man, he will kiss your feet in gratitude. If you choose to execute that man later, he will be made to lay his head on a stone. Should I tell you the rest?"

"I think it might be good for me to hear it, Wally."

"You recovered quickly. I like that. He will be made to lay his head upon a certain stone, and there it will be smashed with a club. You will be queen, and I will be your king whenever I am there. Think about it."

"I will." Cassie swallowed. "I'd like to take the show to Broadway first."

"Of course." In the screen, Reis nodded. "The two are not mutually exclusive. There will be a film, as well. You, Queen Cassiopeia of Takanga, will star in that film."

"You know my r-real name."

"I know a good deal, Cassie. For a man in love, study of that kind is a pleasure. Now the gift. There is a sort of bag built into the door on your left. It's in there. You can take it out now."

She did, noticing that the box wrapped in gold paper was the same shape as the first, although not as heavy. "All right if I unwrap it?"

"Please do."

She slid the ribbon of gold lace off and laid it on the seat. The stiff gold paper followed; the leather of the box it had wrapped was the color of old gold, and as soft as butter to her touch.

"Open it, Cassie."

She did.

And felt that she floated in space above some immense rectangular city. That she sailed through the night sky above a city whose countless lights were far too bright for stars.

Too bright and too near.

WHEN Cassie looked up the door of the limousine was shut and the limousine in motion; she tried to speak and failed, coughed, and whispered, "I've never seen so many diamonds. Or such big ones."

"Few people have."

"It's hard—very hard—to keep my eyes off it." She closed the jewel box. "You promised you wouldn't shut your car door, Wally."

"Your expression gave consent. Are you frightened?"

She shook her head.

"You're right. There's no reason why you should be. We're simply taking you to your hotel. Since you'll be wearing that bracelet when you go into the lobby, Carlos will accompany you as far as the door of your room. I think that's a wise precaution and hope you'll agree."

"I'd rather not take it out of the box." Cassie felt she was strangling.

"If you want to hear my news, which you may consider moderately important, you'll have to put on my bracelet, Your Majesty. It concerns your friend Dr. Chase."

Cassie opened the box, took the bracelet out, and fumbled with the catch.

"Thanks. Someone tried to kill Dr. Chase, but only succeeded in wounding him. You know that, and you probably think I was behind the shooting. Chase himself may well be of your opinion, but you're both mistaken. That's my first news item. I hope you'll agree it was worth the labor of putting on my bracelet."

Cassie did not speak.

"My second is that I'm trying to find out who the shooter was and who's behind him. The identity of the man who pulled the trigger is not really important. What is, is the identity of the person who got him to do it. That may matter a great deal. In time I'll learn it, I promise you. When I do, I'll probably tell you. That isn't a promise, but I think it will work out like that. I'll tell Chase as well—or you can."

"I still think it was you."

"It wasn't. Chase is only a minor threat to me, and I rarely wish those who are dead. Anyone strong enough and clever enough to be a threat to me is someone I'd prefer to win over. I try, and succeed in most cases. When I fail, I can generally draw their fangs without killing them."

"I'm not strong, Wally. I'm not clever, either."

Reis smiled. "Do you really think I want you, Cassie, for the same reason I want Chase?"

GIL CORBY

The telephone woke Cassie at ten minutes past eight.

She sat up, rubbing her eyes and wishing with all her heart that the noise would stop, stumbled out of bed, and at length realized that (this being a hotel) there was a telephone on a nightstand beside the bed.

On the other side.

It had rung ten times, perhaps, when at last she picked up the handset and said a sleepy hello.

"It's me, Cassie. Sharon. Sharon Bench. Remember me?"

"Yes." Cassie yawned. "Yes, I do, Sharon. What do you want? I was asleep."

"Sorry. But you made me a promise, Cassie. I checked my voice mail here at the office, and I checked my answering machine at home. I can dial into it."

"Uh huh."

"And you hadn't called. But you promised me you'd tell me the next time you dated Wallace Rosenquist. You were to let me know and tell me everything about it. And you didn't."

"That's right." Cassie yawned again. "I didn't."

"So tell me now! You owe me."

"I didn't date him. I haven't even seen him." She paused. "This is crazy."

"What is?"

"I dreamed about him, and now it seems like you're still in my dream. I'm awake—I know I am. I'm awake and looking around my room at the downtown Hyatt, but you're stuck in my dream."

There was a long pause. "Tell me about it, Cassie. If I'm in a dream I'd like to know what's going on."

"I was riding in this enormous white car. It was as long as a bus."

"I've got it."

"Wally's head was in there, too, sitting in front of me. Just his head. He kept telling me he was going to make me a queen, and finally he handed me a long narrow box, sort of gold. I thought it was going to be a crown, Sharon. I did! It was going to be a crown, and I would wrap it around my head and fasten it in back. I opened it and there were a jillion huge diamonds in there."

"Cassie? Are you sure you're awake?"

"Of course I am."

"I want you to do something for me. Will you please? I want you to stand up."

"All right." Cassie rose.

"You're standing up?"

"Yes, but I'm going to sit down again in about one second."

"Answer a couple of questions first. Did you go to the theater last night? Do the show?"

"Yes. Yes, I did. Five songs and three encores, and I just about danced my cute big feet off. No wonder I'm so tired."

"Okay. How did you get back to your hotel?"

"I—"

"Yeah? How?"

"Maybe I walked. . . ."

"After dancing your feet off?" Even over the phone, Sharon sounded irritated.

"I guess I flagged a cab. That was it. I got a cab, and there was this nice driver who wanted to know how he could get tickets. I said I couldn't help him, and he said if only he could get tickets he could sell them for four times the box office price. Then . . . No, that wasn't last night. . . ."

"I didn't think so."

"It's hot in here, and the windows won't open. Can you wait a minute while I turn up the air-conditioning?"

"Sure."

Back at the phone Cassie said, "I think I remember it, but it's crazy. How do you think I got back here?"

"Let me tell you why I called, Cassie. I've got a contact at your show. I can't tell you who she is—I gave her my word I wouldn't do that. But I do. I've done this person some little favors, and this person does me little favors now and then. Last night this person called and told me that when she left the theater Wallace Rosenquist's limo was waiting outside. It had to be waiting for you."

"It was," Cassie said, "but Wally wasn't in it. I didn't date him, so I didn't break my promise to you."

"He wasn't in there?"

"Nope. He'd just sent his driver. His driver's name is Carlos."

"That's not exactly hot news."

"I never said it was." Thoroughly awake now, Cassie smiled. "Wally was just being nice. He sent his driver, and I got in and his driver took me back to the hotel and even walked me up to my room. I don't know why I couldn't remember that."

"Neither do I."

"Now I'm going back to bed, Sharon. Please don't call again. Not this morning."

They said good-bye and Cassie lay down once more, but did not sleep.

The telephone rang. She sat up—on the correct side of the bed this time—and lifted the handset. "Casey Answering Incorporated. What can we do for you?"

"This is Zelda, Cassie. Can you meet me for breakfast at nine?"

Cassie glanced at the clock radio. "No."

"Nine fifteen? Please? I'm buying."

"*You're* buying? This is a dream. Got to be."

"I'm buying. Nine fifteen in the coffee shop. Don't be late."

"Nine twenty," Cassie said, but Zelda had already hung up.

After a moment's hesitation, Cassie pushed the button for the hotel operator. "Please ring Margaret Briggs."

Beyond the hotel window, the world had turned to gray while she slept. Once—no, twice—rain lashed the glass. Fall, and the show was nowhere near ready for New York.

"Margaret? I didn't wake you up? I was afraid I would."

"No, Miss Casey. I always get up at seven."

"That's great. Come here? Eleven oh nine. I'm sure you remember, and I'll buy your breakfast after. No, I'll make Zelda do it, but it's the same thing."

"I'll be right there, Miss Casey."

"Wait. Did you call Sharon Bench last night?"

"No, Miss Casey."

"The truth, please. I won't be mad, and it may be important? Did you?"

"No, Miss Casey. Honestly, I didn't."

"Thanks. Come as soon as you can. I have to get dressed in a tearing hurry, and we're going to have to search this room before we go. I'll start without you."

"MARGARET is a genius," Cassie said as she sat down. "She should be a detective. Margaret Marple. I didn't think we'd find it at all, but she found it in about a minute and a half."

Margaret stared down at her plate.

"Found what?" Zelda looked from one to the other.

"The bracelet from my dream. See, I dreamed about Wally last night. I dreamed he'd given me a bracelet."

"You have to see it," Margaret whispered to Zelda. "Miss Sinclair had nothing half as nice."

"I want to."

"Only when I woke up this morning," Cassie continued, "I wasn't exactly sure it was a dream. I felt like I'd had a box, not very big, and hidden it before I went to bed. And so—"

Zelda rapped her water glass. "I didn't think Wallace Rosenquist was here. India would have said something while we were negotiating the recording contract."

"He isn't. But I saw him last night in his car and he gave me this bracelet."

"In your dream?"

"Right. Only when Carlos took me back to my room, I put on all the locks—the security bar and everything—and hid the bracelet box."

"You ought to get a thing at the bank, Miss Casey. A safety deposit."

"I will, only back home. Not here."

"That fits perfectly." Zelda nodded to herself. "Thank you, Margaret."

"Fits what?"

"In a minute. Here's the waitress, and you haven't even looked."

Cassie glanced up. "Do you have buckwheat cakes?"

The waitress nodded, and Cassie ordered buckwheat pancakes with a side of bacon.

"I've been eating breakfast in here ever since we came," Margaret told Zelda. "I don't have to see a menu. Yogurt and fruit, please."

Zelda ordered a Denver omelet. "Now tell me about the bracelet. No, don't. Have you got it? You didn't leave it up in your room, I hope."

"You do *not* get ten percent of my bracelet." Cassie was firm.

"Swell, let me see it."

"Not yet. Margaret came, and I told her I thought Wally'd given me another bracelet and I'd hidden it. She said what about the safe? I didn't remember there was a safe in the closet—that's where I'm going to put it—until she said that. So I said probably not, because I'd forgotten about it, but she wanted to look."

"The numbers were scrambled," Margaret explained. "Mine was set to all zeros when I got here. That will open it until you reprogram it."

"Mine was locked," Cassie went on, "and Margaret wanted to know whether I'd changed the combination. I didn't know you could, so Margaret said I probably hadn't. She turned the numbers zero-zero-zero-zero and it opened. There it was!"

"Hooray." Zelda looked impatient and sounded the same way. "I wanna see the bracelet."

"I'll take it out of my purse," Cassie began, "and hold my arm under—"

The waitress returned bearing food, coffee, tea, and a program from *Dating the Volcano God*. "Would you sign this, Miss Casey? It's for my boss."

Cassie did.

"And could you sign my arm, too? I want to show it to people, and there's a tattoo place down the street."

IN Zelda's rented car, Cassie asked, "Will your hopper hold us all? Three people? I've heard some of the little ones only seat two."

"Yes and no." Always a fast driver, Zelda was driving faster than usual. "It seats four, so it'll certainly hold the three of us. Only Ebony's coming and bringing a tenor for the duets. So that'll be five if Margaret comes."

"Margaret's coming," Cassie said firmly. "I want her there."

"Let's hear it from Margaret. Ever warped through hyperspace, Margaret?"

Margaret shook her head, and Cassie said, "She can't see you there in back. You'll have to speak up."

"No, I haven't, Ms. Youmans."

"Scared?"

"No, Ms. Youmans." Margaret looked frightened.

"I was the first time, too. The saleswoman took me up for a test run, and I was scared to pieces. She talked me through it a dozen times, and after the third one I saw it was a piece of cake."

Cassie said, "Ebony won't take up much room. She's as thin as a soda straw."

"Bucket seats, so it doesn't matter. Only there's cargo space in back. You know. The tenor can sit back there."

The airport was small. Ebony and the new tenor were waiting in the lounge, and looked at least as rain-soaked as Cassie felt. Ebony said, "This is Gil Corby. Gil, this is Cassie Casey, our star. She's the one you'll be singing with."

They shook hands while Corby stared at Cassie's new bracelet. Afterward, Cassie studied Corby's rain-washed face while he met Zelda and Margaret.

Zelda said, "You'll have to sit in the cargo space, Gil. The whole thing will only take ten minutes. Is that okay?"

"Certainly."

As they were scampering across the tarmac, Margaret gasped, "I'll never understand how these things fly. They haven't got wings."

Zelda overheard her. "Does an apple need wings to fall out of a tree?"

Margaret shook her head.

"Well that's how a flier works. It falls, only it falls up."

Margaret looked more baffled than ever.

"It's what the saleswoman said, and the owner's manual says the same thing. I don't understand it either."

Corby struggled to keep the green golf umbrella he had bought in the airport above Cassie's head. "What makes the apple fall?"

Ebony said, "Gravity."

"Really? What's that?"

Cassie said, "I don't know either, Gil. What is it?"

"It's the name we give the property of warping space possessed by matter. All matter has it, even a feather. It's just that in the case of a feather, the amount it has is very, very small."

"You'd better get in first," Zelda told him. In spite of her hooded raincoat, rain was trickling down her cheeks.

Awkwardly, Corby clambered into the cargo space.

Wondering whether Corby's umbrella and her sopping jacket would hurt the upholstery, Cassie took a seat. "This is smaller than a lot of cars."

"Just a li'l pink bug," Zelda admitted cheerfully, "but I can drive to Mars if I want to."

Ebony, seated in back with Margaret, turned to speak to Corby. "Do you really understand these things?"

He shook his head, and suddenly they were rising through the rain, buoyant as a cork in a thousand feet of water. Margaret shut her eyes.

"We're warping space now," Zelda told Cassie. "If you can't imagine that, here's an easier way to think of it. We're grabbing the space over us and throwing it behind us, and that makes us go—less space ahead, more space behind. Are you a physicist, Gil?"

"Hardly."

Cassie said, "He's an actor and a singer, aren't you, Gil?"

"Correct. But like most of us, I've held a great many odd jobs when I couldn't find work."

Ebony said, "Wait 'til you see him dance, Cassie!"

The rain had vanished while Cassie gawked at the instrument panel. "Are we really at fifty thousand feet? Why haven't my ears popped?"

"I have no idea. Okay, folks. We're up high enough that the hop-bang won't break any windows. Here it comes!"

"I didn't hear a bang," Margaret said. Her eyes were still shut, tightly clamped against a glorious sun that darkened windows and windshield.

Cassie said, "I didn't either, but I think the lights flickered."

"We were gone before the bang." Like Margaret's, Corby's voice came from behind her. "It wasn't loud anyway, because the air was so thin."

Ebony giggled. "You can open your eyes now."

"I'm not opening my eyes," Margaret told her firmly, "until we're down."

Cassie had turned in her seat to stare at Corby. "You remind me of somebody I know. You even look a little like him."

Corby grinned. "Handsome, huh? I'd like to meet him."

"I'll introduce you," Cassie promised, "if you're still around."

His grin widened. "I'll wait. Zelda, do you have a big car?"

Zelda shook her head. "It's not much bigger than this."

"In that case, Cassie and I will take a cab to the studio. We'll meet you there."

"Cassie stays with me. Why don't you and Ebony take the cab?"

Margaret asked, "Are we falling? I think I'm going to be sick."

"Not very fast." Cassie reached back to pat her shoulder. "You won't mind riding with Ebony and Zelda, will you?"

Before Margaret could answer, the pink hopper pitched forward, then seemed almost to correct itself. Below, as Cassie could see more plainly than she liked, rolled a vast sea of pearlescent cloud. Above that sea, thousands of feet below, flew something that might have been a monstrous bat. As she watched, horrified, it dove into the cloud and vanished.

IN the back of the cab, Corby whispered, "Why did you want to talk to me?"

"Who said I did?" Cassie favored him with a sidelong glance. "I wanted to smell your aftershave. If you think I'd rather be in a crowded car with three other women than ride in a cab with a handsome man, you need to get to know me better."

"I'd like to. But you may wish to keep your voice down. The driver can overhear us."

"Naturally. If I have to say something he shouldn't hear, I'll tap your arm in code. One tap for A, two for B, three for C. You know."

Corby took a deep breath. "I do want to talk to you. I want to talk to you more than I can say. Miss Casey, I need this job. You'll get royalties on the recording, and thousands up front. I get five hundred for singing with you. If—"

"That's not fair. I'll speak to Zelda."

He shook his head. "It is fair. I agreed and signed a contract. The thing is that my contract says I must be acceptable to you. If I'm not I won't get paid. I want you—I need you—to understand that."

"All right, I do." Cassie hesitated. "I'll tell you what. If I've got to dump you, I'll give you five hundred myself."

"I won't take it."

Cassie turned to look at him. "I thought you said you were hard up, Gil."

"I am." Something unflinching had crept into Corby's face. "I am, but I won't take charity. I'd sooner steal than accept money you gave me because you pitied me."

"If you say so. By the way, lunch is on me."

His grin returned. "That I'll take—and repay the favor just as soon as I can."

"Right you are. What about steak today?"

"Steak will be just the beginning. Is that bracelet real?"

"I don't know." Cassie made a tiny, helpless gesture. "I want to have a jeweler look at it."

"So you think it might be."

"If I had to bet, I'd give you two to one it is. But not three to one."

"Wallace Rosenquist gave it to you." Corby sounded positive.

"How did you know that?"

"I didn't. I guessed. He's a billionaire, according the newscasters, and a friend of mine who knows him says he's, well, crazy about you. Deeply in love with you, in other words."

"Your friend knows him." Cassie was staring out at the suburban houses that had replaced the farmland nearer the airport.

"Yes, but I don't. I wish I did."

"You move in high-class circles just the same."

Corby laughed; he had a good laugh. "My dear Miss Casey! At this very instant I'm sharing a cab with the most desirable woman on any known planet, and you think I move in exalted circles because I know someone who knows Wallace Rosenquist."

"You know physics, too."

He shook his head.

"You knew about the hopper. How it worked."

"I do not, though I wish I did. It warps space, just as gravity does. Any child could tell you that much. Ask me how it does it, and you'll see me at a loss. Any good physicist could tell you, presumably. I can't."

"Nuclear energy. I think somebody said that."

"Perhaps they did. It may even have been me who said it. Warping space and nuclear energy are just words, and anyone can say them. An astro-explorer named Chuck Finney discovered that Woldercan was home to an intelligent race. I can say that quite easily. Finding another planet with an intelligent native race would be rather more difficult. Wouldn't you agree?"

Cassie smiled. "Here's a bunch more questions. Could Zelda really go to Mars in her hopper?"

"That's one I can answer easily. Yes."

"Could she get out and walk around when she got there? Throw rocks? All that stuff?"

"If she had an air helmet, yes. She'd need the helmet because the Martian atmosphere is still too thin to support human life. They're working on that."

"One time I saw a diagram of a hopper, Gil. It had a big airlock, and the caption said how it worked. Zelda's little hopper doesn't have an airlock."

"Actually it does, because those little hoppers are all airlock. When Zelda was suited up, she'd tell the onboard computer. A compressor would suck up most of the air in the cabin and store it. When it had finished, she could open the hatch and step outside. When she came back in—reassemble in reverse order, as the manuals say. She would shut the hatch, release the stored air, and take off her helmet. Clear?"

"Perfect. Next question. You said that like most of us you'd worked at all kinds of jobs when you couldn't get a part. What were they?"

"Oh, Lord!" Corby shook his head in dismay. "It would take me an hour to go through them all. Have you ever been a waitress?"

Cassie nodded.

"Good tips, I bet. Well, I've been a waiter. I've been working at a little diner down the street from your theater. That's my most recent job."

"Well, by golly. . . ."

"What is it?"

"India was talking about getting somebody new to play the mate, and the man who was bringing our food said that there had been somebody in there earlier who might fill the bill. I thought he meant a customer."

"I was in there earlier," Corby said. "Mitch—that's his name—relieved me. When you had gone, he phoned and told me about it."

"India wanted him to send you over."

Corby nodded. "Mitch told me that, too."

"All right, besides a waiter. What else?"

"City planner. Teacher and substitute teacher—"

"Ah ha!"

"It pays well and I like working with students, but the bureaucracy and paperwork drive you insane. To say nothing of having a camcorder looking over your shoulder every minute."

The cab braked hard as Corby spoke, and the driver growled, "Trouble!" Then, *"No es cierto!"*

He swerved down a side street, but not before Cassie had glimpsed Zelda's old, familiar sedan. Zelda, Ebony, and Margaret were standing behind it, surrounded by four men.

One of the men held a submachine gun.

Cassie fumbled in her purse for her cell phone, only half aware that Corby was shouting for the driver to stop.

FOURTEEN

ASK OUR FRIEND

"I've been questioned already," Cassie told the detective. "Questioned by you and by that ugly man with the cigar. I've got to get back to Springfield—"

The detective (his name was Ed Quintin) raised a hand. "I know, ma'am. One more, and I don't think it will take long."

"Where's Mr. Corby?"

"He's been released. The lieutenant you're going to see now finished questioning him and let him go. From what he said as he went out, he's probably trying to get you a lawyer. Satisfied?"

Cassie nodded and rose. They went down a gloomy and rather old-fashioned hall to an elevator and up one floor. "No interrogation room this time," the detective told her. "You're going to his office."

It was a corner office with four windows. Its chief furnishings included a large modern desk faced by a small chair, and file cabinets whose tops were heaped with what were, presumably, souvenirs.

The big man behind the desk stood and offered his hand. A slight twitch at one corner of his mouth might have been a suppressed smile. "Pleased to see you again, Miss Casey. I'm Detective Lieutenant Aaberg, but you can call me Scott if you're more comfortable that way."

"Oh! Oh, my golly!" Cassie sank into the chair facing his desk. "Why didn't I see this coming?"

Aaberg laughed, a laugh as deep and rasping as his voice. "I ask the questions in this room, Miss Casey, and it's a good thing I do. I couldn't answer that one."

She filled her lungs, determined to look and sound like a woman of great courage. "Suppose I ask you one I know you can answer, Lieutenant? Suppose I say—and yes, I'm saying it—that if you'll answer I'll cooperate in every possible way. But if you won't I'll tell you to go to blazes."

"Margaret Briggs was your employee? You liked her?"

Cassie shook her head. "I'm not answering questions."

"Suppose your stubborn refusal to cooperate costs her life?" Aaberg grinned. "You don't have to answer that one."

"I don't have to answer anything. I can demand a lawyer, and tell you to take a hike until I get one. But I'll say this. I've told every last thing I know to two officers already. I don't think they listened to most of my answers, and I don't think you will either. Want to hear my question?"

He nodded.

"Three or four months ago, while I was still in my apartment, I spotted a man across the street who seemed to be watching my building. When he lit a cigarette, I could see his face—your face. What were you up to?"

"You'll cooperate if I give you a full, honest answer to that?"

Cassie nodded.

"Then I will. I don't think we're being overheard, but I'm going to try to do it without telling anybody who might be listening more than they ought to know. One time a friend of ours asked me to pick you up at an ice cream parlor and drive you to the place where he'd parked his car. I won't ask whether you remember that. I know you do."

Reluctantly, Cassie nodded.

"He was worried about you, and after he told me why he was worried, so was I. I assigned a couple of men to look after you, and I joined them myself whenever I could, and stayed around as long as I could, too. Nothing happened, so eventually I took my men off. Mind if I smoke?"

"Mind if I cough?"

"Not at all." Aaberg's lighter flared; he inhaled, and blew smoke to one side. "Have I answered?"

"Not quite. Are you working for our friend?"

"Getting paid, you mean?" Aaberg shook his head. "The city pays me. Our friend helps me out sometimes, and I repay him whenever I can. There's a lot of that in my business."

"I understand." Cassie hesitated. "All right. Yes, Margaret works for me. She's my dresser. Yes, I like her a lot. I'd be turning the whole city upside down to look for her right now, if I could. You could, but you're not doing it."

"We are, but we're keeping it as quiet as we can. If they're still here— which I doubt—we don't want them to know how hard we're looking for them."

"You don't think she's here? Why not?"

"That's not very interesting, even to me. What I want to know is whether you've got a good reason to think I'm wrong. Do you?"

"I guess not."

"I wish you did. It might be helpful. Make up one."

"Are you kidding?"

Aaberg shook his head. "You saw them and I didn't. You know Mrs. Briggs. I don't. Let's hear you make some sort of reason up."

"I suppose it would have to be because of something she could do here that she couldn't do anyplace else."

"That sounds good. Keep going."

"She's been a dresser for years and years, and she lives here. She knows the theaters here, and knows a lot of theatrical people. She's bound to."

"Right. Go on."

"I can't. I can't even imagine what they're trying to do."

One of the three telephones on the large, modern desk rang. Aaberg picked it up, listened for a moment, and said, "That's right, sir. Yes, she is." After listening again he added, "I will," and hung up.

Turning back to Cassie, he smiled. "That was the mayor. He's afraid I'm planning to take you down to the basement and beat a confession out of you."

"But you're not?"

"Of course not. If you mean literally, we never do that. If you mean fig-uratively, we're certainly not going to try sweating a confession out of you. A confession to what?"

Cassie shrugged. "I've noticed you guys can always find something."

"I suppose that's right. But believe me, we can't always make it stick. Let's start back at Springfield. You were in a show there last night?"

She nodded.

"How did you get here?"

"In Zelda's hopper. Zelda's my agent, and she just got one. It's little, but all five of us managed to get into it."

"Name the other four, please."

"I've answered all this."

"Sure. But it will take us a lot longer to argue about it than it will for you to answer. You promised to cooperate, remember?"

"I did, and I will. I'm just sorry I've got to cooperate with an idiot."

"Okay, here's one you haven't been asked. Who else is in your show? An actress, if there is another one."

"There is. Norma Peiper."

"Suppose you and Norma read the same line. Would you sound alike?"

"No. Not even if we tried to."

"Sweet. I want to hear you say the names, Miss Casey, not read them on my screen. I need to see your face as you hear my questions, and I need to watch you as you answer them."

"I'm an actress. I could screw you up."

"But you won't. Not if you want your employee back alive."

"All right, you've got me. Zelda drove. Or flew the hopper. Whatever you call it."

Aaberg nodded. "Zelda's last name is . . . ?"

"Youmans. I sat beside her in the shotgun seat. Ebony White sat in back of her. Ebony's our assistant director."

"Keep going."

"Margaret sat behind me. Margaret Briggs. She's my dresser. Have I said that?"

"We'll get back to her. Go on."

"Would it be all right if I opened my purse and got out my hankie? I'd like to tie it in knots while I talk. It might relieve my feelings."

Aaberg grinned. "Got a gun in there?"

"No, I don't. Honest Injun."

"Then go ahead. I like to watch your bracelet move, anyway."

"Gee. I thought it was me."

He nodded, although it was not clear to what he was agreeing. "Go on."

"Gil Corby sat in the luggage space behind the backseat."

"Tell me about Corby."

"He's a tenor. That's what Ebony says. He was supposed to sing the duets with me when we recorded."

"What else?"

"Nothing else. I'd never seen him until today. India picked him to sing with me, so I assume he's pretty good."

Aaberg grunted. "I should have made him sing while I had him in here. I fell down on that. Maybe later. You'd never seen him until today?"

"Right."

"But you—never mind, I'm getting ahead of myself. Zelda's hopper landed here, at the airport."

Cassie nodded.

"Couldn't she have landed on top of the building that houses Sy-More Studios?"

"What?" Her eyebrows rose. "Can they do that?"

"I'm asking the questions. Could she?"

"I don't know. I never even thought of it."

"I see." Aaberg leaned back, his fingers forming a steeple. "For your information, Miss Casey, a hopper can land just about anywhere. They don't do it because it's against the law. The law says they've got to land at airports. That's because there can be midair collisions with other hoppers. With planes, too. For safety's sake, the law wants them to land and take off where they'll be under air-traffic controllers."

"Makes sense."

"Criminals don't obey the law. If the men who took Margaret Briggs had a hopper, they wouldn't have to take her to the airport, and they could be anywhere by now."

"I see. I didn't realize it was so—hopeless."

"I don't think it is. Just tough. Where were you the first time you saw Corby?"

"In the airport lounge. That was where we met. Gil and Ebony came separately, I don't know how but probably in a cab. Margaret and I rode out with Zelda. She had a rented car. Avis? I think that was it."

"Sweet. You said he had to ride in back."

Cassie nodded.

"Did he argue about it? Object?"

"No. He's not a big man, of course, so it was pretty easy for him. You've seen him. He's not nearly as big as you are."

"You like him?"

"Are you asking if I'm in love with him? No."

"I meant nothing more than what I said. Would you say he's likable?"

"Yes, very much so. He's nice-looking, friendly, and polite. Knowledge-able, too."

"Knowledgeable about what?"

"Hoppers, actually. I didn't know a thing about them. Zelda's the first person I've ever known who owned one. He explained a lot of stuff to me."

"The first person you've known who owned one? You're sure of that?"

"Why . . . ?" For a second Cassie froze, her mouth open. "No. You're right. I don't know this man very well, but I'm sure he must own one. Maybe several."

Aaberg grunted. "What's his name?"

"Wallace Rosenquist. He's backing our show."

"So I've heard. Read, too. You don't know him well?"

Cassie shook her head. "I've dated him a few times. I've accepted gifts from him. But that's all."

"I'm going to ask you a very frank question." Aaberg paused to clear his throat. "Before I do I want to remind you that you promised to cooperate fully."

"You're right, I did. Besides, I've been asked a bunch of rude questions."

"I suppose you have. Try to understand that I've got a good reason for asking it. Have you ever gotten into bed with Rosenquist?"

"This is the bracelet, isn't it?" Cassie raised her arm and watched it sparkle in the light streaming through Aaberg's windows. "All right, I can see how you might think that. No, I've never had sex with Wally."

"Would you?"

"I don't understand how this can help you find Margaret."

"It may not. Are you going to answer?"

"I can't. Not really. But probably not."

"It isn't out of the question?"

Cassie took in air. "I'm going to tell you more than you want to know. It won't help you, but it may help me."

"Shoot."

"He's older than I am, he's kind of fat, and he's big. I told you once that you look like my ex, Scott. Scott was big, and I've had it with big men. Wally's bossy, too—the in-charge guy. But . . ."

"Go on." Aaberg had leaned back in his chair. "I'm interested."

"People say money's an aphrodisiac, and maybe they're right. Wally's been very successful. Everybody says so. He's a tough businessman, but that's not such a bad thing. Scott was an awful businessman—so bad that even I could see he was simply awful, and I don't know anything about business."

"And . . . ?"

"Wally's strong, really strong. We're not supposed to like strong men, but we do. Or most of us do. I do. I know too many wimps already. Wally says he loves me, and he means it. I can tell. It's hard not to like somebody who loves you."

Aaberg nodded. "It is. You see, Miss Casey, I'm trying to find out why these men wanted Margaret Briggs. You saw them. How many were there?"

"Four, I think. It could've been three, but I think four. Of course one could have been out of sight."

"How were they dressed?"

Cassie paused to think. "One had on a suit, I think it was a birch suit with those black stripes. I don't know about the rest."

"Might you recognize them if you saw them again?"

She shook her head.

"Not would you. Might you."

"No. I barely saw them. I don't know how long it was, but it couldn't have been more than half a second. Probably less."

"I've got it. Corby said pretty much the same thing."

"Another detective—I've forgotten her name—told me Zelda and Ebony were all right. She said you had them and they hadn't been hurt."

Aaberg glanced at his cigarette and ground it out. "I wasn't going to get into this now, but I will."

Another telephone rang. He listened for perhaps two minutes, then said, "Tell them to go to hell. She's not under arrest, and she's not going to be. She's cooperating voluntarily, and I'm going to send her back to Springfield in ten or fifteen minutes." He hung up.

"That was about me, wasn't it?"

He nodded. "Corby's back with a lawyer. They seem to think we've got you in a cell."

"You said you weren't going to do that."

"I'm not. I'm going to explain a few things, ask a few more questions, and let you go. You may not think you can trust me, Miss Casey, but you can."

"That's nice."

"About Miss Youmans and Miss White. You're right—they got a good look at those four men. They talked to them and heard their voices. I told them I was going to put them in protective custody unless they promised to stay in town and agree to bodyguards for as long as I felt it was necessary. Youmans agreed. She's been released with a policewoman to look after her. White won't agree, so we've got her in custody."

"But not me?"

"No, Miss Casey. Not you. I'm sending you and Corby back to Springfield." Aaberg paused to get out a fresh cigarette. "Corby bothers me. Why were you in that cab with him? Why not Youmans's car?"

"Zelda must have told you."

"I want to hear you tell me."

"All right. It was going to be jammed with all of us in it, and Gil said he and I would take a cab. I see what you mean. It looks like he knew what was coming. I don't believe that, but that's how it looks."

Aaberg nodded as he flicked his lighter. "It does. It looks like he was tipped. He says he wasn't."

"I believe him."

"What did they want, Miss Casey? We know what they got. They got a sixty-year-old woman nobody ever heard of. A woman with just enough money to feed herself and rent a hall bedroom. I can't believe that's what they were after, so what were they?"

"You're the detective."

"Right, and I've been thinking a lot about this one. What was it? I've got two answers, and it seems to me it has to be one of the two. They were after your bracelet or they were after you. It's real?"

"I don't know," Cassie said. "I think so. . . ."

"So do I. I've been looking at it every time you hold your arm so I can see it. After the third look—"

"Yes?"

"It wasn't important. You thought of something just now. What was it?"

"Am I that transparent, Scott?"

Aaberg grinned. "Not to most people, Bubbles."

"He called me Cassie."

"Fine. So will I. What was it?"

"I told you Wally gave me this. Well, he'd given me another bracelet earlier. A big gold bracelet. I wasn't sure I wanted to keep it, so I gave it to Margaret. Gave it to her to take care of, I mean. To hold for me."

"So they might have thought Margaret had the one you're wearing?"

"Yes . . . yes, that could be it."

"I'll keep it in mind. Would she know where you kept it when you weren't wearing it?"

Cassie shook her head. "I hadn't decided—wait, she would, sort of. Last night I put it in the little safe in my hotel room."

"And she knew that?"

"Yes, she . . . Yes, she did."

"Sweet. The other possibility is that they were after you. You think Rosenquist loves you, and maybe he does. What's for damned sure is you're the star of a show he's backing. Would he pay to get you back? Hell, yes! This Margaret who works for you could tell them a lot about you, things they'd like to know. You weren't in the car, so why not take her?"

Aaberg rose. "You live here, so you must bank here. You and I are going to your bank. You're going to rent a box in the vault and put that damned bracelet in it while I watch, understand? They'll give you a retinal scan and two keys. After that, a police hopper will take you and Corby back to Springfield."

"WHERE'S Dean?" Cassie asked.

"Dean's history." India looked as though she might kill Dean and eat him afterward. "He found out I was thinking of replacing him and quit, effective immediately. I said what about the show tonight, and he slammed down the phone. So history. He'll never work for me again."

"We're canceling?"

"Hell, no! We're going to do the show with Gil here as the mate."

"What about the one-legged guy?"

"Gil *is* the one-legged guy. Didn't he tell you?"

"It's a prosthesis, Cassie. They have wonderful prosthetic limbs, and I'm wearing one."

Cassie reached down to touch his leg.

"Not there. Below the knee. The doctors were able to save my knee. Of course I'll wear the wooden leg Mitch and I made onstage."

Nodding mostly to herself, Cassie glanced at her watch. "Have we got time to go over the big dance number?"

"Just barely," India said. "I'll get Pfeiffer while Gil's changing legs."

There had been time for the most difficult passages and nothing more, yet her trepidation vanished as soon as Corby took her in his arms and they glided toward center stage.

"Ever waltzed with a cripple before, Mariah?"

"I've never waltzed with anyone," she told him, "and I'm not waltzing now, Mr. Sharpy. I'm just walking in time to music."

"What music?"

"The wind and the waves. You know. These lovely trees, the birds in them, and the sand beneath my feet. The moon."

Their spotlight took a bluish cast.

"I thought the moon was in charge of lighting."

"She sings her way through the sky." They whirled, and Mariah spun alone across the stage, followed by the blue spot.

Sharpy pursued her in a series of leaps, at once incredible and clearly painful. When he held her again, she whispered, "Wally's in the audience."

WHEN she had taken her last bow and accepted a huge bouquet of orchids, India was waiting in her dressing room. "You were terrific, both of you."

"Were we?"

"Yeah. You're always terrific, and Gil's a big improvement. Got a vase for those?"

Cassie shook her head.

"I'll send somebody. Dammit, I miss Ebony."

Cassie nodded.

"Don't cry! Why'd I have to shoot my mouth off? You miss Margaret. I've got it. Oh, Cassie! Cassie!"

Suddenly the orchids were on the floor, and India (bigger than most men but far less rough) was hugging her. "It'll be okay. You'll see. Don't cry, baby!"

"I'm sorry. . . ." There was a box of tissues on her dressing table. When India released her she got it, and sat in the black-wire chair in front of the mirror mopping tears.

"Hey, I've got big news. That's why I'm here. We're going home."

The telephone rang, and when Cassie did not pick it up, India did. After two soft blowings of Cassie's nose, India covered the speaker. "Some doctor. You want to talk to him?"

Cassie nodded, and the phone changed hands.

"Miss Casey? This is Dr. Chase."

"Gid? Oh, my God! It's so good to hear from you. How are you?"

"Fit as a new fender. You don't have to worry about me. You must be worried about Mrs. Briggs, though."

"Oh, yes! Have you—did you . . . ?"

"I haven't spoken to her, if that's what you mean. Or seen her, either. But I know who has her, and I know she's all right. She'll be released in a few days."

"They'll let her go? That's wonderful!"

"It is. This phone is being monitored, by the way, so both of us have to be careful not to say too much. The one in your hotel room, too."

"Is it . . . our friend?"

"No. The people who've got Margaret. By the way, you've probably forgotten, but once I told you our friend had someone watching me. I've found out who it was."

"So have I, or I think I have."

"Really? Eventually we can compare notes, but not on this line. What I want to say now, before I forget, is that you'd better not go outside late at night for a while. If you have to, take somebody with you. Two people, if you can."

Cassie felt a thrill of fear. "You mean they might take me, too?"

"No, this is something else—some things else. I don't want you to see them. Just your seeing them would be bad, and it might even be the worst part. Don't leave your windows open."

"In the hotel? They don't open. Tell me!"

"Face-to-face, later. Now here's the big one. You haven't forgotten you're in for a cut of the money? One hundred thousand, minus the twenty thousand I've given you already."

"I remember." A slight sound made Cassie look behind her. A stagehand was picking up the orchids and putting them, one by one, into a blue vase encircled by sinuous yellow dragons. An envelope lay among them. She tapped his shoulder, pointed, and held out her hand.

". . . the big one. The reason I called. Our friend is going to ask you to go somewhere with him. This could be it, our best chance to wrap this up. Will you go, Cassie?"

"I don't know." She accepted the envelope and laid it on her dressing table.

"You've taken some major risks already. You may not know it, but you have. This will be no worse. Will you? Please?"

She kept her voice down. "I'm going to have to know more, and I can't even ask you questions. There are people in here."

"Ask our friend," the voice from the other end of the line advised her, and hung up.

FIFTEEN

DEATH AND DEATH'S
VISITORS

"What was all that about?" India inquired when the stagehand had gone.

"A man I know has heard rumors about Wally. He wanted to know if I'd heard anything. I said I hadn't."

"You said you couldn't ask him questions. I remember that."

"About what he'd told me. He said this was what he knew and he didn't have time for questions. Then he began quizzing me."

"What was this about somebody taking you, too?" The chair squealed a soft complaint as India leaned forward.

"Wally. He'd heard that Wally and some of his people—I suppose a secretary and maybe his lawyer, people like that—that Wally and these staff people were going on a big trip, out of the country. He thought maybe Wally would want me along."

"Wow!"

"Right. I'd be paying for the bracelet, I guess. Did I show it to you?"

India shook her head. "You didn't, but I saw it. I was there when he gave it to you."

Cassie let the misunderstanding pass. "Anyway, I don't know. That's what I told the doctor on the phone, and that's the truth." She hesitated, seeking to measure her own courage. "I—I'm no virgin."

"I never thought you were."

"Not for a long, long time. But I'm not a whore, either. . . ." She fell silent.

"Penny for thoughts?"

Cassie heaved a sigh. "I was just thinking that I've slept with some awful losers, and it might be nice to sleep with a winner for a change."

"That's the spirit! Your friends will be counting on you."

"Yes, there's that." Cassie smiled. "I won't forget you. What's your news? You said you had big news. We're going home?"

"Bet your ass! Everybody knows that Wally's got a major hit here, and that includes Wally. So we're getting new costumes, bigger and better scenery, and a bigger cast. It's too late to take *Volcano* to Broadway this season, so we're going home to work the kinks out of the new stuff at the Tiara."

"That's good."

"You bet it is. It's wonderful, and don't you forget it. The ship gets ten more sailors, and Tiny gets twenty more natives. Fifteen girls and five boys. The whole damned show gets a humongous ad campaign featuring you. I figure a couple months to audition new people and rehearse. The new sets could make that three. Then we play the Tiara for the rest of the season." India licked her lips. "We ought to be able to open a week or two before Christmas. There's nothing like Christmas."

Cassie, who had only half heard her, nodded. "I've been worrying about Margaret's apartment. What if she has a cat?"

"She'd have gotten somebody to take care of it, that's all."

"I hope so, somebody to come in and feed the cat, clean the cat box, and water the plants. But sometimes people don't."

"Margaret isn't people. I've seen enough of her to know she'd have done it. Aren't you going to open that envelope?" India pointed.

"Not 'til you're gone."

"It's probably from Wally."

"I'm sure it is." Largely to herself, Cassie nodded. "It's probably just personal, though. If it says anything you ought to know about, I'll tell you."

"Got it." India grunted and stood up, a moderately lengthy operation. After a final curious glance at the envelope, she went out.

Cassie herself rose as soon as she was gone, and bolted the door.

My Darling, do you know how much I love you? You will close in Springfield in two days. In three you will be the Queen of Paradise. I will send a friend to you. Three times he will use a word to remind you of me. Go with him. He will take you to me and I will bring you to Paradise, where you will see how much I love you.

W.R.

Cassie laid the note aside, wishing desperately that she had someone to talk to. Margaret was gone, only God knew where. Gid was gone as well. Much of what Gid said might be rubbish, but . . .

Should she burn it? She had no matches, and might set fire to the theater if she tried. She picked the note up again.

Do you know how much I love you?

Someone was rapping on her door. Cassie called out, and a familiar voice answered, "It's me, Norma. Want to split a cab back to the hotel?"

"Just a minute." She opened the door. "I haven't changed yet, but . . . but I hope you'll wait. I'll be as fast as I can."

"I'll help."

The help included holding Cassie's navy-blue wool coat while she slipped into it. "Cold out there, Norma?"

"It's bound to be, this late. The rain's stopped, though. I looked out the window."

"So did I, but I didn't even notice the rain. I've got a problem. A big one so complicated I don't even know if I can tell you about it. Make it clear, you know? It's not clear to me."

"Let's hear it."

"Just like that?" Cassie realized that she was miss-buttoning her coat and started over. "I thought maybe you had something."

"I do, Cassie, but you first." Norma smiled, warm and friendly. "You're our star."

"All right." Had she worn her beret? She glanced around and decided she had not. "Let's start with this. Wally scares me."

Norma nodded. "Me, too. He scares everybody."

"Can you love a man who scares you? I feel as if I shouldn't be able to do that, but . . ."

"You like him."

"You're right." Cassie sighed. "I do. He's a stand-up, no buckshot guy. That's how he seems to me. Is it all right if I say *buckshot?* Everybody else says *bullshit*."

The smile became a grin. "They talk it, too. Sure. Say whatever you feel like saying."

"He wants me to go someplace with him. He's promising a lot, but it sounds crazy."

"Go where?"

"That's it. Or part of it. I don't know."

"Some terrible place, right? Death Valley in the summer."

"Please don't make jokes. He says it's paradise."

"That means a resort. Great weather, surfing, maybe scuba diving. You know. Great food and a spa. You're not married, are you, Cassie?"

"Not now. Divorced."

"Me, too. I used to be married to the volcano god. Did you know?"

"Vince? I'm ready to go if you are." Cassie gestured toward the door. "That must have been weird."

"We were both younger then. It wasn't too bad. After a couple of years I explained that what he really wanted wasn't a wife, it was a servant who screwed. We split, and there were no hard feelings."

For a moment, Cassie gnawed her lower lip. "Are you sorry now?"

"Sometimes." Norma finished buttoning her own coat; it was black wool and a little longer than Cassie's. "But not mostly."

The theater was silent, the audience gone. Where it had been, the ushers would be cleaning up—collecting programs, and the plastic cups in which the cash bar served drinks between the acts.

"I'm sorry about Herbie, sometimes. Never about dumping Scott."

"What's that, Cassie? I didn't quite catch it."

A dancer trotted past without a word, hurrying home, perhaps, or hurrying off to the Pink Lemonade Stand for a drink with the boys.

"I said Wally took me to dinner at Rusterman's one time. Did I ever tell you about that?"

Norma shook her head.

"I met him there. He said he'd been hoping to take me himself, but he couldn't make it. He'd be there as soon as he could."

"Sounds bad."

"I don't know." Cassie stopped, held where she was by her own feelings. "He'd made a reservation, and they took me to the table and treated me like the Queen of Sheba. Then my doorman phoned. My place had been broken into and the police were on the way."

"Are you saying it was him? Mr. Rosenquist?"

Cassie nodded. "This is confidential. Please. If you let it out you might ruin us."

"Right. I understand."

"I know it was him. He told me when he joined me at Rusterman's."

"He admitted it?"

"He did. He has enemies, and he felt he had to check up on me. He didn't take anything. So I thought of the show, and you and me and India and everybody. And I smiled and said, fine now you know you can trust me."

"Good for you!"

"We sparred around a little. No, we sparred around a lot, and when dinner was over we got up and I took his arm—you know how you do—and we walked out of our private room and through the restaurant. And I was holding on to this big important man, almost a foot taller than I am, in a thousand-dollar suit. Everybody looked, and everybody was impressed. I'd been drinking wine with dinner, but that was better than any wine I ever drank. This wasn't just some handsome twit. I've had three or four of those. This was a—I don't know."

"The alpha male," Norma supplied.

"Right. A Man with a capital M. He told me after how proud he was because every man who saw us wanted to be him. I've never told him I felt prouder than he did."

The security guard touched his cap and opened the stage door.

"He's an alpha male," Cassie continued, "like you say, if that means what I think it does. He can be hurt, just the same. I could hurt him at least as easily as he could hurt me. As tough as he is and as smart as he is, he's terribly vulnerable. Oh, darn it, Norma, I like him! I do, and I can't help myself. I don't want to hurt him. Should I go with him? Go with him to his crazy paradise? Tell me."

Norma nodded. "I would. I heard about the bracelet."

Cassie breathed deeply, drawing in the cold, stale air of the alley. "Somebody I trust told me once that he was—was . . . Well, never mind."

"Bad, huh? That bracelet didn't sound bad."

Cassie nodded. "It's devastating, really, and then there's the kidnapping. You must have heard from Gil. Zelda and Ebony are still back home, and Margaret—Margaret . . ." She felt she was choking, and paused to push aside an empty beer can. "Another darned old alley!"

Norma gestured. "Come on, if we hike up to Fifth Street—"

"I know."

"Well, sure. Listen, Cassie, we will be getting a whole bunch of new people. It's not just Gil for Dean Heeny."

Wearily, she nodded. There were few pedestrians at this time of night; the street, which had been glutted with traffic an hour ago, was almost deserted as well. A black-and-white police cruiser glided past and was gone.

"You're solid, naturally. My guess is that Vince and Gil are solid, too. Probably Tiny. The rest of us are on the bubble, and I was hoping—"

That was as far as Norma got before the bullet doubled her over.

HOURS later, back in her room with the door locked and the hotel operator under strict orders to block incoming calls, Cassie reflected that *hoping* had been the last word Norma (who had spoken so many lines flawlessly) had ever said. Had Norma heard the sound of the shot? Could she have guessed, before the shot . . . ?

No. Norma had bent forward, her knees buckling, and the sound had come after that, as if the intention to kill had killed.

POLICEWOMAN: "What do you know about rifles, Miss Casey?"

Cassie: "Nothing really. I shot a twenty-two one time."

Policewoman: "I'm glad you're feeling better now."

SIGHING, Cassie unlocked her next-to-largest suitcase and took out the small pistol she sometimes strapped to her thigh. There was nothing reassuring about it tonight; she returned it to the suitcase and turned the key in the lock.

Dialing Zelda got a recorded voice: "You have reached the Youmans

Theatrical Agency. Our staff is otherwise engaged. Please leave a message at the tone, and we'll get back to you as soon—"

Cassie was cradling the hotel telephone when her cell phone played "Pigs in Paradise." Wearily, she pressed the incomprehensible symbol that let her answer. "Hello."

"Cassie? This's Sharon. There must be a couple dozen reporters trying to get hold of you. Have you talked to any of them?"

"No. I don't want to."

"Will you talk to me? Please? We've been friends for years. An exclusive? Please?"

"I have to talk to somebody." Cassie sighed, and felt the sigh turn into a sob. "I'll talk, if you don't ask me questions."

"Fine! I won't. Girl Scout's honor."

"When I got back here, I called the hotel operator and asked her to block calls. She said she would. After that I cried. After that I took a shower and cried some more. I know you don't want to hear all this, but I've got to say it to somebody."

"I do want to hear it. Trust me, Cassie. I really do. Go on."

"After that I thought, 'Thank God! I don't have to talk to anybody.' Only as soon as I thought it, I knew I wanted to talk to somebody."

"I'm here for you, Cassie. I'm listening."

"So I tried to talk to God, but I got his answering machine. You know what I mean?"

"Sure. Go on."

"Gid says there's no good and no evil, and it took me a long time to understand what he meant by it. Mariah believes in God. That's who I am in the show—Mariah."

"I've got it."

"Mariah believes in God, but we don't. Add nothing to God and you get good. Does it make sense to you, Sharon?"

"It does to you, and that's what's important."

"Wally isn't here. He's supposed to be, but he isn't. I thought of talking to him, even if he was in South Africa or someplace. I tried and tried, but I couldn't find him. It was like everybody in the world that I know had died with Norma."

"That must have been awful."

"I couldn't think of anybody else. My mom's dead, and my father wouldn't care. Somebody stole Margaret and there didn't seem to be anybody left for me. I thought of Gid, but I don't have any way to get hold of him. His phone's turned off and I don't know where he is. So I thought of Gil Corby. He wasn't in the theater and he wasn't at the diner where he used to work. I tried to call India, but she didn't answer."

"She's probably talking to the police. I don't know who Gil Corby is, but I'll help you get hold of him if I can."

"He plays Mr. Sharpy. I don't know him, but I like him. Can you like somebody you don't know?"

"Sure. I'll try to find him for you."

"Then I cried again, and after that I tried to talk to Zelda. I got her answering machine, too."

"You've got me," Sharon said. "I'm right here."

"Yes." Cassie swallowed. "Norma's dead. Do you know about that?"

"I heard. Norma Peiper."

"She was my Aunt Jane in the show, and she was walking next to me when they sh-sh-shot—Excuse me."

When Cassie picked up the cell phone again, she said, "I had to go into the bathroom to get—it doesn't matter. My nose was running. It still is."

Sharon said, "No problem."

"Thanks. I remember the shot. How it sounded when it hit her and the bang right after that. I was beside her on the wet sidewalk, on my knees yelling and yelling. After that I was in a police car and Norma was gone. The woman said I was hysterical and I wanted to say I wasn't, but I couldn't stop crying. I . . ."

"Sniveling. Isn't that what you call this? What I'm doing now? I'm sniveling. You'd probably like to kick me for it and I don't blame you, but I feel all hollow inside. No grit, no grit at all. I'm terribly, horribly scared."

"Anybody would be, and I'd like to hug you. I wish I could."

"A rifle can kill somebody three hundred yards away. Did you know that? A woman told me. A cop. They think he was on the roof of a building almost three hundred yards away, with a digital scope on his rifle. He shot her the way you'd shoot something on vid, and she was dead, and he went down in an elevator and out to the street. Wouldn't people see his gun, Sharon?"

"He didn't leave it behind?"

"I don't think so. They said they found an empty case—that's the brass part that holds the gunpowder. She explained it to me, and—" Cassie thought of her own gun, the silver-tipped bullets she could count through the clear window in its neat plastic magazine, and the brass cases that contained them.

Those brass cases were tarnished again, although she had taken them out and polished them once. Aloud she said, "Oh, never mind."

"Then he hid it some way." Sharon sounded confident. "He might have put in one of those long cardboard boxes, for instance."

"Norma was from Maine. She'd grown up there, I mean. Some little town in Maine. She could do the accent, too. I talked to her a few times, and I wish we'd talked a lot more. She took me out to lunch before we left town, but I never took her back and now I feel terrible about it. She was from Maine and she did stand-up comedy in clubs when she couldn't get a real part, stand-up comedy with drunks yelling and trying to ruin her act. And that's everything I can remember about her, every last bit. One more thing—India thought she smiled too much, and I r-remember th-th-that."

Sharon said, "Don't start crying again."

"I w-wish I could. Crying would make me feel better. Norma died for me. She died in my place. I know it, and it's tearing me up inside. Someone paid that man with the rifle. We were walking side by side, two women about the same size, and he shot the r-r-wrong w-w-one."

"Who'd want to kill you, Cassie?"

SHE had said, "Nobody! Nobody at all," but now, as she prepared for bed, she wondered whether that answer had been the right one. Bill Reis was a murderer and Wally Rosenquist was Bill Reis. But her? Did you give diamond bracelets to women you meant to murder?

Someone had tried to murder Gideon Chase, and she was working for him, supposedly. And for Wally, who was really Bill.

Did the police kill people? That lieutenant—she could not recall his name—had seemed capable of any number of murders.

Berg? It had been something like that. . . .

SHE was sitting in a hard wooden chair with a writing arm. Before her, the teacher rapped her desk with a ruler. The teacher was frowning, her frown was deeply disturbing, and the tapping never ended.

SHE sat up in bed. There had been gray light through the scrim when she had switched off the bedside lamp, the mixed contributions of headlights and taillights, of ugly yellow streetlights and many-colored electric signs. Her window was dark now, night-black glass behind the scrim, night solidified.

On which someone or something tapped.

Throwing aside sheet and blanket, she stood up. The tapping continued.

"Who's there?"

There was no answer.

"What do you want?"

There was only the tapping. Step by step she made her way across the dark room to the window and pushed aside the scrim.

They might have been vultures, if vultures stood taller than men and possessed towering pale helmets with elongated visors like caricatures of human faces.

She screamed. One of the tall figures gestured and she screamed again.

Her suitcase was locked and she had forgotten where she put her keys.

The door opened an inch or two—and stubbornly refused to open farther.

Dumping her purse on the floor revealed jangling keys. Suddenly compliant, her suitcase flew open. She crouched beside it trembling, gun in hand.

SIXTEEN

NORMA AVENGED

Knocking awakened Cassie. It was cadenced and polite, yet firm, the resolute knocking of someone who assumed she was asleep and had not the least intention of leaving until she woke. Yawning, she sat up, threw back the blanket and sheet, and stumbled over to the peephole in the door.

Seeing a familiar face, she threw it open. "Ebony!"

They hugged.

"Come in! I was still in bed. What time is it? Ten fifteen? Well, no wonder! My call's for eleven."

"I'm sorry." Ebony looked contrite. "Oh, God! It sounded like such a mess. I thought I might help."

"I would have gotten up at seven to see you," Cassie announced firmly. "Six! Five forty-five, but no earlier than that. When'd you get out?"

"This morning. I guess it was—oh, I don't know! But early. I was in the chow line, and a cop came in and pulled me out. He said I was going to be released, and—listen, Cassie, I'm practically starved. Throw on some clothes and I'll buy you breakfast and tell you all about it. Only then you'll have to tell me, okay?"

Underwear, slacks, and a sweater. A quick trip to the bathroom that included a brief encounter with a toothbrush, shoes, and they were almost out the door. "I warn you," Cassie said, "I haven't had a chance to put on makeup, so I'm going to do it while we wait for—"

The telephone on the nightstand rang, and she stopped to stare at it. "It shouldn't have done that."

"Want me to get it?"

It rang again. Cassie shook her head and picked up the handset. "Hello?"

A familiar voice she could not place said, "Is that you, Cassie?"

"Who's asking?"

"This is Scott. I need to talk to—"

"Hold it right there. Is this the lieutenant?"

"What?"

"Hold on." Cassie covered the speaker. "What's that police lieutenant's name, Ebony? Big guy, seems important, smokes?"

"Lars Aaberg."

"Thanks." Uncovering the speaker, "Is this Lieutenant Aaberg?"

"This is Scott, Cassie! We used to be married."

"Oh. It's you. I thought we were finished. I've got a hungry friend waiting, so I'm cutting this short, Scott. I'm not going to lend you money. Not one dime. I'm not going to invest in anything you've got doodilly squit to do with, either. Clear? Don't call me again."

She put down the handset and gestured urgently to Ebony. "Let's split before he does."

The telephone rang again as she followed Ebony out; she slammed the door, muttered something her mother might not have liked, and hustled Ebony down the corridor to the elevators.

"Mind my asking who that was?"

"My ex, a handsome no-good bum who was my leading man in—oh, never mind!"

Chimes announced an elevator.

"What I want to know is how much he had to slip somebody to get his call through. I told them to block incoming, and they said they would."

They boarded. As the bronzed mechanical doors slid shut, Ebony murmured, "I guess I missed a lot while I was in the slammer."

"You were lucky."

"Norma, you mean. Zelda told me. She said it was all over the news."

Their elevator stopped at the eighth floor. The doors slid open and thus revealed Scott, big, erect, and handsome in a summery bone-white-and-Chablis seersucker suit. As he stepped in, his right eyebrow lifted in a way Cassie found unexpectedly painful. She said, "How the heck did you know I'd be on this one?"

"I didn't."

The elevator doors slid shut behind them, and the elevator resumed its swift descent.

"You said your friend was hungry, so I thought you might be going downstairs to get something. Lunch is on me, but I get to talk to you."

"The heck you do! My blasted phone wasn't supposed to ring. Ever. Nothing but my wake-up call, and I get a call from the one person in the whole world I'd jump out the window not to talk to."

Ebony muttered, "Glad you two parted friends."

"You're half right," Scott told her. "I'll always be Cassie's friend. I'm Scott Zeitz."

"Ebony White." She did not extend her hand.

"It's a pleasure to meet you. Perhaps you can explain to my onetime bride that call blocking blocks only calls from outside. A wake-up call and other in-house calls aren't blocked, as they don't go through the operator. I'm staying in this hotel, so I had no trouble calling."

Grinning, he turned to Cassie. "Another friend of yours was shot yesterday. It was meant as a warning to you. If you'll have lunch with me, I can tell you more about that."

"It's breakfast, and I'm heading straight to the police if you killed Norma."

"Breakfast, then. An early lunch for me. Will you?"

As the doors opened, Ebony said, "The cops don't scare you much."

Scott shook his head. "You're right, they don't. I have a get-out-of-jail card." When neither woman spoke, he added, "I checked in last night. Anybody know where we can get a meal?"

A smiling hostess seemed very happy to see them, and ushered them to a table for four in the middle of an almost empty restaurant. Cassie said, "You serve breakfast 'til noon, right?"

The hostess paused in the distribution of menus to say, "Right, Miss Casey."

Scott watched her hips appreciatively; when she had returned to her station, he turned to Cassie. "They know you here. It must feel good."

"They ought to know me. I woke up half the hotel last night."

"That doesn't sound like you."

"I had a bad dream and screamed, and somebody called the police. Tell me about Norma."

"Your friend who was shot? I never knew her, and I certainly didn't kill her. Let's—"

Ebony said, "But you know who did."

"If I have to speak to that sort of thing, we'll be here all day." Scott waved to a waitress. "I assume you serve club sandwiches. I want a club sandwich, turkey and bacon on lightly toasted white bread. Mayonnaise in a cup on the side."

"A club sandwich?" The waitress got out her order book.

"Listen up, bitch! What did I just say?"

Cassie intervened. "He wants a club sandwich. If he doesn't like it, he can send it back. I'll have the fruit plate and yogurt."

Scott said, "That doesn't sound like you either."

Ebony ordered biscuits and gravy, with a side of sausage and a side of ham.

Cassie asked, "Don't you have frosted flakes and orange juice? I thought I remembered that."

"I've been eating jail food." Ebony sighed. "I've been up since five, and I was waiting in line for their god-awful oatmeal when that cop pulled me out and let me go. Want to hear the rest?"

Cassie shook her head. "I want Scott to tell us who shot Norma. I also want to know whether he knows who has Margaret."

Scott said, "Who's Margaret?"

"Margaret Briggs."

"I never heard of her."

"She ordered fruit and yogurt every morning." Cassie spoke mostly to herself. "That's why I ordered it now. I miss her something awful."

Scott tried to pat her hand, but she moved it away.

"A man who said he knew told me that the people who kidnapped her were going to let her g-g-go soon. They haven't. Not yet. When will you let her go, Scott?"

"I haven't got her."

Ebony cleared her throat, a gentle sound just loud enough to make itself heard. "Before this goes any further I ought to say something. The cop who pulled me out of the chow line got me into a corner and said now listen, sister, we're turning you loose. But if you raise a stink, you just might find yourself locked in here again. After that, they gave back my stuff and shoved me out the door. Your agent doesn't have a bodyguard anymore, either."

Cassie said, "This means something to you, Scott. I can see it."

"Not a thing. I'm out of showbiz, Cassie. Just a tired businessman on a little business trip." He launched into a humorous description of his current lifestyle that included nothing about the nature of his business, and was about to light a cigarette when their food arrived. "My friend here would like a big glass of O.J.," he told the waitress. "She forgot to say that."

The waitress nodded and hurried away.

"Let's get down to it." He replaced the cigarette. "Like I said, I've been living in South Florida. I have a nice little business going there—a very, very profitable business. There was a little bit of trouble about it, and a couple of nice guys came by to see me. They told me they worked for Arthur Thomas Franklin."

Cassie said, "Who the heck is that?"

"It's what they work for, and that's all you're going to know. This'll go one hell of a lot faster if you don't ask questions."

"All right." She shrugged.

"They wanted me to work for it, too. No salary, but plenty of expense money. *Capeesh?* And if I did it I could stay in my nice profitable business and nobody would bother me. I said sure."

Cassie nodded slowly. "Why did Arthur Thomas Franklin want you?"

The empty chair between them moved back as though Scott had nudged it with his foot.

Ebony touched Cassie's arm. "They wanted him because he used to be your husband."

Scott nodded. "That's right. You're my in, and in a minute I'm going to show you a picture someone copied from a webzine. Not right now, but soon."

The waitress returned with Ebony's orange juice.

"I want a cup of mayonnaise," Scott told her. "Not salad dressing—real mayonnaise. If you won't bring it, I'll go into the kitchen and get it myself."

Cassie murmured, "Give me a chance to get away."

He turned back to her. "That wouldn't be smart. Your friend, the dead one—"

"Norma Peiper." Ebony supplied the name.

"Norma Peiper died, Cassie, in order to show you that we're serious. We're after a man you've probably never heard of, and the key to our finding and killing that man is a man seen with you not long ago."

The hostess was seating a new couple; another was waiting at her stand. "You better keep your voice down," Cassie said.

"I hope you heard it."

A new waitress appeared beside Scott. "Somebody here want mayonnaise?"

"He does," Ebony told her.

"You've been approached by the FBI. We know all about it. They may threaten you, but they're just playing games. Arthur Thomas Franklin doesn't fool around, and your friend died yesterday so you'd understand that. Do you?"

"Yes." Smiling, Cassie turned to Ebony. "Do I look brave?"

"Absolutely!"

Cassie cleared her throat. "Do I sound brave, too? Really brave?"

"You sound great," Ebony assured her.

"Virgin Mary great or Joan of Arc great?"

"Joan of Arc all the way."

"Fine. I'm starting to feel like her, too. Scott, did you put those big black birds—or whatever they were—on my windowsill?"

Scott shook his head.

"Or giant bats? I'll bet they were giant bats."

"You've been using something, Cassie, and I think I know what it is. I've gone there myself, and I'm telling you right now that you've gotten to the place where you'd better go back."

"That's good." Cassie turned to Ebony. "They were horrible, but I had this crazy notion that they wanted to be friends. If Scott had sent them, that couldn't be true. But he didn't, so maybe it is."

Ebony said faintly, "Giant bats, Cassie?"

"Something like that. They had tall heads like pointed caps, and their faces looked almost human. They wanted me to let them in. Only the windows won't open."

The new waitress arrived with their food. She glanced around at the occupied tables nearest theirs before she whispered. "Mister here has been cutting up rough with Elouise. If he cuts up rough with me, I'm going to the manager."

"You ought to hear what he's been saying to Ms. Casey here," Ebony told her.

The waitress left without another word, and Ebony whispered, "I'll bet she spit in the mayonnaise."

"I'm not threatening you, Cassie," Scott said. "Not me personally. I'm simply telling you how it is with the people I'm working with. And your friend's right—they recruited me because I've been your husband. They asked me a lot of questions about you. That was the first thing they did, and I answered all of them as well as I could."

Ebony looked disgusted. "But they won't put the arm on you to kill her. Oh, no."

Cassie said, "I hope they do. I hate your double-dealing insides, Scott, but I'm afraid of the people who killed Norma. Not you. Let's see you try it."

"Let's hope nobody has to." Scott took a picture from a pocket of his seersucker jacket. "This is a photo of you with Gideon Chase, Cassie. Tap it if you want to hear the music."

Cassie said, "What?"

"On the back there's a list of phone numbers." Scott displayed the back of the picture. "When you know where this Gideon Chase is, all you have to do is call any number on the list and give the information to whoever answers. As soon as you do that, you're in the clear. But, Cassie, you have to understand something. These people don't have a lot of patience. If you don't call in a day or two, it could be bad. Very bad. You watched what's-her-name die. In two or three days, Ebony here could be watching you."

Ebony, who had been eating hard and fast, looked up. "Show us the picture."

"Yes," a new voice said. "Show us the picture." It was a familiar voice, deep and harsh.

Openmouthed, Cassie struggled to speak—but failed. Reis sat between Scott and Cassie herself, facing Ebony.

Scott goggled, and Ebony gaped. Cassie hid her face behind her napkin. No one broke the silence until the new waitress returned. "Would you like to order, sir?"

Then Cassie giggled.

Reis shook his head and gestured toward Scott. "He hasn't touched his sandwich. I'll eat that."

Shrugging, the waitress turned away.

Scott said, "Who are you?" He sounded as though he were choking.

"I'm your replacement," Reis told him. He took the photograph, glanced at it, and passed it to Cassie.

In it, she waltzed with Gideon Chase through a sea of blue light. She wore Mariah Brownlea's spring-green gown. Gideon was costumed as a seaman, in white trousers, a blue jacket, and a jaunty, nautical-looking cap; his right leg ended in a wooden peg.

There was an exclamation near the entrance to the room, a murmur of voices and the scuffle of chairs being pushed aside. A gray-black beast that might have been a huge dog was leading a man Cassie had never seen before, pulling him along at the end of an absurdly thin leash.

"Don't worry." It was Reis's rough whisper. "You're perfectly safe."

Then the beast's paws, each as large as a man's fist, were on Scott's shoulders. For a moment that Cassie felt would never end, the two stared into each other's eyes.

Scott rose. As he did, the beast dropped lightly to all fours. Turning with almost feline fluidity, it trotted off through the tables and chairs and staring diners, and out of the coffee shop. The man who held its leash walked after it, his hard face expressionless.

Scott followed him.

"OhmyGod!" Ebony had risen, too. "A woman tried to pet it. Did you see that?" She sat again.

"This needs Russian." Reis was examining Scott's sandwich.

At the third try, Cassie managed, "What was that thing? That animal?"

"A wolf. You've probably seen them in zoos. Aren't you going to ask where I came from?"

Cassie shook her head, richly auburn curls bouncing. "I know where you came from, Wally. I figured it out the first time you took me to dinner, remember?"

"I do, and it will save a lot of explanation."

"Well, I don't." Ebony still sounded breathless. "I don't mean to piss you off, sir, but I don't know where the holy hell you came from or how you got here."

"From Melbourne," Reis told her solemnly, "by hopper."

Cassie touched his hand. "It's your wolf, isn't it? You had it come here."

"Nobody really owns a wolf." Reis smiled. "And I certainly don't own that one. He's his own wolf. Scott's going to die for the same reason your friend Norma died. His death will worry you, I know."

"Is he? I don't think I'll cry."

"That's good. Your life will be better with him out of the way."

Reis turned to Ebony. "Scott said in your hearing that the agency he was working for had killed Cassie's friend Norma—"

"She was my friend, too, Mr. Rosenquist. She was in your show and I liked her a lot."

"They shot her so Cassie would know they were serious. The agency that shot her has to learn that some others are serious, too."

"Mr. Rosenquist, sir, I don't understand any of this about agencies. When they let me out of jail, I went to Zelda Youmans's agency. I knew she had a hopper, and I was pretty sure she'd help me."

"I don't think it's that kind of agency," Cassie said weakly.

"A government agency." Reis signaled a waitress by holding up his empty cup.

"Are you saying that guy Scott was working for the government?"

Reis shook his head. "He was working for the agency, and it's part of the government. But it doesn't actually cooperate with the other parts. Most agencies don't. A man I know was with the State Department for a while. It did pretty much as it chose, regardless of the president's policy. That was true even when it knew what his policy was, which it seldom did because he rarely had one. It had rivals, and cooperated with them only under duress."

As the new waitress filled Reis's cup, Cassie asked, "Is this the FBI?"

"No." Reis paused to ask the waitress for Russian dressing.

When she had gone, he said, "This is one of the FBI's competitors. You met men claiming to be Bernard Martin, an FBI agent."

Cassie nodded. "I think the second one was really him."

"You're right. The first was working for that man I know who used to be with the State Department. I wanted to clear that up before you jumped to the conclusion that the first was one of Scott's friends. He wasn't and he isn't. Now tell me about the bats."

Cassie swallowed. "I'd almost forgotten them, and they scared the bejabbers out of me. Are they yours?"

"I'm trying to make them mine, if you want to put it that way. I'd like to, and I will. What did they do?"

"Knocked on my window, that's all. My room's on the eleventh floor, and they were standing there, eleven floors up. Can they fly?" Cassie hesitated. "Forget that. Of course they can, and I even saw one flying once. I'd just about forgotten. It was before Margaret . . ."

Reis nodded to the waitress bringing his Russian dressing. "Yes?"

"Did you do that, Wally? Kidnap Margaret like that?"

"No, but I've been told about it." Reis sipped his coffee. "Let me think. You were in a cab with that man you sing with. Margaret was in your agent's car. Isn't that right?"

Ebony said, "So was I, Mr. Rosenquist."

"Of course." He was spreading Russian dressing. "I had forgotten. That was why you were in jail, Miss White. You were a witness, and you wouldn't promise to stay in the jurisdiction. Is that right?"

"They let her go," Cassie told him.

"They just called everything off," Ebony said. "It was crazy, like there had never been a kidnapping."

"They warned you to keep quiet about it," Cassie reminded her.

"I'm not afraid of them!"

"Wally . . . ?"

He chewed and swallowed. "What is it?"

"At dinner that one time I told you I'd try to keep tabs on Gideon Chase for you."

"You haven't done it."

"Because I didn't know where he was. Or you either. I can't tell you things when I don't know where you are, but I'm going to tell you something now. Dr. Chase phoned me at the theater and told me that Margaret hadn't been hurt and they'd let her go soon. He didn't say who had her, but he seemed to know."

"You're worried about her. All right. I wasn't going to get into this, but I will. If the local police acted the way Miss White here says they did, it was because they had found out that your Margaret had been taken—arrested, they'll say, not kidnapped—by another police agency."

Slowly, Cassie nodded.

"We can probably assume that it was a higher-ranking agency, the State Police or one higher than they are. Did Scott say anything about his friends having her?"

Cassie shook her head.

"Then they don't. He'd have made use of her if they did. There's another police agency involved in this, the one Bernard Martin belongs to."

Ebony asked, "What do you mean by 'this,' Mr. Rosenquist?"

"The shooting of a featured actress of ours, among other things. I can't tell you with certainty why Cassie's dresser was arrested, but my guess is that the people who arrested her wanted to question someone who knew a good deal about Cassie. When you want to compel somebody's cooperation, all sorts of facts can be useful."

Reluctantly, Cassie nodded. She was spooning up yogurt.

"A rival agency—what was it that fellow called it? Arthur Thomas Franks?"

"Franklin," Ebony said.

"Thank you. Arthur Thomas Franklin decided to copy their approach— that's typical of them, by the way—and enlisted Cassie's ex-husband. Many husbands know a lot about their wives. Was Scott one of them? He didn't seem the type."

"You're right," Cassie said. "He wasn't."

"Having talked to him, they decided they might get what they wanted by stupid brutality and shot one of my employees. I think we can be certain they were the ones, not only because Scott admitted it but because it's also typical of them. It's the way they do business."

After a glance at the potato chips that had escorted Scott's club sandwich, Reis dismissed the plate. "Cassie, I said once that I'd send a friend who'd lead you to me. Remember that?"

She nodded.

Ebony said, "I've got one more question, Mr. Rosenquist. It's part of my job."

He brushed it aside and stood up. "Not now. I have to go."

Cassie said, "I've got one, too. Why did you come?"

"I've got extensive business interests. A financial empire is what some fool on vid called it. Do you know how such things are run?"

She shook her head. "I have no idea."

"I'll tell you, and what I'm going to tell you is worth a semester at Harvard Business School. The man at the top—me—has to spend half his time, and half his effort, finding the right people and persuading them to join him. When he finds them, he gives them the authority they need and turns them loose. You know India Dempster, and she's a fine example of what I mean."

Ebony said softly, "I see. . . ."

"That's good. I wanted somebody to organize a show, choose a good cast, and stage it. I found Miss Dempster, offered her an excellent salary, and turned her loose when she accepted it. The result has been outstanding, proving she was the right person for that slot."

Reis lowered his voice and leaned closer to Cassie. "He spends the other half running around stamping out fires, handling the things his people can't deal with. When some bastard shoots somebody who works for me, that's a fire. I've come to stamp on it, and I will."

She had not expected him to kiss her; but he did, crouching until she rose, bending low even when she stood. Much too soon he released her and was gone, threading his way among the tables—

Until he vanished.

Ebony was openmouthed when Cassie sat down. "Did you see that?"

"I guess I did." The pineapple was good, and Cassie ate a piece. "I've heard of people disappearing into a crowd, but I don't think I've ever seen it done before."

"What in the world . . . ?"

"It might not be good to talk about it. What was it you were going to ask him?"

"About this picture." Ebony held it up.

"Whether I'm going to call those numbers? No."

"This man you're dancing with. I've seen him on vid, and there were stories about you two a while back. Isn't that Dr. Chase?"

Cassie pretended to study the picture more closely. "I think it must be."

"He's got Gil's wooden leg! And you don't dance with Dr. Chase in the show. You dance with Gil."

"That's right, I do." Cassie decided on the honeydew melon. "What's Gil's last name anyway? I've forgotten."

"Corby. He's Gilbert Corby."

"Thanks. How does anybody take a picture, Ebony? You have them talk, snap your camera, and stick the wire into your computer. It prints your picture out for you if you want a print like this, or stores it if you don't. I couldn't play around with a picture in a computer if my life depended on it, but there are people who can make a computer do anything they want it to. Dr. Chase has been photographed a lot, so putting his face on Gil ought to be pretty easy."

Ebony nodded. "I guess so."

"Now put that away and tell me all the stuff I ought to know if I'm ever sent to jail."

SEVENTEEN

THE NOT SO SILENT WOMAN

The curtain rose for the final time with Tabbi Merce as Jane Brownlea. Gil Corby stumped over to stand in the wings next to Cassie. "She's great, isn't she? Pure gold!"

Cassie could only murmur, "I wish we had Norma back."

Later, he said, "Hear that applause? That's box-office gold."

And still later, while they danced, he whispered, "I think the spot's the wrong color. They say that in the South Pacific, the moon is gold."

"Come by my dressing room," Cassie replied. "I need to talk to you."

HE knocked, and she rose and let him in. "I bought a new camera," she said. "My old one's back home, and it's not as fancy as the new ones anyway. This could even be too fancy, come to think of it. Will you help me fig-ure it out?"

The camera was on her dressing table. She sat, and bent over it. "The little book says to press this in and twist this, then select the mode. How do you select?"

"Ebony showed me the picture," he said.

She glanced up at the mirror, and saw Gideon Chase standing behind her. When she turned in her chair, Gil Corby stood there.

"I had to hide." He sounded hopeless. "Surely you understand, Cassie. They were trying to kill me."

"You could have told me."

"You're right." He sat down. "I could have, and increased my risk enor-mously. It would have been of the greatest benefit to you."

"It would have shown you trusted me."

"It would. But if we were overheard, or a telephone you thought was safe wasn't, I would have died. Besides, I thought it might be Reis, and I've learned that he can walk unseen. You know about that. Ebony told me when she showed me the picture."

"Oh, my gosh! Is she blabbing it around?"

"I hope not. I warned her it might be fatal, but she said she'd already told India."

"India won't talk." Cassie relaxed. "Do you know how he does it?"

"In general, yes. He does it in much the same way I changed my appear-ance. What I did is called a glamour in English. Sir Walter Scott defined it as well as anyone ever has, calling it 'the power of imposing on the eyesight of the spectators so that the appearance of an object shall be totally different from the reality.' If you're asking whether I can do it myself, I can't. Not presently."

"But you could learn?"

"Perhaps. If I tried for a year or two, I could probably master it. As it is—well, I haven't had to evade arrest as much as Reis has."

Gideon waited for Cassie to speak. When she did not, he said, "Have I answered your questions? About this matter, I mean."

She shook her head. "It's just that I don't know what questions to ask."

"Then let me say this, although what Reis does is akin to a glamour, it isn't actually the same thing. It's much like a glamour in that the change is wholly in perception. There is no change in reality. If Reis were somehow to become perfectly translucent, he would cast no shadow. He would also be blind, although that's another matter. If I were to cast a glamour on that window so that it appeared to be a featureless section of wall, it would still admit light. Reis still casts a shadow. Is that clear?"

"It's an illusion," Cassie said. "I used to know an illusionist. He was a fun guy, and I let him saw me in half one night when his assistant didn't show up."

"Exactly. Real magic isn't stage magic, and stage magic isn't real magic. Or at least, not often. But they have a lot in common."

"Is he good? I mean Wally? Is he a good magician? What do you think?"

"I don't know. All right if I wash my face at your bowl?"

"Makeup? I thought you'd taken that off already."

Gil shook his head. "The glamour. You suspected me as soon as you saw rain on my face. Remember? Washing's one of the best ways of breaking the spell. That may be the origin of baptism—another thing I don't know, though I'd like to. Washing, striking the face with a hazel wand, striking with cold iron, and so on. Just crossing running water will do it sometimes. Wouldn't you rather I were Gideon Chase?"

Cassie nodded.

"Then I'll try, with your permission."

As he was scrubbing his face with her washcloth, she said, "You're working for Wally now, aren't you?"

"Yes. For Bill Reis. I'm not a permanent employee, you understand. I'm a consultant, as I was earlier at a much lower figure."

Something new had occurred to Cassie. "Suppose this room's bugged?"

Gideon looked up from his ablutions. "I've been assuming it was. By whom, do you think?"

"The FBI."

He chuckled softly. "That certainly feels better. Do I look like my old self again?"

"Yes. All right if I kiss you?"

For once he was speechless.

Half an hour later, in a caramel coupe he had just rented, he said, "This should be safe. May I explain about the bug?"

Cassie nodded.

"First, there was one. I destroyed it some time ago. People who want to bug a room often plant two bugs, one being fairly obvious. There was a wise man not too long ago who used to talk about needles and haystacks."

"Finding one, you mean?"

"Finding several. He said that if you told most people to find a needle in a haystack, they looked until they found a needle. Then they stopped. He would search the entire haystack, trying to find all the needles. I won't boast that I'm like him, but I try to be—sometimes, at least. I've been looking for other bugs ever since I found the first one. I haven't found them, which means they're good if they're there. Of course it's always possible that new bugs were planted after my last search. Thus I tried to be circumspect. I also unplugged your phone as soon as I came into the room."

She turned to stare at him. "I didn't see that."

"You were looking at your new camera, and I tried not to be obvious. That's all that stage magic is, more often than not—a thought-through attempt not to be obvious. I disconnected your phone because a telephone is one of the very best places to put a bug, and there are special phones that will let someone listen to the room even if the phone isn't in use."

"What about magic?"

Although his eyes never left the empty street they were traversing, he grinned. "I didn't think you'd think of that."

Her hand found his thigh. "I get lucky sometimes. I'm not smart, but luck can be just as good."

"Better. Yes, it could be done. I have good reason to believe that Reis can't do it, but I could be wrong. He got all his powers on Woldercan, or so I think. . . ."

"Only you're not sure?"

"Correct. I'm not sure he got everything there. He learned to turn base materials to gold there; there can be no doubt of that. Everything I know about his operation indicates he's using their method. The art of vanishing has been known here for thousands of years, however."

"Really?"

Gideon nodded solemnly. "Yes. Really. A hundred and fifty-odd years ago there was a man called Cranston who was quite famous for it. But it's also known on Woldercan, and I think it most likely that's where Reis picked it up. If he were using their method of listening from far away, I'd have detected him. Would have or should have."

"He wouldn't like my kissing you," Cassie said thoughtfully.

"Correct. Or at least I don't think he would. That's why I got you out of there fast."

"Can I change the subject? Where are we going?"

"To a nice place I know where I can buy you dinner. Or a snack at least, if you don't want dinner. I'm hungry, I confess, and there's no one I'd rather look at and talk to while I eat. After that I'll take you back to your hotel. You can pack tonight. Or in the morning, if you'd prefer. We'll leave after lunch."

"You're the person Wally said would come for me, aren't you?"

Gideon nodded.

"I thought so. When you said 'gold' the third time I caught on, or thought I did. Only I thought Wally wanted to kill you, so I didn't think it could be you."

"An excellent reason for choosing me."

"I know we're going to Wally, but where is that? Where are we going?"

"We'll land at Kololahi, on Great Takanga. I don't suppose you're familiar with the Takanga Group. It's a remote Pacific island chain."

Cassie shook her head. "I—" She hesitated. "I was about to say I'd never even heard of it."

"There's no reason why you should. It produces a few pearls and some copra, and serves as a vacation spot for Australians who are really serious about getting away from it all. Beyond that . . ." Gideon shrugged.

"Have you been there?"

"No." He braked and turned down a side road. "Can you drive? I should have asked sooner."

"Yes. Can't everybody?"

"No, but we're going to switch cars here, and when we return I'll need you to drive this one back to the rental agency. Just follow me, and I'll show you where it is. After that, I'll drive you to your hotel."

The side road had, perhaps, been a highway of some importance at the turn of the century. Its pavement was cracked now; dark weeds and shrubs sprouted from the cracks. One of the desolate buildings they passed might have been a body shop fifty years ago. Another had, just possibly, housed poultry.

"Spooky!" Cassie whispered it, and spoke mostly to herself.

"It's a decayed agricultural area," Gideon said. "There are a lot of them."

She nodded. "I suppose all this was wilderness once."

"It was, and in the long history of Earth that was only the blinking of an eye. Now it's largely wilderness again. Would you like to hear a wolf howl?"

"No." Cassie shivered. "I saw one already today, and once was enough. Ebony must have told you."

"A little, yes. Wolves were never the most dangerous animals here. Grizzly bears denned here, as they do again. Go back a few blinks further, and you'd find lions."

"This is North America, Dr. Chase. Are you trying to fool me?"

"Panthera leo atrox has been extinct for no more than eight thousand years. He was still around within living memory, in other words. He may return—or something like him may." Suddenly, their coupe swerved to the right, and Gideon wrenched the wheel.

"What are you doing?"

"Making a U-turn, of course. It seemed wise to scout ahead a little before stopping." He jammed the accelerator to the floor, throwing Cassie back into her seat as he added, "And if we're being followed, we may find out like this."

She was too frightened to ask any more questions until they screamed to a stop at the abandoned body shop. As he left the car she managed, "Do you know what's in there?"

He did not reply. A few seconds later, a bleary yellow light flickered inside. And died away.

A door closed, a metallic bang that made her think of Ebony and jail.

There had been no sound of an engine starting, but a black sedan, oddly angled and a good deal larger than the coupe in which she sat, rolled through a ruined doorway. When Gideon opened its door, no light kindled inside.

He motioned to her. She left the coupe and took his arm as he guided her toward the passenger side of the black sedan. "You know," she whispered, "I'd almost forgotten this."

"Let's hope others have forgotten it as well."

"Aren't we going to dinner? You said we were."

"We are," he told her, "at the Silent Woman."

Then she was in the black car, snuggling into downy-soft upholstery she found she remembered very well. The black car itself was speeding—and jolting—along the ruined highway.

Until it was not. There were stars (and nothing but stars) beyond its windows. They crept along the glass as though the car were rolling in the sky. "Am I supposed to be afraid?" she asked.

"Certainly not. Are you?"

"Nope. This car of yours is a hopper, too."

"Certainly it is. I'm surprised you didn't guess it earlier."

"I didn't know you could do that."

"You can't, legally."

"Since it is, couldn't we have hopped to that mountain in Canada?"

"We could have, and I intended to. But I wanted to get out of the city—away from all the settled areas—before I went up."

"You said you were watched, or you thought you were."

Gideon nodded.

"You were. It was the man you sent to get me at the ice cream store."

"You're right. May I ask how you found out?"

"I didn't, really. But he's Detective Lieutenant Something—"

"Aaberg."

"And the mayor called him to tell him to be nice to me. After he let me go, I started wondering why the mayor cared, and it had to be because Wally had phoned him. So if he could do that—"

The stars jumped. And steadied.

"He said he had been watching my building to protect me. That didn't make a lot of sense. What did was that he wanted to catch you."

"You're correct. As I was saying, I had to get away from the city where someone might have seen us. Then you woke, so I had to drive. I didn't know how far I could trust you back then."

"You trust me more now?"

"I have to. I love you too much not to."

"Really?"

"Yes, really. You already trust me much more than you have reason to. The least I can do is to trust you every bit as much."

"What if you're wrong? Or I am?"

"You know the answer. You're not wrong about me, though. Am I wrong about you?"

For a minute or more, Cassie stared out at the stars, and at treetops growing at a pace that slackened moment by moment as the onboard computer slowed the descent of the black hopper. "I don't know," she said at last. "I hope not."

"I hope not, too." Gideon cleared his throat. "This place we're going to is called the Silent Woman. Perhaps I said that."

"I think so."

"It doesn't mean you've got to keep quiet, but be careful what you say. There are people there, and things there, too, who have sharp ears. The lowest whisper will be overheard by someone."

"I'll watch it. You laughed when I said the FBI might be bugging my dressing room. Why was that?"

"Because I've been cooperating with them—up to a point. If they were, I would surely have been told about it."

"You're on their side?"

The black sedan was settling through the trees.

"To a degree, yes."

"You're working for Wally, too?"

"So are you." The computer eased them to the ground with the smallest possible bump. "I don't think you'll need your coat. Want to leave it in here?"

"If you say so."

She had unbuttoned her coat already, and she slipped out of it when he opened the door for her. "Where are we?"

"Here." He pointed. "See those colored lights? That's the Silent Woman."

"I get eighty thousand if we catch Wally and turn him over to the FBI. Is that right?"

"It is." Gideon's voice was just above a whisper.

"Please don't be mad, Dr. Chase. But I'm not sure I want to do it."

"Nor am I."

"Really?" Cassie felt that a weight had been lifted from her heart.

"Yes. First because I'm working for him. I'm doing it now, I'm very well paid, and I may be working for him for some time to come. Ethically, I can't possibly turn him in while I continue to accept his money."

"I can see that. You're a good, good man. I always knew it."

"And second—you might as well hear this, too—because my negotiations with the government haven't been going as well as I would like. The money's fine, and so are the honors. There are strings on them both, however. Onerous restrictions on my future operations."

"I see . . ."

"There are other complications, too. But here we are."

The ancient inn looked older than Carnac, a structure of odd angles, many dormers, and inscrutable projections, small-windowed and secretive, its stone walls furred with black moss. Tables and chairs had been set outside beneath towering trees whose lower limbs bore strangely shaped lanterns, grass-green and sea-blue.

The ears of the bowing waiter summoned by a snap of Gideon's fingers were hairy and sharp. "Madame. Monsieur. Will there be more?"

Gideon shook his head, and the waiter led them to a table for two.

The bill of fare was in a language Cassie failed to recognize, one that might possibly have been Russian or Greek, although she had the feeling that it was neither. She studied hers for a second or more before she put it down. "I can't read this."

"Don't worry," Gideon murmured. "I'll suggest a few dishes."

"He spoke English to us. Was it because he recognized you?"

"Possibly. Or because you look Irish. Or for some third reason. Do you think you might like a nice duck with truffles?"

Memories of Rusterman's came flooding back. "You know what we ate. Wally and me."

Gideon glanced up. "Actually, I didn't. I simply thought you might like duck."

She shook her head.

"The lentil soup is superb, believe me."

"Tell me about your leg, Gid."

He grinned. "That's the first time you've called me Gid since I washed."

"Hurray. You were in a lot of pain right after it happened, but you said it would be all right."

"I thought that it would be. The antibiotic I'd been given didn't work, however, and it became infected. I had a violent reaction to the next one—you'll pardon me, I'm sure, if I don't tell you who was treating me—and nearly died. After that I told them I wasn't going to take any more. Other methods didn't work either, and in a few days they had to amputate my leg below the knee."

"You're still wearing the wooden one you wore onstage."

"Correct. I had reasons for remaining Gil Corby when I went to your dressing room, the first and foremost being that Gideon Chase had no business being backstage. Is that enough?"

"The man who hurt your leg . . . ?"

"Who shot me. There's no reason you shouldn't say it. I'd be happy to give you his name if I knew it. I don't."

"You talk about a man named John. He's phoned you a couple of times, or I think that's what you've said. Could he have been the man who shot you? Or one of his friends?"

Gideon shook his head. "I saw the man who shot me. He didn't resemble John. It wasn't his face or his body type. As for it being a friend of his, I doubt it very much. His friends are good shots, and this man wasn't."

"I see." Cassie nodded.

"Organizations act according to patterns, patterns from which they deviate only rarely. John and his friends are careful men, violent only when they have no choice. That doesn't sound like the man who shot me, or the people who sent him to do it."

Cassie nodded again.

"In addition to what I just said, John has compelling reasons to want me alive and active. You may give that more weight than I do, however. I've been involved with our government more than once, and know how often it acts contrary to its own best interests."

"What about the man who bought me truffles?"

"That's much more plausible, I admit." Gideon picked up the menu. "Do you like Hopfenkäse?"

"I have no idea. What about our friend? The one I just asked about?"

"It's a cheese. People usually eat it with beer, which I rarely drink. I just thought you might like it."

Cassie shook her head.

"Our friend is a lot more plausible, I admit, and for twenty-four hours or more I felt reasonably certain he had done it. Then I found out that he was looking for me in the hope of protecting me and getting me better medical assistance."

"Really?"

"Yes, really. It showed that he was still anxious to enlist me, if he could— that we were just haggling about price, in other words. If I were indebted to him, I might feel obligated to do as he asked. A tall man in a gray suit visited me, one who had visited you earlier. He told you he was from the FBI and tried to get you to call him if you saw me or heard from me. Remember that?"

Cassie nodded. "Did India tell you?"

"No. He did. Now tell me about the wolf."

"You must have heard about that from Ebony."

Gideon nodded. "What she told me was sketchy and subjective. I'd like to hear it from you. Everything."

"All right. I'm sure I'll be subjective, too, but I can't help it. My second husband showed up. He said he was working for somebody named Arthur Thomas Franklin. Do you know who that is?"

Gideon said, "Go on."

"He gave me a picture of us dancing in the show, you and me. I told Ebony it'd been faked—Ebony was with me. That's what I said, but I didn't believe it."

"The names, I suppose."

"Yes. You two were about the same size, and certain things Gil Corby said made me think of you. I decided to buy a camera and try it myself. I was going to take a few shots of you there in my dressing room. Only I couldn't figure the camera out."

The waiter returned, and Gideon ordered lièvre à l'Allemande for them both. "Wine?" he asked Cassie.

She nodded. "I could use a drink. A nap, too."

"Champagne, in that case." When the waiter had gone, he added, "Three glasses should do it, and you can sleep on the way home."

"Three glasses and you'll have to carry me back to the car."

"With food? Nonsense. Get to the wolf."

"I'd rather get to the waiter. He's not—well, he's not like us."

Gideon nodded.

"So what is he? Somebody from Woldercan?"

"I doubt it. Their ears aren't pointed, as far as I know. Or hairy, for that matter."

"A werewolf?"

"Certainly not. Werewolves are human."

Cassie sighed, spotted the waiter returning with their champagne, and sighed again. The waiter opened it. Gideon sampled and approved it, and the waiter poured for them. Gideon sipped and said, "The wolf now, please."

"Do you ever feel like you're in the wrong show?"

He sipped from his glass again, and set it down. "Just what do you mean by that?"

"It's a nightmare I've had. Maybe a nightmare I'm having. I'm onstage, I've got no idea what the play's about, and the audience is always behind me. I'm in a restaurant that can't possibly be in one of those guides you can read online, the waiter's not—shouldn't this place serve dragon's eggs? Stuff like that?"

"Certainly not. They're poisonous."

"You've tried them?"

Gideon looked disgusted. "It's common knowledge, that's all. If you don't believe it, you eat them."

"All right. Pink clouds with spun sugar. Delicious!"

"Not to me. Too sweet. Let's talk about the wolf."

"Right. We were having breakfast. That's Ebony, my second husband Scott, and me. Scott was there because he had promised to tell me who killed Norma. It was Arthur Whatshisname. That's what he said."

"Truthfully, I'm sure."

"He pulled out our picture, and all of a sudden Wally was at our table, too. Can I say Wally?"

"You just did."

"Then the wolf came in with a man holding a leash and pretending it was a dog. It was bigger than any dog I've ever seen. It looked like it could kill a bull moose all by itself, no problem. The wolf looked Scott in the eye, and he looked at it. When it went out he followed it. I don't know why, and he didn't say a word."

"But Wally did, didn't he? Think carefully, please, because that's my key question."

"I don't think—wait! Yes, he did. He said not to worry, we were safe. Then, after the wolf was gone and Scott, too, he said his sandwich needed Russian dressing."

"Fine. You've met the werewolf. Met him in his human form, I mean. He works for Wally, and I'd guess that Wally told him what to do before he became visible at your table. The man in the gray suit."

Cassie sipped her wine, paused to think, and sipped again. "He works for Wally?"

"Correct. He's an ex-cop and a private investigator, and our friend Wally owns the agency that employs him. Not as our friend. Another name. He was trying to find me, because our friend wanted to help me, as I've told you."

"But he's a werewolf."

"If you mean our friend, no, he isn't. If you mean the man in the gray suit—"

"Yes. Him."

"Correct. He is."

"He told you?"

"He did not." Gideon paused. "I hadn't intended to get into this, but I will. There are several signs; when an individual exhibits two or more, it's safe to assume lycanthropy. Hair on the palms of the hands is the classic indication, mentioned as far back as the Middle Ages. One almost never sees that today, because they shave it off. Luckily there are a number of others. The ring finger is often the longest on the hand. They're sensitive to odors and insensitive to colors. There's often a swift loping walk, even in women. It's hard to describe, but once you see it you'll remember it. They tend to dress in wolf shades: gray, black, and white. There are others, but those are the most common."

"I changed." She waited for him to speak; when he did not, she said, "Or you changed me."

"You changed. I assisted you, and called upon others who assisted you, too. Going up is a lot harder than going down. I think I told you that once."

"Yes, you did. I'm not a good student, Dr. Chase, but some things stick with me."

"You learn your lines, and learn them very quickly from what I've heard."

She ignored it. "How can you tell if someone is like me?"

"Again there are several signs, some of them seldom seen and rather obscure. Often, one sees spontaneous flashes of the higher form; and that was what I saw in your case. I attend the theater as much as I can when I'm not on campus, you understand. Call it a guilty pleasure."

"You'd seen me onstage?"

Gideon nodded. "I had, in several productions. Nine-tenths of the time you seemed a very ordinary thirtyish actress, but there were flashes of something more—of an indescribable something that electrified me and, I believe, the whole audience. I marked you then."

"But you weren't going to help me?"

"On the contrary, I was going to help you as soon as I found reason to. That's our food coming, I believe, so let me say before it arrives that another sign is desire. One sees that in werewolves, too. They want the wild and a liberation from human morality. People like you want to be the higher thing they cannot quite become. I tested you on that score, and you said that you'd walk barefoot all day and all night if it would make you a star. Remember?"

Slowly, Cassie nodded. "Two more questions?"

"Yes, but only two. What are they?"

"Why was the wolf so big? And—"

The waiter was setting down his tray on an empty table.

"Why did Scott follow him like that? The wolf never said a word to him. Can they talk?"

"Sometimes," Gideon told her, "and that's three questions. The wolf was so big—thank you."

Cassie had received the first covered dish. When she removed the cover the aroma made her mouth water in actual fact.

"The wolf was as big as he was," Gideon said, "because Al is. He's not fat, but he must stand at least six foot two. When his cells have repositioned, they make a large wolf. I told you about that, too, once."

Cassie nodded, her mouth full.

"You can charm people. You know you can. You charmed our friend, for example. The wolf charmed Scott. That's one way to put it."

Cassie chewed and swallowed with great pleasure. "I try to charm you, too, but it doesn't work. Is it because you saw me before I changed?"

"Quite the contrary. You do charm me. If you didn't, I wouldn't have written that twenty-thousand-dollar check; and you charm me all the more because I saw you before you changed."

She grinned. "I've been waiting to say this, Gid. Get back to the wolf."

"Indeed. People attacked by tigers often do nothing to defend themselves. They simply stand there until the tiger kills them." Gideon took a bite of sour cabbage. "The tiger has told them they are tiger food, you see."

EIGHTEEN

A REMOTE PACIFIC
ISLAND...

"I saw their sign as we left," Cassie said as the black hopper that doubled as a sedan lifted off. "It's a woman with no head, and it ought to scare me. Why doesn't it?" She was full of roast hare and spätzle, champagne and Black Forest cake, and felt relaxed, sleepy, and perhaps a little romantic.

"Because it assures you that women should talk as long as they're able to."

"Really?" She considered. "I don't think so."

"You may be right. You've had my explanation . . ."

They hopped.

"What's yours?"

"That was it, wasn't it? We're back home."

"More or less. High enough that the noise shouldn't bother anybody on the ground much, and low enough to be under the radar—I hope. Over a thinly populated area with an old timber road running through it."

"You love me, Gid?"

"Much, much more than I should."

"You trust me, too. We've already talked about that, so I won't ask. I'm going to say right now that I won't touch anything you tell me not to touch or do anything you tell me not to do. I won't hop or go up. Not an inch off the ground."

For a moment he turned to glance at her.

"When we go back to the rental, I want to drive this. You can show me the way in the rental. When we get to the agency and you've turned it in, you drive this to my hotel. All right?"

"No."

She stroked his arm. "Please, Gid?"

"Absolutely not. You don't know what you're asking."

"Last chance. Please?"

"No, and I don't think there's anything you can do or say that will make me change my mind. I'm saying no for your sake, Cassie."

Gently, the black hopper landed on two faint tracks that wandered away among trees. As its tires took its weight, the headlights came on.

"Well, I'm going to try. I wasn't going to tell you yet, but it's the only thing I've got. I had company last night—company that scared me half to death. Maybe they were trying to be friends. I hope so. But I don't want to sleep alone in that hotel room tonight. I was going to ask you to stay with me, but I won't now. I'll call Ebony and try to talk her into coming up to my room and sleeping with me."

"You weren't going to do that?" The black hopper rolled silently forward.

"No. I wanted you there in the bed with me."

"If I would let you drive this?"

Cassie sighed. "I'd want you anyway, Gid. Ebony wouldn't be much fun, and if those bat-things came back, she'd probably be as scared as I was."

"They look on you as a friend, I'm sure."

"That's scary, too. Please, Gid? I'm a good driver, because I don't drive enough to get confident. I'll drive very conservatively, stop at all the stop signs, and never speed, I promise."

"Why do you want to do it?"

Seconds passed before she answered, and when she did her voice had fallen almost to inaudibility, becoming small and frightened. "Well, because

I want to feel, just for a little while, that I belong with you and Wally. You can't understand that."

"I think I may."

"You're not a woman, so you can't. I want to be—I want to matter. I want to be somebody, not because I'm Wallace Rosenquist's woman or because I'm Gideon Chase's woman. Because I'm Cassie Casey."

"You *are* someone, Cassie. You just don't know it."

"If I were, you'd let me drive."

Silence descended. Shadowy trees appeared to jog past them, moving rapidly and purposefully while they bumped and jolted. At last Gideon said, "I'll stop and get out. You get behind the wheel so I can coach you."

"How far do I get to drive?"

"All the way into the city."

"In this?" She smiled.

"No, when we get the rental you'll drive that." He braked. "We can change drivers now."

She shook her head. The smile was gone.

"You'd be alone in this car. It would be a terrible risk."

"But I can drive it now?"

"Yes." He opened the door and got out. "Until we come to the place where we left the rental."

She hesitated, then nodded.

They met at the front of the car, where blue-white beams from the headlights fenced them on both sides. Gideon caught her there and kissed her, released her, and felt her cling to him.

When the doors had closed again, Cassie sat behind the wheel. "Now tell me what I mustn't do. Tell me that first. After that you can tell me how it works."

"There's only one thing you mustn't do. Don't start the computer. Hopping and warping require it, both of them. Leave it off, and you've got a very simple car that employs a micropile to generate electricity. An electric vehicle like this is actually easier to drive than a hybrid or an all-fuel."

She nodded.

"There's a motor for each wheel; and the wheels are A, B, C, and D, starting left front and going clockwise. The four little gauges up top are giving you information on those wheels individually. Don't worry about them. That big dial in the middle is the speedometer, of course. Keep it below ten until we get on a better road. If this one gets any worse, keep it below five. By now you've already found the accelerator and the brake pedal."

She nodded.

"I've been using them, mostly because I need to train myself to drive using my left leg. You can use them, too, but you don't have to. Now say 'ten' loudly and firmly."

"Ten!"

The acceleration was gentle and very brief. When the virtual needle touched ten, it ceased.

"It will steer itself if you tell it to, but that will be tricky, especially on a road like this. I'd stick with manual steering, if I were you."

"What if I want to use the pedal or the brake?"

"Just do it. The car will respond normally. The only way you'll have a problem is if you try to give a verbal command at the same time. Hit the accelerator and shout 'Stop!' for example. It will obey one or the other, but there's no way to tell which. Don't do it."

"I won't." She crossed her heart while thinking of what she might do.

"The doors lock automatically when you start and unlock automatically when you stop. If you want to keep them locked, just say 'Lock.' "

"It's not responding to you when you say those things, is it?"

"No. For one thing, I'm not saying them loudly and firmly enough. More importantly, I'm not sitting in the driver's seat. If you want to test it, make sure you're going to like what happens when it obeys."

"Let me try. *Seven!*"

The car slowed, the virtual needle creeping down.

"What else do I need to know?"

"How to reverse. Here's the switch. Throw it, and the car will slow down and back until you brake. Or you can say 'Reverse.' When you do, the switch will change positions automatically."

Cassie smiled. "I've got it."

"To go forward again, push the switch the other way or say a number. In reverse there's a top speed of two miles an hour."

She studied him. "You could back faster than that."

"You're right, but I'd have to use the computer to change the setting. You're not going to turn the computer on. Are you?"

"No. I'd be in over my head, and I know it. Is it much farther?"

It was not. The timber road joined the neglected side road, she tripled the speed of the black car, and the onetime body shop where they had left Gideon's rented coupe came into view. She pulled the black car alongside it, leaving room enough for him to open his door.

He got out while she was still fiddling with her seat belt. As his door closed, she said, "Ninety!"

The black car shot ahead, its acceleration pushing her deep into the soft upholstery. For moments that seemed like forever, it was all she could do to steer. At last she said, "Fifty!"

The black car slowed to a speed that was almost sensible, and she smiled and relaxed. A minute or two later she tapped the computer screen. "Hey! Wake up!"

The screen remained dark.

"Come on, Sleepy!" She steered with her left hand while her right pressed keys at random. "On!"

A voice from the backseat—a voice that might almost have been the soughing of a weary wind—whispered, "Say 'Computer.' "

Cassie stared into the rearview mirror, seeing nothing. "Who the heck are you?"

There was no reply.

The neglected side road joined the main road from which Gideon had turned, and that main road quickly became a suburban street. As she braked for a traffic light, she said, "Computer!"

Lights flickered across the screen. "Start-up comprete." The computer spoke with the simulated voice of a Japanese woman. "How may I serve you?"

"I have questions about this car. Can you answer those?"

"Many, but of not are. What are your questions?"

A small voice near the dome light, secretive and somehow tinny, suggested, "Ask how to hop."

"I haven't found the turn signal. Where is it?"

"Turns are signared by brinking the rear rights and running rights."

"But how do I do it?"

"You do not. The hopper does it."

"You?"

"No, the hopper. Thus they are operative when I am off."

"It knows when I'm about to turn?"

"It knows when it is about to turn."

"I—see. Can you provide coffee? Or tea?"

"Which would you prefer?"

A deep voice behind her suggested, "Ask for whiskey."

"Tea, please. Hot tea. Diet sweetener, if you have it. Milk, if you have that."

"I do not. Cream?"

Cassie shook her head, and the tinny voice near the dome light remarked, "She can't see you."

Cassie nodded. "But you can. What's your name, computer lady?"

"Your servant is Com Pu Ter."

"Got it. Just sweetener in my tea, please. No cream."

An instrument vanished and her cup appeared, extended by a simple gripper. It was very good, and almost too hot to drink.

"Com Pu Ter? I want to ask about the windows. How do I put them down?"

The tinny voice giggled. "Bad windows! You're dirty! You're scratched!"

The computer asked, "Manuarry, automaticarry, or orarry?"

"The easiest way." Gideon's caramel coupe had appeared in Cassie's rearview mirror.

"Ask me to."

"Then put down the one nearest me. Would that be Window A?" Pushing hard on the accelerator, she beat the next traffic light, crossing the intersection on amber.

"Yes." The window at her elbow slid down swiftly and silently.

"Thanks, Com Pu Ter. There are voices in here—"

The tinny one near the dome light giggled.

"Three, anyway. Maybe more. Can you tell me who they are?"

"Your servant is Com Pu Ter, a Revel One artificiar interrigence, a product of Yokosuka Bell Raboratories. The rest I do not hear."

"You can say 'Bell.' "

"Arso many more things."

"One of you others say something. I want Com Pu Ter to hear you."

The tinny voice giggled again, but did not speak.

When she stopped at the next traffic light, the caramel coupe pulled up beside her. Its right front window was already down; through it, Gideon called, "Are you all right?"

"I'm fine!" Cassie gave him the thumbs-up sign. "You're just in time. Lead the way to the rental agency. I'll follow you."

He gave her a look that should—were justice ever to prevail on planet Earth—have fried her. His right front window slid up.

WHEN Cassie was settled in the passenger seat of the black hopper and they had pulled out of the rental agency lot, she asked, "You know how to get to my hotel?"

"Certainly." Gideon paused, apparently to bring himself under control. "I have questions."

"Fire away. The Amazing Cassiopeia knows all, tells all."

"Where did you get that tea?"

"Your Japanese lady gave it to me. She makes good tea."

"I know. You weren't supposed to turn on the computer. You promised me you wouldn't."

"That is not a question, O seeker of wisdom, but the Astonishing Cassiopeia will answer anyway. Just don't push your luck. You're right, I promised not to turn on your computer. You're wrong, I didn't. I happened to say the word *computer,* and wham-o! Here she was, and she made tea for me."

"You merely chanced to say 'computer'?"

"Bingo. I was chatting with one of those invisible people in your rear seat. They really opened up once you were gone. He—I think it was the man, but it may have been the bug up on the roof. He started talking about your computer. I was talking to him about it, so of course I used the word *computer.* Alakazam! Here was this Japanese lady—voice only—asking what she could do for me. So I said how 'bout some tea? and she made this for me. Next question?"

"You didn't warp?"

"Nope. I wouldn't know how."

"Or hop?"

"Without warping up first? You know darned well you would have heard me if I had." Cassie took a final sip from her plastic cup. "Where do I put this?"

"Just drop it on the floor. I'll get it later."

"Seems terribly messy. Can't I drop it in back?" She did. "They're really quiet back there now."

"If they are wise, they'll keep it like that. Am I still going up to your room?"

"Well, I certainly hope so. If Ebony couldn't make it, I was going to phone Donny Duke. Don't look at me like that, Gid."

"I don't believe you."

"Fine. Who would you call? Wally, sure, only Wally's not available. Vince? He's creepy enough when there are other people around."

"India, perhaps."

"Point A. She'd take up three-quarters of the bed. Point B. She and Ebony are splitting a room. Ebony says she snores—which I can easily believe. Point C. Since they're together in the room she'd know right off that she was second choice."

"How about Tabbi Merce?"

Cassie shook her head. "I don't want to talk about that."

"Let me think. . . . Because of Norma?"

"Yes. Let's talk about something else."

"The voices didn't bother you?"

"They were kind of nice, really. Gave me somebody to talk to."

"I keep underestimating you." Gideon sounded a trifle awed.

"I'm glad somebody does. There's my hotel, on the right and a block and a half."

"I know. We need to find a public garage where I can park this myself."

Cassie smiled as she struggled into her wool coat.

When her wake-up call came at eleven, he was gone. There was a note on his pillow:

> *I will never forget this night, Cassie. Never.*
>
> *Please remember that we must hop to Kololahi this afternoon. You have to pack. Do not leave anything behind, because I will not be available to hop back and get it for you. You will want to check out of the hotel.*
>
> *Bring money. You can change U.S. dollars for Australian there. Everybody takes Aus. You will need to buy tropical clothing, a lot of it. Fortunately it is inexpensive.*
>
> *Be in your room about 2:30. I will phone you then. If you are not there, I will have you paged.*
>
> *It sounds juvenile, I know, but I cannot wait to be with you again. I have loved you for years but never more than now. I shall always love you with all my heart.*
>
> *G.C.*

She smiled as she read it. Now she nodded to herself, still smiling, and got up. When a dressing gown had covered her, she dialed Room Service and ordered chicken nachos with a glass of skim milk.

What was it Gid had said? She had turned off the lights, saying she would not undress with them on, and he had said, "One day after you get to

Kololahi, you'll be wearing a bikini that covers three square inches. And every man who sees you will foam at the mouth."

She giggled softly and sat down in front of the best mirror to put on makeup.

When she answered the room-service waiter's knock, she saw that an envelope had been pushed under her door. She picked it up, but scarcely glanced at it until the waiter had gone and her nachos and skimmed milk were on the little round table that had stood beside the desk.

The note on the front of the envelope had been put there by a woman whose handwriting was clearer than her own.

Hi, Cassie!

This was in the paper I read at breakfast. You were still asleep, I'm sure, so I cut it out for you. It gives me the willies, but I have no idea how you'll feel about it. Good, I hope.

Ebony

Cassie opened the envelope with a nail file.

VISITOR KILLED BY DOGS

The body of Mr. Scott R. Zeitz, a resident of Marco, Florida, was discovered yesterday in woods near County H. He appears to have been attacked and killed by the pack of feral dogs reported sporadically in that area.

Sheriff Blunden's office informs us that Mr. Zeitz was a guest at a hotel in this city, having arrived from Florida on Tuesday. The sheriff's office has made no further comment, but confidential sources have revealed that portions of the body were devoured.

NINETEEN

GREAT TAKANGA

"I have questions," Cassie said as the black hopper left the curb. "Do you have answers?"

"It depends," Gideon told her. "Probably not. Try one and we'll see." He was watching the computer screen.

"Did you know the wolf would kill Scott?"

"Did he?"

"Yes. By which you mean you didn't know he would?"

"I suppose. I admit it seemed probable."

"If you had been sure he would, would you have tried to save him?"

Gideon glanced up. "That's a hypothetical."

"Would you?"

"By the time I learned the wolf had taken Scott—which was when you told me over dinner—he was almost certainly dead. Knowing that, and feeling quite certain Bill Reis had set everything in motion, I would have done nothing unless you asked me to."

"Does your computer still make tea?"

"Certainly. Tea, please, for the lady you served last night. Prepared in the same way, I suppose."

Cassie nodded.

"More questions? Would you like the grid coordinates for Kololahi?"

"No. Here come some tough ones. You're still working for the government?"

"For the president, in conjunction with the Federal Bureau of Investigation. Correct."

"They want you to . . . ?"

"Arrange for them to capture my employer, Bill Reis, alive or persuade him to give himself up." Cassie's tea had emerged, and Gideon handed it to her.

"You're trying to do that?"

He nodded. "Yes to both."

"Arthur whatshisname just shot Norma like you'd spray a fly. Couldn't they do that?"

"Probably, although I don't know with any certainty. I'm reasonably sure they've never tried."

"Why not?"

"Because they want to learn what he knows. When I spoke to the president, he simply wanted to know how Reis had penetrated some supposedly secure research facilities. Nothing was said about invisibility, and I don't believe they knew about it then. They do now, because I've told them."

"Are we going where we went up from last night?"

Gideon grinned. "Is that one of the tough questions? Yes. If you know of a better place, tell me and we'll go there."

"I just wondered. It seemed like it." Cassie sipped tea. "I'm not really going to put on one of those bikinis, you know. I'm too fat."

"You have a question you're afraid to ask. How's your tea?"

"Like the questions. Almost too hot. Are you really trying to get Wally caught?"

"That depends on what you mean by trying. Twenty! Ten! Stop!"

The black hopper halted for a traffic light.

"Suppose you'd wanted to stop faster?"

"I'd have said it louder and twice."

"You've been driving with your right leg. You said—"

"I was wearing the wooden one. This is the modern prosthetic, metal and polymer, thought-controlled. I need to practice using it, too. That time I was thinking of something else, and talking was easier."

"Can I ask what you were thinking of?"

"Certainly. What the question you're afraid to ask is. Let me finish." He touched the accelerator, and the black hopper glided smoothly through the intersection. "I'm not actively trying to get Bill Reis captured, because I don't see a way to do it as things stand. He's been out of the country pretty steadily, and by the time I learn he's reentered, he's gone again. I hope you'll help me with that."

Cassie said nothing.

"I've been trying to persuade him to give himself up, however, and trying to persuade the president to offer him better terms. I'm getting close there, or think I am."

"What's my next question?"

"What I'm doing for Reis. Pretty much the same thing. I keep him informed as well as I can about Washington and what the various agencies there are doing that bears on his operations. What the people who shot Norma are up to—when I know. What the CIA's doing, and so on. The FBI feeds me a lot of that information because John and his friends don't want their rivals to win."

"But you're spying on them, too."

"Of course I am. Don't think they don't suspect it."

They sailed through the last traffic light on green, and Cassie said, "I'll be in the real South Pacific in just a few minutes? I can't believe it."

Gideon nodded. "I can do it, but I can't make you believe it." He hesitated. "I can't make you go, either. Won't. If you don't want to go, just say so."

"Wally will think you talked me out of it."

Gideon shrugged. "Perhaps."

"Then he'll try to kill you. Since you're working for him, it'll be a snap. I want to go, Gid. Let's not talk about that anymore."

"I meant everything I said in my note."

"I know you did." Her lips brushed his cheek—and were gone. "A while back, you told me the president wanted to know how Wally disappears."

He sighed. "Correct. It would be a grand tool for espionage, both international and domestic."

"Doesn't he care about the gold?"

"He certainly does. Even more than he cares about invisibility. He says he simply wants to stop Reis from making it, because he's unbalancing the world market. The truth, I feel quite certain, is that he wants to make gold himself. He just won't admit it."

"None of this makes sense, Gid." Cassie paused. "Did I just sound plaintive?"

"Very."

"Good. I felt plaintive, so I thought I might. I have trouble with plaintive onstage, sometimes."

"You're the only one who's noticed."

"I'll be a little bit better now if I can remember just how I did that." Cassie sipped more tea. "What they really want from Wally is what he knows. Isn't that right? They want to learn how he disappears and how he makes the gold."

"Correct."

"Well, why bother? If he found out how to do those things on that crazy planet—"

"Woldercan."

"If he found out on Woldercan, why don't they go there and find out like he did?"

They had turned onto the abandoned highway as she spoke. Now Gideon braked to a stop and turned in his seat to face her. "You thought of that for yourself."

"Sure. Anybody would."

"Believe me, that's far from true." He seemed about to smile. "This is one of the things I love about you. You're not at all intellectual—we intellectuals are, for the most part, fools—but every so often you show the most marvelous penetration."

"You mean I'm right?"

"Certainly you're right. I've been trying to persuade the president to appoint me ambassador to Woldercan. With the authority of the office behind me, I could go there and learn those things just as Bill Reis did. He doesn't want to remove the current ambassador. He wants me to go there as his special representative or something of the sort—wants me to make his win cheap and easy for him, in other words."

"Will you?"

"No. Absolutely not." Gideon grinned. "Want to hear the secret of my success? Not that you need to."

"You bet I do!"

"It's cheap and easy. Never set yourself up to fail. Never!" He turned back to the road, and the black hopper glided forward again. "Do you have any more questions, Cassie? We haven't long."

T H E air of Kololahi Aerodrome was warm and humid and stirred by a hundred breezes. They carried the salt tang of the sea, and soon had Cassie wondering what the airport at Springfield had smelled like. If it had smelled of anything but rain, she could not remember what it had been.

This smelled of salt waves and salt spray, and spoke of lazy mornings spent paging through fashion magazines under beach umbrellas.

She had brought three suitcases and a garment bag. After making sure that she had also brought money Gideon Chase found her a porter, a bronze-toned man somewhat larger than most refrigerators and somewhat smaller than most trucks. He crouched before her and kissed the ground at her feet, a mountain of rolling fat and bulging muscle; and by the time she had recovered from that, Gideon was gone and the black hopper rising into a cloudless sky. It shrunk to the size of a bird.

And vanished.

Seconds later, the faint boom of its vanishing reached her, and she was alone.

The porter rose. "Go hotel?"

Cassie nodded. "A good one, moderately priced, please."

The porter shook his head. "You are high queen. High queen go Salamanca House." He touched the name embroidered in red on his sleeveless white tunic. "Salamanca House most fine. I am Hiapo. I show you." He hurried away and returned with a baggage cart on which was a folding chair.

At his insistence she accepted the chair on the cart. He stacked her suitcases behind her, draped her garment bag over one enormous arm, and pushed her slowly across the tarmac, down a narrow but well-paved road and along streets (in which tourists in shorts and big hats stared at her open-mouthed) to a sprawling and somewhat decayed white building of many spindly pillars and flourishing palms.

"Salamanca House!" he announced proudly.

Cassie thanked him and would have paid him, but he was already hurrying up a wide, white staircase with her bags.

She found him inside, speaking urgently to the girl at the desk in a language that was certainly not English. She tried to pay him again.

He backed away, managing to indicate by gestures and facial expressions that it was an honor to have served her, an honor that would be diminished were he to accept money for it.

"You are our queen," the girl behind the registration desk whispered. This girl appeared to be about eighteen; she wore a hibiscus behind one ear and had huge brown eyes in a broad face of lighter brown. India Dempster would have looked small beside her.

Cassie cleared her throat. "I have no reservation, unless perhaps Dr. Gideon Chase made one for me? My name's Cassie Casey."

The girl smiled. "The royal suite has been prepared for you, O Queen."

"I would imagine the royal suite is a bit more than I can afford."

The girl looked shocked. "There is no charge for the royal suite, O Queen."

"My bags——"

"Have preceded you. Hiapo took them, O Queen. I will show you to the royal suite. Will you require one maid or two?"

The elevator was a large and luxuriously furnished cage of gilded, overwrought iron. It appeared to be at least two hundred years old.

"We have not yet a private elevator for the royal suite," the immense girl whispered. "We proffer abject sorrys for that. This is ordered, but a ship have not arrived that carry him. Very soon." She let down a dully shining gate of twining iron vines with a scarcely audible clang.

Cassie said that was quite all right.

"You are most kind, O Queen. This we are told, and so it is. True? I am manager. I am Naylay. What you wish, O Queen, I have for you."

"Nelly?"

"Yes." The girl smiled. "Naylay." She patted her ample chest, found a name badge that appeared to designate her right breast, and displayed it: *Nele*. "Will our high queen require both maids now?"

SHOPPING was not so much easy as ridiculous. Cassie exchanged five hundred American dollars for a larger sum in Australian dollars. After which, she visited four shops in which whatever she liked was given to her without charge.

Now these gifts were spread on the enormous bed in what had proved to be the hotel's penthouse: five flowered gowns of gauzy material, a gleaming white purse amply large enough to hold her little automatic with much else, and two pairs of white sandals with low but distinct heels. Three of her five new gowns had plunging necklines; all had full skirts.

She had particularly liked the pale yellow one with the foliage and red flowers. After showering and drenching herself with Lily Delight she put it on and posed before the pier glass in her new boudoir. She did not look like a queen, she decided. Most especially, she did not look like the queen of a nation whose children rivaled linemen in the National Football League.

But she looked quite nice.

She had never used much mascara, and did not use much now. A little face powder and a touch of New Rose Number Ten. Her hair, she decided, needed a good brushing. The hand bell summoned Ku'ulai, who brushed it thoroughly and reverently.

"How should I wear it, Ku'ulai? I want to get it up off my neck."

"I show." Ku'ulai began to rearrange.

"Will the high king come for me?"

"Who can say, O Queen?"

"Not me, obviously. Not so long ago—it seems like years now—Gideon Chase wanted to know if I had any more questions. I said no, not having asked a one that I should have asked. But he probably didn't know, or he would have told me." Cassie glanced at her watch. "It's evening now, where I came from."

Ku'ulai giggled.

"Very late, and winter's coming on. Here it's what? A little past lunch, I suppose. I should have asked them at the bank."

"Like eat?"

"Much too much," Cassie told her darkly.

THE answers came slowly and from a variety of sources, but they came. The bank knew a little. The Office of Tourism probably knew a great deal more, but he (an elderly man who sat fanning himself slowly behind a desk piled with brochures) had difficulty understanding her questions, and she had even more understanding his answers. Nele was too polite to be particularly informative, and Ku'ulai was too provincial to understand why her high queen should inquire about things everyone knew. The tourists positively scintillated with information, much of it contradictory; even worse, they overflowed with questions.

After three days, she felt moderately secure with the following:

- There were seven (or six or nine) inhabited islands in the Takanga Group.
- No one knew exactly how many uninhabited islands there were. Inhabitation depended upon the availability of fresh water.
- Kololahi was on Great Takanga, the largest island.
- Kololahi was the only city in the Takanga Group; it was a bit smaller than Alice Springs.
- There were innumerable villages on the inhabited islands. Each was ruled by a king—occasionally by a queen.
- The nation was ruled by its high king. All of the people had seen him. None of the tourists had seen him. All kings were sacred, the high king most sacred; he had been chosen by God. Or by the gods. Or by certain gods.
- The high king ruled from Takanga Ha'i. It was the most mountainous island in the group, and could be seen from the top of Mauna Makani to the northeast.
- The high king ruled from the Island of the Dead, under the sea north of Takanga Ha'i.
- The high king's wife was the high queen. She was very beautiful and mistress of many magics. Her head was on fire. ("I feel the same way sometimes," Cassie told the tourist who told her that.)
- The people were Christians, belonging to a variety of Protestant sects.
- The people were pagans, worshipping many gods.
- When people became Christians, God came but the old gods did not go away. (This from Ku'ulai.)
- No one knew the names of the gods. They were called the Thunder God, the Blind God, the Shark God, the Volcano God, the Storm King, the Sun God, the Sea Goddess, and so forth.
- The names of the gods were too sacred to be pronounced.
- There was no ferry service to Takanga Ha'i.

She bought sunblock and a bathing suit. It was not as small as Gideon had suggested but was very small indeed. Salamanca House controlled a considerable stretch of beach and furnished its guests with beach umbrellas and beach chairs. The water was warm, hospitable, and very clear. There had been no shark attacks along that beach for two years Hiapo told her proudly. After that, she continued to swim but swam somewhat less.

On the fifth day, it occurred to her that it might be possible to reach the United States by cell phone. She found hers in a drawer and put it in her beach bag. On the beach a kind woman from Perth informed her that a good many people, herself included, called home often. There was a tower, she said, on a hilltop outside Kololahi. From it, calls were beamed to a satellite in Clarke orbit.

"Calling the States might be a bit costly, though," the woman from Perth mused. "Dog charges, you know. Rover, or whatever they call him."

"I don't care," Cassie said. "I'm going to call India."

"Oh, you've friends in India?"

Somewhat later, Cassie did.

"Hello! Who is this?" India sounded testy.

"It's Cassie. How are you?"

"Cassie? Ohmygod! I was just about to phone you. I'm sitting on the john."

Cassie grinned. "So of course you thought of me."

"No, no, no! I've been calling and calling. You've been out of service."

"I turned it off," Cassie confessed. "I turned it off and forgot it. What's up?"

"We're almost ready to go. Just about, nearly. The thing is, I want rocks for the second dream. Pfeiffer says they'll get in the way of his dancers. I say dancers ought to be able to dance around a rock. I'd love to have you and Gil dance there for him. I don't think Gil will have any trouble, even with his saw-log leg. Do you know where he is?"

Cassie decided that explaining "Gil's" identity would be too complicated. "No idea," she said. "I haven't got him. Honest Injun."

"Okay, do you know where you are?"

"Sure. Only I've got a feeling it would be better not to tell you. Wally wouldn't like it, or I don't think so. Ask him."

"You haven't got him either?"

"Huh uh. I'm waiting for him to ride up on a white horse. I've been waiting for a week."

"In the middle of some swamp, I bet. Poor baby!"

"Not really." Cassie grinned. "Luxury hotel. Great meals, great beach. Great big hunks. You know."

"Holy snot, Wanton Woman, you must be suffering the tortures of the damned."

"You've got it. I keep eating and eating and chugging piña coladas. I know darned well I'll be way too fat to get into my costumes when I get back. Roast pork is the specialty here, and it's to die for. The roast pork and the fruit. They bring me this whole big tray of fruit, all cut up and arranged to make it look like a sunrise, and the colors are so bright it looks like a tray of jewelry."

There was only heavy breathing from the other end of the connection.

"The rest of it's pretty ordinary except for marvelous seafood." Turning away, Cassie stifled a giggle. "For my first two dinners I had rock lobster in drawn butter——"

A soft click from the other end of the connection told her no one was listening.

She called Gideon Chase, and to her considerable surprise got him. "I'm at Salamanca House, Gid. That's the big hotel here. They treat me like a queen. Wally hasn't come for me, so why don't you come and take me home? You did what he wanted and so did I. He left me high and dry."

"Two reasons. No, three. First, because Reis may be waiting to see whether that happens. You're being watched, Cassie. I guarantee that. I don't know who the watchers are, but there are some."

"India needs me."

"She should talk to Reis. Not to you and certainly not to me. Second, because I'm in a ticklish situation. I know how it sounds, but everything could blow up in my face if I took a day—and it would require at least that—to access my car, drive it to a safe spot, hop, pick you up at your hotel, and all the rest of it. Third——"

"Don't bother. That's enough."

"Third, you may be of great value to me where you are now. If you were in Kingsport, I'd have to rely on Aaberg to outmaneuver the people who killed Norma. He's good, but I'm not sure he's that good."

"I love you, Gid. Thanks for letting me drive your car."

"I love you, too, Cassie." He hung up.

ONE of the great big hunks she had mentioned to India seated himself on the sand next to her beach chair. He was, she decided, at least six foot eight and remarkably good-looking, but strictly local talent. She leaned back, closing her eyes behind large sunglasses she had been forced to accept by the hotel's gift shop.

She swam in water that might almost have been blue air, the hunk beside her matching five of her strokes with one of his. A wall of coral rose to the right, coral of a hundred shades of rose and green; the fish that swam before it were yellow and electric blue, each hardly larger than a quarter but so bright they seemed to burn.

The hunk touched her arm, smiling, and pointed behind and below them. She turned to look, and the great white shark that swam there was larger than many fishing boats. She knew she should have been terrified—but knew also that the shark had come to protect them from a horror that stirred in darker waters far below. A horror that waited, that gathered its—

She woke with a start. Everything had changed except the hunk, who was still beside her and still smiling after having touched her arm.

"I—I . . ." She struggled to collect her thoughts. "You were there. You were with me."

The smile became a grin; his teeth appeared to have been filed to points.

"We didn't have scuba gear, but we didn't drown. We didn't need it." Cassie paused, struggling now to catch her breath. "Wonderful! It was wonderful!" It sounded terribly inadequate even to her.

"I am Hanga." He extended his hand, apparently unaware that men are not supposed to initiate handshakes with women.

She accepted it, and they shook. "I'm Cassie Casey, Hanga. Pleased to meet you."

For a time they sat in silence, side by side, staring out at the sea. At last he said, "Which is more beautiful, Cassie Casey? Is it the sea or the land?"

"They're both so lovely. . . ."

He nodded.

"Which do you think, Hanga? You've seen more of them than I have."

He chuckled, a deep and echoing chuckle like surf on a rocky shoe. "What I think is not important, Cassie Casey. I say after."

"But what I think is?"

He nodded solemnly.

"All right. The sea is very, very beautiful. I just had a dream about it, the most beautiful dream I ever had in my whole life."

He nodded again.

"I adore this sea. It's the South Pacific, right? It's like the sky, like the sky had a sister. It's as beautiful as water can possibly be. But the land is my home. You've got to love your home best, because it's home. Does that make any sense?"

"You are wise, Cassie Casey."

"I'm not, but I'm smart enough to know I'm not. We had a puppy once. He wasn't wise at all, but he knew he was just a puppy and he would beg me sometimes to take that into account. He had chewed my shoe, but he hadn't known he wasn't supposed to. Are you smart, Hanga?"

He shrugged. "There are many things few understand that I understand. There are many things many understand that I do not understand."

"I've got it."

"It does not trouble you that I am on this beach, Cassie Casey?"

"Heck no. Why should it? It's your beach."

The chuckle came again. "It is the hotel's beach. The village people may not use it. The people of Kololahi may not use it. Only guests of the hotel. Only them, Cassie Casey. Not even those who labor for the hotel may use it."

"Are you a guest?"

"No. They do not see me." He sounded amused.

"And you're afraid I'm going to tell them. I won't. Honest Injun."

"I am not afraid."

"Good! You shouldn't be. These are your islands. I'm here as a guest, Hanga. If you and your people don't want us here, you have a perfect right to tell us to go home."

The voice of the woman from Perth reached her, faintly but distinctly. *"She keeps talking and talking."*

"I guess I do talk too much," Cassie said. "You talk, Hanga."

"Would you wish the hotel guests gone, Cassie Casey? All save you?"

TWENTY

AT SEA

"So I said, no, of course not," Cassie told Zelda Youmans thanks to the miracle of cellular-telephone technology. "And he said I was the high queen, and if I asked the hotel they'd do it."

"You're high queen?" Zelda sounded incredulous still.

"Of these little islands, that's all. Wally did it somehow, and I'm pretty darned sure he's high king. Only this hunk——"

"Hanga."

"Yes, Hanga. He never called me queen. All the others do. Can I say natives or is that insulting?"

"You can say it to me."

"Fine. They're my people and I don't want to insult them, besides they're awfully nice and scary big. You've seen Tiny."

"Sure."

"He'd be an average guy here. There's plenty bigger than him—than he is. Only it seemed like I'm not Hanga's queen, he just knew I was. Then he told me a whole lot of spooky stuff about the Storm King and how this darned Squid God—that's what he is—has it in for Wally and me. For the high king's what he said. He told me the Storm King's real name, but I've forgotten it and couldn't pronounce it anyway."

"You said this was scary."

"It is. I just haven't gotten to the scary part yet. When you sit on the beach here, a waiter comes about once an hour and asks if you'd like a drink or something to eat. You can order and he'll bring it. Hiapo—that's my waiter—came and I thought it would be nice for me to order Cokes for Hanga and me and charge it, because I was pretty sure Hanga wasn't staying at the hotel and wouldn't have much money. I don't think the people here—they're Takangese, that's the word. I don't think these people care a lot about money."

"They probably don't need much," Zelda said.

"Right. So I ordered a Diet Coke and started to ask Hanga what he wanted. Only he was gone. He was nowhere in sight. . . ."

"He just left quietly, Cassie. That's not scary."

"He was a great big man, like a linebacker. He'd been sitting on the white sand right beside me, only there were no marks in it there. They rake it at night, Zelda. To get all the footprints out and rake up the junk the guests have left. Cigarette butts and swizzle sticks. All that stuff."

"I've got it."

"And there were no marks where Hanga'd been sitting. None at all. I could still see the rake lines."

"You fell asleep, Cassie, and had a dream. He was something you dreamed. You just thought you were awake. It was really the waiter who woke you up."

"When he was gone," Cassie said slowly, "this woman I'd met the other day came. I'd forgotten her name, but I remembered she was from Perth. It's in Australia."

"I know."

"So that was how I thought of her then, the lady from Perth. Only I learned her name afterward. It was Florence McNair. She said I'd been chattering away, and at first she thought I was on the phone. Then she saw I wasn't, I was just sitting there with my head turned to the left, talking and talking."

Zelda said, "You were talking in your sleep. A lot of people do that."

"I explained that there'd been a Takangese there with me, and I'd been talking to him. But she just looked at me funny and went down into the water.

I watched her swim—she was a really good swimmer—and then she went under and d-didn't . . ."

"You're getting ready to cry, aren't you?"

"Not me, Zelda. I'm tough."

"Right."

"So I jumped up and started yelling and ran out into the water, only t-two guys grabbed me and carried me back. There was a siren, like for a t-t-tornado or something."

"You're not in Kansas anymore, Cassie."

"You mean I'm M-M-Mariah. I guess I am, only older and maybe a little sm-smarter. And n-not as l-l-lucky."

"You don't have to tell me this."

"I want to. I kept yelling that a woman was drowning out there, and they showed me the lifeguard's boat. It was like a canoe with a m-motor and a thing out to one side to k-keep it from t-turning over, and he was going a m-mile a minute."

"Take it easy."

"The s-siren w-was so l-l-l-l-loud—"

"I'm going to hang up now," Zelda said. "You can call me back later if you want to, or I'll call you."

The siren had filled her mind, precluding all thought. A middle-aged tourist with a beer belly had her left arm, a younger, leaner tourist her right. Someone had shouted, "He's found her head!" and they had turned her away so that she would not see it.

That evening, as she went to the dining room, she had seen a weeping man escorted by friends. She had asked another tourist, a soft-featured gray-haired woman who was surely somebody's grandmother, who the man had been; and the grandmotherly woman had said he was the dead woman's husband, and that the dead woman was Florence McNair.

One of her waitresses, a girl fully as large as Nele, had asked politely where she had been when the shark alarm sounded.

And she had said, with a feigned confidence that surprised her, that she had been on the beach.

THAT night, the death of Florence McNair was replayed in her dreams. The siren screamed, no one seemed willing to help, and her legs would not obey her—an instant stretched, almost, until she snapped.

She got up, opened the drapes as stagehands open a theater curtain, unlatched her French doors, and stepped out into her private garden, where tall figures with long, almost human faces waited among the palms and azaleas, wrapped in leathern wings.

"Hello," she said. Then, "I'm Cassie Casey." And after that, "I suppose you know."

"Our touch frightened you," one whispered.

Cassie nodded. "I suppose it must have. I doubt that it would now."

The one who had spoken laid his hand on her shoulder; he was taller than she. It was a small hand with three fingers and a thumb, and its back was covered with dark fur as soft as down.

"I suppose you're wondering why I've come out."

Another whispered, "It is enough that you come."

"I've always felt you were friendly—friends I didn't want. Friends I was deathly afraid of."

The first whispered, "We understand."

"Now I'm afraid of something else. Terribly, terribly afraid, and I don't think it's friendly at all. When I was little I was scared of dogs—just ordinary, neighborhood dogs. Pets. Isn't that silly?" She giggled.

None of the winged ones spoke.

"My mother married a new man, and he was—was just horrible. When she was away, he made me do things for him, and he said over and over he'd kill me if I told her. One time I was home all by myself, and I saw him coming up the walk. I ran out the back door and went through the hedge into a neighbor's yard and hid behind their garage. Only their dog had seen me. He came into my hiding place and licked my face and hands, and let me hug him. Does this make any sense?"

"He whom you fear was a god once," one of the winged ones whispered.

Another whispered, "We might be gods, too. Such gods as he. We do not desire it."

"You already know what I'm afraid of?"

There was a sigh of assent from them all. "We do."

"Then tell me, because I don't. When—when I dreamed I went swimming with that Takangese—there was something horrible way deep in the water. When the lady from Perth was killed, I thought it had killed her."

The winged ones watched her in silence.

"But it was only a shark. It's real, isn't it? The thing I dreamed of. The Storm King."

"It is not a god." That was one of the winged ones who had not spoken, save when they all spoke.

"So it's real, and I'm a lot more scared of it than I ever was of you. I know you don't want to hurt me."

"We are your friends."

"I know it. Would you like to come inside?"

"Would you like us to carry you through the air?" The whispered reply carried no hint of humor.

"I've got it." Cassie managed to smile. "No thanks. You said the Storm King wasn't a god. Not really. What is he?"

"One who came to this world sooner than we."

"An alien?"

"Yes," whispered one.

Another added, "Here."

And a third, "Even as we."

"Is this a dream? Am I just dreaming I'm out here in this warm night, talking to you—" She made a quick count. "To you five in my nightgown?"

The first whispered, "Does it matter?"

"Maybe not. I won't ask why the Storm King wants to kill me. What can I do about it?"

"Does he wish your death?" the first asked.

Another added, "Not so soon."

And a third, "He wishes you."

Cassie tried to smile. "Monster lusts for beautiful Earth woman? I think I watched the movie. What can I do about him?"

"Go home," one of the winged figures whispered.

"He can't reach me there?"

Another whispered, "He has long arms."

"I know they do. I've seen pictures."

One was standing upon the back of her stone bench, although she had not seen it climb. *"We will save you."* It spread vast wings and seemed to float up like a kite.

"Trust those who love you." That whisper was the first. A moment later it too was gone.

"Only them." One remained. It stretched a furry, clawed hand toward her. She took it, and it pressed her hand, very gently, between its own. "You are our cub." Its long, hard face was without expression, but its eyes held a palpable warmth.

"I can trust you," Cassie said. "I know it."

It nodded solemnly, then gestured toward the graying sky.

She nodded, too, and backed away. After a last look, she turned and stepped back into her suite; when she turned again to close the French doors, her garden was empty.

SHARON answered on the first ring.

"This is Cassie. I owe you a call."

"You owe me a dozen. Cassie, please, where the hell are you?"

"You mean you don't know?"

"Dammit, you vanished without a trace. You checked out of the hotel and that was it. Nobody I talked to had any notion where you went. I checked the hoplines, both airports."

"Did you talk to India?"

"For God's sake, Cassie! She was the one who told me you'd disappeared."

"I phoned her. Did she tell you that?"

"No, damn her!"

"I called to let her know I was all right, but I don't think I told her where I was. I know I didn't. What time is it where you are? I know it has to be different, but I have no idea how much."

"Where are you, Cassie?" Sharon sounded ready to throw whatever might be within reach.

"I asked first. What time is it there?"

"Almost lunchtime."

"I see. I just ordered breakfast. Room service, you know. They have all this weird tropical fruit. I think I told India."

"You're in a hotel. Where is it?"

"I don't know if it makes you fat, but boy does it make me feel healthy. The thing is, Sharon, I'm out of the country and I haven't got a passport. Am I in trouble?"

"Hell, yes."

"Maybe there's, you know, diplomats or something."

"An American embassy."

"Right, I'll ask. Nelly will know. Only I wanted to say, Sharon"—Cassie grinned—"that I might have to hang up to let the waiter in."

"Don't you dare!"

"Can I tell you about my dream? There were tall flying things in my garden. Remember Batman? These were Manbats. Menbats. Only I think one was a woman bat."

"Where are you, Cassie?"

"On this cute little chair. It looks very French, to me anyway. I don't know much about furniture. It's all spindly and gilt, with an ashes-of-rose plush seat. I've got the drapes pulled back and the glass doors open, and the ocean's so darned warm and beautiful you can't believe it. Only the shark signs are up, so there's no swimming except in the pool."

"For God's sake! Cassie, either you answer this one or I'm hanging up. Is Wallace Rosenquist with you?"

"I'm happy to give you a full and honest reply. No, he isn't. I haven't seen him in quite a while, and I have no idea where he is. Will that do it?"

"Have you ever heard of William Reis, Cassie?"

"Say again?"

"William S. Reis."

"Oh, you know, I have heard of him. Not lately, but Gid said something about him a while back. Dr. Gideon Chase did, I mean."

"Is Rosenquist tied in with him? To the best of your knowledge?"

"Oh, golly! Sharon, all these big financial types know each other. You ought to know that. Don't you want to hear about my dream? If it was a dream, I mean."

"No!"

"Wait a minute." Cassie cocked her head as though listening. "I think that's my waiter. He's pretty close to a giant and I think he carries a gun, but he knocks so softly I miss him sometimes."

She pressed the button to hang up, turned off the phone, and snapped it closed.

The hotel phone rang before she had time to return her cell phone to her beach bag.

"King Kanoa has come for you, O Queen, with many, many warriors." It was Nele.

Not knowing what else to say, Cassie said, "That's good."

"It is, O Queen. He comes to bring you to the high king on Takanga Ha'i."

"Fine. What about my breakfast?"

For a time so long that Cassie finally hung up, she could hear only voices conferring in a language of many vowels, *M*'s, and *L*'s.

When her breakfast arrived, she smiled at the waiter, wondering whether he really carried a gun. "Has King Kanoa eaten?"

"He eats. His men eat also. Bon appétit, O Queen."

"I'm sure it's wonderful. I'm going to miss you, Hiapo."

"I go with you, O Queen, for a time at least. This hotel dispenses my service? I shall seek new employment with our high king."

"I—see. Don't let the tourists see your gun, Hiapo."

"I shall not, O Queen."

"You might tell King Kanoa the same thing."

"I shall, O Queen. He knows, and his men also. It can do no harm if I repeat your words, even so."

King Kanoa was waiting for her in the lobby. He was, as she had somehow expected, the biggest man she had ever seen. His violet loincloth was long, wide, and elaborately embroidered; his crown of crimson and gold blossoms simple but strangely becoming. Seeing her, he bowed until its perfumed petals brushed the carpet. "Greetings, O Most Glorious Majesty!"

His voice, Cassie reflected, would have filled any theater on Earth and shaken the light fixtures. It was as if an orchestra composed solely of bass drums had spoken. Aloud she said, "Greetings, King Kanoa. Thank you for your welcome."

"The office does me honor, High Queen Cassiopeia. I am come with the cream of my people, eager to serve you." This pretty speech carried more than a trace of British accent.

As soon as he had finished speaking, there was a loud murmur of assent from the gigantic warriors and huge women who had followed him. Enormous though they were, he made them look small.

A party of tourists, Cassie noticed, had come into the lobby; they stood gaping at the spears. She smiled in a way she hoped might reassure them. "Don't worry, it's just a guard of honor."

"My lads will clear the road for us." King Kanoa's voice had fallen to mere thunder. "Walk behind them, if it please Your Majesty. I shall walk one step behind you, to your left. Near enough to converse, should you wish it."

"I certainly do."

"Gratifying, Your Majesty. Most gratifying." King Kanoa spoke to his followers. Four trotted away, spearmen so big they could not use the revolving door.

Smiling, Cassie followed.

From behind her, King Kanoa rumbled, "We ought to've contrived a sedan chair. We still can, if you wish it."

"Are we going far?" Some Takangese were watching, and looked ready to cheer. She waved, and they did.

"No indeed, Your Majesty. Only down to the marina. Okalani! Parasol!"

Abruptly, Cassie walked in shade.

Three big catamarans waited for them, double-hulled vessels with two masts mounted on each hull. A platform between the hulls of the lead catamaran carried a high and very painted chair for her and a lower, davenport-wide one for King Kanoa. "I'm not used to boats," she confided to him. "What if I'm seasick?"

"No fear." He sounded more confident than she felt. "Sea's like glass, you know, and we cast a spell on your chair. It should keep you feelin' tiptop."

As forty paddles dipped into the water as one, their catamaran put out more smoothly than any motorized craft.

When the ocher sails had unfurled and Cassie had grown accustomed to the boat's rhythmic pitching, she asked, "Do you know somebody named Hanga?"

"Several."

"He has pointed teeth. Like a shark."

"Does he?"

"Yes. He's the only Takangese I've seen with pointed teeth like that. Are there others? What does it mean?"

"Can't say, I'm sure. Not my peck, eh?"

Cassie changed tack. "Why do you sound so English?"

"Public school, you know. Eaton after and all that rot. Cambridge, only I didn't cop the gown. Pater passed, so I did a runner. Perfect excuse."

"I'm sorry to hear it."

"I wasn't." King Kanoa fell silent staring out to sea. "Ought to have been, eh? But no."

"What can you tell me about the Storm King?"

King Kanoa sighed, a sound that might have been more appropriate (so Cassie felt) to a Clydesdale or a bull. "Not a thing, really, Your Majesty. A few legends and a smatter of folktales. Not cricket to quiz royalty, is it? I'm royal myself, and I know. But we might progress if you told me what Hanga told you."

"Some of it's pretty fantastic."

"I dare say. This Hanga had pointed teeth, you say?"

Cassie nodded.

"Good swimmer, too, I'll wager."

Cassie considered. "Well, I can't be sure. I had a dream, and he was a super-duper swimmer in my dream. Then I talked to him when I was awake."

"Interestin'. Put me over the moon to hear more, Your Majesty."

"Only I don't think he was really there, because there were no marks in the sand where he'd been sitting. He sort of disappeared, though. If he was there—I don't think he can have been, really—the only way was for him to slip into the water fast while I was talking to Hiapo. Slip in and swim away underwater."

"Hiapo didn't see him at all, I'll be bound."

"I don't know. I guess I should have asked."

"I'll answer for him, Your Majesty. He didn't twig. I, um, fenced with you a moment ago. Shouldn't have done, and I apologize. You know who your Hanga was, I'll be bound. Askin' to get confirmation. Do the same myself betimes. I give it now. Let's not talk about him at present. Not kosher, eh? Heard a Yank say that in a film. Not cricket. The, um, other gent either. Don't speak his name, for my sake?"

"I couldn't," Cassie admitted.

"For the best. The high king has friends, eh?" King Kanoa struck his chest, a resounding thud. "Good man, our high king. Kindly chap. Very decent, but—ah—tough. A good friend but a dangerous enemy. Has some and they know it."

"Do you mean that—"

King Kanoa interrupted her. "Yes. Allow me to tell a whopper. Native legend, eh? We've ever so many, we silly blighters. With your leave."

"I'd love to hear it."

"You shall. My gaffer was a great wizard. Friend of ghosts and spirits. All that. That friendly chap you met sent his soul off on some errand or other, and the gaffer caught it. Locked it in a bone 'bout so long—I've seen it. Ran a bit of string through the eye to hold it. Your friend walked small after that, knowin' the gaffer had his soul. If he bothered this one or that one, the gaffer'd lend the charm. Problem solved, so it would seem."

"Only I imagine something went wrong."

"Bang on. Oh, bang on! Silly blighter borrowed the charm and untied the cord. Your friend's friend forever, eh? Fine for him, but the gaffer was eaten by a shark. Biggest anybody'd ever seen, they say. Bigger than this boat."

"I—see. . . ."

"Your friend was the friend of our village afterward. Twig?"

"To be honest I don't believe I do." Cassie was no longer looking at the sea or the high sea-girt island they were approaching, but into the water. It was smooth save for a slight roiling by their steering paddles, and seemed as clear as glass. Yet blue. Blue far below, and dimmer and darker there.

"Gaffer held the spirit of our village. He'd loved it and done his best for it. Your friend ate all that when he ate him. His son—my pater that was—wanted peace and sent all sorts of gifts. Honored him every way he could think of and some that some others thought up for him. Welcomed him to our feasts, you know. Gave him anything he asked for. He's a good chap at heart, twig? Bit peckish at times, but aren't we all."

"I liked him," Cassie admitted.

"There. You see?" King Kanoa sounded relieved. "Fine chap, Hanga. Keep it so, I beg you."

"Do you still want to hear what he told me?"

TWENTY-ONE

TAKANGA HA'I

"You don't know whether the high king is here?" Cassie asked.

King Kanoa shook his head. "He nips in and out very quick, Your Majesty. With a private hopper and no need to watch expenses, one may do so. At times I wonder when he sleeps."

"I'm wondering where. Does he have a house in this village?" She indicated the cluster of palm-leaf huts.

"That I shall show you, Your Majesty. Do I sound self-satisfied?"

"Just a little, maybe."

"I feared it, though I come by it honestly. By His Majesty's generosity, I am accorded my own apartment in the palace, a large and commodious one. I am the only lesser king in our nation who can make that boast."

King Kanoa paused, looking thoughtful. "I offered to contrive a sedan chair for you in Kololahi. You graciously declined it. I offer it again here, and urge you most seriously to accept. The road up the mountain is long and steep."

"But you're going to walk?"

He nodded.

"Then I'll walk, too."

"You are a delicate woman, Your Majesty, as befits a queen. I am, as I've proven repeatedly, the strongest man in my village."

Cassie decided to be charitable. "One who has no need to lose weight. I've been fattening on hotel food for ten days. If the high king were to see me now, he'd put me on bread and water, and hold the bread."

King Kanoa smiled. "You are as beautiful as you are kind."

"Thank you. I'm also fatter than I am beautiful and kind put together. I'll walk. On the good stretches, I may joggle. That's jogging when you jiggle."

"The sun is warm, I warn you."

"I see Okalani is still with us, with her parasol. Can she walk up? All the way?"

"You may make book upon it."

Cassie set her jaw. "Then I can, too."

"I propose a compromise. Let my folk lash up a sedan chair for you. You and I will go up there, have a seat on that log out of the sun, and watch 'em. They'll carry it behind you. If you grow weary, you may ride. What's the harm, eh?"

Cassie nodded, and King Kanoa gave orders.

"You didn't have to threaten anybody," she said when he was seated on the log beside her.

"I never do." He smiled. "Now and then I may raise my voice, Your Majesty. That's as far as it goes."

"I've been watching to see if they resented me. They don't seem to. Everybody smiles if they see me looking at them."

"For the remainder of their lives—I trust I sound sincere, because I am very—they'll boast of havin' formed a part of your escort today."

"We're friends, aren't we?" For a moment or two, Cassie collected her courage. "At least I hope we're friends."

"I'm your friend and your most loyal subject, Your Majesty."

"And I'm the queen of—of paradise. I can't get used to it. Maybe I will, eventually."

"Here's a coconut." It had been half buried in the sand. King Kanoa pulled it out and displayed it. "There will be a little milk still, I judge, and the meat should be refreshing and delicious. If Your Majesty would consent to sample it?"

She nodded, and he gestured to a man standing just out of earshot. The man handed him a large knife, shorter and heavier than most machetes. King Kanoa's powerful fingers stripped away the husk, leaving the hairy brown nut Cassie had seen in supermarkets. A single blow from the heavy knife decapitated the hapless nut. "Your Majesty will find the milk cool, I believe, though there's but a swallow." He presented it to her.

It was cool and delicious. She drank it and handed it back to him.

He split it with another deft blow and presented her with a bit of coconut meat on the point of his borrowed knife.

She thanked him. "I've been thinking about this place. People who aren't smart, and I'm not, shouldn't think too much. Only sometimes I do. Wally—the high king came here and made himself king."

"He did." King Kanoa nodded solemnly.

"He had to kill people to do that, I'll bet."

King Kanoa nodded again. "He did. Bad men and far too many bad women, perhaps a thousand altogether."

"Not your people? What Hanga said was right?"

"It was. The Storm King gathers worshippers from every nation on Earth, Your Majesty. Too often they come here to be near him." King Kanoa fell silent.

"He lives here?" Cassie shuddered.

"There's a city under the sea." King Kanoa's voice had fallen, still deep but faint. "This is what I've been told. Haven't seen it myself, and pr'aps no one has. It's miles south, but ours is the nearest land."

"He's there? In that city?"

King Kanoa nodded. "So they say. He dens in the tower from which he ruled before the first man walked."

"Wouldn't archaeologists . . . ?"

"Be expected to go there, poor chaps. More would. Dive in suits or pr'aps little subs. A few have. Didn't come back, eh? None did. Another brought a robot diver. Camera on it, lights and all that. Quite neat, you know. I saw it."

"It didn't come back either?"

He shrugged. "No one knows. Ship sunk. Lost at sea, eh? Never a distress call, so it was fast. Ever look at old pictures, Your Majesty? Woodcuts? Squid bigger than the ship it's attacking?"

Cassie shook her head.

"Pity. Have a look sometime. They knew, back then. Not now. Been forgotten, and he likes it so, eh? Less trouble. No depth charges."

She blinked. "Depth charges?"

"Like bombs, eh? For subs. Set your depth and push 'em off the ship. Might work—I've noodled it. Prob'ly get you killed, though. Couldn't do it myself."

"Only the high king could?"

"Bang on. Scads of pelf, eh? Filthy lucre. He could. He might. Storm King's afraid he will, and that's enough. If he—" King Kanoa broke off to stare upward.

Far above them, a gray hopper had sprung into being, moving slowly south. Cassie, staring up as well, squinting through her sunglasses, could just make out the painted letters on its side: USN 1110. "What's that doing here?"

King Kanoa chuckled. "Technically, violatin' our airspace. We complain about it all the time. Doesn't do a bit of good."

"Are they doing it just to annoy you?"

"Failure, eh? I'm amused, not annoyed. You see, Your Majesty, I know what they're lookin' for, and I know they won't find it. Don't exist. If they'd ask, I'd tell 'em straight out. Not that they'd credit me."

"What is it? Is it a secret?"

"Not at all." King Kanoa chuckled again. "Gold. Our high king knows how to make it. I can see you knew."

Cassie nodded slowly. "Somebody told me."

"Told you right. He does. Radioactive, eh? Not much. Wouldn't hurt you unless you had lots of it. But—"

"Or wore it," Cassie interrupted. "Massive jewelry would."

"I suppose. I haven't got it and I don't, so I don't care. But suppose there was a lot. Hundredweight or more hidden in a cave on one of these islands. I say suppose, 'cause that's what they seem to think. Clever chaps could find it, eh? With instruments. Metal detectors, pr'aps, like shootin' coins. Or pick up the radiation. Should work, eh? So they . . ." He pointed to the hopper. "Have 'em on board, and good 'uns. Goin' to find our high king's hoard, only there isn't any."

"There isn't?"

"No indeedy. They should think a bit, eh? S'pose there was. Be dangerous to come too near. How'd he ship it out all at once? Lead boxes? Lead's heavy as sin, and so's gold."

"I think I see."

"So he don't. He makes little bars. You could pick one up with one hand.

Hides 'em in shallow water, all scattered 'round, so there's not much radiation anywhere. Don't have many anyhow, not at one time. When he wants 'em we dive down for him and bring 'em up. Off they go, one or maybe two. No more than that. Told me once he never keeps more than six on hand."

Cassie thought. "Suppose somebody wants to buy a lot?"

"Oh, they get it, Your Majesty. But not all at once. One little bar at a time. What they do when they've got it's up to them."

LATER, when they had begun the climb, Cassie asked, "Why is the Squid God called the Storm King?"

King Kanoa smiled. "A legend, Your Majesty. Just a legend, though I happen to believe it myself. I'm a native at heart, you know, and blood will tell. He can fly, they say. Swim through the air, or whatever you want to call it. Hanga does it, too, and others. You don't have to believe any of this."

Cassie remembered wide leather wings and long-faced bats who rose like kites. "I believe everything so far. He can make it storm?"

"Bang on. He flies high and lets fly a cloud of ink." King Kanoa paused, hiking up the steep slope manfully for all his two hundred kilos. "Had a class in astronomy once. Had to take it. Requirement. Clouds in space, eh? Dark clouds. Nobody's sure what's in 'em or how they got there. But I know, or think I do."

Cassie shuddered, but said nothing.

"Ink blots out the sun, eh? Darkness over land and sea, cools the air under, and the winds come. Draws 'em, though I don't know how. Winds bring rain, and the rain makes thunder and lightnin'." He smiled. "Had a chap at Cambridge explain that once. Drops blownin' up and down. Makes 'em charged. Static electricity. Ever stroke a cat in the dark?"

Cassie was still trying to think of a reply that would keep him talking when they rounded a point of rock and she caught sight of the palace.

Terrace after terrace rose up the topmost third of the mountain, garden terraces flaming with flowers and accented with palms, each with a white stone balustrade. There were white stone buildings scattered among them, buildings that did not quite look Greek or Roman, low and solid-looking buildings dotted with arches and striped with wide pillars.

"Oh, my gosh!" She spoke without intending to, and knew the inadequacy of any words of hers in the following instant. "Oh, golly!"

Close behind her, King Kanoa said, "Welcome home, Your Majesty."

"I—I . . ."

"It makes me feel like that each time I see it. My people built it, you see. It was our high king's money, that's true. He furnished the materials and paid for their labor. But it was our hard work and our skill. And he's our king, after all. We chose him, we lesser kings. The tourists . . . Well, he won't let 'em gawk at it. I hope he'll change his mind someday."

The wind, and the sound of the surf far below, mingled with Cassie's sobs.

"Don't cry, Your Majesty. I can't put my arms 'round you, 'eh? Mustn't dare. But Okalani can."

He spoke in his own tongue. Cassie's shade vanished, then reappeared. Okalani's arms, larger and more muscular than the arms of most men, embraced her; and she gasped and sobbed against Okalani's soft breasts, breasts that smelled of sweat and the sea.

"I feel the same," King Kanoa told Cassie when at last she had dried her tears. "Pr'aps I said that. It's not my house, but I feel it even so. It's the palace of *our* high king. Ever so many of us live in there to serve him, and I come 'round whenever I wish. When I do, my quarters are ready and waitin', and there's always somebody to welcome me."

"The taxes . . ." Cassie gulped. "Not from you, I hope. From the shops and things in Kololahi? It must have taken a lot."

King Kanoa's booming laughter echoed from the rocks. "Not a dollar, I assure you, Your Majesty. No bl—No ruddy taxes here. I'm s'prised no one told you. Our king pays us, twig? Better 'rangement all 'round. Hires a good many of us, and slips a shillin' or two to us lesser kings. To be used for the public good, as 'twere."

Cassie could only stare.

"Good for us, eh? Steel knives, steel heads for our spears, cloth for the ladies when they're goin' to Kololahi and don't want their bubbies showin'. Hospital for those who need it. Good for him, too. High king. Loved by his people. Got his ambassador at the U.N. All that."

"I—well, maybe I do see."

"King Wiliama 'Aukailani. That's how the U.N. knows him, when it does—what I call him in public, too. Bill in private. No side, eh? William, the Sailor of Heaven. As decent a chap as ever I've met."

"I—please, King Kanoa. Would it be all right if I rode in the chair?"

"What it's for, eh? The chaps who made it would be hurt if you didn't. They want to carry you and have been waitin' ever so. Who carried Her Majesty to the palace? Why, I did. Me an' three mates. All that, eh?"

The very painted chair had been unshipped from the catamaran. Bamboo poles lashed to its legs on either side (inside those legs, so that the seat rested on them) neatly fitted the broad bronze shoulders of two men before and two behind. These men, each of whom might readily have been a lineman for the Seahawks, carried Cassie and her chair with transparent pride, seemingly without effort. Okalani's parasol, woven of green palm fronds, waved above her head like a banner; and she felt, felt truly and for the first time, that she was in fact a queen, chosen by fate to judge her people and to stand proudly before their gods as their representative.

"King Kanoa's Tiny Penniman," she told herself. "And I'm Mariah Brownlea. I only hope I never meet Vince." But when at last she was able to tear her eyes from the palace, its beauty and its splendor, she glimpsed another mountain beyond it—a mountain from which rose a plume of smoke, soon whipped away by the wind.

"YOU are not to sit up," a dark voice told her. "I am here and I will continue to talk until you wake and talk to me, but you are not to sit up. I have a silenced pistol, and I have these glasses so I can see in the dark. There will be a sound like the striking of a kitchen match, and a flash rather smaller than the flash of a cigarette lighter. A flash that will be gone at once. Before it is gone, the bullet will strike you. You may not feel it for a moment or so. Shock does that. Though you may not feel it, it'll be in your lungs if it's not in your heart. If you don't want to be shot, don't sit up and don't scream. You're awake now. How much of this did you hear?"

"I heard you say I wasn't to sit up," Cassie said.

"And why? Why are you not to sit up?"

"Because you'll shoot."

"Right on. I will. Do I sound like an American?"

Cassie nodded, wondering whether the figure at her bedside could indeed see her.

"Good. I am. I was chosen, in part, for that. I'm a fellow American, and I was chosen in order that you might know that we're everywhere. Suppose I say to you—I wish to confirm that you are truly awake—number one eighty-one East Arbor Boulevard, apartment three-oh-one. What does it mean to you? Anything?"

"It's my address. I live there."

"You live there, but you may die here. Or there. To us they are the same. Who was Brian Pickens?"

"Brian Pickens?" She searched her memory. "Why do you want to kill me?"

"We do not. I'll explain in a moment. We do not, but we will unless you do precisely as I instruct you. I will or somebody else will. You'll be just as dead either way, Queen Cassiopeia. Can I call you Cassie? I'd like that."

"No. Who's Brian Pickens?"

"Who was, not who is." The dark voice giggled. "He's no longer with us. What a shame!"

"Are you a man or a woman?"

"I never saw you onstage. I regret it. One of us did. You danced a horn-pipe in a grass skirt, with flowers on your tits. The very exemplar of royal dignity. As for me, I saw you in Kololahi. Your beachwear was amusing, I concede. It ought to have had a little skirt to hide your thighs."

"I thought you were a man," Cassie said, "until you laughed."

"Would a man frighten you less? Then I'll be a woman for you. The Sisters of the Secret Sea. How cozy! Have you recalled poor Brian?"

If I can just keep her talking, Cassie told herself, *someone may come.* Aloud she said, "I'm afraid not."

"He was a paralegal, tall and gangly, with a big nose. I killed him." The dark voice giggled again. "He had the apartment over yours, and—"

"Oh, Lord! Yes, I remember."

"Well you should, Cassie dear, since he died for you. His apartment is ours now. Should you return to your old home, you'll find us above you. It won't be pleasant."

Cassie sighed. "It's bound to be more pleasant than this. Who are you?"

"A member of a fighting faith. Can't you guess our god?"

"You said something about a secret sea. So yes, I think I can." Her thoughts whirling, Cassie tried a ploy that might, she hoped, release a flood of words. "It's Hanga. It's the Shark God."

"Hardly, and you know better. An actress, with no more vocal control than that? Perhaps I may tread the boards myself someday. I couldn't be worse. You know our god. Are you going to follow my instructions? To the letter?"

"It depends on what they are."

"Not really. It depends on what will happen if you disobey. I thought I had made that clear. It also depends on the reward you shall have for obedience. First, your life will be spared. Second, you shall rule your little kingdom as its sole monarch, with no pernicious interfering husband. If you like men, you may have a hundred. Or a thousand. If you prefer women, the same. You will be subject, of course, to divinity. As we all are. You'll find him a kindly master, though one whose precepts must be obeyed to the letter."

"It's that dirty Squid God."

Something hard struck Cassie's head, leaving her dizzy, in pain, and half stunned.

"You didn't cry out." The dark voice was approving and amused. "That's very well. I would have had to shoot."

"Early training." Cassie felt her own warm blood running from between her finger. "My stepfather punished me again if I yelled."

"A man after my own heart."

"Yeah. He was. What did you swat me with?"

"The barrel of my gun. The barrel from which the bullet that will take your life shall come, unless you obey. Listen!"

"All right. I am."

"High King Willy will return tomorrow. You'll explain that you wish to swim in the sea, something your people do every day. He'll agree, and have you carried down this mountain. You'll return to the sea daily, or almost daily. In the sea, you'll be instructed further, and tested."

"Hot dog," Cassie muttered.

"When your instruction is complete, you'll speak to your husband of the bestial lust you and he hold so dear. You wish to couple with him in the sea, to couple alone amid the waves. By 'couple' I intend the satisfaction of his most dearly held desire, regardless of the form it may take. You'll do it—there—however filthy it may be."

"Let him suck my toes?" Cassie tried to sound serious.

It was ignored. "You'll hint, oh, most enticingly, of the many delights you offer. He'll come with you, and at the moment of climax he'll be taken. Leaving you, glorious High Queen Cassiopeia, the black throne. Do you understand what I said?"

"Better than you do, maybe. Did you give that poor paralegal a fighting chance? I'll bet you didn't."

"Nor will we give you a fighting chance," the dark voice told her. "You'll die like the stupid cow you are. A cow in a slaughterhouse."

"Got it. Have you yourself, personally, ever had normal sex? I think you're a woman. Not a woman like me, but a woman. So have you ever done it with somebody you loved? Somebody who loved you?"

"Pah! Fah!" The dark voice might have been that of an angry cat. "Juvenile posturing! Breeding! Do you think I want to learn what billions already know? My steel dildo is in your face. One moment more, and its ejaculation will blind an eye if it does not pulp your brain."

Cassie glimpsed a faint gleam on the oiled barrel and grabbed for it.

The pistol fired at once, its weakened flash burning her left cheek. The sound of the shot was lost amid the crash and rattle of broken glass.

The pistol fired again as they wrestled for it. Then its owner had it and fired a third time, not at Cassie but toward a door that had flown open. A woman so large she filled the doorway screamed.

The terrace door, which ought to have been closed and bolted, was neither. For an instant, a slender figure was silhouetted there against tropical stars.

There was another shot, not muffled in the least and followed by three more in quick succession. Then silence. Cassie found her robe on a chair not far from the king-size bed.

The lights came on. "You are hurt! O dearest queen, where do you bleed?"

"I don't think I do." Cassie paused, waiting for some indication of a wound. "My face is burned, maybe."

The maid spun like a bull in the ring and was gone before her flying hair had fallen to her back.

Cassie tied her belt and walked out onto the terrace. There was no one there, but an angry voice sounded from the terrace below. From the balustrade she saw an enormous man bent above a much smaller figure sprawled on the flagstone.

"Hiapo?" Blood trickled into her left eye. She wiped it away.

He looked up. "I here, O Queen."

There was a faint groan, not Hiapo's.

"Stay there until I get there."

A wide stairway, far from steep, led from her terrace to the one below. Afterward, she could not recall taking those steps, only speaking to Hiapo across the sprawled figure. "You shot her."

"I must, O Queen. She shoot at me."

"Did she hit you? You'd be hard to miss. Move your left hand."

He did, and she touched the place where it had been. Much more blood, warm and sticky.

"Give me your gun." She held out her hand.

He hesitated, then obeyed.

She pushed down the safety, dropping the hammer. "I don't sleep with mine. I guess that's a mistake. Go find the doctor, Hiapo. Dr. Schoonveld. Send him to me when he's through with you."

Hiapo pointed toward the sprawled figure. "This one, O Queen, may overpower you."

"While I'm standing here with a gun in my hand? I doubt it. Where's her gun, by the way?"

Hiapo found it and presented it to Cassie, who dropped it into a pocket of her robe.

After that she was alone with the sprawled figure, which moaned from time to time, though not in a dark voice, and once struggled to rise. Cassie tried to craft an adequate remark now that they were alone again, with roles reversed. *I need a writer,* she thought, and remembered one named Moe Zuckerman. Moe could have given her the perfect line, but he was not there.

"Your Majesty?" Dr. Schoonveld was leaning over the balustrade.

"Here!" she called, and recalled saying the same thing in school.

He hurried down. "Where were you hit?"

"On the head, but my cheek hurts worse."

For a moment his small chromed flashlight played on it.

"It's a powder burn, I think."

He nodded absently, already rummaging in his bag.

His nurse arrived, a tiny Japanese. After her, like elephants following a hare, came five hulking warriors with pistols and short black assault rifles.

Cassie dropped Hiapo's pistol into her robe's other pocket. "Look after her first."

"There are times," Dr. Schoonveld murmured, "when even royalty is not obeyed. This is one of them." He swabbed her cheek with a soft something that he dipped into a fluid that was neither water nor alcohol.

"She's dying!"

"That is so. It may be also that I kick her so that faster she dies."

"She may be able to tell us something."

"Lies, Your Majesty. Only lies she tells." Dr. Schoonveld motioned to his nurse.

"I feel sick," Cassie said, and as she spoke realized that it was so.

IT was almost dawn when she returned to bed. That bed had been made in her absence, with clean sheets and clean pillowcases. The drapes were closed over the window that the first shot had broken, though its broken pane remained. Outside it, a massive warrior with a black rifle scanned the terrace. She had expected not to sleep at all, but fell asleep as soon as her head touched the pillow.

In the corridor outside two men sprang to attention, their bare feet silent on the thick carpet, their rifles rattling as they presented arms. The door—hadn't she locked it?—opened and closed again, softly.

She heard the snick of the bolt, and knew the embrace of large, strong arms and the spicy scent of some cologne. A rough voice, kind and almost familiar, said, "Go back to sleep, Cassie baby. You've had a tough night."

And she did, feeling warm and safe.

HE was gone in the morning, but there was a note on the pillow next to hers.

My darling, I have been married twice but I have never loved anybody the way I love you. No woman I have ever known has been as beautiful or as brave and good. I am a king but I will kneel at your feet very soon. Last night I held you in my arms. I can't wait to hold you again. Did you feel my kiss? I'm hungry for yours!

Wally (Bill)

Bill Reis held up his hand. "I'm giving you my word, Kandy. I will not attack the Storm King, or his city, with depth charges. Or attack them at all without telling you what I plan."

King Kanoa nodded and thanked him.

They were gathered around a circular table in a room she had not seen before, King Kanoa, Hiapo, Reis, and Cassie herself. She had said not long ago that she could not be certain she had locked her bedroom door, but thought she had.

Now Reis returned to it. "What about the bolt? Did you use it, too?"

"I don't think so."

"Then that settles that. She was carrying lock picks, though to pick that lock she'd have to be good with them. What about the outside door, Cassie?"

"I locked it. I know I did."

Hiapo rumbled, "It was opened before the woman I shot came out, O High King. I see that it is opened. I was not watching when it open. I think our high queen does it."

Reis nodded. "An escape route. She'd try to get to the beach and into the water, I think. Kandy?"

"I concur." Looking thoughtful, King Kanoa cleared his throat. "I talked to Iulani. She was the maid who was shot at."

"She wasn't hit," Cassie put in.

"She was grazed, Your Majesty. Nothing serious, just tore the skin. Had it been a bit to the right . . ."

Reis asked, "What did she have to say?"

"She hadn't known the door was locked, and said it wasn't locked when she opened it. She had no key, she says."

"That fits. This woman—we need something to call her."

"The assassin? Good as anythin'."

"Right. The assassin picked the lock, came in, and shut the door behind her leaving it unlocked. Another escape route in case Hiapo came in from the terrace."

"Devilish good locks those are, Bill. Warren and Hardcastle? Best in the business."

Cassie said, "She's a woman, then. I thought so."

Reis flushed, his big face—already sunburned—redder still. "We'll call the doctor in before we're through."

"Fine. Then I want to know why King Kanoa doesn't think she picked my lock."

He adjusted his huge frame in his oversized chair. "Don't seem likely, that's all. Little bit of a thing, eh? Tallish for a Yank, but thin. Saw an expert try to pick a Warren and Hardcastle once. Rare book room. Librarian chap had locked himself in and shot himself. Body in there putrefyin'. He gave it up, eh? The expert chap. Ten minutes or so. Said it could be done but might take all afternoon. Drilled it out instead. Had a diamond-coated bit for the job, and needed it."

Cassie nodded.

"Assassin would be on her knees out in the hall, with people goin' up and down. Silly twit to try pickin'."

Reis said, "Then how'd she get in, Kandy?"

"Walked in, I'd say. I talked to Iulani. I say that? Well, I did, and she aired out the room before Her Majesty retired. Open windows, open terrace door, eh? Let in the fresh air. Let in the assassin, too. Easy as pie, 'cause Hiapo here was watchin' our queen and not her room. Little bit of a thing, dark clothes, hid in the shrubbery sneakin' from terrace to terrace soon as the sun was down. Peeped into the room, saw Iulani was gone, and popped in through the door. Not just a bedroom, is it?"

Cassie shook her head. "There's a bathroom and a—I don't know what you call it. A little private sitting room with big windows. A room for getting dressed and having my hair done with lots of closets, and a kitchenette."

"There you have it." King Kanoa raised his hands as if presenting a tray. "Dozen places to hide. She hid in one and waited 'til you'd gone to sleep and things quieted down. Then out she popped, unlocked both doors, and had a talk."

"I want to talk to her, this spy the Storm King sent here to threaten me." Cassie turned toward Reis. "Can I, Wally? Please?"

He nodded. "Before dinner, if you want. But I want all four of us to talk to Dr. Schoonveld first."

Cassie took a deep breath. "That's great, but I want to talk to you, too—to talk to you for a long, long time when the two of us are alone."

TWENTY-TWO

THE CITY UNDER THE SEA

"I will give you answers to the best of my ability," Dr. Schoonveld said as he and Cassie left a warm bright terrace for a corridor redolent of antiseptics, a corridor that seemed filled with cool twilight. "My answers are not apt to be satisfactory. Of this I warn."

"Why is that?"

"Let me repeat myself. It is because there are many things I do not know but wish to know. I have sent DNA to Amsterdam, but there is yet no report. This is one example of many."

"I'll start with an easy question, one nobody asked in the big meeting room or whatever you call it." Much to her own surprise Cassie found herself wishing for a pencil and notepad. "What's her name?"

"It is easy, Your Majesty. I do not know."

"She won't tell you?"

"She has told me half a dozen, none of which I credit. Most recent is Diana Diamond. Do you like it?"

Cassie shook her head. "Just for the record, I really am Cassie Casey. For lawyers it's Cassiopeia Fiona Casey, but I've been called Cassie all my life."

"You I credit. Perhaps I would credit Diana Diamond also, if so many others had not preceded it."

"Is she really a woman, Doctor? You seemed doubtful in the meeting."

"I am more than doubtful, but to speak of her we must call her one or the other. Woman is closer. There is no reason my opinion should interest you, but it is that she was once female and human."

"He can do that? The Storm King can?"

Dr. Schoonveld shrugged. "There is one other patient that has asked of you. This is one of ours, a woman your husband sent to spy. Will you see her? Afterward?"

"If you want me to, yes."

"Good." (It was nearly *goot*.) "I want it."

They had stopped before a door that appeared more solid than most. Dr. Schoonveld unlocked and opened it. "Alone you wish?"

"I don't care."

"Then I stand by."

Cassie went in. The slender figure chained to the bed appeared asleep. Its face was less white than the sheet drawn up to its waist. Its free arm lay at its side; above it, a flask dripped pale yellowish fluid into its veins through a slender tube.

"Do you hear me?" Cassie asked. "I'll keep talking until you wake and talk to me, but you're not to sit up."

Eyes too nearly colorless to be labeled "brown" or "blue" flew open. "That's not exact, but you're close." The voice was dark still.

"I'm a quick study. Should I call you Diana?"

"I don't care."

"Then I will. You hunted me."

"No . . ."

"Of course you did, you wanted to catch me. Now we've caught you. You people were all over Great Takanga and two or three other islands. That's what I've heard."

The figure in the bed said nothing.

"My husband came here and brought soldiers. They—"

"Mercenaries . . ."

"You mean they were paid. Of course they were. They hunted you down and killed most of you. Isn't that right?"

"Not all."

"I said most. They also captured a few of your people who were badly wounded. Dr. Schoonveld here patched them up so they could be questioned. After that, they were shot. That's what I was told."

The wounded woman's eyes were closed again; there was no sound but her breathing, and her breathing was scarcely audible.

"A friend told me once that my husband was a murderer. I think that's probably what he meant. I understand why he did it, but I still don't like it. So I'm offering you a deal. If you'll cooperate with me and answer my questions fully and honestly, I'll do everything I can to save your life. I can't promise I'll be able to, but I'll try, and try hard. What do you say?"

There was a long silence. At last the quiet figure said, "He's here. The doctor . . ."

"Yes. He is."

"I'll have to whisper. Bend down."

Cassie did, and the still figure in the bed spat in her face.

THE saliva, thick and faintly green, was off Cassie's face now, and that face had been thoroughly washed twice. "I still feel dirty," she told Dr. Schoonveld as they sat at a small table in the lounge.

"I understand."

She flipped open the red plastic compact she had bought at a chain drugstore in a time that now seemed infinitely remote. "She ever do that to you?"

"No."

"I feel like somebody who started school in the fourth grade." Cassie inspected her face in the compact's powder-dusty mirror. "I know the advanced stuff, but I don't know the basic stuff. How do I look?"

"Most lovely, Your Majesty. You are an astonishingly beautiful woman."

"Thanks, but this mirror doesn't believe you. I need eye makeup. It's all gone, every bit of it."

"Your eyes are most beautiful."

"Thanks again, but you can't see my eyelashes from a foot away." She got out mascara. "She worships the Storm King?"

Dr. Schoonveld nodded.

"Why? Why would anyone want to? What draws them to him?"

"Three things." Dr. Schoonveld pursed his lips. "Three at least. Three I know. First to be accepted and welcomed. They are outlanders, you see, those their own folk will not have. A man is born in China. Let us say this. His parents are Chinese. His brothers and sisters, also. Yet all look upon him and say, 'This is not one of us.' In your country and mine, the same. Once these were called changelings. For witches they are burned sometimes. The Storm King welcomes them, and these qualities that make others say no, no! he treasures."

Reluctantly, Cassie nodded.

"That is the first. Here is the second. They are made to feel a secret superiority, most strong. They are the masters of the hidden knowledge which turn the world. They have a friend—a patron—greater than any had by those who reject them. A queen? They spit in her face. What is a queen to them? What is any queen next to them? Dust and rubbish."

"When I was a little girl"—Cassie spoke mostly to herself—"he said that pride was the greatest sin, but that I could be proud of good grades and new clothes, that there was no sin in that. I knew from what he said that there was another kind of pride, but I don't think I ever really knew what it was. . . ."

"It is that, Your Majesty. You are most correct. There is a third reason. Would you hear it?"

"Yes, of course."

"They are given power. They may take life at their discretion. They are taught how to do it, how to do it without being taken. How to escape if they are taken. They are given a thousand comrades who will rescue them from any menace of law."

"She hasn't escaped."

Dr. Schoonveld shrugged; he had an expressive shrug. "I advised His Majesty to cut off her feet, and when he would not I offered to do this. He would not permit it. Perhaps he was right, but I think me."

"There must be some middle ground. I'll talk to him."

"That is good. Do you comprehend why the Storm King's worshippers come?"

"No. He's a monster. At least he sounds like one."

"He is an immigrant from the farthest stars. He comes before the flood." Dr. Schoonveld paused, and cleared his throat. "In all our history, we have found but one race of intelligence."

"The Wolders?"

"This is correct. Many such have found us, however. Many have made

Earth their home, though in small numbers always. Why do they not make themselves known to us?"

Cassie had finished work on her right eye and was starting on her left. "Because they're intelligent, I suppose."

Dr. Schoonveld smiled. "This is wise, what you say. Yet think. So many races, and all to the same conclusion? We think ourselves knowing, too. We find Woldercan, and a knowing folk there. We make ourselves known to them, and trade with them. We teach them, too, and learn from them. These things I have read. I have not been there."

"Neither have I."

"So. There is a difference. You agree, Your Majesty? We do not act there as others act here. Why?"

"You're a lot smarter than I am, Doctor. You tell me."

"I can say what I think. Only that." Dr. Schoonveld paused to glance around the room. There was no one in it save themselves. "He is the difference. The Storm King. He comes first, before all the rest. He is mightier than they, so they fear him. We are his, his cattle, and have been his since we came to be. They live here as mice in his barn. He was here before the first man stood erect to look up at the Host of Heaven. . . ."

"You're afraid of him?" Cassie was studying her own eyes in her little mirror.

"Him I have never seen," Dr. Schoonveld whispered. "But, yes. I am."

"So am I."

Dr. Schoonveld nodded. "You have more right than I. He has sent no one for me."

"My husband sent a woman for him. That's what you said."

"Yes. She has come back to us, broken and ill."

"Do you know what she found out?"

"That I do not." Dr. Schoonveld shook his head. "I do not ask. It is not my affair. I am to make her well—if I can. My nurse told her you had come. She would wish to speak with you, I said I would bring you if I could. I cannot make you go."

"I'll go, of course. What can you tell me about her?"

"Only this little. For me, her name is Jane Doe. It is the name I have been told to use. She is young, only not a child. She was instructed—His Majesty has told me this. In California she was to enter into the Storm King's circle. Have you been there?"

Nodding, Cassie opened her lipstick.

"Then you know. It is a place of strange beliefs. Spiritualists, Buddhists, pagans to prance naked beneath the full moon." Briefly Dr. Schoonveld smiled. "These do little harm, I think, but there are worse. There was a circle of fools to pay homage to the Storm King, but quite small. Also Satanists, and their groups became one. This was larger and grew quickly."

"Sounds bad," Cassie said.

"His Majesty wished to know who was there and what was planned. He found Jane Doe, who would see for him. One of our guards discovered her on the beach. He telephoned, and she was carried here. This is all I know."

"She's not talking?" Cassie inspected her lipstick in her little mirror.

"To me, no. To Izanami, more. To His Majesty, yes. To you more still, I think."

"How do I look?"

"Beautiful. No man could resist you."

"Thanks." Cassie smiled. "Lipstick on my teeth?"

"No. None."

"If she talks to me, I may not be able to tell you everything she told me."

"This I understand, Your Majesty."

Cassie rose. "But if she tells me anything that seems like it would help you treat her, you'll get it."

FOR a moment, the room seemed very different from the small, stark one in which the assassin lay; flowers will do that. Orchids and hibiscus, Cassie decided after studying the big bouquets. Orange blossoms, or something very like orange blossoms. Passion flowers? She tried to remember how passion flowers were supposed to look. Bougainvillea.

The woman in the bed lay upon her side, her face turned away from the door. A tall woman, Cassie thought, though the rangy body was hidden by a sheet and the long legs drawn up.

"Hello?" Cassie spoke softly. "I don't want to disturb you, and if you'd rather not talk to me I'll go. But the doctor said you wanted to see me."

She sensed that the tall woman was awake, though there was no sound and no movement.

"I'm Cassie."

Still nothing.

"I—I'm afraid I'm the queen here. Queen Cassiopeia, if you want to be formal."

The tall woman rolled over. The eyes in her wasted face appeared large; their stare was hypnotic.

"I don't know what happened to you, except that it was very bad. Whatever it was, I'm sure my husband didn't intend for you to be so—so hurt."

Slowly, the tall woman was sitting up. Long, bare legs slipped over the edge of the bed. The sheet was thrown back to reveal the usual inadequate hospital gown. White, in this case, with bloodless pink stripes.

"If you need some favor . . . Well, I can't promise anything, but I'll do what I can."

The tall woman stood, swaying, hands outstretched. Cassie took them, knowing somehow that it was what was asked.

And woke.

It had been only a dream, all of it. Her girlhood in San José, college, her work in the agency, the midnight meetings in strange places, and the strange visitors who sometimes appeared at those meetings.

There was only . . .

This.

This warm water, these bubbles spiraling slowly toward the surface with each breath she drew.

Less breath each time. Breaths more and more widely spaced. What was the value of breathing? Once she had known. Now she groped for the answer. Of what use was breath?

The world changed, silently, subtly, reversing as old-fashioned negatives are reversed. Light was darkness, and darkness light. Night lay below her, making dim her bright being with its starless self that was all shadow, the land of the murk-marred soul.

Above her the city shone, a city on the sun, its proud towers streaming with coruscant banners of holy vegetation that fluttered and snapped in crystal currents.

She removed her mask and the clumsy tank that held the air she did not need. They neither floated toward the city nor sunk toward the surface, but remained motionless where she had been. She herself made haste to meet those who made haste to meet her, angels too high and holy to serve any other god. They swarmed around her, larger—yet far smaller than she, kissing thighs and buttocks, sucking her ears and licking organs she had not known she possessed. Might she someday be as they?

Yes. He could do it. Would do it. . . .

He was the city, and the city he, his supple arms wrapping this world, warm and knowing, subtly favoring those who served him.

As she had served him to betray him.

I have come to see him and speak with him. She spoke to herself and thus to those who swarmed about her, swarmed like buzzing blue-backed flies, like minnows, like graceful gray slugs come to devour the dead, like lions circling an elephant whose blood soaks the soil on which he stands, an elephant whose strength is of the past, kept standing by pride, by the inborn knowing. It was—it is—the true king. It is royal and will remain royal even as carrion.

"Wheresoever the carcass is, there will the eagles be gathered together."

I have come that I may behold his face, and he mine.

Their reply came on the rush of the current. *You may not enter, much as we love and hate you.*

I must, or die.

Their laugher blew her upward, toward the city they denied her. *Already you are dead.*

She held her hands before her eyes. They were whiter than any chalk, hands molded of snow traced with blue—and that myriad who had swarmed her was no more. So soon as she no longer saw them, they were no more. She lowered her hands and swam, and they were back. She willed not to see them, willed as the man with the living beard, the six-fingered man, had taught her, had taught them all. Willed away, they were gone.

I am dead, bringing my bones to lay upon the heavens in tribute to him. This she spoke to herself, and thus to the keeper at the gate.

And you are . . . ?

Shalimar of the circle am I, Pat Gomez of Presidio Security, Patty Darling, Sweetheart, and Baby. All these.

The keeper of the gate remained erect; the gate bowed low. *Enter!*

The city was the god, the god the city. She entered into it as a man enters into a woman, triumphant in defeat.

They lay on white slabs all about her, his living dead. She wandered among them, changed by each, stronger in body and mind and less trusting of her strength, the storehouse of strange skills of language, murder, art, and love. She gloried in her strength and longed for the day when he would send her forth to rend his foe.

Long and long she waited; then the torture began. There remained in her, somewhere and somehow, the seed of humanity. A spore unseen but real; a thing that valued life in all its wild fantasies, standing awed before the slime mold and the butterfly. To root out that spore he broke her, scattering the bits from pole to pole.

Reassembling them in strange ways, scraped, washed, and cleaned. Broke her again, sifted the rubbish that remained for burning.

Until at last it came to her that if it continued she would come to hate him whom she had loved so briefly. And afterward that such hatred was proper, was right, was what he sought. Armed with the knowing, she rebelled. She would not hate him, though she wiped him from the world.

This was her first case, for which all the others, the skips and the shoplifters, the frauds, the cheaters, and the missing heir had been mere practice.

No, entertainment. Busywork . . .

Once she had made chains of colored paper, snipping out each link with clumsy, careful scissors, welding each closed with fubsy fingers that knew but little of tape and nothing of chains.

She escaped—or was rejected. Too dead to drown, she was cast up by the surf and nibbled by sea-green crabs that scuttled away when the footfalls sounded.

A man as large as any wrestler rolled her over. He might have had her there, there on the strand. So she thought and prepared herself to be violated, promising him that she was no longer sea-chilled but warmed now by the sun, sun-warmed and dead and welcoming his love. Surely there were those who spent their seed in the dead, who caressed cadavers such as she and struck them afterward in the corruption of their love?

He was not of their number. He took her in his arms, cradling her as he might have cradled a child, and carried her to the tiny cemetery behind the infirmary, went inside and told a nurse that he had found a body, a *haole wahine,* a white woman, dead.

The nurse had gone to look at her and had him carry her into an examination room. There she had lain faceup, salt water trickling from nostrils white as snow, as though the snow melted under the bright lights, melted in the cool air of the infirmary as it had in the warm sunlight of the beach.

There Dr. Schoonveld had tried this and that, a mask that breathed deep for her who did not breathe, stimulants injected directly into the heart muscles, shock.

He declared her dead and returned her to the cemetery, where she had vomited salt water, groaned, and wept for the grave this vomiting, these groans, denied her.

CASSIE started, and found herself alone and trembling, staring down at the dead woman who had . . .

Clasped her hands, if it had not been a dream. She shook herself and shivered, suddenly lonely for the strong arms that had held her through the night, for the furry hands of winged friends who grasped strange knowledge.

The arm of the woman who lay before her was limp. The wrist held no pulse save for one single weak beat that was almost certainly a mistake, a blunder by the stupid Cassie Casey she had tried so hard to forget, by the silly stagestruck woman who knew less of medicine than any drugstore clerk.

That stupid Cassie Casey who was in fact herself and no queen at all.

She found Dr. Schoonveld and told him his patient was dead, had been dead when she came into the room, although her hands had been clasped by that same dead patient, whose name was Pat Gomez.

CASSIE herself left his infirmary and stood staring up for a long minute at the Navy hopper that cruised grayly against the high blue vault, aerodynamically impossible, bristling with guns and antennae, yet flying as it seemed without effort.

Were they looking for her?

No, King Kanoa had said they were looking for Reis's gold, but would not find it. After a time she was joined by Hiapo, whom she sent looking for Reis.

After a still longer time, she was joined by the Japanese nurse, who feared she might be ill.

"No, I'm just trying to get over finding Pat Gomez dead. That was a jolt."

"You know her?" The Japanese nurse smiled politely. "Doctor, he say the king say it was her name."

"No," Cassie said. Then, "Yes. Yes I suppose I did know her. I played her for a while."

TWENTY-THREE

A STROLL ON THE BEACH

"I know you love me," Cassie told Reis, "and gosh knows I love you. I know you're busy, too."

Reis nodded.

"So what I'm asking for is a big gift, but I'm going to ask for it anyway. I want some time alone with you. Now. Two or more hours at least. Three might be better. I've got questions, and I think it's time we really got to know each other. Can I have it, Bill? Please?"

"Yes." He glanced at his watch. "Starting this minute if you like. I'm flattered. I hope you know that."

"I don't believe it, but I sure would like to. I want us to take a walk together. Down there on the beach would be too dangerous, wouldn't it?"

"The beach here in front of the palace would, yes. Absolutely. What about another beach, would that do if it's a nice one?"

Cassie nodded. "It might be better."

"In that case, there's no problem." Reis spoke into his watch; half a minute later, a hopper popped into being far above them. As he turned off the cell phone function, he said, "Our beach is watched, I'm sure of it. Not by the Storm King himself but by his worshippers. Luckily for us, there are thousands of islands in this part of the Pacific. They can't possibly watch them all, so they don't."

"WHERE are we?" Cassie asked as the hopper rose and boomed into nothing above them.

Reis smiled. "Let's not be overly specific. We're outside the Takanga Group. This could be Tuvalu or the Solomons, or a lot of other places. We'll be a little bit safer if I don't say it, perhaps. If you want the name of this particular island, I don't know it and it may not have one. It's uninhabited as far as we know."

"Except for the volcano."

Reis's smile widened. "Yes. Except for that. I'm glad you remember."

"So am I. Did you write that show, Bill?"

"Yes, with a collaborator. I knew what show I wanted and he knew how shows ought to work. I suppose I ought to say I sweated blood over it, but it was fun. I enjoyed it. I didn't compose the music, you understand. For the most part I sketched out the plot and told my collaborator what ought to happen in various scenes. Are we going to walk along the beach?"

Cassie said, "I hope so. That's what I wanted."

"In that case I'll take off my shoes." Reis found a shady spot beneath a palm tree and sat.

Nodding, Cassie sat beside him. Her canvas sandals were off in a moment. They kissed, and when both his shoes stood beside hers, they kissed again.

She rose. "Want a hand up?"

"Not particularly." He grinned. "But I know you want to talk. So do I. What is it you want from life, Cassie?"

"That's a big one. All right if I think about it?"

Reis nodded.

"What is it you want, Bill? I know you must have thought about the answer before you asked me."

"You're right. I have." He stood. "Everybody dies, Cassie."

"Sure."

"I wish it weren't like that. But even if we didn't age, we'd die anyway, sooner or later. Accident, disease, suicide, war, murder . . . Something would get us."

"Uh-huh."

"We'd have two hundred and fifty years, perhaps. Some would. Three hundred at most." Reis drew a deep breath. "So here's what I want. I want to be a very powerful man, and I want to use that power for good. A lot of people think I'm a bad man."

Cassie nodded, remembering. "Dr. Chase certainly seemed to think so."

"The rich are his clients. Rich people, governments—they're all rich, never let anybody tell you different—and rich corporations. Nobody else can afford his fees. He takes the money and does what they want. Sometimes it's good. Sometimes it isn't. He's a wizard. I'll give him that. I've got him on my team now, and I'm damned glad to have him."

"Do you trust him?"

Reis shook his head. "I trust very, very few people, and Gideon Chase isn't one of them. You can never trust a wizard, my darling. They know too much and they're too complicated."

"I trusted him." She began to walk.

He followed her, keeping his steps small and slow to match her speed. "You're a trusting woman, and I love you for it. That doesn't mean I'd put you in an executive position. I wouldn't. It's not what you're cut out for."

"I know. . . ."

The sea was blue and gentle. She found a dried starfish, examined it, and tossed it back into the water. "I've been thinking about what I want."

He nodded. His face serious. "Are you going to tell me?"

"Pretty soon, I think. You disappear. Want to say you don't?"

He shook his head.

"That's good. I watched you do it in Springfield. I asked Dr. Chase after that, and he said yes. You could do it, but he couldn't."

Reis said, "Then it seems he told you the truth. May I show you something?"

"Yes, if you want to."

"Watch me. Look hard." She did, and he vanished. Unseen, his hand touched hers. "I'm still here."

"Yes." She was smiling.

"And you're still beautiful. Now look behind us."

She turned, and saw their shadows paint a romantic silhouette on the sand, a big man clasping the hand of a smaller woman.

"As a general thing," he said conversationally, "I try to stay clear of sunshine when I do this. Of bright light from any single source."

He was visible again, and she rose on tiptoe to kiss him.

When that kiss ended, another began.

At last they separated. "You make gold, too, Wally. Is it all right if I call you Wally sometimes?"

He nodded. "The gold made you think of that first bracelet. I understand."

"I guess it did. We've already talked a little about the gold. Radioactive gold."

"We have."

"And vanishing. So you're a wizard, too."

He chuckled. "I suppose I am. I've been called a financial wizard often enough. I should have thought of that."

"You told me once that you could be trusted. You said your word was always good."

"Did I? I probably did. Certainly it's true."

"Do you love me, Wally?"

"Yes. As I've never loved anyone else." He sighed. "I only wish you loved me as much as I love you."

"I want to. Because that's what I want from life. Remember asking me? I want love. It's why I liked doing *Dating the Volcano God* so much. I could get out there onstage and be Mariah Brownlea, and the whole audience loved me. It's why I married two pretty terrible men, because I thought they loved me. They said they did, and I believed it. When I found out Scott didn't—and Herbie not enough—I dumped them."

"I don't want to be dumped. Do you believe me, Cassie?"

"Sometimes, but there are things that bother me."

"The gold, of course. Do you know the dragon legend? How dragons hoard gold, amassing more and more? Sleeping on a bed of gold?"

"I saw a vid about that once."

Reis nodded. "I called it a legend because that's what everybody calls it. It isn't really a legend at all. There are dragons, Cassie. Real dragons."

She stared out to sea, then turned back to him. "A year ago I wouldn't have believed you. Now . . ."

"You don't know."

"Right. Dr. Chase took me to a place called the Silent Woman. Have you ever been there?"

Reis shook his head.

"It was a storybook kind of place, but they had good food."

He smiled. "They often do in storybooks."

"I suppose. Anyway, I told him they ought to serve dragon's eggs, and Dr. Chase said they couldn't, eating dragon's eggs would kill you. He talked like there really were dragons. Both of you do."

"Because there are. Some are human beings, Cassie. Some aren't. The Storm King is a dragon in the sense I mean, and one of the worst. A dragon, and not remotely human. May I tell you about my gold?"

"I wish you would."

"I sell it in small bars, little bars that you could put in your purse. They weigh about as much as a bag of groceries. Gold's heavy stuff."

"I know that bracelet was."

"You're right. My customer may buy only one. Or a hundred. If he buys a lot, he gets it delivered in dribs and drabs, one or two little bars at a time."

"King Kanoa said something about that."

"Kandy? Yes, he knows. Sometimes my customer is a dragon who hoards it all. If he isn't, it will fall into the hands of a dragon sooner or later. Most of it, if not all of it. They keep it together and they keep it near them, because they're afraid it may be stolen."

"I—see."

For a time they walked together in silence, looking out to sea, or up at the towering peak of the volcano, or just along the beach, an utterly deserted beach of white coral sand.

"People lived here once," Cassie said at last.

"How do you know?"

"My eyes keep looking for footprints in the sand."

"Have you seen any?"

She shook her head. "Only ours. But I wouldn't look for them if I didn't know, down deep, that there had been people here."

"You may have seen the blocks without really noticing them."

"What blocks?" She had stopped, and turned to face him.

"Squared blocks of coral back in the jungle. I saw them when I stopped to take off my shoes. Someone built something here once, even if there's nobody here now."

"Don't be mad, Wally. Please don't. But would it be all right if we go back so I can look at them?"

"Of course it is. This is your walk."

His watch chimed; he answered it, saying mostly yes and no. Once he said, "Go ahead," and once he chuckled.

When he had hung up, Cassie said, "I think my walk's almost over, and I haven't even gotten to the important stuff. So I'm going to bring it up right now. Pat Gomez is dead. Do you know who she was?"

"I do. I got her killed, though I didn't intend to. What do you know about her?"

"Only that she was working for you, and that she went down to the Storm King's city. They must've done horrible things to her there, because it seemed like she was crazy."

"You talked to her?"

Cassie ignored the question. "I liked her, and she died while I was there with her in her room."

"I can't say that I liked her," Reis said, "but then I only saw her twice. Before she was dumped on our beach, I mean. She seemed competent, and I didn't think they were likely to suspect she was a plant. That was what I wanted, so I hired her. She was an operative with a little agency in Oakland. She was supposed to join the Storm King's cult in San Francisco and tell us who belonged to it and what they were planning. She did it for about six weeks. After that she dropped out of sight. The agency didn't know what had become of her and neither did I."

"I asked Dr. Schoonveld how they bury people here. It's pretty simple. No embalming. They just wrap them in plastic and bury them in a hole in the sand."

Reis nodded. "For us, yes, though not many of us die here. Kandy's people have their own customs, and we turn their bodies over to their relatives."

For a handful of seconds it seemed to Cassie that the palms, restless as they always were in the trade wind, were whispering to her: dark secrets she had no desire to hear. "You make sure they're dead?"

"The doctor does, yes. You said she died while you were with her."

Cassie managed to smile. "That's true, Wally, but I'm not really a nurse. I just play one sometimes."

He smiled in return.

"Hiapo found the man who had found her body for me, and brought him to me. He was sure she was dead when he picked her up. So was she . . ."

Reis put his arm around Cassie's shoulders. "This is just making you unhappy, and I hate seeing you unhappy. What would you like me to do?"

"I don't know!"

"Then let's talk about something else. Isn't there anything else you'd like to talk about?"

"In the meeting—oh, Wally, I hate to say this."

"The meeting today? That was when you said you wanted some time alone with me."

"Right." Cassie forced herself to stand straight. "The Storm King sent that awful woman, Wally. Sent her to try to make me hand you over to them."

"Go on."

"And I felt sure you'd be angry. But in the meeting, right at the beginning, you promised King Kanoa that you wouldn't do anything about it."

Reis shook his head. "I did nothing of the sort."

"Yes you—"

He raised his hand. "I did not, Cassie. I know what I said, even if you don't. I promised Kandy I wouldn't attack the city with depth charges. That was what he was afraid I was planning to do. Think back and you'll find that I'm correct."

"It's the same thing!"

"No. It really isn't. Still, you're right in one way. I'm not attacking it. Or him. Not attacking isn't the same as doing nothing. Have you ever offended gypsies?"

She stared. "I don't even know any."

"Neither do I, but a man who works for me got some gypsies seriously angry at him. They put stolen goods in the trunk of his car and phoned the police."

For several dozen steps, Cassie considered that. At last she said, "I'm so lost. . . . What do you mean, Wally?"

"The Navy's been hunting for my gold for two years. I told you about that."

She nodded.

"They're good men, and they've been working hard. It's pretty mean of me, when you come to think of it, to keep them flying around with nothing to report. I've decided to let them find some."

"Do you know," Cassie asked, "you look exactly like a little boy with both hands in the cookie jar?"

Reis chuckled. "You see right through me."

"Maybe I do. The police found some stolen goods, right? In the trunk of your guy's car?"

"Exactly. We know, you see, where the Storm King's sunken city is. We've known for a year at least, and Kandy's been afraid I'd try to blow it up ever since we found it."

"Does he like the Storm King?"

"No. He's afraid of him. He fears him even more than he fears me. With good reason, I'd say." For a few steps Reis was silent. "I've killed some people, Cassie. Killed them myself, I mean. A good many more have been killed at my order. I think I had good reasons in every case. The Storm King may think the same thing, though I don't believe he does."

"What does he think, Bill? Do you know?"

Reis shrugged. "Ever lived on a farm?"

"No. I'd like to try it someday."

"I haven't either, but I stayed on one for a while as a young man. A company dinner was almost always chicken. Real free-range chicken. The farmer's wife would catch one and wring its neck. It didn't bother her. They were just chickens."

"I think I've got it."

"I've wandered way off the point, but I'll get back now. Today we start dropping gold bars into R'lyeh. We'll be dropping one a day, mostly. Sometimes two. Sometimes none. That will depend on what other uses I may have for the gold. The Storm King has people down there. Hundreds. A thousand, maybe."

Remembering, Cassie nodded.

"He may not know about the gold for a while, but they certainly will in a day or two. They'll collect them, and keep them together."

"The radiation . . . ?"

Reis grinned. "Long before the radiation, the Navy. I don't know how much gold they'll have to have at that depth before the Navy picks it up. It could be twenty bars. It could five. But they'll pick it up, and when they do, they'll go after it. My guess is that they'll send down robot submersibles. They have some good ones, designed for underwater rescue and salvage."

Cassie asked, "The kind with operators somewhere else?"

"Exactly. The operators will be in ships on the surface, but they'll see the images transmitted by vid cameras on the submersibles. Those images will be of the Storm King's sunken city, lit by the powerful lights the submersibles carry." Reis grinned again. "Which one do you think will be the most surprised?"

"I don't know, but the Storm King . . ."

"Will find that he has a much more dangerous enemy than I am."

THE squared coral blocks, when they found them, led them to an image, also of coral: a squat, wide-mouthed king or deity remarkable only for its size and the ruin wrought by weathering.

"I don't like him," Cassie said.

"I don't think you're supposed to," Reis told her. "You're supposed to fear him and like me."

They kissed; and soon after, on the beach and half in the surf, they did a great deal more.

ABOARD the hopper that would return them to Takanga Ha'i, Cassie asked, "Are you going to marry me, Bill?"

He looked pleasantly surprised. "If you'll have me, darling. Yes. As soon as we can arrange whatever kind of wedding you want, and I'll give you a rock so big nobody will believe it's real."

He gulped, and though Cassie could not hear the gulp, she saw his throat move before he said, "I was about to tell you I didn't know what you wanted from marriage. But I do. You told me. You want love. You'll get it—shaken down, pressed down, and overflowing. I would die for you, Cassie. I really would."

"Don't talk like that. Don't even think like that." She shivered. "Put your arms around me."

He did. "I don't do this as much as I'd like to. I don't want to embarrass you in public."

"I like it. I don't care whether they envy my rock. It'll have to be in some bank most of the time anyway. I want them to envy my man, and they will."

He hugged her, very gently.

"Can I tell you what kind of wedding I want?"

"Yes. Tell me."

"Nothing complicated. I've been married twice already. You know that." Reis nodded. "So have I."

"But I want a bridal gown. Pastel green. White is for virgins, and I'm not trying to fool anybody. Aren't there preachers on the big island? Missionaries?"

"Yes. Half a dozen, probably."

"Well, one of them can perform the ceremony. I want it to be in the city somewhere. I mean Kololahi. A place where there's a wide green lawn, and a white building in the background. I want King Kanoa there, and hundreds of our people. Would that be all right?"

"Absolutely. They'll be delighted."

"And I'd like you to fly in a few of my friends from Kingsport. India and Ebony for sure. Tiny, and Dr. Chase. Sharon Bench. Of course you can invite your own friends and family."

Reis nodded, his face serious. "You don't have any family do you, Cassie?"

She shook her head. "It was just Mom and me. That was all the family I ever had, and she's dead now."

"I'm sorry."

"So am I. But it's not like she died yesterday, or even last year. I'm used to it."

"I—I have a son from a previous marriage. May he come? Would that bother you? He's sixteen."

She smiled. "Of course not! He should come, and I want to meet him."

Reis kissed her.

THAT evening, Hiapo asked leave to speak with her. She agreed and made him sit down in her little drawing room. "Something's bothering you." Her tone was as kind as she could make it. "If you're afraid I'll be angry, I won't be. You've got my word."

He adjusted his position, his nervousness freakish in so large and stolid a man. Distrustful of her graceful chairs, he was sitting on the floor. "I am not afraid you will be angry, O Queen. I am afraid you will be afraid."

"But you think I ought to be told."

Hiapo nodded solemnly.

"My guess is that you're right there, but wrong about me being afraid. What is it?"

"The woman die."

"The woman I was talking to in the infirmary?"

"Even so, O Queen. This woman who die. They bury her. Over her is sand and dirt, made smooth like beach."

Cassie nodded. "I've got it."

"This morning, no longer smooth. I say we must look. They do not like, but I dig."

Cassie took a deep breath. "She's gone, right?"

"You say true, O Queen. They wrap her in—" Hiapo hesitated. "Sarong of dead."

"A plastic sheet."

Hiapo nodded. "I find it in grave at bottom, but no woman there is, O Queen."

TWO days later, when they were inspecting possible sites in Kololahi, Reis said, "I have good news and I have bad news. The good news is very good. Or at least I think so. The bad news is only a little bit bad, but I admit I'm disappointed. Which would you like to hear first?"

"The good news, naturally. I'm a good-news girl."

"Rian's coming. That's my son. Rian Reis." Reis cleared his throat. "His mother named him."

Cassie nodded. "I'd say she did a pretty good job of it."

"Thank you. She raised him, and I've got to say she did well with that, too. He was very ill as a child. A defective heart valve was what they said, although I think it was really something else. His mother got your friend Dr. Chase. Chase fixed it, whatever it really was. I'd never heard of him until then."

"He's well now?"

Reis nodded, smiling. "This is his final year at prep school, and he's their starting quarterback. Now you'll ask if I've ever seen him play. I have. I've seen every game."

"My gosh, Bill! Isn't that dangerous?"

Reis's smile became a grin. "I said I'd seen them, which I have. I didn't say I was seen at them."

She kissed him, a fleeting kiss like the touch of a finch's wing. "Now the bad news. Should I sit down?"

"That shouldn't be necessary. I doubt that you've ever heard of Harold Klauser."

Cassie shook her head.

"He was my predecessor as American ambassador to Woldercan, and he stayed on for a month after I got there to show me the ropes. I don't have many friends, Cassie. Wealthy men rarely do. Harold Klauser's my closest friend, though, and very close indeed. He wanted to come, but his doctors say he shouldn't risk the trip."

"We could vid it, and send him the card."

"You're right. I should have thought of that myself, and I'm surprised you did."

Cassie grinned. "Showbiz. Remember?"

Later that day, they were shown the broad lawn of the New Zealand consulate, a close-cut carpet of green running down to a rock-strewn beach and the clean, blue Pacific.

TWENTY-FOUR

THE STORM—AND THE CALM

Hearing stealthy noises as she composed herself for sleep, Cassie opened her eyes, sat up, and found a woman on either side of her bed. To her right, the assassin's large, pale eyes seemed luminous in the dim light; a faint smile played around her mouth.

On the other side, the dead woman stood erect and motionless, her face a mask, her eyes two darker stains upon that mask.

"Mate in three moves." The assassin tittered. "I've come to tell you the game's as good as over. That it *is* over in the intellectual sense. It's over, dear, darling, sweet, plump Queen Cassie, and you'll be a widow before you're ever a bride."

Cassie stared. "How did you get in here?"

"How could you keep me out?"

From the other side of the big bed, the dead woman whispered, "I unlocked her chain."

Cassie turned to look at her. "Why?"

"A witness. I must write my report."

The assassin tittered.

"I don't understand."

"When I've written it, I will have peace."

The assassin said, "We are the halves, Cassie dearest. Together we make a whole. I'm the hunted, she's the hunter. I'm the vixen, she's the bitch baying on my trail. Without a fox she's just a pet, one who'd soon be replaced by a poodle like you. Without a hound, what glory would I have in the court of the Storm King?"

The dead woman said, "We're going to steal Reis's hopper. We'll return to the Bay Area."

The assassin tittered again. "I to San Francisco, she to Oakland. But first, we visited you. You don't have to offer refreshments."

"Really? I'm sure you'd like a nice glass of blood."

The dead woman said, "You're my sister. You've seen what I saw. You felt what I felt. Please find my grave, in Oakland or Orinda. I may not be in it, but I'd like you to lay flowers there."

"She'll die, too!" The assassin snarled.

"You will live. Lay the flowers."

"I will," Cassie whispered. "I promise."

"We've won!" The assassin's hand, small and thin, grasped Cassie's shoulder. "Listen! What do you hear?"

Cassie did. "The wind. Only the wind." Although her windows were closed, it seemed to her that her drapes were stirring.

"Yes, the wind!" There was no giggle or titter now, but the wild, unnatural laughter of a thoroughly bad child. "Come out on the terrace. Tell us what you see."

The dead woman was already pulling down the sheet. Cassie rose and found her slippers. The dead woman and the assassin held her robe. She recalled it long afterward, and nothing in all their strange interview seemed stranger than that.

When the terrace door opened, the song of the wind filled her bedroom; the wind itself ballooned her robe and knocked over something in another room.

Outside, she felt she had gone blind. She struggled to keep her feet, while her robe snapped behind her like a banner. The assassin and the dead woman who had been Pat Gomez had vanished into the howling night.

She was putting on her shoes when the lights went out. Her watch swore that it was day; no daylight came, only the crashing of waves not far enough below.

A window blew in, showering the room with broken glass.

She fled into the hall and ran toward the only light she saw. Hiapo held it, a clumsy lantern in which the flame of a fat candle flickered and smoked. He said, "You are dressed, O Queen. That is well."

"Why should I be dressed?"

"We would dress you." He whistled, abrupt and shrill. Two women came and took her arms. When she protested, he said, "These are needful, O Queen. These are needful. You must go with us."

She had recognized one of the women and whispered, "What is this, Iulani?"

"Justice, O Queen. You bring the judgment of the Sky Gods."

Only that, of all her questions, evoked an answer.

They left the palace for a rough tunnel cut into the living rock of the mountain, and left that for a long, worn stair that mounted up and up, turning and sometime coiling upon itself like a snake—or so it seemed to Cassie. Her little Italian automatic was strapped to her right thigh; had it been back in Kingsport, it could not have been less accessible.

The wind screamed. She heard it faintly at first, but nearer and louder with each step they mounted, a wind that shrieked in agony like a witch in labor. *The devil's son,* she thought, *will be born tonight.*

And found herself shouting it, not at the women whose strong hands pinioned her arms but at Hiapo's broad back. "The devil's son! Listen to me! The devil's son is born tonight!"

If Hiapo heard her, he gave no sign.

The arch at the top of the stair appeared, fitfully lit at times by vagrant beams that slipped away—swallowed by a night blacker far than any night should be.

The wind was terrible, alive with cold anger.

Then her arms were freed. She used them to hold down her skirt, which threatened to climb about her waist. Her hair had become a red mop—or so she thought, and did not care. As she saw now, the fitful beams came from hundreds of big lanterns of pierced tin lanterns held by warriors Hiapo's size.

Then Hiapo was gone, and King Kanoa was coming toward her. "You have not been injured, I hope." King Kanoa's face was in shadow; his booming voice, which so often held a smile, was not smiling on this black morning. "Are you hurt?"

"Scared," Cassie admitted. "Just scared."

"You needn't be. No one here intends you harm." He took her arm. "I shall protect you. Come with me to the seat of justice."

More steps, narrow and steep and lit from below by the flickering beams, steps she surmounted one by one on legs that already ached.

The seat of justice was of stone; when she was seated upon it—with her arms pinned to its armrests by the two women—her fingers found carvings.

"This," King Kanoa told her, "is the ancient throne of my ancestors. It is here that our high king or high queen sits to announce to our assembled nation the justice of the Sky Gods." His tone was conversational but not light. "At present the only god in our sky is the Storm King. He has raised this typhoon. Do you recall the village where we landed?"

Cassie managed to say yes, although it was difficult to make herself heard above the wind. "Yes, I do."

"It is gone, every stick of it. At this point I would guess that a hundred such villages have been destroyed and two thousand or more of us drowned."

"How terrible!"

"It is." He had moved behind her now, but Cassie felt sure he was nodding. "You have a good, loud voice, as is to be expected of an actress. I had hoped this wouldn't be necessary. Close your mouth, please."

She did not, but his powerful hand closed it for her, forcing her chin up until the back of her head was firmly against the high stone back of the throne, then farther until her teeth locked. A moment later, a strip of tape covered her mouth.

"You can still breathe, I hope. I'll take that off as soon as this is over. Or you can."

Suddenly his voice boomed forth, speaking his own tongue. Clearly, Cassie decided, he had a microphone, and there were loudspeakers below—loudspeakers that had not lost power when the palace had, or to which power had been restored.

Minutes passed. King Kanoa finished, and was cheered wildly. Several men fired into the air.

"Let me speak English." For the second time, his voice thundered from the speakers. "There are those here, our high king among them, who do not understand our tongue. They, too, deserve to know."

Cassie's eyes searched for Reis, but did not find him.

"In righteous anger, the Storm King has raised this typhoon. We, his devout worshippers, perish. We have begged him to mitigate his displeasure, and he has answered us. If we offer our greatest sacrifice, his storm shall abate. Here we do as he asks. Our high king will die for us, his people."

Cassie struggled, but could not free her arms from the women's grip.

"Bring him forth! *Lawe mai Mo'i!*"

Below them, the crowd of huge warriors parted. Reis, a big man, looked small beside them. Very small, Cassie thought, but proud and unafraid. His hands seemed to have been tied behind his back.

The last of the warriors who accompanied him carried a painted club the size of a softball bat, with a great knob of wood at its head.

King Kanoa spoke again in his own tongue. Then: "You cannot speak as we, O King, but you may now address those who wait in English speech."

"I don't want to," Reis said. "I couldn't make myself heard anyway." He paused. There was fear in his eyes, but something else as well. "Can you hear me, Cassie?"

She could not reply, but she nodded.

"This storm isn't even intended for us. We're on the fringe here. The Navy's gone after the Storm King, and he's hoping to sink their ships. He's probably sunk a few already."

"Faster," King Kanoa told Reis. "We haven't got a lot of time."

"Remember what I say, Cassie. I did what I could for humanity. I wanted to be of real help, and never gave a damn for what anybody thought of me. I succeeded. I love my son Rian. Tell him if you can."

Cassie tried to nod, but King Kanoa's hand had closed around the back of her head, holding it immovable.

"I love you. Don't forget that, either. I loved you in life, and I'll love you in death."

King Kanoa spoke, and Reis was thrown down. At once he vanished, then reappeared only to vanish again. Visible or invisible his captors held him, positioning his head on a wide, dark stone near Cassie's feet.

The warrior with the club moved to stand beside it, his club raised.

King Kanoa spoke again, his words followed by wild cheering and more shots. The beam of every lantern found her. It was as if she sat onstage, the target of hundreds of feeble spotlights.

During those cheers, King Kanoa had switched off his microphone; when he spoke again, in English, his voice was normal and only just loud enough for her to hear him above the shrieking wind. "How must it be, O Queen? Speak now. The high priest watches. Must High King Wiliama 'Aukailani die this day to save his people?" His hand forced her head down, raised it, forced it down again, and freed it.

The club struck; the thud of the blow and the sound of breaking bone would stay with Cassie as long as she lived.

King Kanoa spoke, and the women freed her arms. His strong fingers freed her mouth of the tape with a quick pull. "You remain our high queen," he told her. "Thinking solely of your own good, I advise you to marry someone thoroughly familiar with the local situation who can assist your rule."

Then her gun was in her hand and King Kanoa's broad chest stretched before its muzzle. Afterward, she could not recall how many times she fired, only that the number was greater than two and probably greater than three.

Something seized her and jerked her upward, and her gun was no longer there.

Magically, the wind vanished. Driven by it, they were scudding over a tumultuous sea, and there were wings before them, wings darker even than that dark day.

THEY landed her upon a coral beach in sunshine. "We can carry you no farther," the tall being who had held her explained, "and could not have raised you as we did if it had not been for the wind. You may be happy here."

Cassie could only gasp her thanks.

Then they were gone, flecks of black dwindling against a blank turquoise sky; she sat down and stared at the waves for a time, rose, found shade, and sat staring again. It was not until the sun touched the horizon that she shook herself, unstrapped the empty holster from her thigh, and threw it into the waves.

Fresh water trickling down to the sea betrayed itself by a chuckle. Cassie drank long, and slept on the beach. She slept soundly that night and spent the following day in search of food; but the next night was different.

After that, each day was like the last. She looked for food, always finding some but never finding enough. In time, it occurred to her that she should keep a tally of the days; but many had already passed, and she could not say how many. She would be here until she died, which would be soon. Wasn't that enough? When she died, the gulls would peck her corpse. How would the number of her days on the island matter?

It was not until she caught sight of the burning mountain that she realized where she was. After that she walked in good earnest, searching for the place where they had seen the coral blocks, the place where Reis had left his shoes.

She found it at last, took off her sandals, and went barefoot thereafter.

After three days she returned to the spot, drawn by memories that were sweeter and more real there. For a time she followed a regular schedule, returning every third day to sit where they had sat together. When she closed her eyes, it seemed to her that Reis sat beside her. She could hear the soft sigh of his breath, and catch the spicy scent of his cologne.

Until at last she remembered the image they had found, the squat, worn image that devout hands had carved in coral long ago. She looked for it again.

And found no image, but Vincent Palma seated on a weathered block of coral.

His skin was almost black with tattoos; his headdress, which ought to have been of long red and yellow feathers, was now of leaping flame. And yet it was surely Vincent Palma, taller than most men, with his too-cunning eyes and tomcat smile.

"Vince!" she gasped. "Ohmygosh, Vince, what in the world are you doing here?"

"I've come to give you something, Cassie." His voice was just as it had always been, a voice that made whatever he said sound important.

"You've given me plenty just by coming. I've been so lonely here, Vince. You can't imagine how lonely." She reached out to touch his hand, but it was so hot that she jerked her own away.

"I know it only too well," he told her. There was a rumble less distinct than the surf, a deep drumming like distant thunder, from the burning mountain behind him.

"Remember the show? The banquet you made for me? The way you danced with Gil and me?"

"No . . . No." He sighed, and it seemed to her there was a loneliness as deep as her own in the sigh. "May I ask a favor, Cassie? A great favor given freely to one who will afterward present you with a gift that will be precious to you?"

It sounded dangerous. "I can't promise I'll do it when I don't know what it is."

"But may I ask?"

Hesitantly, she nodded.

"We used to dance, you say. Dance with me now."

"I—well, of course I'll try, Vince. But there's no music."

"Listen. Only listen! How can you say there's no music?"

She did. There were drums in the waves and a thousand strings in the palms. Sunbeams winded trumpets through the dark green leaves. She began to dance, and discovered that she could no longer dance as once she had, though she did her best for her partner's sake, keeping time to the music and moving with quaint grace.

He rose and leaped higher than her head, circled her with a breathtaking series of leaps, seized her in hands that smoked where they touched her ragged dress and tossed her into the air so high that she turned head over heels at the apex.

And caught her as she fell.

It freed something that had been bound before; after it she danced as he did while the burning mountain pounded a kettledrum and birds of a hundred brilliant hues joined the music with strange songs. So they danced, and it did not matter to them that no one saw them, because they saw themselves.

Until at last she fell panting, and could dance no more.

He kissed her as she sprawled upon the black jungle loam—burning lips that brushed her own—seated himself once more upon his weathered coral block, and waited.

At length she sat up. "I'm awfully sorry, Vince. I gave out." And then, "You're not really Vince, are you? You just look like him."

Sadly he shook his head.

"I like you better, whoever you are. I never liked Vince, or not much. But I like you a lot."

"Then you will do as I ask." He smiled Vince's smile. "Gather wood, Cassie. Pile it on the sand. You know the place. Twigs and fallen branches. Driftwood. It may be wet or dry. That will not matter."

She nodded as she rose. "How much?"

"You will know when there is enough."

Something held her. "Will I ever see you again?"

"I think you may. Leave flowers."

"All right," she said, and began to collect wood. When the pile was as high as her waist, and night had come with the breathtaking rush that only the tropics know, she searched for more wood by moonlight.

When she returned, her pile was ablaze.

AFTER that she had fire, a fire that she kept burning always, sometimes larger, sometimes smaller. She learned then to make a spear, burning the end of a hardwood sapling and scraping away the charcoal with a shell. It took hours of patient fishing to spear a fish. Little by little her aim improved, and she learned which kinds tasted best when wrapped in green leaves and roasted in the coals.

DAWN, and she woke to see a white ship. She screamed and leaped and waved, and piled all her wood onto her fire, which seemed almost to go out before it sprang up roaring.

And miracle of miracles, a boat, a swift white motor launch, put out from the ship. Then she raced through the jungle picking flowers and piled them at the feet of a weathered coral image, and met the boat on the beach with an armload more.

The launch's crew of three, three lean, sun-bronzed sailors who spoke a language that Cassie felt sure was not French, smiled their welcome and patted her back gently. The young officer who commanded the launch was English, and reserved with that young man's reserve that is at least half embarrassment. "Shipwrecked, I'd say?"

It seemed safest to nod, so Cassie did.

"Bit of a time, I'd say. You look it. Should've brought you a sheet or something. Back aboard and bob's your uncle."

After which he would not look at her.

The captain was American, formerly of the Coast Guard. He made her sit, and there was coffee and a coffee cake well sprinkled with nuts.

"I haven't had coffee . . ." Cassie began, and began to cry.

"You'll have to meet the owner," the captain told her. "She's still in bed, but after her breakfast. Try not to cry, Mrs. Casey. She doesn't like it."

Cassie nodded, and cried the more.

"Want to tell me how you got on the island?"

She shook her head. "You'd never believe me."

"Try me." He sounded serious. "Tell me the truth. If it's the truth, I'll know it."

"May I think for a minute? It seems like a long, long time ago now. What year is this?"

He told her, and she said, "It was last year when I got to the island. I—I was always hungry. Always. Sometimes I could find some food. Fish or fruit, almost always. I don't think I'll ever eat fish or fruit again." She picked up the nearest pastry, bit it, chewed it slowly, and swallowed. "I thought I'd die there. Right there. Do you believe me?"

"I do. You're telling the truth. How did you get there?"

"I was on Takanga. One of the Takangas. Do you know those islands?"

He shook his head. "I know they exist. I've never been there."

"I met my husband there. I mean, I went there and after a week or so he came there, too. He'd been away on business."

"I understand."

"We lived there for a while. Sometimes he'd go away—he had this hopper. But I was there all the time. There was a big storm." Cassie began to cry again.

"I heard about that. Thousands died."

She nodded, dabbing at her tears with a napkin.

"You were in it?"

"Yes." She took a deep breath. "Wally was k-killed. Wally was my husband. I—you must think I'm a terrible liar."

The captain shook his head. "Not so far, Mrs. Casey."

"I'm trying to tell the truth. I really am. Only the truth. My husband's name wasn't Wally. Not really. It was Bill. I called him Wally a—a lot. It was a little private joke we had. Oh, gosh! I hope you understand."

The captain smiled. "I won't tell you what my wife calls me."

"Then you do understand." Another deep breath. "All right. Here's the other thing. A lot of people would have said we weren't married at all. That's not right, but it's what lots of people would've said. It's called common-law marriage. We lived together and told everybody we were married. If you do that, you enter a common-law marriage. Please believe me. It's the truth."

"I know it is," the captain said.

"This is true, too. We were going to have a regular marriage, a big ceremony. One of the missionaries on Great Takanga would do it. We were going to be married on the grass in front of some embassy. Bill had it all set up, and a dressmaker was making my wedding dress. Then the st-storm . . ."

"I understand," the captain told her, "but how did you get on that island?"

"Wally d-d-died, and I was g-going to die, too. I kn-knew it. I wanted to die." Cassie sighed. "I really did. I w-wanted to get it all over."

The captain nodded. "Go on."

"Some friends came. It was v-very unexpected, but they did and they were going to fly me out. Only they were o-overloaded and c-couldn't carry me anymore."

He nodded again. "Did they have a seaplane?"

"N-no. They landed on the beach and told me I'd be all right there, that I might even be h-happy. I guess I thought they would come back for me, but they never did."

"Did it ever occur to you that they might have gone down at sea after they let you out?"

Cassie shook her head.

"A light plane, heavily loaded, trying to fly out through a storm? It could have happened very easily."

THE owner, Madame Pavlatos, was a rake-thin brunette who had once (there were photos and oil paintings everywhere) been a great beauty. Her stateroom was large even for such a large yacht, and where her pictures were not, there were mirrors. Cassie had taken one and one-half steps into the stateroom when she glimpsed herself in one—a wasted face, sunburned and deeply lined, surmounted by dirty, graying hair. A bent and barefoot old woman dressed in rags, with arms and legs like sticks.

She screamed and sobbed and choked, and pounded the little table that held Madame Pavlatos's tray with futile fists, while Madame Pavlatos (that austere mistress of a thousand millions) comforted her like a mother.

TWENTY-FIVE

AFTERWARD

The *Athena* landed Cassie at Cairns, where she lived less than happily in a shelter for homeless women until the United States Government was persuaded to bring her home. Herbie, it transpired, had morphed into an undersecretary in the Department of Education. He had a friend in the Department of State and may have harbored a sneaking affection for the wife who had divorced him not quite ten years ago. So the thing was done.

THE airport was the one in which Zelda Youmans's small pink hopper had once landed. It seemed almost unchanged, a lack of instability that struck Cassie as nothing less than miraculous. How could a little knot of mere buildings have changed so little, when she had changed so much?

Barclays scanned her retinas, and so established her identity. "You'll need new checks, I suppose," the bank officer said.

Cassie nodded.

"You have a box. We've been paying the rent from your account. That's standard here."

Thinking of her lost apartment and all the possessions that had mysteriously disappeared with it, Cassie said, "I wish everyone were that thoughtful."

"Thanks." The bank officer smiled. "Will you need a new key?"

She nodded again.

"If you require immediate access to your box, we can break into it today." Embarrassed, he paused. "There's a substantial fee for that. Five hundred dollars. I don't control these things, you understand."

"That won't be necessary." She sighed. "I'll have a lot to do as soon as I get the checks."

"A credit card? I can give you one of those, too." The bank officer's fingers danced over the keyboard.

"Yes. Please. I have to buy new clothes and find a place to stay. A hotel room for tonight, and an apartment as soon as I can find one. Furniture."

"You lost everything." He looked sympathetic.

"Everything except my life. I even lost my friends, because I don't want them to see me like this. Is that crazy?"

"I don't think so."

"There was a nice little woman who used to work for me. Her name is Margaret Briggs."

He waited.

"I passed her. Walking, I mean. I took the bus from the airport, and it let me out at the Blake. So I walked over. It's three blocks, I think."

"Yes. It is."

"Margaret was walking the other way. I stopped for a minute and sort of stared at her. She just kept going. I know she didn't know who I was."

"There are beauticians . . . I'm afraid I don't know much about those things."

"I do." Cassie managed to smile. "I'll go to them, but it won't be enough."

The bank officer's printer was birthing temporary checks. He turned to it, glad of the distraction. "A new key the usual way will take a week or so, but the charge is only twenty-five dollars. We'll call you when it's ready."

"I don't have a phone," Cassie told him. "That's the first thing I'm going to get."

HER new apartment was old and small, yet she found it very pleasant indeed after the shelter. It was clean and cheap, and had just been repainted. Best of all it was on the east side of Kingsport, across town from her old one. There, when she had finished breakfast on the fourth day, she patted her lips, got out her new cell phone, and made the call she had planned for so many months.

"Miskatonic University. How may we help you?"

"I'm looking for a man who teaches there. I hope you can help me find him." They were lines she had rehearsed a thousand times. "His name is Gideon Chase. Dr. Gideon Chase."

"Oh, don't you know? We're so proud!"

She sucked air. "I'm afraid I don't understand."

"Dr. Chase is on indefinite leave of absence. Our catalog this semester absolutely trumpets it. Our faculty member, the chair of our Department of Modern Gramarye, has been appointed ambassador to Woldercan. The whole school's proud enough to burst."

SELLING the bracelet took far longer than Cassie had anticipated; but when the sale was final at last, she found herself (as an awed manager at Barclays informed her) the wealthiest woman in the state. At which point it was time for another call. She entered a number she had gotten from Directory Assistance the day before.

"Klauser residence."

"May I speak to Mr. Klauser?"

"I'm afraid not. He's sleeping right now." (A reedy voice in the background protested.)

"Will you tell him I called? My name's Fiona Casey, and I was a friend of . . ." Something seemed to have taken Cassie by the throat. "Of the late William Reis. Please explain that I'm going to Woldercan, and I want very much to speak with Mr. Klauser before I leave."

"Wait a moment."

There was a long silence, during which Cassie smiled to herself and stared out her kitchen window. The sky was blue, and the steep roofs and sometimes ornate chimney pots of the old buildings in this part of town were a pleasant reminder of Kingsport's colonial origins.

"Ms. Casey?"

"Yes, I'm still here."

"Mr. Klauser is anxious to meet you. He, ah—" The speaker's voice sank to a whisper. "He isn't at all well. Please don't tire him."

"I'll try not to," Cassie said, resolving to tire him if necessary. "What would be a good time?"

"He lunches at eleven thirty. After that he must rest for at least two hours. I would say—ah—three. Would that suit you?"

"I'll be there tomorrow about three. A friend of mine . . ." (this was stretching it, but Cassie stretched) "told me you were in Myersville. I know that must be right because it's where Directory Assistance found you. Are you in town?"

"Oh, yes. Eleven fourteen Bushong Boulevard. The cross street is Taylor."

Cassie scribbled on a paper napkin.

"You'll have no trouble finding it. It's the big white house on the corner."

SO it was. Cassie rang the bell and told a short, stout woman with a hard, dark face that she had come to see Mr. Klauser.

"He don't see people."

Thankful for her sensible shoes, Cassie put her foot in the door. "I have an appointment. Three o'clock this afternoon."

"He don't see nobody."

"He'll see me," Cassie said, and pushed.

"*¡Fuera!*"

"Phooey yourself!" Cassie pushed harder.

Something banged and clattered inside, and the short, stout woman gave up. The door opened, and Cassie saw an elderly man in a wheelchair. He appeared to be preparing to throw a fork.

"Mr. Klauser? I'm Fiona Casey."

"I know who you are." It was the reedy voice she had heard. "Let her in, Maria."

Cassie advanced, stepping over a plate that had held eggs and around an overturned tray. "It's wonderful to meet you, Mr. Klauser. You were Bill's best friend. He didn't have many, but he thought the world of you."

Klauser accepted the hand she offered. His own was thin and felt pitifully weak. "Push me into the living room, please. Maria will clean this up."

Cassie got behind the chair and pushed, steering around an overturned coffee mug. "I made an appointment, Mr. Klauser. With another lady. I really did."

"That was Roxane. Told you to come at three?"

"Yes. She did." It was a large living room with a high ceiling and a light coating of dust on every level surface.

"Nasty trick," Klauser muttered. "She gets off at two."

Recalling the tray, Cassie said, "I was told you'd be through with lunch."

"Roxane cooks what the doctor orders. Maria cooks what I tell her to. Besides, she's a better cook."

"Did you really throw that tray to make her let me in?"

"Ha! Of course I did. Only way to get her attention. Over there, if you please, so I can see the big maple. You won't mind having your back to the light, Miss Casey?"

She positioned his chair. "Not at all."

Her own was large and comfortable without being soft. "I like this," she said.

"So did I. I got it in Russia and had it shipped back." For a moment Klauser looked so sad that Cassie wanted to hug him. "I'm afraid it's a long story. You wouldn't want to hear it, and I don't want to tell it. Cassiopeia mourns for her children."

Cassie nodded. "That's right. She does."

"You weren't disconcerted by the change in subject."

She shrugged. "Neither were you."

"Bill Reis was planning to marry a young woman named Cassiopeia Casey. I got a wedding invitation, the usual thing. You stuck it in the computer and saw pictures of them smooching. She was a luscious redhead. About your height."

Cassie said, "A little taller."

"Half an inch I would allow. Are you her mother?"

"No. I—I'm a relative. I would prefer not to go into our relationship."

"Meaning?"

Cassie smiled. "Meaning I'd lie, and I don't want to lie to you, Mr. Klauser."

"I was Ambassador Klauser once."

"You're right, Ambassador. I should have been calling you that. I apologize."

"Don't worry, I understand, and I understand about the anticloning laws. Is Bill dead?"

Cassie nodded.

"Is that just what you've been told, or are you certain?"

"I had to call his son and tell him." Cassie gulped. "Please don't make me cry."

"You liked Bill?"

She nodded again. "I liked him a lot."

"What about the Casey girl? The one Bill was going to marry?"

"She's gone, too." Cassie hesitated. "She's passed away, but I'm hoping to bring her back."

"I believe I understand that as well. You won't want to say anything more about it. What would you like to talk about? Why did you come up here? I assume you came up from Washington."

"From Oakland. That's not where I live—not where I'm living now." Cassie glanced at her watch. "I left Oakland two hours ago."

Klauser nodded. "You've got a hopper."

"I do. Yes."

"And you're planning to hop to Woldercan."

"That's right. I want to leave as soon as possible, but first I'll have to hop home to Kingsport and buy the things you're going to tell me I ought to take with me."

Klauser's brow wrinkled. "I'm no hopper expert. . . ."

"Neither am I, Ambassador."

"And I can't tell you exactly how far it is, because I'm not an astronomer, either. Just that the distance is enormous. Inconceivable."

"I know."

"A few government hoppers can make the trip. A few of the biggest. Not many."

"I know that, too, Ambassador. It's how Dr. Chase got there."

"Chase?" Klauser's eyes narrowed. "Are you talking about Bob Chase? Our first ambassador? I replaced him, Miss Casey, and he's been dead for years."

Cassie shook her head. "His son has been appointed ambassador, Ambassador Klauser."

"Really?"

She nodded.

"I remember him. Just a little fellow, but those eyes . . ."

"I know what you mean."

"Tell me something honestly, Miss Casey. No lies. Promise?"

She smiled. "Promise. Honest Injun."

"Is this some kind of nepotism?"

"Absolutely not. I know Dr. Chase quite well, Ambassador. You don't have to believe me, but it's the truth. Do you know him? At all?"

"I don't. I haven't seen him since he was a small boy."

"If you did, you'd know that he wears a watch but never looks at it. He always knows what time it is."

Slowly, Klauser nodded. "I can believe that."

"It's the truth. This is the truth, too. He knows a great deal about Woldercan. He's studied it for years, and of course he has childhood memories. He's a very able man, Ambassador. Ask around, and you'll hear that over and over."

"As able as Bill? Forget I said that. Old men are foolish, Miss Casey."

"So are women." Cassie fumbled in her purse for her handkerchief.

"Here. Take these." Klauser tossed a packet of tissues into her lap.

"I c-can't." She tried to pass them back. "You must n-need them."

"Try to understand, Miss Casey." Klauser coughed. "Giving you those may be the last chivalrous act of my life, and I need one. I need a last chivalrous act far more than I need half a dozen paper handkerchiefs." He waited for her to speak. "I want anchovy toast. I didn't get to finish my eggs. Would you like something? Coffee? A drink?"

"Hot tea." Cassie smiled through her tears. "I'd love some hot tea, Ambassador."

Klauser bawled for Maria to bring anchovy toast and two teas.

"May I tell you about my hopper, Ambassador? I'd love to show it to you, but you'd have to go out to the airport. It's a Jimmy Galactic. Have you ever heard of those?"

"No. I'm afraid I don't know much about hoppers."

"It's the biggest they make. The man who sold me mine said celebrities buy them so they can hop to places where they can't be followed." Cassie paused. "Mine is Lincoln green, and really beautiful. It's seventy feet long and twenty-five feet high. Twenty-five—no, thirty. It's thirty feet wide. I'm not good at remembering numbers, but I do remember those. It can go to Woldercan. The onboard computer told me—her name's Aquilia. Don't you think that's lovely?"

Klauser smiled. "For one who soars like the eagle. Yes, I do."

"It will take a lot of hops, but Aquilia says we can do it. I forget how many, but a lot. Twenty-something. I've bought the fuel rods. I still have to send Dr. Chase an ethermail to tell him I'm coming."

"What if he doesn't want you to, Miss Casey?"

"He does. I had an ethermail from him before I bought my hopper. It's just that I think his ethermail must be a reply to the one I'm going to send him today. Do you know about that?"

Klauser shook his head. "Nobody really knows about it."

"I suppose. Anyway, Dr. Chase told me once. If I don't send mine, his will have to be accounted for in some other way and it's liable to get complicated. So I'll send mine so I don't have to worry."

As Maria came in with tea and toast, Klauser murmured, "The distinctions we draw between past, present, and future are discriminations among illusions."

"Really?" Cassie's eyebrows shot up. "It sounds crazy."

"Albert Einstein said that, and Einstein wasn't crazy. Nor was he joking, Miss Casey. For us, the illusions seem terribly real. The robin another robin fights in a clean window seems terribly real to him, too." Klauser accepted a cup half filled with steaming tea, to which Maria added sugar substitute.

"I can pour for myself," Cassie told her, and watched with satisfaction as Maria left.

"It isn't that she doesn't like you," Klauser said. "She's just trying to do her duty."

"Which would have included pouring hot tea in my lap. What should I take to Woldercan?"

"Women," Klauser said slowly, "have monthly needs. You could use rags, and our great-great-grandmothers did, but if you would prefer not to . . ."

"I—well, I take a certain medicine. I don't need tampons."

"In that case, you should bring along a supply of the medicine. There'll be a doctor at the embassy, and he'll probably give you some if he has it."

"Then again he might not. And he might not have any. I understand." Cassie took a pen and pad from her purse and jotted a note. "A friend of mine's a reporter. She tapes interviews, but she carries these, too. I'm starting to understand why."

"I won't talk about clothing. You'll take too much, women always do. Take two warm dresses and one warm coat. The rest can be light stuff."

She made another note.

"You can eat the same things the Wolders eat, and you'd better do that and learn to like it. You can't possibly bring along enough food for a long stay. Are you staying long?"

"I hope so."

"Then learn to eat their food. The things that look like worms aren't worms, by the way. Have you ever eaten spaghetti squash?"

Cassie shook her head. "I've never even heard of it."

"Too bad. The wormy things are vegetable, just like spaghetti squash. I like stinky cheese."

"So do I."

"Good! That will help. A lot of the food smells bad but tastes good. What weapons are you planning on taking?"

Cassie blinked. "You know, I hadn't even thought of that. I used to carry a little automatic. . . ."

"If it's still in a drawer somewhere, get it out and have a gunsmith check it over."

"It's gone. I—I shot a man. Does that bother you? This was during the storm, when—when . . ."

"When people we won't name died. It was on vid. The storm, I mean, not the people. Those tissues are next to the tea tray. Did you shoot my friend?"

"Bill?" Cassie fumbled for the tissues. "Good gosh no! Bill was already d-dead."

"Self-defense?"

"Yes. Yes, it was, Ambassador. But—but if I told you what he wanted me to do you'd think that I was crazy, and he'd have killed me if I wouldn't do it."

"None of my business. I shouldn't have asked. Get another gun. You'll get two, if you're smart. Two guns that use the same ammunition. You won't need a lot. Two hundred rounds will probably be enough."

"The Wolders look like we do, don't they? I've seen some on vid."

"They do if you don't look too closely." Klauser nibbled a triangle of anchovy toast. "Frankly, they'll be the least of your worries. They . . . well, sometimes they try to seduce human women."

"But not women my age. Or women as homely as I am."

"You're not, Miss Casey, although you may think so. Have you always been so thin?"

She shook her head. "I used to be quite fat. A very nice man described me as luscious once, but women thought I was fat. I'm a woman myself, so I did, too. Then I nearly starved after the storm. I've been trying to stay thin."

Klauser snorted. "I wish you bad luck with it. Your genes will control your weight, unless you get as sick as I am or starve. I . . ."

"What is it?"

"I just thought of something, that's all. Will you accept a gift from me, Miss Casey? A knickknack to remind you of me? It will do you no harm and please an old man mightily."

"Of course I will, Ambassador. Thank you."

"Take it to Woldercan. I'd like that. It won't take up much space and it doesn't weigh much, so bring it along. Please."

Klauser drew breath. "Maria! Come here!"

Maria came, Klauser whispered urgently to her, and she left. "She'll wrap it for you. Wrap it as a gift, which it is. You can open it when you get back home."

"I promise not to peek."

"Good." Klauser coughed. "I've been talking about what you ought to take. That's what you asked about, and I've done my best to stick with it. How you act, where you go and where you don't . . . Those are a lot more important. May I talk about those?"

Cassie said, "I think you'd better."

"Try the anchovy toast. Half is for you."

Reluctantly, she picked up a triangle of toast. "I eat breakfast at a little place called the International House of Toast most mornings. I remember seeing this on the menu."

"You should've tried it. Before we get into behavior, I ought to mention that the laws of physics aren't exactly the same on Woldercan."

Cassie nodded. "A thing I read on the net said that, too. It won't bother me. I don't know what the laws are here."

"We used to believe they'd be the same everywhere." Klauser paused, and for a moment he seemed to be looking far away. "That seems terribly naive these days."

Cassie waited, and he said, "It can throw you off if you go up or down stairs fast. Take it slow until you're used to things."

"All right, I will."

"Don't go into the forests. No ifs, ands, or buts. Don't go. Don't even get close to one."

Popping the last of the triangle into her mouth, Cassie made a note.

"If you absolutely have to go, take a couple of old hands with you. At least two. More would be better."

"Got it."

"There are some pretty awful things in those forests, and from time to time they come out. That's why I advised you to bring two guns."

"I will." Cassie selected another triangle.

"Fine." Klauser hesitated. "The Wolders sometime hybridize with lower animals. The results can be, well, nightmarish."

Cassie nodded.

"If you go fishing don't talk to any fish you catch. That's very dangerous. Release them immediately or kill them immediately. One or the other. Don't go fishing without an experienced companion. How do you like anchovy toast?"

"I like it a lot," Cassie told him. "It makes me think of a time when I was the green goddess."

KLAUSER'S gift was small, flat, and light. Cassie packed it, and did not open it until the engines were recharging after the fifth hop and she was getting ready for bed. Opened, it proved to be a picture. A younger William Reis than she had ever seen stood next to an older man of about the same height who must have weighed at least three hundred pounds.

When she tapped Reis's image with her fingernail, he said, "I'm Bill Reis, the new ambassador to Woldercan, and I'd like to thank Ambassador Klauser for teaching me a great deal I needed to know, and for all the kindness and hospitality he and his family have shown my wife and me."

WHEN the sun was a yellow spark and the blue sphere of Earth less than nothing, Cassie murmured, "Oh, Bill, my poor Bill. Why did you have to die?"

And when the Milky Way was a little band of bright stars, a thing like a diamond bracelet seen from a great distance, "Come back to me, Wally! Please, oh, please, Wally! Come back to me!"

The important players are credited here, with many who take minor roles.

AABERG, LARS   Detective lieutenant on the Kingsport Police.

BENCH, SHARON   Reporter often seen on trivid.

BRIGGS, MARGARET   Cassie's dresser.

CABANA, ALEXIS   Leading lady in *The Red Spot*.

CASEY, CASSIE   Our star.

CHASE, GIDEON   Professor, consultant, and wizard.

COM PU TER   Artificial personality.

DEMPSTER, INDIA   Director of *The Red Spot* and *Dating the Volcano God*.

FERGUSON, JOHN   Official of the Federal Bureau of Investigation (FBI).

GOMEZ, PAT   Private investigator.

HANGA   Shark god.

HERBIE   Cassie's first husband.

HIAPO   Takangese who meets Cassie at the airport.

IULANI   One of Cassie's Takangese maids.

IZANAMI   Japanese nurse at the clinic on Takanga Ha'i.

KANOA   King of a village on Great Takanga.

KEAN, BRIAN   Reverend Brownlea in *Dating the Volcano God*.

KLAUSER, HAROLD   Former ambassador to Woldercan.

KU'ULAI   One of Cassie's Takangese maids.

MCNAIR, FLORENCE   The lady from Perth, an Australian tourist.

MERCE, TABBI   Actress who replaces Norma Peiper.

NELE   Manager of Salamanca House.

OKALANI   Takangese who carries Cassie's parasol.

PALMA, VINCENT   Actor who plays the Volcano God.

PAVLATOS, MADAME   Owner of the seagoing yacht *Athena*.

PEIPER, NORMA   Aunt Jane Brownlea in *Dating the Volcano God*.

PENNIMAN, PORTER "TINY"   Chief in *Dating the Volcano God*.

PICKENS, BRIAN   Tenant renting the apartment over Cassie Casey's.

PRESIDENT, THE   Chief executive of the United States.

REIS, RIAN   William Reis's son.

REIS, WILLIAM "BILL"   Billionaire with a slight touch of megalomania.

SCHOONVELD, DR.   Head of the clinic on Takanga Ha'i.

STORM KING, THE   Squid god.

WARSHAWSKY, JAMES K. "JIMMY"   Security guard.

WHITE, EBONY   India Dempster's assistant.

YOUMANS, ZELDA   Cassie's agent.

ZEITZ, SCOTT   Cassie's second husband.